THE TOWER

J. KENNER

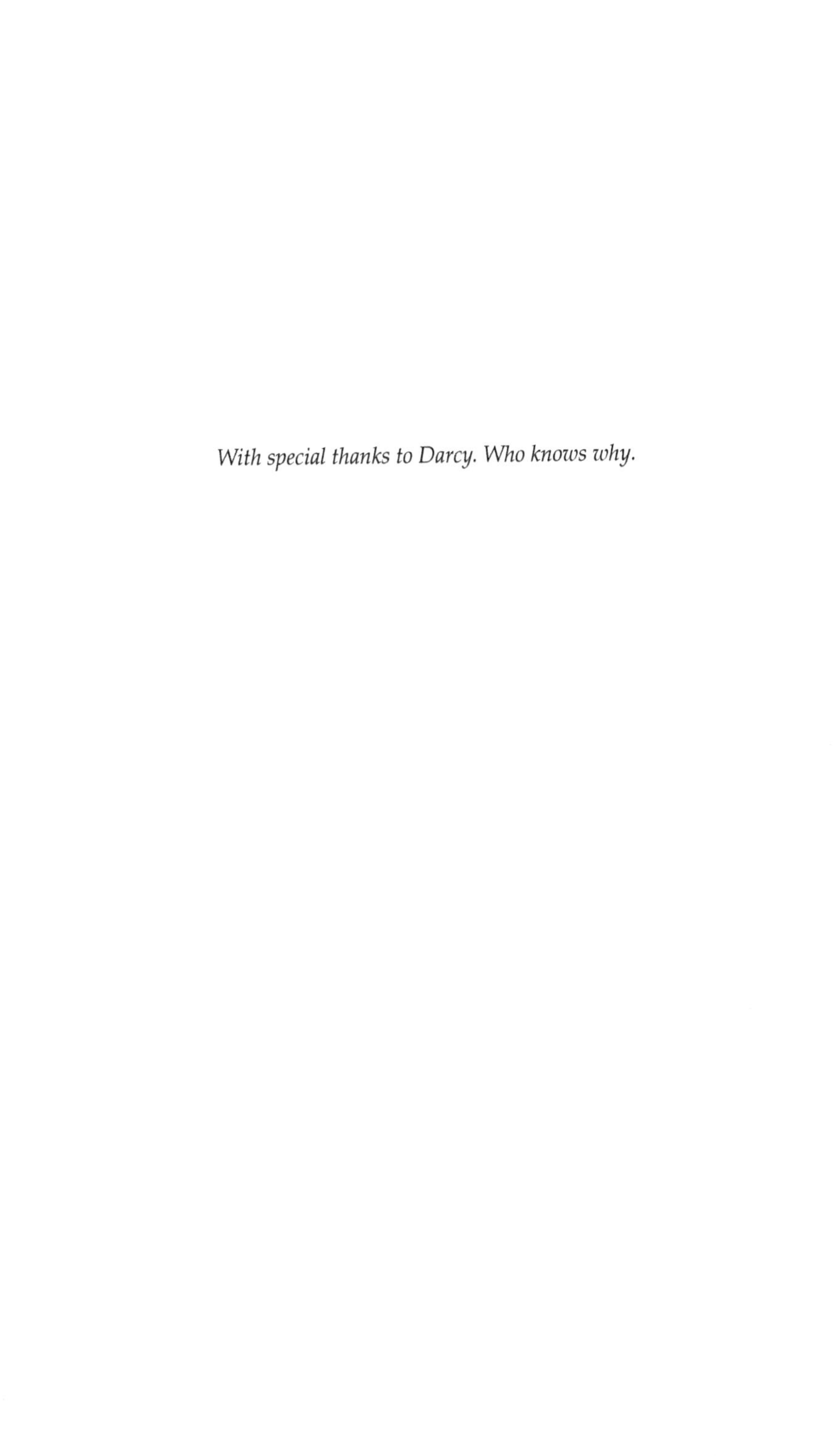

With special thanks to Darcy. Who knows why.

CONTENT WARNING

This dark romance contains elements that may disturb some readers, including:

For readers who crave an intense journey with a dangerous hero who walks the line between protection and possession, this enemies-to-lovers story delivers a raw, unfiltered experience. The darkness is real, but so is the redemption.

Recommended for mature audiences who understand that fiction allows us to explore the shadowy corners of desire safely.

"At first, Rapunzel was terribly frightened when a man, such as her
eyes had never yet beheld, came to her."

ONE
THE ROOF

I'm a captive princess in the highest tower of a castle in the sky.

At least, that's what it feels like. That's what it always feels like. But today isn't just another day of confinement. Today is a special kind of torture.

"Turn just a bit, darling," Adam, the skinny new photographer, says in a pretentious accent that I'm certain is entirely fake.

I comply, and the motion makes the rhinestones on this frothy pink monstrosity of a ballgown catch the late afternoon light, setting them to sparkle like the tears I'm not allowed to shed.

"Lovely, lovely," Adam murmurs, apparently oblivious to the fact that I've taken two steps back in a desperate attempt to put distance between myself and the edge of the rooftop observation deck.

For the briefest of moments, I wish I really were Rapunzel. But with my waist-length blonde locks twisted into an updo and held in place by ivory combs and a helmet of hairspray, I don't have enough hair to get me down even one level, much less forty-three stories to the ground.

Not that it would matter if I did. I could never go through with it. Already, panic threatens to claw at my throat. Already, the world beyond the rooftop reaches for me with invisible hands, waiting to drag me down, down, dow—

"Sasha!"

My father's voice slices through my thoughts, snapping me back to reality. I take five slow, deep breaths, telling myself that it's fine. That despite my unsteadiness and the pangs of fear, I made the right decision not to take my meds this morning—and to flush them down the toilet in case Father sends someone up to my room to check my supply.

The right decision, I tell myself again, with a glance toward Ruby Ryder, my best friend and personal assistant. We've been joined at the hip since we were twelve. That's when she came to live with her grandmother, our housekeeper. Today, her job is ostensibly to hold makeup brushes and extra hairpins. In reality, she's here to silently bolster me if I start to crumble under the weight of my new determination to wean myself off the damn pills Father and his cabal of doctors have forced down my throat since I was seven.

Behind the photographer, Ruby grimaces as she holds up two fingers—a signal that my father is coming.

Ice floods my veins. I turn to see him stalking toward me, weaving through the forest of light stands and electrical cords. His polished Italian shoes click against the roof tiles like a countdown. His face remains neutral—it always does when investors or clients are nearby —but I recognize the familiar fury blazing in his eyes and cringe back the moment he arrives at my side.

"Do you have any idea how expensive this shoot is?" His voice is low, for my ears only. "How important this launch is? Dammit, girl. Everything I do for you—making you the face of this entire campaign, every privilege you live under, the time and money I spend getting you the proper medications—and you can't be bothered to follow directions?"

I want to tell him I've been standing here for hours. That I've barely eaten, much less had water. That the stupid dress weighs a ton, but I can't sit down because, god forbid, it wrinkles.

I've been the face of Reed Cosmetics since I was fourteen, my carefully cultivated image of fragile beauty serving as a cornerstone of my father's brand. A perfect princess in her stunning tower.

I hate it.

I want to scream that I never asked for this. That I hate this role I'm forced to play. That I think the newest Dreams campaign is tacky and stupid.

I want to rage that he knows the roof terrifies me, even with all the meds he forces down my throat. That he promised we'd shoot in our home's elegant ballroom. That instead of the warm protection of four walls and familiar marble pillars, he's positioned me three feet from a barely secure edge beyond which lies forty-three floors worth of terrifyingly empty space stretching in all directions.

But I don't say any of that. Not to Victor Reed, the man who fathered me. The man who repeatedly says he loves me. The man who just as frequently torments me. To him, I can only whisper, "Sorry, Daddy."

He sighs, checking his Patek Philippe Grandmaster watch with theatrical disappointment. "You know damn well we need these shots for the launch. The board is already questioning the budget." He runs a hand through his perfectly styled silver-gray hair. "Fools, all of them. But they'll change their minds when they see our market share."

He points a long finger at my face, so close I can see the manicured nail. "Mark my words, child. The fairy tale aesthetic is a genius maneuver on my part. Maybe they can't see it now, but this campaign is gold. It's going to push us ahead of Lucent."

Lucent.

Just the name of the Grimm family's cosmetics line makes my skin prickle. Sophisticated. Elegant. Dripping with class. Everything our campaign is not.

The irony isn't lost on me—how the vilest family in Manhattan creates the most beautiful products. They lie and cheat and steal to get what they want.

And they kill.

I fight the urge to hug myself as I think of my mother, now nearly twenty years in her grave. I was seven when my father told me Elias Grimm, the family's monster of a patriarch, was the one I'd seen murder her. Worse, he'd gotten away with it. "That family has the police in their pocket," Father had said.

I was too young then to understand what that meant. I only knew the Grimm family had taken my mother from me—that because of them, I'd been left alone with my father, a monster of a different kind.

And I swore that someday—somehow—I would get revenge on Elias Grimm and his entire clan.

If this Dreams campaign had even the slightest chance of kicking

Lucent's marketing ass, I'd be all for it. But instead, we're pushing something tasteless and stale—like poisoned apples wrapped in gold leaf.

I say none of this out loud. Instead, I meet my father's eyes. "We'll get their market share, Father." I say it because that's what he wants to hear. And I'll pay the price if I try to tell him anything else.

He grunts, his expression thunderous. My insides tighten, only to loosen when Adam calls out, holding up his camera and gesturing for me to return to his side.

I start to move, but my father's hand closes around my upper arm. "We need to see that smile of yours, Sasha. That sparkle. This is about making dreams come true."

I lift my face to his and look deep into those emerald green eyes, so like my own. "I wouldn't know about dreams coming true," I say —but only in my head. I gave up on dreams long ago. Now, I have only nightmares. Except for that one lingering dream of escape.

That's a nightmare, too though, because I know it will never happen.

What I say aloud is, "Yes, Daddy."

His mouth curves into a saccharine smile as he nods toward the onlookers. "Dreams," he repeats, his voice booming as he sweeps his arm toward the banner hanging near the catering table. It bears the Reed Cosmetics logo and the campaign slogan: *Make your dreams come true.* "And aren't dreams the reason we're here?"

I want to run, but I know my role in this twisted fairy tale. I rise on tiptoes, then kiss his cheek as the reporters' cameras flash. When I settle back on solid ground, I aim a simpering smile at the onlookers, then hurry toward Adam so we can start the whole damn performance all over again.

I hit my mark and strike the next pose, following Adam's direction. For a few minutes, I manage to lose myself in the fantasy that I'm Rapunzel, trapped in a high tower, waiting for my prince.

But too soon, the fantasy dissolves like mist. After all, I know better than to believe in fairy tales. I'm just a girl playing dress-up, and any rescuing will have to be done by me.

Too bad I don't have a clue how to make that happen.

"A bit to your right," Adam says, and I force my hesitant feet to move closer to the waist-high railing that separates the roof from the void. My insides go ice-cold as I move, and I wish desperately that I'd taken the damn meds. But I tell myself I'm safe—that I won't go over. There's a barrier now, unlike that horrible day when my mother died.

A barrier and concrete firm under my feet. Solid. Sturdy. *Safe.*

I won't go over. I won't fall. I won't get lost in the vast oblivion.

I gulp air, realizing I've forgotten to breathe. I stamp my foot, the heel making a sharp sound against the roof. Solid. All solid.

Except it's not.

It's all just atoms. The same atoms that make up the air, and air won't keep me safe. Air is just something to get lost in. To fall through.

"Tilt your chin up and smile." I hear the edge in my father's voice as he approaches from behind me. "Remember, you're selling fairy tales."

I want to snap that I'm not. I'm selling makeup by being the frothy, pink, fake image of sanitized tales. Nothing like the stories the Grimm family used to publish centuries ago—dark and dangerous and cautionary.

But since I'd have to be out of my mind to say that aloud, I force my lips into yet another practiced smile. Anything to finish this shoot. The sooner it's over, the sooner I can get back inside.

The thought calms me even as fresh terror rises—the promise of being safe inside clashing with the stark reality that I'm outside, with Central Park spreading below me like a verdant carpet. In this moment, I'm reminded of all the open space around me, and vertigo hits with a vengeance. My head swims, my stomach plummets, and I'm suddenly convinced I might float away untethered, tumbling down, down, down to shatter into a million pieces.

It would be a relief. An escape.

It would be over.

No.

I slow my breathing, settle back on my mark, and force my fear-stiffened body to strike the pose—even as I wish I hadn't tossed the damn meds.

So that I can cope, I imagine I'm painting this scene rather than living it. Creating depth and perspective on a flat canvas. Or coding sections of Elysium, my private virtual world where everything is under my control, and girls who tumble off buildings fly instead of fall.

"Take three steps closer to the edge," Adam calls. "I want the skyline rising behind you."

I glance in that direction. Three steps would put me right *there,* where even a deep breath could shift my balance and send me hurtling over.

The possibility locks me in place. I can't move. I'm frozen. Terrified. *Ashamed.*

Then my father is beside me. "Quit being such a child," he growls, pressing his hand to my waist and moving me closer to the void.

No, no. Please, please no.

I'm going to be sick. Surely, they don't want to photograph me like this.

I know he feels me trembling. I know he's using this moment.

Using my fear.

But all he says is, "So lovely. The light hits your face perfectly here."

A wave of nausea crests over me and I spin toward him. "Father, I—"

"Do not embarrass me, Sasha." His voice is low. Cold. Accusing.

I look down at my shoes, hating this reminder that I need him. That I'm not strong enough for the world outside.

I force myself to look up, expecting to meet my father's stern, commanding eyes. Instead, I see the deep lines of his frown as he stares across the roof. I turn, following his line of sight.

That's when I see *him.*

Liam Grimm.

The devil's spawn.

TWO

HIM

H*im.*

Here at my shoot. The man who ripped out my soul just over three years ago.

My stomach twists, and I fight the urge to vomit. I have no idea why he's here, but he stands less than fifteen yards away, just past the small shed connecting the stairwell to the rooftop, watching as I pose and Adam clicks off shot after shot.

His hair is the color of copper, highlighted by gold—so different from the raven-black hair of his father and brothers. Even from this distance, I can see his eyes—the palest of blue, like something super-natural. Something predatory.

He wears his perfectly tailored dark suit as if he's the one who should be in front of a camera. Or in a boardroom. Every inch of him radiates command, but this is no benevolent ruler. Liam Grimm is dangerous—just like his half-brothers. Just like his vile, outlaw of a father.

Elias Grimm may be the person I despise most in the world. But his son Liam falls solidly into second place—not only because every-thing I've heard suggests he's a chip off the old block, but also because of what happened at a charity gala three years ago. Words he whispered for my ears only. Words I'd anticipated would be sweet but turned sour and rotten. Taunts that I was nothing. That I'd tried to damage the launch of Lucent's newest product by spreading lies.

That I was my father's little marionette doll who only knew how to dance the tune he played. And that, like my father, I would lie and cheat to get my way.

I'd told myself he was only trying to hurt me—that he was the liar, not me. But it didn't matter. He'd made me ashamed that I'd let myself crave him even for a moment. I'd wanted to lash out, to scream that he didn't know me at all—but I knew him. Knew exactly what his family had done.

Knew the blackness of their souls.

But he'd slipped back into the crowd before I could find the words, much less my voice.

Now, a shiver races up my spine. Part of me wants so desperately to escape that I consider leaping over the barrier and taking my chances with the air and atoms. But another part—some foolish, hidden part—can't help being perversely intrigued. And the longer I watch him, the more I want to confront him and demand answers.

I turn to where my father stands just out of camera range. "Why is he here? Why is there a Grimm at our shoot?"

"Industry courtesy." Father's smile doesn't reach his eyes. "I invited Elias to see our new campaign. I knew that bastard would send a proxy."

"You *invited* him? Why would you do that?"

Father shrugs, his manner infuriating, given what Elias Grimm did to my mother. "I was curious to see who he'd send in his stead. Looks like Liam may be in the running to be the next CEO."

A dangerous smile tugs at his mouth as he turns to Adam. "Done?"

"Yes, sir."

"Then get ready for the next set-up."

When Adam nods, Father turns his attention back to me. "And you go change before we lose the light."

He hurries away before I can ask another question. That's probably for the best. I'll confess—if only to myself and Ruby—to having lusted over Liam Grimm in the past. But that was before his whispered taunt … and nothing more than a fantasy.

In the real world, Liam Grimm is not a man I care to know. Or to know anything about.

Ruby hurries over with Mindy, the wardrobe coordinator, and

despite the urge to look back, I keep my eyes forward as I follow them into the small tent that serves as a changing room. "Did you see him?"

I grimace. "Father invited him. Can you believe that?"

Ruby's mouth twists, but since Mindy's pulling a dress over my head, I miss the rest of her expression. The rustle of stiff material blocks out her words, too.

"… surprised."

"What?" I say, catching only the tail end.

"I said that considering the circumstances, I'm not too surprised. That your dad invited him, I mean."

"The circumstances?" Clearly, my bestie has lost her marbles. "He's a competitor. Giving him early access to our ad plans? It might be a stupid campaign, but that doesn't mean Father should—"

Ruby holds up a hand. "What are you talking about?"

"Liam Grimm," I say with a glance toward Mindy, who looks uninterested. "His father murdered my mother, remember? Their Lucent brand is Reed Cosmetic's biggest competitor. Ringing any bells?"

She cocks her head, her forehead furrowed. "All sorts of bells. But what does that have to do with—?"

"Father invited Liam Grimm to the shoot," I snap. "How can you not think that's insane?"

"Wait. What?" She gapes at me. "Liam Grimm? Your dad invited Liam Grimm?"

"Yes! What have we been talking about?"

She runs her fingers through her tumble of auburn curls. "I had no idea. It's just him, right? None of his brothers?"

"Just him," I assure her. Years ago, Ruby made the mistake of dating Leo, the youngest and wildest of the Grimm brothers. To say it hadn't ended well would be the understatement of the century.

"But if you weren't talking about Grimm," I ask, "then who …"

"Desmond Bane." The name hangs in the air like icicles as Mindy extricates me from the rest of my princess garb.

I shudder. "Why were you talking about him?"

"Duh. He's here."

Bile rises in my throat. Desmond Bane is a walking horror movie with the Midas touch.

Everyone in my family's social circle knows he's the vilest human on the planet—and that he's had a thing for me since I was fourteen.

Seeing him here on the day of my shoot is really not a good sign.

I'm in only a bra and panties now, and I yank a robe off the rack, waving away Mindy and the hanger overflowing with the next costume.

"Back up," I say to Ruby as I slip on the robe and tighten the belt, as if the flimsy silk could provide any real protection. "Tell me all of it."

Ruby shrugs. "That's all I know. He's here. He's an investor, right? So I guess it makes sense."

"Has he been talking with Father?"

"Mostly he's been watching you and rubbing his hands together like some creepy, evil mastermind."

I shudder. She's exaggerating the evil mastermind part—probably —but that doesn't change the fact that Desmond Bane has a reputation for breaking his toys. And his favorite toys are his ex-wives and mistresses.

"Father's probably convincing him to invest another mil or two," I say, as much to convince myself as Ruby.

"An investment," Ruby repeats, as Mindy helps me into the next wearable torture device. "That must be it." Ruby's frown suggests she doesn't believe it. Then again, maybe she's frowning at my outfit—yet another overly sugary princess dress.

I scowl, then poke her.

"Ouch!"

"What aren't you telling me?"

"I—it's probably nothing. Okay!" she adds when I give her *the look*. "It's just that earlier today, Anita told me that he had a breakfast meeting with your father in the small dining room. She was the one serving them, and you know how they talk when the help's around, like Anita's invisible and stupid. So she heard a lot when she wasn't back in the kitchen."

"And?"

"They were talking about tomorrow's gala. She said your father mentioned some big announcement."

"About what?"

She shakes her head. "I don't know. Not for sure."

"Not for sure?" I repeat. "That means you think something."

"Just—Desmond's been hot for you since forever, and your dad wants access to his bank account."

"And you think, what? That Father's going to sell me? Money in exchange for a ring on my finger?" That's absurd. Except it's not, and Ruby knows it, too.

She drags her fingers through her curls. "It's only—Sasha, I've got a really bad feeling. Can you get out of going to the gala?"

I just cock my head. She knows the answer as well as I do.

She lets out a long breath. "Well, at least I'll be there, too."

I nod, remembering that she's going to be working as a waiter for the catering service. "It's probably nothing," I say, but even as I speak the words, I know they're wrong. With my father, it's never nothing.

He has some horrible new plan for me. Which means that tomorrow night, I need to be ready for anything.

Mindy ducks out of the changing tent and I'm about to follow, but Ruby tugs me back. "So? How are you feeling? You ditched them, right? Do you feel any different yet? Everything I read said it might take a while to get out of your system."

I'd read the same thing, and so far, it's true. I tell her how my phobias feel more potent—heights and open spaces. It's harder to stand where the photographer wants than it was the last time we shot on the roof. "But I feel more ... I don't know ... *here*, I guess. It comes and goes. One minute I feel grounded, and the next, I almost feel like I'm floating. I think that's normal, though, because there's still crap in my system."

"Well, if anything feels really off, you take them, okay? Your father's an ass, but surely even he wouldn't pump you full of drugs you don't really need."

"I'm fine," I say, which isn't an answer at all. But this isn't the time or the place to tell her she's wrong. Besides, she already knows it. She just doesn't want to believe that anyone would drug his own daughter just to make her more obedient.

And maybe he's not. I don't have any solid proof. Just the way I feel when I take the meds compared to when I don't. And not just about how I feel. On the few days I've risked going without my meds, I've come close to remembering my mother. Not just the horrible day when she died, but snuggly moments on the couch and laughing moments as we played games on the floor.

I want those memories back all the time. And I know it's the meds that are keeping them away.

But Ruby's right. Nobody would drug their own child without a good reason. So something must be wrong with me. Either that, or something is very wrong with Father.

Finally, I can't hide out in the changing tent any longer, so with Ruby beside me and Mindy holding the dress's train, I head back into the open. Sure enough, there's Desmond, tall and sandy-haired, with the blank good looks of old money. He's attractive if you don't know anything about him. And if you don't look into those dangerous golden eyes.

"He keeps glancing this way," I murmur.

Ruby cocks her head, indicating the other side of the roof. "So does Liam Grimm."

I risk another look at Grimm, now standing mere inches from the barrier. For one horrible moment, I imagine the barrier breaking and him falling, falling, falling into the void.

I gasp, surprised when I realize Ruby's holding my arm. I can see from her face that I'd fallen into the fear again and almost let it drown me.

But what baffles me is that it was the vision of Grimm tumbling over that had pushed me deep inside myself. After all, it's not as if I care if he lives or dies.

Frowning, I turn just enough to see him, still casually flirting with that terrifying void. He's chatting with the art director, but his head turns toward me as if he's caught my scent. I meet his eyes, then stumble, shocked by the zing of electricity that seems to sizzle across my skin.

The man's an arrogant asshole, but there's something about him. Something both compelling and terrifying about this man who flirts with the edge. Who can look into the abyss and not fall.

Or maybe he's already fallen. The man truly is a devil, after all.

"You okay?"

I turn to find Ruby studying me. We've arrived at the makeup tent, and as I sit in the chair, Ruby puts her hand on my shoulder. "What is it?"

"Just tired," I lie. "I'll be fine."

She doesn't look convinced, but she doesn't press. Soon enough, the makeup artist drapes me, and I'm grateful to have something else to think about. She adds more glitter to my cheeks, and I can't help but swallow a sardonic smile. I'm twenty-six years old, shooting an ad for cosmetics aimed at adults, and I'm being dressed like a third grader's fantasy of a fairy princess. It's one of those moments where you either laugh or cry.

Or throw yourself off a roof.

"Places in five," Adam's assistant announces, and the moment I'm released from the makeup chair, I head toward the refreshment table. I want one of the bagels slathered in cream cheese, but until we wrap, I'm allowed nothing but water or apple juice. Can't risk staining my teeth, spilling on my dress, or—god forbid—bloating.

I'm sipping juice through a straw when I feel a tingle up my spine. The kind of sensation that warns you of danger. That survivors will say protected them from the car that jumped the curb or kept them from getting on the plane at the last minute.

When I look up, I see the danger staring back at me, predatory and calculating. Liam Grimm. Something dark and magnetic pulls me toward him, and I'm by his side before I can stop myself.

"Mr. Grimm," I say, my voice as sharp as steel. "It's been three years. Have you finally come up with some new insults to toss at me?"

His mouth curves into something predatory. "Ms. Reed. Still playing dress-up for the man who owns you?"

I stiffen, hating that his words mirror how I've been feeling all day. Victor Reed's pretty little dress-up doll.

"I see your daddy's still sending you off to sniff out the competition. I guess that makes you little more than an errand boy." I flash my most charming smile. "Not surprising. Lucent's a diamond. And Daddy wouldn't want to give too much responsibility to someone who's nothing more than ordinary quartz."

It's a low blow, but he deserves it. After he cut me off at the ankles three years ago, I made a point of learning more about Liam Grimm. Including that he's the product of an affair, that his birth mother is dead, and that except for Leo, his brothers and stepmom haven't exactly welcomed him into their loving embrace.

I watch his face as I speak, but I see nothing. No twitch in his cheek. No darkening of his eyes. No narrowing of his gaze. As far as I can tell, my words haven't fazed him at all.

Well, damn.

"You're hardly one to speak of quartz, Ms. Reed. Especially since we both know your campaign is a far cry from a jewel." His eyes move slowly over me, and for a moment, I'm lost, trapped in the power of that dark, commanding gaze.

Trapped, yes. But at the same time, I have no desire to break free. Not yet.

And that is what makes Liam Grimm truly terrifying.

I draw a breath and lift my chin. "Like what you see?"

The corner of his mouth quirks up, revealing a dimple that softens the hard planes of his face. My body relaxes, unwittingly sliding into complacency by the hint of compassion I think I see in his eyes.

He glances down, then lifts his gaze slowly, his eyes moving over me like a caress, the sensation so oddly intimate that I can barely breathe. When he meets my eyes, I see a hint of warmth there. But that heat turns frigid as he holds my gaze, the frost cold enough to make me shiver.

Then he takes a single step backward and, with a slow movement of his hand, indicates the hideous ball gown. "You're wearing the proof of your father's debasement. That man will steal and destroy anything." His eyes once again sweep over the gown. "Even my family's legacy."

I hear the hard edge of fury in his voice and have to bite my tongue to keep from shouting that I hate it, too. The ridiculous fluff that makes up the dreams we're selling.

But I won't say it. I won't align myself with this man in any way. Not after what he said. What his family's done.

I blink, trying to force back tears as I think of my mother. Of the night when Elias Grimm crept up to the roof. The night when I watched helplessly as he sent her tumbling over the edge as my father tried to grab her in time to save her.

But it was no use. She was gone. Down, down, down into the void.

I shiver, then hug myself, trying not to think of the fear she must have felt. I'd been only seven, and my mother had been my world.

The Grimm family had taken her from me.

I force myself to stand straighter, then take a single step toward him. "Your father is a monster," I say. "Do you think I don't know what he did? What he took from me?"

His eyes narrow, and for a moment, I think he's going to simply walk away. Then he lifts his chin, and something savage flashes in those cold, blue eyes. He leans in, close enough that I can feel his breath against my ear. "Careful, Princess. The villain in one tale is often the victim in another."

A twitch of dread runs up my spine, and I step back. I know only one thing for certain about Liam Grimm—the man is at least as dangerous as Desmond Bane. And yet, for some inexplicable reason, I'm drawn to his flame. "Stay away from me."

He meets my eyes, and my breath catches. Then he nods, just a single tilt of his head. "As you wish."

He takes a step away from me, then another. And then, despite my own better judgment, I blurt, "Why are you really here?"

He turns back slowly, and I want to kick myself when I see victory painted all over his face. "To see the girl who haunts my dreams," he answers, his voice dropping to a dangerous register. "To watch the daughter of the man who destroyed my mother be paraded around like a porcelain doll."

"Destroyed?" I shake my head. "That never happened. It was your family—"

"Better be careful, Princess," he says, moving closer, trapping me by nothing more than the force of his presence. "Accusations can be as dangerous as a blade."

Before I can stop myself, I slap him, the crack of palm against cheek startlingly loud. He catches my wrist before I can pull away, his grip like iron, his eyes blazing.

"That fire," he murmurs, his thumb pressing against my racing pulse. "That's not your father in you. That's all Lydia. And your father extinguished her fire, too."

"Don't you dare say my mother's name."

"I'll do or say whatever—"

Ruby appears suddenly, breaking the moment. "They're waiting," she says, her voice like ice and her eyes on Grimm.

He releases me slowly. Deliberately. "Enjoy your tower while it lasts, Rapunzel," he says, then leans forward to whisper in my ear. "Because one way or another, I'm going to tear it down. And you'll have to decide if you're falling or flying."

My skin burns where he touched me, as if I've been branded. Walking back to my mark, I can feel his eyes tracking me—a predator assessing his prey.

I take my position at the edge, the vast openness beyond the barrier no longer the most terrifying thing on this rooftop. That distinction now belongs to the savage current flowing between me and the man my father raised me to hate—a current that feels dangerously like desire.

My father positions himself where he can watch both me and Grimm, his scowl deep. Desmond stands beside him, his predatory gaze making me want to scrub my skin raw in a boiling bath.

"Come on people," Adam calls, his camera already clicking. "We're wasting the light."

Immediately, I twirl, flashing my brightest smile. What choice do I have? I'm the princess in this story, after all. The innocent virgin lost in the woods and trapped between two monsters.

There's no way out. Not for me. Because real fairy tales don't end with happily ever after. They end with blood and teeth and pain.

And I'm beginning to wonder if I'm the heroine of my own story —or the sacrifice.

THREE
THE CAGE

The princess costume lies crumpled on the Calacatta Gold marble floor, the deflated pink fantasy stark against the opulent gold and gray veins that run through the stone. I'd dropped it there hours ago after Ruby helped me escape its clasps and ties before heading off to check on her grandmother.

For a moment, I stand over it, fighting the urge to tear the gossamer fabric into satisfying ribbons. But what would be the point? Another gown would simply appear tomorrow.

I yank open my closet, then bypass the Victor Reed-approved outfits as I reach for the back corner where I keep my real wardrobe. I pull out black leggings and an oversized NYU sweater that Ruby smuggled in for me last year. But even after I've changed into the comfy, familiar clothes, I can't seem to settle. Instead, I find myself pacing my beautiful prison with its hand-painted murals and imported drapes that cover the line of windows overlooking a view I'm too terrified to see.

I'm edgy and antsy, and I don't know why. Maybe it's the meds working their way out of my system. Maybe it's just the never-changing drudgery of a life lived almost exclusively in this room on the forty-second floor.

I don't know. All I know is that I'm more antsy than usual, so I pick up the in-house phone and call Ruby.

By the fifth ring, I remember that Ruby had plans to go to a movie with some friends from college this evening. She'd invited me, but Father had said no. An evening out following a full day of work was too strenuous for someone with my conditions and phobias.

Bastard.

I pace the room, trying to decide if I'd rather paint or play in Elysium. But neither is what I want. Not right now. Honestly, I want to be out with Ruby, living the kind of life twenty-somethings live on television—out in the world, surrounded by friends, falling in love and kissing in dark corners.

That, however, isn't on tonight's agenda—or, most likely, the agenda planned out for, oh, the next seventy or so years.

When I can no longer stand the loneliness, I slip into the hallway and navigate the familiar route to the service stairs. The penthouse residence occupies floors forty-one to forty-three of Reed Tower, with the forty-first floor dedicated to staff quarters, laundry, and the main kitchen. It's also where Ruby shares small but comfortable rooms with her grandmother Birgit, our head housekeeper.

I consider popping in to say hello to Birgit, who's a surrogate grandmother to me, but it's past ten, and I know she must be asleep. Instead, I head straight to my goal—the express service elevator that goes directly from this lowest penthouse floor all the way down to the public lobby of Reed Tower.

This floor is quieter, more comfortable. And mostly free from the ornate touches that dominate the main living areas. Here, the building's original details remain—geometric patterns in the woodwork, chrome and brass accents that gleam like forbidden treasures, and other charming details.

I pause at a window and force myself to look out at the city. I know the thick glass and bricks are protecting me. But even so, my stomach quivers as Manhattan's lights form a glowing tapestry against the night sky.

Out there, people walk freely, unafraid of the vastness around them. People like Liam Grimm, who stood fearless at the edge of the roof today, as if daring the void to claim him.

Will I ever be strong enough to do that? Or am I truly as fragile as my father and doctors say I am?

I force the question out of my mind, afraid I won't like the answer.

As I continue down the corridor, I pass one of the housekeepers.

She nods respectfully, but I catch the sympathy in her eyes. The staff know more about life in Reed Tower than my father realizes. They see everything—including, I suspect, how he treats me when cameras aren't rolling.

A few more corners rounded, and I reach the service elevator. As soon as it arrives, I get on, punch in my code, then press the button for the lobby.

The car doesn't move.

I repeat the process, cursing Gerald, the head maintenance man who's supposed to make sure the elevators are always working seamlessly. Again, nothing.

I'm about to press the call button when a voice pops out from the intercom. "May I help you, Miss Reed?"

"Hey, Edward." I'm trying to get down to the lobby. I want to take a walk in the walled garden."

"I'm sorry, Miss. The lobby's restricted tonight."

"I didn't see a memo about a restriction. Are the floors being waxed?"

"No, Miss. Your father's orders. He doesn't want you outside this evening."

"I see," I say, reining in my temper. If I lose it, Daddy Dearest will hear all about it in under five seconds. "I just want to enjoy a bit of fresh air before I go to sleep. I'm not even going to the pond. Just the walled garden."

The pond is exactly what it sounds like, a lovely pond that houses ducks and turtles and any number of other creatures. It's surrounded by well-tended grass with a walking path. And Edward is right—it's not someplace I can go by myself, especially not at night, with that endless black void hanging over my head as I try to keep myself whole and sane, even as the empty space around me tries to pull me apart.

I shiver just thinking about it. Definitely not on tonight's menu.

"I'm sorry," Edward says. "But you know I can't authorize it."

"But it's a room. It was literally built for me. Flowers. Plants. A table and chair I picked out when I was ten, and all of it set up behind a wall."

"I understand," he says again, and this time I'm certain I hear pity.

"But I can't let you come down tonight. Not against your father's orders."

I want to jam my hand right through the damn speaker panel, but I don't. I also don't say another word to Edward, which is bitchy since it's not his fault, but I'm in an edgy mood and I just don't give a fuck.

It occurs to me that I'm usually much more chill. *The meds.*

Makes sense. Why would my father want to fight with his bitchy daughter when he can keep her mellow?

Oh, God.

Is this really my life?

I stomp back up to my room, but since I'm in my bare feet, the stomping is less than satisfying. I'm about to flip on the television just to have the company of human voices, but for some reason, the campaign's catchphrase echoes in my head: *Make your dreams come true.*

What about *my* dreams? The ones that will never become reality if I'm trapped in this suite, in this tower? If my father is feeding me drugs?

And what will happen if Father learns that I'm not taking them anymore? Because as of today, I am officially done.

He'll put them in your food. Your water. If he figures out you're defying him, you'll never have a choice again.

For a moment, it occurs to me that maybe I'm spinning out. Maybe I really do need all these drugs, and if I stop taking them, the world will crash around me and swallow me whole.

But I have to try. I have to at least take a shot at making my dreams come true.

Back in my suite, I hurry to the far window, the one that opens onto the fire escape. Reed Tower is an architectural landmark, completed during the last great surge of Art Deco construction in Manhattan and renamed by my father. A monument to his ego disguised as respect for history.

The wrought iron fire escape is an original feature. Ornate. Sturdy. And a potential route to freedom.

It takes a moment for my trembling fingers to pull aside the drape and unlatch the window. Then another few moments as I take five deep breaths, rush to raise it, then take two protective steps back.

Cool night air rushes in, carrying the distant sounds of the city below—honking horns, fragments of music, and the constant ambient hum of millions of lives being lived beyond these walls.

I desperately want to be among them.

Do it.

I inch forward

Do it now.

I hold my breath, moving fast as I force one leg through the opening, then the other, until I'm sitting on the windowsill, the metal grating of the fire escape just inches below my feet and my heart pounding so hard my chest aches.

But I'm here. I'm halfway outside. Halfway into becoming part of the world.

All I have to do is step out.

One simple step.

Then I look down.

The city sprawls beneath me, a glittering void. My breathing accelerates, but I can't get enough air. Spots dance before my eyes as the familiar grip of panic tightens around me.

Central Park stretches northward like a deep, dark, mouth, ready to consume me. Buildings rise on all sides, the emptiness between them vast and consuming.

The void whispers to me, the awful vastness ready to swallow me whole.

My body freezes. I'm locked in the space between imprisonment and freedom, utterly paralyzed.

You're not strong enough for freedom.

My father's words slither through my mind. I want to shake them off, but he's right. I'm weak. I'm broken. I'm exactly what he's made me.

With a strangled sob, I wrench myself back through the window, slamming it shut before sinking to the ground.

I stay there, knees pulled to my chest, until my breathing steadies and the panic fades to a familiar background hum. Then I haul myself up and retreat to the one place where I still have some control. The only place in the whole damn tower that is truly—mostly—mine.

My studio occupies the northeast corner of my suite, where the morning light is best. Canvases and paint dominate one half, while my custom-built computer system commands the other.

I stand before my easel, where an unfinished cityscape waits. It's a view of Manhattan from above, but unlike the actual view from my windows, this one doesn't terrify me. On canvas, I control the perspective, the depth, the vastness. On canvas, I can look down at the world without fear of falling into it.

My hand hovers over my palette, but the colors seem wrong tonight, flat and lifeless. The painting won't save me. Not today.

I turn instead to my computer, powering it up with a sense of desperate need. This tricked-out machine is the one concession my father grants me without question. Perhaps because technology serves as another barrier between me and the real world. Or maybe he understands I need some form of escape, even if it isn't real.

As soon as I've typed in the complex series of passwords, Elysium materializes on my screen—not a game but a world. My world. With verdant landscapes and clear blue skies. The one place where I make the rules, where gravity is optional, and doors can open anywhere I imagine. A place where I can touch and be touched. Where I'm not locked away like some virginal princess awaiting sacrifice.

I've been building Elysium since I was fifteen, teaching myself coding through online courses and programming books Ruby smuggles past my father's watchful eyes. What began as a tiny virtual garden has evolved into an intricate realm of impossible architecture and breathtaking landscapes, all stored on off-site servers and protected by a series of passcodes that I'm sure my father can't hack.

I forgot to charge the headset and bodysuit that lets me fully experience Elysium, so tonight I'll be in my virtual home only on the flat screen. That, however, is better than not visiting at all, and I eagerly navigate to the central castle—a structure nothing like Reed Tower. Inside, I've built rooms that couldn't exist in the real world—spaces that defy physics, chambers that expand beyond their apparent dimensions, and staircases that twist into impossible geometries.

In Elysium, I'm free and unafraid.

I send my avatar to the castle's highest tower, where Lydia tends a garden of digital stars. I've given her my mother's name and features, or at least what I've seen in photos: laughing blue eyes and a dimple on her left cheek. Sometimes, I pretend it's really her, watching over me in this world I've created.

"Hello, Vale darling," digital-Lydia says, calling me by my avatar's name. "What shall we build today?"

In answer, I start creating a dark tower with pale blue windows. A man stands to one side, his face shrouded in shadows. But I know him. A dark prince who has visited my realm for over a year. A passionate lover who has yet to reveal himself fully to me.

For months, he only watched me. Then he came closer, and closer still, until finally, we began to walk the paths of my realm together. He refused to tell me his name, saying only that he was a prince in a far-off kingdom. He told me that it was my privilege to name him, and I did—Prince Killiam the Noble.

He'd smiled at that, his shadowed mouth curving just slightly.

I'd tried to see beyond the shadows—hell, I'd tried to alter the code—but I'd utterly failed to learn more about this prince I crave. I only know that the AI that I wove into this world built him for me, this prince who has become my forbidden lover. A passionate man who fulfills all my fantasies in this illicit affair. A romance that will prove deadly if we are discovered.

The king won't allow his princess to be touched by a rogue prince, after all.

My fingers dance on the keys, and I—Vale—hurry closer, bounding across the open field, taking care to ensure that my father, the king, isn't watching.

I crave him, this prince who calls to Vale. *To me.* We know that he's forbidden, and yet we're powerless to resist his touch. His kisses.

My heart pounds, my breasts ache, and a delicious warmth teases between my legs. I slide my hand down, my breath coming ragged, but this isn't me—it's Vale, and I ease my avatar closer, drawn by the intensity of this man who never wavers. This prince who has claimed me so deliciously, so thoroughly.

Closer, then closer still.

A screech rents the sky, and I look up to see my pet dragons circling above, ready to incinerate anything that might threaten me. I lift a hand to wave them off. My prince would never harm me.

But the dragons remain, their enormous wings sending shock waves through the air as I move close enough to finally, truly glimpse my prince.

Except he's gone—a solid man one moment, then a column of mist the next.

My fingers freeze on the keys, my heart pounding with frustration and foiled desire.

Dammit.

I was so close. So close to learning what I crave. What I want.

I don't trust my dreams in the real world—they're too tinged with my father's orders and demands. But in Elysium … that's where I see the real me reflected back.

I need that.

I need to see who really hides behind the shadows.

Because in the real world, it's Liam Grimm who has slipped into my fantasies, and that can't be right. Because other than my father, he is the man I hate most of all.

"Dammit!" I cry again as I slam the top down on my computer. *What the hell is wrong with me?*

The answer comes in my father's voice: *You're a beautiful, broken, sick little girl who men will try to take advantage of. Who needs her father to watch over her. Who needs a strong, guiding hand. Trust your daddy, Princess. I'll take care of you. I'll keep you safe from the dark things in the world.*

Except he won't. My father *is* the dark thing, and I'm trapped here with him, where no one can hear me scream.

FOUR
THE GALA

The Beautify Manhattan Gala is held at the Pershing, a stunning hotel with marble floors and gilded everything. Major players in the industry circle each other like wolves in designer clothing, all pretending to like each other while jockeying for position.

My father guides me through the room, his hand resting possessively on my lower back. "Showtime, darling," he murmurs.

I want to break away from his touch, but I know the kind of punishment that awaits me if I'm anything other than the perfect cosmetics princess tonight. Slightly aloof and pristinely elegant. A walking aspiration rather than a real woman.

Too bad for me, I'm as real as they come, complete with fears that are determined to set me up to fail as the space both stretches and contracts around me. The room is too open, too exposed, and all of my breath seems determined to escape, leaving me weak and helpless on my father's arm. Which is the last place I want to be.

No.

I force in a breath, then slowly release it, all the while regretting not taking my meds again today. What I'd intended as an act of defiance against my father was really me sabotaging myself.

Stop it. This is just a party. Just one more event for Father to show me off. Nothing new here. Nothing I haven't done a million times over.

"Sasha?"

I hear the edge in his voice, and I'm certain he knows I'm spiraling.

But I'm not. I can't. *I won't.*

Not because of the punishment he'd surely render, but because I refuse to embarrass myself that way.

With more effort than it took to get into this damn dress, I lift my face and smile at him. "Lightheaded," I say. "I should have had a bite before we left home."

For a moment, I think he's going to call me on the lie. Then he lifts his hand, signaling a waiter who comes over with a tray of small crystal plates topped with fruit and cheese.

I'm not hungry, but I thank both the waiter and my father. And, of course, I eat the fruit, using the tiny fork as my father continues to parade me through the room, showing me off to anyone looking in our direction.

Once I've finished the snack, Father steers us toward Desmond Bane, standing among a cluster of men, all in tuxedos. He's talking to Leo Grimm, the youngest of the five brothers. And, possibly, an even bigger asshole than Liam Grimm. He's got a lanky build and a relaxed manner, but that's just the exterior of a cold, calculating, and dangerous man. I should know—I was the one who held Ruby's hand when he so brutally betrayed her six years ago.

I glance around, wondering if the rest of the brothers are on site, but I don't see them. Good. I've had more than enough of the Brothers Grimm lately.

My relief fades when Desmond sees us. He smiles as he stalks toward me, slow and proprietary. I shiver, suddenly feeling as if he's the hunter and I'm his prey.

"Sasha," he says, taking my hand and pressing his lips to it. His mouth is hot and damp against my skin, and when he releases my hand, I have to fight the urge to wipe it clean against the folds of my dress.

"It's so good to see you," I say, forcing a smile.

"You as well. You look exquisite as always." His eyes graze over me with such a proprietary leer I actually shudder.

I conjure my most party-ready smile. "Please excuse me. I'm sure you two have business to discuss, and I should mingle."

My father's expression tightens, but he can hardly make a scene.

The further away I move, the easier it is to breathe, and by the time I've weaved through the clusters of Manhattan's elite and spotted Ruby, I feel like myself again. She's serving champagne when she sees me, then nods toward one of the balconies.

I reach it before she does, finding it mercifully empty. Despite the height, I feel less anxious out here than inside. The openness of the night sky is somehow less threatening than the ballroom with Desmond's watching eyes.

Even so, I stand away from the railing, my back to the stone wall and my eyes closed.

I hear the door open, glad Ruby's finally here.

But it's not Ruby who speaks.

"Running away again, Ms. Reed?" The voice is deep, masculine, and disturbingly familiar. A tremor runs through me that has nothing to do with fear, but everything to do with danger.

I open my eyes, turning to see Liam Grimm shut the door behind him before striding across the narrow balcony. He turns his back to the rail so that he's facing me, the black void of sky and city looming behind him.

He stands straight, his posture almost arrogant in a black tuxedo that fits his broad shoulders perfectly. His copper hair gleams in the dim light, like fire against the inky-black sky. A dark prince. Dangerous and compelling.

I swallow, unsure if it's the void that disturbs me or the man. I lift my chin, forcing myself to meet his eyes. "Following me again?"

"Escaping the tedium." He's holding a small plate with a bowl of melted chocolate and several thin, cylinder-shaped cookies. He dips one end of a cookie in the chocolate, then puts it in his mouth, sucking the chocolate off in a way that goes straight between my thighs. Then he bites off the end of the cookie, making me jump as if being released from a dream.

He smiles, his eyes roaming slowly over me, as he holds out the plate. "Care for one?"

"I—no, thank you. I don't eat sweets."

"Don't? Or you're not allowed?"

I say nothing.

"Too bad. I was looking forward to watching you … enjoy yourself."

I lift my chin. "If you don't mind, I came out here to be alone."

"You came out here to meet with Ruby. But I believe she's tied up at the moment."

I stiffen. "How do you—"

"That's quite the statement you're making with your attire," he says, his eyes grazing over the virginal white tent of material that practically screams *storybook princess.* "Your father's choice?"

I should be relieved that he knows I didn't pick the hideous thing. But he's making me so edgy that I snap instead. "What makes you say that?"

Something flickers in his eyes—understanding, perhaps. Or calculation. "Your father has always been a master at manipulation."

"Care to elaborate, Mr. Grimm?"

Instead of answering, Grimm pushes away from the rail and steps toward me. Close. Too close. His scent—dark and primal—envelops me. And the heat from his body mingles with the cool night air, making the space between us seem charged with electricity.

"Tell me, Sasha, has your father said anything to you about his plans for tonight?"

The use of my first name feels far too intimate, and I bristle. "What do you know about it?"

"I make it my business to know what Victor Reed is planning. Especially when it involves using his daughter as a bargaining chip."

He's baiting me, and I tell myself I should just walk away. But I can't. I've been my father's pawn more times than I can count, and every time I've been blindsided. If Grimm has insight, I want to hear it. Especially in light of Ruby's intel that an announcement is coming.

"All right," I finally say. "What are you talking about?"

The corner of his mouth quirks up. "Your father really is the bastard I've always believed him to be."

Panic taunts me, and the night starts to close in. "Just tell me." The words come out as a plea, not a demand, and I want to kick myself for showing weakness.

For a long moment, he says nothing, but I think I hear a hint of compassion when he finally says, "An engagement announcement tonight would be quite the strategic move for Reed Cosmetics. Bane Marketing merging with Reed's empire—very tidy."

I shake my head, not yet certain where he's going with this.

"And since Lucent currently works exclusively with Bane on its marketing, it's also a deviously underhanded way to force Bane to withdraw his services from Lucent. Leaving my family's company in a lurch, your father as the winner, and Desmond Bane …"

He trails off as he deliberately rakes his gaze over me, slow and heated. "Well, I guess Desmond's the biggest winner of all."

He frowns as he strokes his chin, like a detective in a bad movie. "I'm not quite sure where that leaves you, Ms. Reed," he finally says. "But at least you're already dressed for the occasion."

I try to move, but my body's turned to stone.

"You really didn't know," Grimm says slowly, his eyes narrowing as he studies my reaction.

"Just go." I have to force the words past the tightness in my throat.

He stays. "I take it this isn't a happy day for the beautiful bride. White," he adds, appraising the gown with the hint of a smirk. "So, is she a virginal bride?"

My face goes hot. "You can leave now, Mr. Grimm."

"I'm perfectly comfortable here. But you? What will you do now, Princess?"

"Please. Just go."

"You're going to walk back in there and do what Daddy says," he continues, ignoring my plea. "Because that's what you've done your entire, pampered, little life."

Anger flares hot and bright inside me. "You know nothing about my life."

"Don't I?" He steps closer, trapping me like wounded prey, the night sky now visible only over his broad shoulders. "I know that your father has kept you like a bird in a gilded cage for years. I know about your agoraphobia—so convenient for keeping you hidden away. I know about your medications. And I know that they make you dependent on him."

My heart hammers against my ribs, so hard it makes me dizzy. "What? How—"

"I make it my business to collect information. I pay well, and my people know that what they deliver had better be accurate." He studies my face for a moment, and in that short span of time I want to bury him in a blizzard of horrible words and violent screams. But I can't even conjure a squeak.

He leans in closer, and I feel the whisper of his breath as he says, "I know what I know, Ms. Reed."

His nearness is disorienting—threatening and thrilling in equal measure. Part of me wants to shove him away. But some small, hidden part wants to step closer. To see what would happen if I surrendered to the magnetic pull drawing me toward this man.

"Sasha?" My father's voice shatters the moment. He stands in the balcony doorway, his expression a mask of paternal concern that doesn't quite reach his eyes. "Desmond's been looking for you."

I swallow, recognizing the steel beneath my father's polite tone. "I was just getting some air."

"With Mr. Grimm?" His gaze shifts to Grimm, who takes a step back, freeing up space for me to breathe.

"We were discussing business," Grimm says smoothly. "Specifically, the remarkable similarities between Lucent's current branding and Reed's upcoming campaign."

I frown—I'm not aware of any campaign other than our idiotic and saccharine Dreams campaign, and that's nothing like Lucent's historically excellent advertisements.

My father's smile doesn't falter, but his eyes harden. "Creative inspiration is the lifeblood of our industry, Mr. Grimm."

"And theft is the lifeblood of fools," Grimm replies, matching my father's false civility.

The tension between them crackles like electricity, and I'm caught in the crossfire as pieces of a puzzle I can't see take shape around me.

"Now, Sasha," my father says, extending his hand to me. "The presentations are about to begin. Your presence is required."

It's not a request, and I dutifully take my father's hand. As he leads me back inside, I glance over my shoulder. Grimm watches us, his expression unreadable, but his eyes burn with an intensity that follows me long after he's out of sight.

FIVE

BETRAYAL

Father's grip is unyielding as he leads me through the throng. "What the hell were you thinking?" His voice is low, intended only for me.

"He approached me," I say. "I was just getting some air."

"Stay away from him. He's more dangerous than you can imagine." He stops, then looks me in the eye, and for the first time in my life I think he might actually be seeing me. "Promise you'll stay away from that man."

"I—Of course." I'm confused by my father's reaction, but not about his assessment of Grimm. "I have no interest in talking to him again."

I meet my father's eyes, certain he sees the truth in mine.

Except …

I look away, not to let my father see the tiny flutter of doubt … and the more violent twinge of desire.

Before I can analyze my traitorous emotions, we reach the small stage at the front of the room, and a wave of nausea washes over me when I see Desmond standing a few yards away. My father's grip on my arm tightens as we move to join him, my legs reluctantly carrying me alongside my father.

No, no. Please no.

Desmond turns and strides toward us, meeting us halfway with a wolfish grin that makes my stomach twist.

31

"Ladies and gentlemen." The voice of the gala's director booms through the speakers. "If I could have your attention …"

Desmond reaches us, and I stand rigidly between him and my father. Grimm can't be right—he can't. But even as I try to convince myself of that, I know that some sort of trap is closing around me. And I haven't a clue how to escape.

When the director invites my father to the stage, Desmond moves closer, his hand pressing against the small of my back with the casual certainty of an owner.

"After my wife's tragic death," my father says with practiced emotion, "my daughter Sasha became my reason for living. Tonight, I'm proud to announce not only Reed Cosmetics' continued support for this worthy cause, but also a new chapter in our family's story."

My heart hammers against my ribs, and Desmond's hand moves from the small of my back to my upper arm, his fingers tightening enough to leave a bruise.

"You're my crown jewel," Desmond whispers. "I know I'll enjoy you very, very much."

"No," I whisper. "Please, no."

But Desmond only smiles as Father continues. "I'm delighted to share that Reed Cosmetics will be entering a new partnership with Bane Marketing, strengthening both our companies for the future."

I turn, searching the crowd to find Grimm's smug face, but my father's next words make me forget Grimm entirely. "And on a more personal note," he continues, "I'm even more pleased to announce the engagement of my daughter to Desmond Bane."

The room erupts in applause, and I want to kick myself for not racing away when I'd had the chance. Desmond's arm circles my waist, drawing me closer to his side. Cameras flash. I force my lips into a smile even though I want to scream that I never agreed to this. That I'm nothing more than a marionette and Desmond and Father are pulling my strings.

But the words don't come.

All I can do is stand straight and numb at Desmond's side, playing my role just the way I have my entire life.

My father beams at us from the podium, the picture of paternal pride. To anyone watching, this is a beautiful moment. But I feel the bars of my cage contracting, squeezing tighter until I can barely breathe.

Desmond leans down, his lips brushing my ear. "Mine, Sasha," he says, his voice sickeningly smooth. "You'll be coming home with me tonight. I don't intend to wait for our wedding night to get between those luscious thighs."

Bile rises in my throat as he leads me onto the stage to stand beside my father. *This can't be happening. This can't be real.*

But it is, and when he slips a massive diamond ring onto my finger, reality finally crashes over me. My father has sold me to a monster. I'm not his daughter, just something to be traded.

Through the haze of flashing cameras and congratulations, I see Grimm. Our eyes lock across the room. Unlike everyone else, he isn't smiling. His expression is dark. Intense. And though I don't know why, it gives me strength.

In that horrible moment, I make my decision.

I will not be the prize in my father's game. I will not marry Desmond Bane. I will escape my cage tonight or die trying.

I just need to figure out how.

———

THE EVENING PASSES in a blur of congratulations as Desmond and I make the rounds. "You look a bit pale," he says during a rare moment when we're relatively alone.

It's not a legitimate expression of concern, of course. It's a test to see if I'll defy him.

I won't. Not now. Not without a plan. My father only locks me in the tower. I'm certain Bane's punishments will be the kind that leave bruises and draw blood.

"Anything troubling you?" he continues.

"Just overwhelmed," I reply, which isn't entirely a lie. "I should find Ruby," I add, grasping for any excuse to escape him. "My medication—"

"Your father mentioned you might need this." Desmond reaches into his pocket and produces a familiar pill case—my emergency stash of meds. "He said large crowds sometimes trigger your condition."

The realization that they've discussed my "condition" makes bile rise in my throat. I take the pill case, almost wanting to swallow them right now. Wanting to bring back the haze through which I now realize I've always seen the world.

No.

I force myself to smile, then even give his hand an affectionate squeeze. "I'll just go … freshen up."

Thankfully, he doesn't come with me, and I hurry away, certain he'll reappear at my side soon. I spot Ruby clearing glasses near one of the service entrances, and hurry toward her.

"Sasha! Oh, my god. Are you okay?"

I meet her eyes, and she shakes her head, wincing.

"Sorry. Stupid question."

"What about you? I saw Leo in the crowd."

She lifts her shoulders in what looks like a casual shrug, but I know better.

"What can I do?"

"Nothing," she says. "It's fine. That's ancient history, and it's going to stay that way. Besides, he won't bother me tonight. We both know his father will disown him if he talks to the help."

Since she's right about that, I twist the conversation back to my more immediate concern—me.

"I have to get out of here."

She glances around. "Hell yeah, you do. But how?"

"I don't know. Somehow." I flash the hideous ring. "I'm terrified, Rue. I mean, can I really do this? Can I really run? If he catches me, he'll keep me trapped inside forever."

The words hang in the air. We both know they aren't hyperbole.

"Then I guess you're marrying Desmond."

Her tone is matter-of-fact, and I know she's goading me. I also know it's working.

I shake my head. "No. No, I'm not going to let him hand me over to a monster who treats women like possessions he can destroy when he's bored. I want a life. I want *my* life. The one I never got to live."

I didn't even get to go to college when Ruby did. If I had, maybe she and Leo—

No.

I push the thought out of my head. Really not the time.

"I'm running," I say firmly. "I'm getting out of here tonight, because who knows when I'll ever have the chance again?"

She bites her lower lip the way she does when she's thinking. "Okay, so you run. Bold move, but it might work." She scans the room, then nods toward a set of doors. "There's a service corridor through there. It leads to the kitchen, then out to the loading dock. But Sasha … then what?"

I want to say it doesn't matter. I only care about getting out. But of course it matters. I have no money I can access. No place to hide that isn't connected to him somehow. No friends outside Father's orbit.

"I'll sell the damn ring." I don't love the idea. It would feel too much like Desmond was taking care of me. But I don't even have cash or a credit card. Just my phone, my meds, and a lipstick.

I lift my little cocktail purse. "All Father would let me bring."

"Here," Ruby says, pulling a slim wallet from the back pocket of her uniform slacks. She passes me a credit card. "The limit's only ten grand, but it's paid off."

Tears sting my eyes. "Thank you."

"Be careful where you use it. Your father's not an idiot. He'll think about tracking my cards eventually, and—"

"Then I can't take it."

She pushes away the card I'm trying to give back. "I'll tell him you stole my purse from the kitchen. I'll be fine. Take it."

When I hesitate, she crosses her arms and tilts her head. "Take it or I tell."

"You wouldn't."

She smiles and shrugs innocently. I sigh. I know she wouldn't ever betray me. But I take the damn card. "Thank you," I say again, pulling her into a tight hug.

She squeezes back. "Now go."

I nod, and with a final glance at the glittering ballroom, I slip through the service door.

The corridor is dimly lit and narrow, lined with shelves of supplies. I follow the sound of clattering dishes to the kitchen, grateful that the staff is too busy to pay much attention to me. Even so, I skirt along the wall, keeping my head down until I reach the loading dock.

It's a large open area with delivery trucks and a few members of the hotel staff on smoke breaks. The cool night air brushes my face, and I draw a deep breath, eager for this first taste of freedom.

Then I hear my father.

"Well, find her goddammit!"

I jump, then slide into a shadowy alcove beside a stack of crates, terrified that the pounding of my heart will give me away.

"We have people at all exits, sir," someone says over the thud of approaching footsteps. "She can't have gone far."

I twist my head, frantically searching for another way out. I'm about to take my chances and run when a hand closes over my mouth from behind, and in that same moment, an arm like steel captures my waist and drags me backward into darkness.

"Don't scream." The whispered voice is deep. Familiar.

Liam Grimm.

The tension in my body changes from terror to something I can't identify. Relief, I think. Only it's coupled with something even more disturbing than fear.

I nod once, and his hand leaves my mouth, though his arm remains around my waist, holding me against his large frame. I feel his heartbeat against my back, the heat of him so intense I fear I might burn. His breath stirs the hair at my nape, sending a ripple of unwelcome shivers down my spine.

"Are we safe?" My whisper is so low I'm afraid he might not hear it.

"For now. Storage closet. Pressure door. No latch, so it's well camouflaged. And they'll be focusing on exits."

"How did you find me?"

"I saw your face when your joyous news was announced. I knew you'd run." There's a hint of approval in his voice.

"You'll help me get out of here?" I turn in his arms, facing him in the dim light filtering under the door.

Grimm studies me, his expression unreadable in the darkness. "Why should I stick my neck out for you?"

"You already have."

He nods, conceding the point. "I can walk away right now."

"But you won't."

Even in the dark, I can see his brow rise. "Why not?"

"Because you hate my father."

He's silent for so long I fear he's going to say no. Then he says, "And what will you give me in return?"

"Information. About Reed Cosmetics. About any of my father's operations."

He chuckles, and his arm around me tightens, forcing my body to press up against his. "I've been getting that information for years without your help."

"I—well, what do you want?"

He lifts his free hand, then traces my jawline with surprising gentleness. The touch burns against my skin like a brand.

"Everything."

For a moment, I forget how to breathe.

"I don't know what that means."

"Does it matter?"

"Of course it matters!"

He chuckles. "Those are my terms. Everything. Yes or no. But hurry. They'll find us here sooner or later. My money's on sooner."

Yes or no.

The devil who bought me or the devil who's holding me?

"Yes."

The word is barely a whisper, but from his smug, satisfied smile, I know he heard me.

He takes his arm from my waist, and I suddenly feel so vulnerable that I almost beg him to put it back.

"My car's in the underground garage. There's a service elevator that goes directly there. We need to move quickly."

I nod, pushing aside my questions and doubts. Right now, escape is all that matters.

Grimm slips off his tuxedo jacket and hands it to me. "Cover up some of that white." Once I put it on, he eases the door open, then takes my hand. "Stay close."

We slip through the kitchen, Grimm moving with such quiet authority that no one pays much attention to us at all.

At the service elevator, Grimm swipes a key card and the doors slide open instantly. Once inside, he releases my hand, then presses the button for the garage level.

As the elevator descends, reality crashes over me. I'm running away with a virtual stranger—a man my father considers an enemy. I have no plan, no resources, and nowhere to go.

And no idea as to the *everything* I've promised him.

Well, perhaps I have some idea …

I shiver, not certain if the reaction is from fear, revulsion, or desire.

"Second thoughts?"

I hesitate, then shake my head. "None."

"Good. Because there's no turning back now." The elevator doors open onto a dimly lit parking garage. "Once your father realizes you've left with me, he'll come after you with everything he has."

The statement should terrify me. Instead, it somehow steadies my resolve. "I know."

Grimm leads me to a sleek black Aston Martin tucked into a far corner of the garage. He opens the passenger door, gesturing for me to get in.

I hesitate for just a moment, aware that I'm stepping into the unknown. Then I slide onto the leather seat, my ridiculous white gown billowing around me like a deflating balloon.

As Grimm walks around to the driver's side, I stare at the enormous diamond still on my finger. This foul thing represents everything I'm rejecting—my father's control, Desmond's ownership, a life mapped out and paid for without my consent.

Grimm slides in and starts the car. Without thinking, I roll down the window and toss the ring into the darkness of the garage. It makes a tiny, satisfying sound as it bounces across the concrete.

Grimm raises an eyebrow. "That was at least twenty carats."

"It was a shackle."

He studies me for a moment, then nods once, something like respect flashing in his eyes.

"Where are we going?" I ask.

"Somewhere your father can't reach you."

A chill curls through me. I've crossed the line. There's no coming back.

And Liam Grimm, with his dangerous eyes and dark bargain, is my only way forward into the blackness ahead.

SIX
DEVIL'S BARGAIN

As Grimm expertly maneuvers through the dense Manhattan traffic, I sit rigidly in the passenger seat, trying to ignore the way the oncoming headlights sting my eyes. I look down, keeping the layers of my dress wrapped around me like a security blanket as I try not to think about the enormity of what I've done. What Father will do if he finds me. *When* he finds me.

He'll kill me.

Except he won't. I'll be punished, yes. Locked up. My privileges ripped away. No more painting or sketching. No more time on a computer.

No more Elysium.

Death would be more kind.

Oh, god, what have I done?

"You're very quiet," Grimm says, interrupting my mental spin-out. "Having regrets or basking in your victory?"

"No regrets," I say, the words true despite my fears. "But no victory, either."

"No?" He turns and rakes his eyes over me, the slow, heated gaze leaving me more than a little unsettled. Like my father, Liam Grimm radiates power and control. But where my father's control feels suffo-cating, Grimm's feels … magnetic.

And that's what makes him dangerous.

I lift my chin. "I'll claim victory when I'm free. But I'm not, am I?"

"No. You're not."

Everything.

A shiver runs up my spine, but I'm not cold. On the contrary, I feel an unwelcome heat spreading through me as I think about that one and only condition for his help. A condition that teases uncomfortably close to fantasies I don't want to admit.

Unsettled, I turn toward the side window, as if another view might somehow increase the distance between us. "Where are we going?" I ask again, but I get only silence in response. I want to shout the question, but why waste my breath? When I fled with no plan and no resources, I'd placed myself at the mercy of the devil himself.

My hands shake with what can only be nerves. All things considered, it's possible I was too hasty.

Then again, between the devil and Desmond Bane, I'll take the devil. Especially if he can protect me from my father.

I close my eyes, letting myself drift as the events of this very crazy day settle in my mind. I'd assumed he would take me to Grimm Tower, but we've been driving in the wrong direction for at least half an hour. I'm sure he expects me to beg him to tell me where we're going—and I do desperately want to know. Just not enough to give him the satisfaction of asking.

Then again, as far as tonight's events are concerned, I think Grimm wins any competition that might exist between us. But I don't care. All I care about is that he's taking me away from my father and Desmond. And despite my doubts and fears, I'm more than happy to simply sit here and bask in that lovely new reality.

I only realize I must have dozed off when he brakes hard, and my eyes fly open, my heart pounding. I see a dog racing off into the dark and Grimm gripping the steering wheel like a vise. "Sorry. It bolted right out in front of me."

"Nothing to apologize for," I say, oddly reassured that he didn't hit the dog. Considering what I know of his family, I wouldn't expect any of that clan to go out of their way to avoid a toddler, much less an animal.

I shift to look in the direction the dog bolted and find myself staring at Grimm Tower, its dark presence both threatening and compelling.

Whereas Reed Tower has an Art Deco vibe—sleek lines, geometric patterns, and gleaming metal—Grimm Tower is Gothic, with towering spires, shadowed archways, and carved stone gargoyles.

Both sit on the Central Park perimeter, with my father's lair dominating the east and Grimm Tower looming over the west side near Columbus Circle.

"One of the first skyscrapers in Manhattan," Liam says, and I recall that Grimm Tower was built about a decade before my family's home. "My great-grandfather commissioned it when the family publishing business expanded."

"It's beautiful." I don't begrudge the Grimm family the admission. There's an elegance to Grimm Tower that has always drawn me in. I've even battled my own fears and curled up in the window seat on the west side of my suite for the pleasure of admiring the way the sun gleams off the copper-green of the spires.

I shift to look at Grimm more directly. "We could have walked here from The Pershing in less than twenty minutes. Why on earth have we been driving around for an hour just to end up—*oh*." It's like a cartoon lightbulb brightens above my head. "If they were following, you wanted to lose them."

"And I wanted them to see me heading out of the city. I have property in Connecticut. Let them try and get past that security."

He looks so amused by the idea that I almost laugh, my humor bolstered by another cartoon image. This one of my father electrified on a protective fence like some vile version of Wile E. Coyote.

"Something funny?" he asks, but I just shake my head and bite back a tiny smile, feeling more relaxed than I have all evening.

That feeling of comfort lingers only for a few more minutes. That's when Grimm turns off the road and navigates the car into the Tower's underground garage. He doesn't slow as he expertly steers the Aston Martin down the winding driveway to the lowest level—one with a second gate, more cameras, and who knows what other security measures.

Clearly, this is the area where the family parks.

"Do you live here?" I ask as we head for the elevator.

"When it suits me," he says, in a tone that makes clear I won't be getting more specifics.

Like the penthouse level at home, this elevator requires both a key card and a fingerprint scan. Unlike Reed Tower, it also requires an optical scan. The technology is sleek, expensive, and speaks of serious security concerns.

I don't know why I'm surprised. I've known for years that many of the Grimm family ventures aren't exactly squeaky clean. Seeing this level of security, I'm thinking those mysterious ventures are positively caked in mud.

I don't look at Grimm as the elevator sweeps us up into the sky. He's my savior, yes. But I'm savvy enough to understand that he's my captor, too. For all intents and purposes, he now owns me.

Everything.

The word echoes in my mind, both ominous and enticing in a way I don't want to think about. But I still don't know what he means by that. Does he want sex? Information? Or does he have some darker plan to hurt my father, and I'm nothing more than a pawn he's willing to destroy?

I shudder, my hands shaking. What the hell have I done?

When the doors slide open onto the fifty-seventh-floor apartment's opulent entryway, I can't seem to move. He's been standing behind me, but now steps around and faces me. He extends a hand.

I don't take it.

"It's okay, Sasha," he says in a voice designed to coax a kitten. "I won't let him hurt you."

I believe him. I do. And yet …

"Will you?"

His eyes lock on mine, and I see a glimmer of something dangerous. "Perhaps."

My body goes strangely warm as he takes one long step toward me so that he's standing right in front of me. He slides one hand against my waist as he moves in even closer. "If I do," he murmurs, his breath hot on my ear, "I have a feeling that you'll like it."

Then he turns his back to me and continues across the entry toward the living area, where floor-to-ceiling windows showcase Manhattan spread out below, the city lights glittering like stars beckoning me to come fall with them.

I tense as that familiar tightness presses against my neck, like an invisible hand threatening to cut off my air. The doors begin to close, and I reach over, jabbing the button to open them again. Then I close my eyes and step into the entryway, my heart pounding against my ribs as I trade the captivity of one tower for the possibilities of another.

I miss the safe, close walls of the elevator, but I couldn't let it descend, taking me alone into the world of Elias Grimm and the family that has been my lifelong enemy.

And even if I reached the lobby safely—even if I bolted out into the night—what good would that do? I'd be alone with my father's men hunting me, ready to trap me and toss me into that horrible maw that is Desmond.

Everything.

The word whispers through me, and once again, I feel that shiver up my spine. That's what awaits me if I catch up with Grimm. *Everything.*

I tell myself that while the thought of Liam Grimm touching me is vile, it's less vile than the thought of Desmond's hands on me.

And that's true. So very, very true.

But it's also a lie.

Because even though it terrifies me—even though I would shout from the rooftops that Liam Grimm is horrible—my dark, terrible secret is that despite the odious things he said to me at that charity gala three years ago, when I slid my hand between my legs that night, it was his fingers I imagined stroking me. His lips breathing life into mine.

And the thing that I most hate about him now?

That despite his cruel taunts and insults, he still has a starring role in my dreams.

———

"WOULD you like me to block the windows?"

I've taken one step out of the elevator and am looking at the floor when his voice washes over me, so low and gentle that I almost wonder if the speaker is someone other than Grimm.

I know better, of course, and yet that tiny show of compassion settles inside me, warm and comforting. I hold onto it as I look up, then focus on his face and not the floor-to-ceiling windows beyond.

"I—" I press my lips together, uncertain what I'd intended to say. Part of me wants to lift my chin and tell him that I'm not nearly as weak as he thinks I am. The other part wants to crawl back into the elevator and hide in the corner. Because yes, I truly am that weak.

He studies me with those eyes that somehow see all my secrets. Then he lifts his arm, taps something on his smartwatch, and the windows instantly turn opaque.

"Oh," I say, the word hanging foolishly in the air. "Thank you."

"The windows are triple-reinforced. The building would shatter around us before the windows saw even a crack. You're safe," he says, then cocks his head. "From that, anyway."

There's a dark heat in his voice. A warning not to trust him. A reminder that acts of kindness don't mean he's kind, and that I still don't understand his full agenda.

That basic reality makes my stomach churn, and I take a deep breath, trying to get back on steady ground. I nod toward the windows, then force a casual smile. "Triple-reinforced, huh? Are you anticipating a bombing?"

A single brow rises along with the corner of his mouth. "Now that I've taken you from your father and Mr. Bane, perhaps I should be."

I dip my head to hide my smile, then look back up when his choice of words registers with me. "Taken?" I repeat. "I seem to recall making a choice."

"No." Those predatory eyes lock onto me like lasers. "You didn't."

I open my mouth to argue but close it again. He's right, of course. As much as I may despise the entire Grimm family, between running away with Liam and staying behind to marry Desmond, there was no choice at all.

"That's only semantics."

"No," he counters, stepping toward me. He takes my hand, his slightly calloused, and for a moment, I wonder if this man is more than a billionaire heir whose only work consists of sitting behind a desk making decisions.

"No?"

He moves toward me. "Let me be clear. I will protect you, Princess, but only so long as you fully comply with our agreement. From here on out, you will do as I say—*what* I say. And each and every *yes* that slips through those famous lips represents you choosing to remain under my protection."

I tug my hand away. "What exactly do you want me to do?"

His smile is wolfish. "*What* isn't part of this equation. You agreed to everything. I expect you to live up to that bargain."

I tilt my head down, not quite able to meet his eyes when I say, "You're talking sex."

"Look at me," he demands in a voice that makes clear I have no choice.

I look up to see that he's stepped even closer, so close that I can see the hard lines of that gorgeous face and the ice in his pale blue eyes.

"Sex is too soft a word, Princess. Love is a fairy tale, and sex is a release. And the love of a good woman won't fix a bad man. My mother learned that the hard way. So did yours."

I want to ask what he means, but he continues on. "I don't do relationships. I don't have sex as if I'm having tea. I fuck. For the foreseeable future, I'll be fucking you."

Oh, I say. Except no sound actually comes out.

"I'll have you, Sasha. And I will take the *everything* you pledged to me. But have no illusions. I'll keep you safe from Victor because that was our agreement, but we are not riding off into the sunset when the curtain comes down."

As if I'd want to! But I can't get those words out, either.

"And I'll tell you a little secret, Princess," he adds, taking my hand and pulling me close. He puts one hand on my breast, the other over the lace of my dress, right at my core. He pushes the material between my legs so that I gasp at the pressure of his finger at my entrance. I stifle a moan, unwilling to let him see any reaction from me at all.

"I want to fuck you," he whispers, that damn finger now teasing my clit and making my thoughts spin wildly. "I want to taint you. Not because of you, Princess. But because you're the one pure thing your father has. I'll take you and use you to get back at him. But I won't keep you." He steps back, breaking contact, and for a horrible, hateful moment, I mourn the loss.

"And that's a good thing, he adds, "because I'm a man who would destroy you." He takes a single step toward me. "I'll use your body to get off. I'll use you to get revenge. But I won't hurt you—or if I do, I promise you'll like it," he adds with the slightest twitch of his lips. "And I'll help you get free from your father and get Bane out of your life." He pauses as if letting all that sink in.

"Then I'll cut you loose, Sasha. I'll set you free. But you're going to pay the price before I do, and the price is *everything*. Mind. Body. Soul."

His gaze rakes over me in a way I fear will leave my skin burned. "I'll have you in my bed, Princess, and I intend to defile Victor Reed's little girl in every way I can imagine. I want to see that famous face contorted in passion. I want to look down and watch you sucking my cock, with you knowing you're locked in this tower with me."

He reaches for a hip-length lock of hair that has come free of the clips and pins. Slowly, he runs it through his fingers. "Those are my terms, Rapunzel. And they're non-negotiable. Do you agree? Or should I take you back to the gala?"

I lift my chin and force myself to meet those cold eyes, trying to parse out what he really wants from me. It can't be sex—this is a man who could have any woman he wants, which means he wants me for some other reason I don't yet see.

I start to ask, then hold my tongue. Because in the end it doesn't matter. I need him, and that's the bottom line. But that bottom line is underscored by a single, horrible truth—whatever his motive, I want him, too.

I want to be touched by fingers other than my own.

I want to know what it feels like to be real, and not merely a pretty little dress-up doll.

"Everything," I finally say, taking pride in the way his eyes widen just a bit in subtle proof that I've surprised him.

"Everything and nothing, and that's fine by me." I slide my hands down the dress, then clutch the material, trying to keep them from shaking. "You're the devil, Grimm. But this is the one time the saying is wrong. Because you're the devil I don't know. And compared to my father and Desmond Bane, you're still the safer bet."

For a moment, he simply studies me. Then he nods. "I'm glad we've reached an agreement. Make sure you stick to it. Break my rules—push me away, disobey—and you'll find yourself on the street." Amusement flickers over that sculpted face. "Perhaps you should have held on to that ring, Princess. It could have bought a lot of groceries."

"Stop calling me that," I snap, irritated that I'd thought that very thing about the ring. But it had felt so damn good when I'd tossed it.

I glance at Grimm, expecting him to argue. To say that he won himself a fairy tale princess, and that's what he expects me to be. Instead, he takes a step closer, everything about him exuding dark power as he says, "My rules, Princess. Unless this is your way of asking to be punished?" His gaze rakes over me. "And wouldn't that be fun?"

I force myself not to tremble. But it's not Liam Grimm who scares me. It's my reaction. The unnerving, unexpected thrill that races up my spine. The way my nipples tighten. The heat that floods the secret parts of my body.

And all from the way he pronounced that one horrible word: *punish.*

Because he didn't pronounce it like a man about to dole out a beating, but as a man about to give a caress.

I sag a little, realizing that my legs are trembling. Not surprising since I've barely eaten a bite today. Combine that with adrenaline and Liam Grimm, and it's no wonder I'm unsteady.

"All right," I say, forcing myself to keep my chin up and look him in the eye. "I accept your condition."

"You'll obey me?"

I give the slightest tilt of my chin, then meet his eyes, daring him to make me say it out loud. To my surprise, he doesn't. Instead, he gestures for me to take a seat in a plush armchair before heading to a bar on the far side of the room.

He looks back at me over his shoulder. "I believe your drink is Scotch?"

"I—yes. But how—?" I let the question hang there. Right then, I'm not sure I can handle the answer. Because as far as the world is concerned, I only drink white wine—and only at formal dinners or special events, like tonight's gala.

That, of course, is my father's depiction of me. In reality, Ruby and I discovered a love of Scotch when we were seventeen and she decided to start smuggling in various alcohols so we could try them out.

"Glenfiddich 50-Year-Old," he says, handing me a glass with the golden liquid and a single ball of ice. It's a label I'd seen in my father's liquor cabinet, and I'd been curious enough to look it up. So I know that a bottle costs upwards of thirty grand. It's amazing how much mundane information you can learn from the Internet when you live your life inside a gilded cage.

Despite the content of my father's bar, I've never had anything more expensive than the Dewars that Ruby smuggles in. How could I, since I have hardly any money of my own? Why would I need it, not being able to go into the world without an escort?

I lift the glass, eager to taste this rarefied treat, and not at all surprised that a man like Liam Grimm has such a bottle. He settles back into his chair, watching me in a way that makes this moment feel like a test. I take a casual sip and almost moan. It's like I'm drinking liquid gold.

"Better than Dewars, isn't it?"

"How did you—?"

I cut off my question. I'm a quick study. Apparently, Grimm is, too. And it's clear he's been studying me.

He moves to the window. I watch as he taps the control on his watch. Immediately, the glass shifts back to transparent. Even from across the room, I feel the pressure of that emptiness against the glass.

He looks over his shoulder at the dark and deadly vista, standing so close I'm terrified the glass will fall away and he'll be sucked out into the night.

Then his attention returns to me, and he holds out his hand. "Come here."

Oh, hell no. I shake my head, my breath catching as cold tendrils of fear twist inside me.

"I thought we were clear about your position here. I say jump—you ask how high."

I shake my head again.

"Very well. I'll call your father. He can pick you up at the entrance to the garage."

"You bastard." My words are only a whisper, but they are heavy with loathing.

"I've been called worse. Now come here."

It's anger that pushes me to my feet. It's fear that keeps me from moving.

He crosses to my side. "Two steps. Hold on to me."

He takes my arm. I jerk it roughly away. "Prick."

"You're pissed? Good. Use it. Use it to fight your fear."

"You goddamn, sanctimonious asshole," I snap, turning so that I'm not only facing him, but so my back is to that terrifying void. "Why are you doing this? Do you just want to humiliate me? What the hell do you want from me?"

Panic rises in my chest as tears flood my eyes, making my vision blur. But not so much that I miss the tiny bit of sympathy that crosses his stone-chiseled features. It's gone in an instant, so quickly I might have imagined it. But I didn't.

It doesn't erase the fear. It doesn't make me trust him. But it does calm me. A little bit, anyway.

"It won't suck you in," he whispers, and I tense, shocked that he understands how I feel. And the truth is, he's right. I know he's right. I know perfectly well that I'm safe. That the glass won't fall away. That I won't be sucked into the dark.

That I won't fall to a horrible death.

Except maybe I will.

I want to scream and run. I want to do what he says. I want to close my eyes and sleep for a hundred years, like a princess under a spell. But who knows what new horror I'd wake up to?

I turn back toward the window, my eyes on the floor, then take one more tiny step. "Good girl," he whispers, but I don't know if it's because he's proud of me or because I just took the first step into whatever unseen plan he's concocted. Because, of course, he has a plan. And somehow, I'm at the center of it.

"Now two more," he says, releasing my elbow. I go tense, immediately reaching for his hand. I expect him to pull away, but he doesn't. "Two more," he repeats, as I tighten my hold.

I draw a breath, then take one step toward the void.

"One more. But look up as you walk."

But I can't. The gaping maw is too close now. I feel its pull. Its hunger. Any closer, and I'll fall in. I'll lose myself in the dark. And I'll never find my way back.

"No." The word is a whisper, and I tilt my face down, concentrating on my satin shoes that peek out from under the hem of my dress. Shiny and white and festive, so unlike the night that wants to claim me.

"You can do this, Sasha." His voice is firm and without pity. "If you want my protection against your father, you have to."

My head snaps up. "Bastard."

"In so many ways. Walk, Princess."

"I told you not to call me that."

"Too bad you're not the one with the power. Now walk."

Prick. But I don't say that aloud. Instead, I swallow, my hand tightening around his as I force myself to look through the glass at the lights of the city, so like the lights that twinkle up in space. A vacuum. Unsurvivable.

But I have to do this. I need his help to stay hidden and protected from my father.

He starts to loosen his grip, but I squeeze tighter. Small windows I can handle. Mostly, anyway. But this expanse … it's overwhelming. I'm still at least eight feet from the window, and I already feel like I'm about to teeter. Like I'm going to fall.

Just like my mother did.

Except she was pushed. You know she was pushed.

I shudder, and it's only Grimm's hand in mine that keeps me steady.

The irony isn't lost on me.

I take one step, then another and another. I try to take one more, but my feet won't move. My body is stone, and I close my eyes, terrified that he's going to demand I open them and take two more steps. And like a hammer falling against a salt pillar, those words will shatter me completely.

Instead, his voice has a hint of gentleness when he says, "You did well. Open your eyes."

I hesitate but comply, then sag with relief when I see that the windows are opaque again.

"Congratulations," he says.

"Screw you," I snap, but the words aren't hard. I want them to be, but I'm too drained. And yet …

Despite the fear and exhaustion, there's a tiny flicker of glee. Because I did it. I walked toward the void, and I wasn't sucked into hell.

That's good, right?

Then again, maybe I couldn't get sucked into hell because I'm already here, trapped in Grimm Tower with the devil himself.

SEVEN
REVELATIONS

"What game are you playing?" I ask after I'm seated again and have taken one—actually, two—more sips of the Scotch. "Why do you even care if I can walk toward your windows?"

"It's not me who's playing games with you," he says. "That would be your father."

I want to argue out of principle, but, of course, he's right.

"As for why I care …" He trails off with a small shrug. "The truth is, I've watched you for years."

I lean back, startled by the statement.

"I've seen what your father has done," he continues, his tone so icy my body feels chilled. "The mind games he's played with you."

"What are you talking about?"

"Has anyone ever talked to you about the way your mother died?"

"My mother?" The words feel like ground glass, and my eyes sting as I blink back tears. "Who the hell are you to ask about my mother when your father is the one who murdered her?"

"That's a lie you shared with the entire world three years ago," Grimm says.

I shake my head, fighting off his words. "It wasn't a lie. I was there. I saw what happened."

"You did, yes. But you told the world a lie."

"You're insane."

He shakes his head, his words coming hard and fast like gunfire, and just as brutal. "My father is a bastard who couldn't even buy his way into heaven and will give Satan a run for his money when he waltzes into Hell. But he didn't kill your mother."

His words land like a slap. Sharp. Unexpected.

"Don't," I whisper. "Don't you dare." My voice is steady, but my hands aren't. "I saw what he did. I saw him push her. I saw—"

The words break apart somewhere between memory and breath. I turn away, blinking fast. My fingers swipe at the tears before they can fall.

I don't want to go there. Not now. Not with him.

But the edges of that day are pressing in—the roof, the scream, my mother's body swallowed by the void. My father's arms around me. His voice thick with tears, just like my own.

I believed him. Of course, I had. Because that was the one story that made sense. And her loss is the only thing I've ever shared with my father. The one thing that has ever given me even the tiniest hint of closeness with him.

Now Liam Grimm wants to tear even that from me?

I turn back, forcing the words out as tears trickle down my cheeks. "You don't get to rewrite what happened."

Grimm doesn't move. Doesn't speak. Just watches me with that maddening calm. Like he knows what he just cracked open.

Like he's waiting to see if it breaks me. But I can't afford to crumble around this man. Not when I don't even understand what I've agreed to.

That's why he's talking about her. That's what his game is. To break you. To make you smaller than you already are.

"I can't do this," I whisper. "I don't want your help."

He tilts his head toward the door. "Go. I won't stop you."

I stand up, grab my tiny purse off the coffee table, then hurry toward the elevator. I pause just inside the vestibule to open the clutch and make sure my phone and Ruby's credit card are still there. I can take a taxi. Or the subway. And I know Ruby's PIN, so I can get cash.

My head pounds, and my mind keeps spinning as I tell myself I can do this.

And as another small voice tells me I'd be an idiot to get into that elevator.

Screw that. I step forward, then press the button to call the car. I glance at the monitor—it's ten floors away.

I can do this. I can do this.

I can do this.

I even know a hostel where I can crash for a night or two. A model I'd worked with for a Reed Cosmetics campaign had stayed there. The Twenty-Seventh Street Hostel. I'll go there. Then I'll make a plan. I'll get out of New York. Pay cash. Take the train.

And then what?

I turn just enough to look over my shoulder. Grimm is standing in the middle of the room, his back to me as he faces the opaque windows.

I shiver.

Four floors away.

My father will look for me. Grimm will tell him I'm gone. And Father will release his dogs, real and metaphorical. They always find what they're looking for.

They'll find me, too.

I close my eyes, hating the bitter truth—with Grimm, I have a chance. By myself, I'll be locked in my suite by sunrise. I'm a fairy tale princess who escaped her tower. And the evil king will put me there again. But this time, there will be no visits from Ruby. No computer. No phone. No canvases and jars of paint. No sketchbook. No Elysium.

Because real fairy tales have dark and scary endings.

Ding.

The elevator doors slide open, and I use the back of my hand to wipe away the tears that have streaked down my cheeks. Then I turn and walk back to the chair I'd vacated. I sit, looking down at my hands, folded primly in my lap.

As if no time has passed at all, I say, "I saw Elias Grimm push her. I saw my father try to save her. But he was too late. She slipped from his fingers."

I shiver, the memory like ice. "She plummeted into the dark," I whisper. "And the void consumed her."

"Is that what you remember? Or is that what your father told you?"

"I remember," I say. "Of course, I remember."

"Do you remember what my father was doing on the roof of Reed Tower?"

"No, but I was only seven. It was probably a business thing."

"Because our fathers did so much business together. On roofs. Without their lawyers present."

I shake my head, ignoring his dripping sarcasm. "I don't know. I just know he was there."

"But how?" Grimm's voice is surprisingly gentle. He comes to crouch in front of me. "Victor Reed wouldn't have invited my father to a hanging, much less his rooftop. So how did my dear father get past Reed Tower's security? Think about it. He couldn't have made it into the lobby, much less to the roof. We both know that."

"I told you. I don't know. I was just a kid." I want to scream the words. Because why the hell is he interrogating me about something that happened almost twenty years ago? And why does the *how* matter, anyway? He was there. I saw him. And that was the end of the story.

Wasn't it?

"For that matter," Grimm continues, making me want to throw something. "You know there's no love lost between me and my father."

I hug myself tighter. I do know that. Gossip runs wild in my father's circle, and it's common knowledge that Liam Grimm is the black sheep of the family. He's the child of Elias Grimm and a secret lover. She died, though, and although Marge Grimm let her husband raise the literal bastard, the whole world knows that Liam Grimm is very firmly stuck on the bottom rung of the family ladder.

"My father thinks you're going to be the next CEO of Lucent. Why else would they have sent you to the shoot?"

"Your father is a fool. A dangerous fool. And my father is a dangerous son-of-a-bitch. That is something I have never denied. So why would I defend him now?" He rises, then paces the room before dragging an ottoman in front of me.

He sits, then leans forward, his elbows on his knees as he says, "Think about it, Princess. If my father murdered your mom, I'd be the first one to say he should be locked in a cell." I look down, not wanting to meet his gaze. I feel twitchy. Confused. I want to curl up with my feet under me, but in this stupid dress, that's impossible.

"Why are you doing this?" I cringe, hating the needy, weak sound of my voice.

"Why am I telling you the truth? Don't you think you deserve the truth? Your father damn sure doesn't."

"But it's not …" I trail off, hugging myself, realizing I don't know what's true. Not anymore.

"Have you ever read an article accusing Elias Grimm of killing your mother?"

I haven't. Not one. "I was only seven," I say.

"But surely you've looked since then. Every article says your father tried to pull her back before she jumped. *Jumped*. Not a mention of my father. Seems odd, doesn't it?"

I don't nod. I don't have to. He knows I can't argue.

He slides off the ottoman and crouches in front of me again. This time he puts his hands on my armrests, his eyes focused on mine. His proximity makes me feel trapped. Jittery. Strangely aware.

"Your father told you lies, Sasha. You were a traumatized little girl and he told you what to see, over and over and over until it became your truth. But not *the* truth."

"Stop," I beg, then push him back as I force myself to my feet. "Please, please stop."

His expression is hard, and for a moment, I think he's going to press more, shoving me back into memories I don't want and theories I don't understand.

But then he tilts his head in silent acquiescence as he stands. "Sit back down. I'll get you something to drink. There are other things we need to talk about."

He starts to walk away, then pauses to open the ottoman, revealing a compartment full of blankets. He hands me one, and I wrap myself in the soft warmth, strangely grateful.

A few minutes later, he's back. And though I'd expected more Scotch, this time he offers me a mug of hot cocoa. I sniff, then smile as I take a sip.

Right now, I really do feel safe. I know it won't last, but it's real. And for this one fragile moment, it's mine.

I close my eyes, exhaustion warring with adrenaline and the rattle of unanswered questions. I drift, Grimm's accusations twisting around me. My father is vile, but I know what I saw. My mother at the edge of the roof looking out at the city lights. Me sitting on a blanket playing with Kitty, a teal stuffed cat that was my constant companion, gone now, just like so many other happy things I'd had before she died.

And there's my father standing behind her, giving her one firm shove. My mother going over. My scream renting the night as she plunges forward. My father standing at that murderous edge as he watches her fall and fall and fall while my screams fill the air to bursting.

In my mind—*my dream?*—I look around, searching for Elias Grimm. But it's just Father and me. And the deafening silence that a moment ago was my mother's scream.

After what feels like an eternity, Father turns and slowly walks to me. He reaches down and pulls me to my feet as Kitty falls from my lap.

"I tried to grab her sweater. You saw me. I tried to pull her back, but I couldn't save her." His words are low and measured. "I'm sorry, sweet girl, but you saw that bastard, Elias Grimm. He came here. He took her from us. Elias Grimm is a monster. You saw him murder your mother. You saw it with your own eyes, just like I did. Tell me, precious girl. Tell me you saw."

"I saw it," I say as hot tears spill from my eyes.

"He's a monster," Father says. "And he murdered your mother."

"A monster," I whisper. Then, "*Mommy!*"

My scream pulls me from the dream—the memory?— and Grimm rushes to me, studying my face. "You believe me," he says softly. "You remember how she really died."

"Maybe. I don't know. Maybe."

"It's true. You know it is."

He's right. But I say nothing.

"And the rest? Do you know why you didn't remember before? Why you thought my father was there?"

"He drilled it into me," I whisper. "Over and over and over." It's the root of my agoraphobia and my fear of heights. My father killed my mother in front of me. He broke me.

And for years he's been using me.

I shiver, then brush away the tears that have dampened my cheeks. I want to scream that I don't believe any of this. Except I do. Of course, I do. I know better than anyone alive what he's capable of. I've looked into my father's eyes. I've been the recipient of his ego, his pride, his manipulation, and the fallout from his ambition.

"He played with my memory," I whisper.

Grimm nods. "And your meds keep the memories suppressed." He tilts his head, studying me. "You didn't take them yesterday, did you?"

I shake my head, my mind turning his words over and over. *My father's been manipulating my memory.*

I hug my knees to my chest, trying to breathe. "Why do you care about any of this?" I finally ask.

"Let's just say that I have as much reason to hate your father as you do."

It's not an answer, but I know it's the best I'll get tonight. It also has the ring of truth.

His eyes lock on mine. "Your mother fell to her death from the roof of your home. A place where you should be safe. "But you've never been safe there, have you Princess?"

I want to snap at him for calling me that, but I remember the damn rules. So I just glare instead.

He ignores me, pushing on. "Your mother fell into the void," he says, his voice surprisingly gentle. "And that fall was one of the building blocks of your fear. Your father knew it would be."

I hug myself. I don't know where he's going with the conversation, but I'm certain I don't want to follow him there.

"But that wasn't enough for him to be sure," Grimm continues, his words drowning out my whispers to "stop, stop, oh, please, stop."

"Victor Reed's a clever, manipulative man. And it's you he manipulated most of all. Then he locked in your fears and anxieties with one more incident. You know what I'm talking about, Princess. This time, you tell me."

I press my lips tight and shake my head. Just tiny movements as I try to find someplace to hide. Like Elysium, only in my mind.

But at the same time, some part of me doesn't want to disappear.

That part wants to hear more. To maybe, finally, understand what kind of monster my father truly is.

"That's it," he says, apparently reading my face. "Tell me what happened when you were eight."

"How—" My voice comes out weak. Shaky. I hug my knees tighter. "How do you know about that?"

"My father would have been a fool not to research the competition. And I would be a fool not to review his files." A smug grin tugs at the corner of his mouth. "I don't have a damn thing to do with Lucent, Princess. My business is information. And I know how to get what I need."

I stay silent, and after what feels like an eternity, he says, "When you were eight, you got separated from your nanny. You were lost in Rockefeller State Park for hours. That contributed to your condition as well. Being out in the open. Alone. Afraid. Unable to anchor yourself to anything. Unable to find help."

I close my eyes, blocking the hazy memory. The joy I'd felt watching a huge hawk in a tree. Then the terror when I'd turned around, only to find that Jennifer, my nanny, was gone. The fear that had washed over me when I'd wandered for hours, only to have the night creep up on me like death.

The way the trees extended their arms to grab me and hold me there. The way my screams went unanswered, as if I were the only one on earth. I was going to starve. I was going to fall to the ground and die. Then my body would decompose and I'd be nothing, just like the corpse of a decomposing rat I'd once tripped over in the basement.

"I was terrified," I admit, my voice small.

"Of course you were. And when your father found you, he should have soothed you. Helped you. Instead, he yelled at you."

Grimm's right. I still remember my father's shouts that I was disobedient and stupid. That I'd never learn, and it would have served me right for him to have left me there.

I swallow, then look straight at Grimm. "How do you know that?"

"I've been ... intrigued by you for some time. I asked around. There were several people in the search party who witnessed your father's tirade and agreed to talk to me. And once I located Jennifer and assured her that her story would stay between the two of us, she told me your father had paid her to leave you there. He told her it was a rite of passage, and you would be fine. She didn't want to do it, but she was afraid he'd hurt her son if she didn't.

I hug myself tighter, not sure what to say or how to feel. It's Liam Grimm telling me this. A man I've despised for years, from a family I've grown up hating.

I draw one breath, then another, hoping to calm my racing pulse. I don't like being fragile. And I like even less showing that weakness to this man. This enemy.

"It's been a long day," I say. "Is there someplace for me to sleep?"

I cringe and look down as soon as I say it, realizing it's a stupid question.

Everything.

Of course, he's going to want me in his bed.

"There's a room made up for you just down the hall."

"Oh." I stand, feeling strangely hollow. I tell myself that the feeling is relief.

I point toward my tiny handbag, now on a side table. "I guess I should take my meds."

I don't want to. I like how my mind felt clearer at the shoot and then even more so today. But not being able to approach Grimm's window ...

I shake my head. I don't want to be weak. Not around him. And if the meds can make the phobias more manageable, then maybe I really should be taking them.

"No." He stands, then moves to my side so that there's only the tiniest bit of air between us. So close I can feel the warmth of his breath when he says, "Haven't you been listening? Your meds are bullshit. A way to keep you manageable."

My pulse kicks up. "Maybe, but Father's not here. And you don't understand what it feels like when the world wants to swallow you. The phobias, I—they help."

"Do they?" His voice is flat. Entirely devoid of inflection. A total contrast to my rising fury.

"You don't know a thing about me or my medical history or anything. You hate my father. You hate me. And now you're going to try to gaslight me? Make it so I can't even sit across a room and look at the view out the window? Well, screw you. It's not going to work."

"I'm not gaslighting. Quite the opposite. I'm trying to help you."

"Why does this matter to you, anyway?" I snap. "And how the hell do you know so much about it?" I cross my arms and glare at him. "Oh, right. You've been watching me. That's not even remotely creepy."

Instead of looking pissed, he looks amused. Which, frankly, makes me even more pissed.

"You're right. I pay attention," he says in a soothe-the-angry-puppy tone. "To everything." His eyes lock hard on mine. "But mostly, I search out anything that might give me enough leverage to destroy Victor Reed. Anything, Princess," he adds, his expression as hard as stone. "Whatever it takes."

My body feels both cold and hot. I lick my suddenly dry lips. "What are you talking about?"

His brow lifts, and his mouth curves into a half-smile as he inches even closer. I draw in a sharp breath, willing myself not to scurry back away from him.

"Let me be very, very clear, Ms. Reed. I'll help you conquer your fears and break your dependence on pills because it suits me. But you are not my goal nor my priority. I need your meds identified and analyzed. And I need you clear-headed. Therefore, I will make you that way. I will do that and whatever else is necessary to take your father down, including using you in whatever way I deem fit."

I search for words but can't find any. His brutal honesty has surprised me too much.

"Bottom line? I don't like Victor Reed." His mouth quirks into a half-smile, and I see a flicker of humor in those cold blue eyes as he adds, "I don't think you like him either." He steps even closer, his proximity making it harder to think. "That may not make us friends, but it does make us allies."

"Really?" I keep my head tilted down, afraid if I look up at him, I'll lose my words. "How does that work? You've pretty much told me I'm your slave."

"True." He takes a step back, his eyes roaming over me once again. "But I think you'll enjoy it."

My cheeks heat, as does the area between my legs.

He notices my blush, of course, and that devilish smile returns. "Oh, I have plans for you, make no mistake. And you will comply with *everything* in our agreement. But in our few minutes of free time, I think we can help each other."

I fight the urge to hug myself, not sure if the tightness in my body is a longing to run or something far more complicated. "Help?" I try to keep my voice casual. "So, you're helping me out of the goodness of your heart because my father is mistreating me?"

"I know you've been sheltered, but are you really that naive?"

"Dammit, just tell me why you're helping me." I want to add *you son of a bitch*, but I force my lips together.

He tilts his head. "This is good."

"What?"

"You're stronger than I thought you'd be. Considering everything he's done to you, I thought you'd be broken."

"Maybe I am, but you can't see it because you're even more broken."

"Maybe," he says without irony.

I swallow, more unnerved than I should be. "Answer the question. Why are you helping me?"

"Because, Princess, you're the perfect weapon to bring him down."

"Oh." The bluntness is almost refreshing after years of my father's subtle manipulations. "And you want to destroy my father because ..."

"That's not your concern."

I frown, but he's right. And frankly, if he wants to take my father down ... well, faster Pussycat! Kill! Kill!

"So, I'm a means to an end," I say.

"As I am to you." Grimm's smile is sharp. He spreads his arm to encompass the room, the entire tower. "Didn't I bring you to a sanctuary? I think that gives us mutual ground upon which to move forward, don't you?"

I nod, even though we both know I have no choice.

"Excellent." He's perched on the edge of the ottoman, but now he gets up, goes to the bar, and returns with fresh drinks. He passes one to me, then holds his out as if for a toast. "To our arrangement," he says, raking a wolfish gaze over me. "May it be both productive and ... entertaining."

I square my shoulders, anticipating an order to strip, his words from earlier ringing through my head. *I want to fuck you. I want to taint you.*

Any moment now he'll demand payment, and my horrible, hated, secret truth is that I want him to.

Which is why when he finally escorts me to a small bedroom, then runs his fingertips gently over my neck and down my bare arm, my breath hitches and my body fires in a way that is both unfamiliar and strangely—terrifyingly—welcome.

Then he taps my chin with his fingertip, politely says goodnight, and walks away, leaving me standing like a fool in the doorway, not sure if I want to laugh or cry.

EIGHT
AWAKENINGS

After squashing down a mountain of mortification, I tell myself to get it together. Then I close the door behind me with a sigh and wonder what the hell is wrong with me. I don't want Liam Grimm. He's hot as sin, but he's a Grimm, and just because I'm here doesn't mean I trust him.

"Idiot," I mutter, even as I mentally call myself half a dozen more interesting names.

The next thing I do is glance around. The guest bedroom is both elegant and drab—neutral tones, expensive linens, and not a single personal touch. Like everything else in Liam Grimm's world, it's carefully curated to reveal nothing he doesn't want revealed.

I open my handbag, intending to pull out my meds and my phone.

Neither are there.

Instead, there's a note in a bold, masculine hand: *You don't need them. And Ruby can wait for tomorrow.*

It's so ridiculous I actually laugh. Then I remember that I'm pissed off. Not so much about the meds—all things considered, I'm leaning toward believing everything Grimm's told me. But taking the phone
…

That bites. Because it's been a hell of a long day, and I really want to call Ruby.

63

And if wishes were horses then I'd have been way the hell and gone from Manhattan years ago …

I grimace, then distract myself by exploring the room. After a day like today, I should be passing out face down on the bed, but I'm too wired to sleep. Instead, my mind races with questions … and with the memory of Grimm's soft caress.

I shove that memory right back down where it belongs, then start opening doors. The closet is empty and pristine, with padded hangers just waiting to perform their duty. The bathroom is so bright it makes my head hurt. Fortunately, I can dim the light, and still enjoy the way it sparkles and smells vaguely of lilacs. The countertop displays an array of toiletries, like the kind you'd find in a world-class hotel— only times ten.

There's a fluffy white robe hanging behind the door, and I eagerly strip out of my fairy-princess meets captive-bride outfit—resisting the urge to stomp on it, as if grinding the thing into dust would finally make me real.

I stand naked for a moment, letting my physical appearance mirror my mental state. Because for the entirety of this day, I've felt on display. Examined. Judged.

So, yeah, big, fluffy robe? That sounds pretty nice.

I sigh as I slide into it, but it takes a moment for me to cinch the tie since my hands are shaking. *Nerves*, I think as I stare at myself in the mirror. The robe is beyond casual, while my hair in its fancy up-do looks like I'm heading to a coronation ball, even with the few strands that have escaped the hairpins. With a surge of unexpected fury, I start ripping those damned pins out and tossing them in the sink. I'm so sick and tired of being a dress-up doll for everyone's pleasure but my own.

Each tiny clatter in the basin feels like a punch — another piece of my father I'm tearing off and throwing away.

Rip out the pins. Rip out the lies. Rip out the girl he built for show.

When the pins are out, I bend over and run my fingers through my hair, loosening the braids and twists and whatever else the hair-stylist did earlier today.

I shiver. *Was it really only today?*

I straighten, thinking of all that has happened since I woke up in my bed. Technically, that was yesterday morning, but as I haven't slept, I figure it's all the same.

I give myself a mental pat on the back. Today's the day I walked out of hell. And no matter what happens next, that's something.

I meet my eyes in the mirror and nod, as if in solidarity. My normally straight hair hangs almost to my waist, the kinks and curls from the twists and the braids giving me a wild, almost beachy look.

The mass of hair is heavy and time-consuming, and I've considered cutting it so many times, but my father wouldn't allow it. I'm a little princess, after all. And my hair is my crown.

If that were the only factor, I'd shave my head and suffer the consequences. But the truth is, I like my hair, too. Despite the major pain-in-the-butt factor that comes from care and styling.

Now, I do nothing more complicated than tucking it behind my ears as I pick up the dress, then head barefoot back into the bedroom to continue my exploration.

I randomly open dresser drawers, finding extra sheets, a box of tissue, several drawers of nothing at all, and then—strangely—a sleek, silver laptop computer.

I start to close the drawer, assuming Grimm's last guest had left it behind. But then I change my mind. This is my room now. And if there's even the slightest chance that any of Grimm's information is on that computer, I want to see it.

As soon as I'm settled on the bed with the lid open and the device plugged in, I know there won't be any secrets here. The screen isn't even locked. It simply says, "Have A Pleasant Stay."

A bit more polite than I'd expect from Grimm, but then again, what do I know? Maybe he's a pussycat around everybody but me.

I dim the brightness to stave off the headache that's determined to invite friends. Then I poke around the hard drive, but there's nothing installed on the computer except for a couple of web browsers.

And isn't that interesting …?

For a moment, I debate logging in. After all, it's just sitting there like a trap, all bright and shiny, like tin foil to attract a blackbird.

Doesn't matter—I'm going in. I head over to Instagram first, then leave a *U There?* DM for Ruby. When she doesn't answer right away, I assume she's asleep. A reasonable assumption since it's almost 3am.

Ruby, however, never turns off her phone ringer. According to her, as my PA, she needs to be available to me night or day. And since my father switches out my phone number every few weeks without warning—because god forbid someone I meet at a shoot should call me socially—she lets any and all calls ring through.

Thankfully, I don't have too many three a.m. crises. And I don't bother making friends on shoots anymore. That never works out.

It takes no time to create a new Internet-based number, then to dial hers from memory.

Ring. Ring. Ring.

I frown. She usually picks up right away.

Ring. Ring.

A message pops up to tell me my party hasn't answered—as if I couldn't figure that out on my own—and I click the button to continue ringing.

Ring. Ring. Ring. Ring.

I'm about to give up and just try again in the morning when I hear a click and then a breathy, "Hello?"

"It's me."

At first, she doesn't do anything but breathe, but I can practically feel the relief melting off her. "Where are you?" she finally demands, her voice so low I can barely hear her. How are you?"

"I'm okay," I say. "I'm still with the devil."

"I know. Your father tracked your phone. I overheard him talking to Desmond. He said you're at Grimm Tower."

"Yeah. I don't think Liam lives here permanently, but apparently, all the brothers have apartments on site."

"I've never heard his voice like that. He's beyond furious."

I hug myself. Of course, he is. "Do you know what he's planning?"

"Not specifically," she says. "But—"

"Yeah. I know. He's going to send some of his goons to get me."

Reed Cosmetics is only one tiny piece of Reed Industries. And those much larger pieces demand a highly trained security team. The kind that recruits from covert government agencies and could extricate a damsel in distress before breakfast.

Fortunately, Grimm International has a similar status ... and a similar security team. My father can't send goons into Grimm Tower without risking a full-on war, and my father's not a man who takes risks without first considering every other option.

That buys some time, but not much. Because my father wants me back, and Elias Grimm won't stick his neck out for his estranged third son.

So sooner or later, those two will strike a deal, and Father's men will converge on this place. I don't want to be here when they do.

"I don't know where I'm going to go," I tell Ruby, "but I have to get out of here. And I have to ditch the phone. Keep the number I called from. I'll try to log in when I can."

"I will. And Sasha—never mind." I hear the mix of hesitation and fear in her voice. It's easy to notice since it sounds like mine.

"What?"

"What if we're wrong? What if Liam isn't helping you? What if he brought you back to win points with his dad? Toss Victor Reed's daughter at Elias's feet. That would be one hell of a peace offering if Elias Grimm wants a detente with your father."

A wave of fear crashes over me, and I draw in a sharp breath even as I shake my head and say, "No. No, that's not what he's doing."

"You're sure?"

"Yes," I say, though I'm not sure at all. But I really, really don't want to believe it. Weirdly, I've started to trust Liam Grimm. At least a little.

But maybe that's just Stockholm Syndrome. Now that she's mentioned it, turning me over like a trophy sounds like a very Grimm family type of plan.

And that's not good.

"Sasha ..."

"I'm sure," I snap, then immediately cringe. "Sorry. I'm just tired and stressed. And it's not like I can do anything right now."

"Sleep," she says. "You need to be able to think straight tomorrow. And call when you can. If I learn anything, I'll text you at this number and leave a message in Elysium, too."

"Love you," I say.

"Love you back," she whispers, her voice cracking with what I know are nerves. "It's going to be okay," she says. "You're going to get free."

"I know I am," I say, but for the first time since this adventure began, I'm starting to doubt that I'll be able to make that fantasy come true. I'm just one princess in a tower, the monsters are readying to cross the moat, and there's no dragon prince to burn them to cinders and whisk me away.

I'm not in Elysium.

I'm not in a fairy tale.

I'm not even sure if this is my story. Because as far as my father, Elias Grimm, and Liam are concerned, I'm expendable, and not the heroine at all.

———

As soon as I end the call, I close my eyes and take a deep breath. Of course, Father is tracking my phone. I can't believe I didn't think of it before. Then again, I've been a little bit overwhelmed, so maybe I should cut myself some slack.

Grimm? Not so much. Surely that's something he should have considered before bringing us here. Especially since there are only three ways out of this place—the elevator, the stairs, or parachuting out a window.

I drag my fingers through my hair as I pace the room. I can't imagine Father will try to raid Grimm Tower tonight—there's too much planning involved. Not to mention that if he makes a move, Elias Grimm will strike back.

No, this is a situation in which he'll ask permission. Favors will be traded. Pacts formed to later be broken.

That will take time, so it's a fair bet that I'm safe here for the night. For tomorrow, too, and probably the day after, at least until dusk. Because this is the kind of infiltration that will happen at night. When commandoes in black will enter the building, put Grimm out of commission, and take me back with them whether I want to go or not.

The irony?

I'm basically a hostage here, completely at Grimm's mercy. Yet this is where I want to be.

I need to tell Grimm.

The exhaustion of this long day fades in the face of my new resolve as I pull open the bedroom door and step into the darkened hallway, my bare feet silent on the hardwood as I move through the shadows. The living area is empty, the windows still mercifully opaque. I call out for Grimm, but my voice merely echoes through the space.

I continue exploring, stopping at an open door. *Grimm's bedroom.* The space is dominated by an enormous bed with rumpled dark sheets that whisper of restless sleep—or active non-sleeping. My stomach twists, and an unwelcome image of Liam Grimm rolling in those sheets with a woman flickers into my mind.

I push that thought firmly away, but remain in the doorway, my gaze raking over the room. Unlike the rest of the apartment, the bedroom feels lived in, almost primal. A faint scent hangs in the air, something masculine and evocative that makes my pulse quicken. I step back quickly, as if I'd just brushed up against something forbidden.

I continue exploring, then realize that I'm hearing music—a haunting cello piece that seems to glide over my skin, making me want to close my eyes and soak in the beauty of the notes.

It's coming from behind a door that's partially ajar. Curious, I push it open just enough so that I can peek in—then gasp at what I see. Liam Grimm. Shirtless and moving in slow, hypnotic patterns, his back to me. He's wearing only low-slung gray sweatpants that cling to his ass and thighs like a lover's hands. My mouth goes dry, and a flush of heat blooms beneath my skin.

His back is a masterpiece—broad shoulders tapering to a lean waist. Muscles shifting like liquid steel beneath golden skin slick with sweat. A tattoo I can't quite decipher curves sinuously along his left shoulder blade—dark, jagged lines forming what looks like a broken crown, the sharp tips splintered as if it had been shattered by force. The same force that seems to move through him now, every slow, hypnotic shift of his body a silent promise of strength and danger.

Each movement is deliberate, almost sensual, as if he's making love to the air. And yet at the same time, the movements are underscored by a strength that seems coiled beneath the surface. A dangerous power, contained and controlled by the will of this man. Like his body's a weapon, and he's barely keeping it leashed.

I know I should leave. I shouldn't be watching this private ritual, shouldn't be letting my eyes trace the contours of his body like fingers. And I definitely shouldn't be wondering how those muscles would feel flexing beneath my palms.

And yet here I am.

"Enjoying the view, Princess?" He hasn't turned, hasn't missed a beat in his slow, fluid movements.

"I—" My voice is traitorously husky. I clear my throat. "I talked with Ruby. My father is tracking my phone. He knows I'm here."

Now he turns, and the front view steals whatever breath I had left. That well-defined chest now glistens with sweat. Those stunning abs ripple with each breath. And a crazy-sexy trail of dark hair disappears beneath his waistband like an arrow pointing to sin itself.

I have zero experience with men other than in my fantasies, but there is no doubt in my mind as to how this man would feel beneath my fingers.

With firm determination, I force myself to lift my gaze to his eyes, only to find something predatory looking right back at me.

"It will take them a while to get their shit together," he says, cutting to the chase and ending up where my own thought process had landed.

He reaches for a towel and drags it slowly across his chest. My eyes follow the movement helplessly.

"I've been monitoring the situation."

"Oh," I say stupidly as he walks toward me with the fluid grace of a jungle cat. "That's good to know."

He stops just inches from me, close enough that I can feel the heat radiating from his body and smell the salt of his skin. "Shall I take you back to bed?"

My cheeks flame as forbidden images flash through my mind. "What?"

"You need to sleep," he says, but his eyes dance with amusement. "You're exhausted. And tomorrow will be demanding."

"Right. Sleep." I'm not sure if I'm disappointed or relieved. "Goodnight, Grimm."

"Liam," he says firmly, but I just shrug, then turn and head for the door.

"Good night, Princess. We'll talk in the morning."

I slip into the hallway, my body burning in places it shouldn't as I think about his voice, his eyes, and that small smile that always seems to promise things I really shouldn't want.

Get a grip, girl!

In my room, I drop the robe, then slide naked between the cool sheets, my body humming. I close my eyes and see him again—the fluid grace of his movements, the controlled power in every muscle, the way his sweats hang so low I can see the sharp cut of his hip bones.

I hate him. I want him. I hate that I want him.

I slide my hand down my bare stomach, lower and lower—then yank it firmly away. That's not what I want. Not my own touch, familiar and flat.

And yet … well, there are other ways to escape.

I roll over and grab the laptop from where I left it on the bedside table.

I lift the lid, then type in the URL for Elysium.

NINE
ELYSIUM

I navigate Elysium's simple landing page to the corner where I've hidden the secure portal that lets me log in even away from my computer at Reed Tower. All I have to do is ride Grimm's WiFi like a giant waterslide all the way to the secure servers that provide the boundaries of my digital haven.

I hold my breath, expecting firewalls, digital barriers, *something* to jump in the way and keep me from my goal. But to my surprise and relief, Elysium's elaborate silver gates appear, along with the familiar message requiring "the magic word" to enter.

I type in the complex password—a combination of letters and numbers which, if properly decoded, spell out the message Welcome to Freedom.

I bite my lower lip, still not believing it could be so easy. But sure enough, the loading sequence begins, unfurling a swirling pattern of stars that coalesce into verdant landscapes beyond the gate with the central castle rising like a dream from digital mist.

Relief washes through me, so intense it brings tears to my eyes. My father may control my body. Grimm may control my circumstances. But here in Elysium, no one controls me but me.

The moment the virtual world finishes forming, the gates swing open, and I'm swept inside, the world now appearing from my—well, Vale's—point of view.

"Welcome, Vale." The system's voice is tinny through the laptop's tiny speaker, and I ache for my bodysuit and headset back at Reed Tower. I miss the way the sensors trace my skin, translating every touch, every kiss, every stroke into electric pulses that fool my body into thinking they're real.

With something like hunger filling me, I navigate through my territories—the Crystal Garden, the Floating Islands, the Mountain Sanctuary—each one a testament to countless hours I spent coding, creating, escaping. But none is my destination tonight.

On impulse, I summon Ember, one of my dragons. Her scales ripple between crimson and obsidian as she lands beside me, extending a wing to assist me onto her back. Soon we're soaring above the digital realm, Vale's shoulder-length hair streaming behind us.

As the tension eases from my real-world shoulders, I guide Ember toward a secluded lake nestled between snow-capped mountains— our most intimate sanctuary, where my prince awaits me.

The first time he came to me here, he'd stayed in the shadows, watching as I bathed in the moonlit lake.

Night after night, he'd crept closer, until the weight of his gaze felt as potent as a touch. Eventually, he reached out a hand, and when I folded my fingers around his, he pulled me to him. He became my secret, my solace, my forbidden dream.

In his arms, I found a world where I wasn't caged. Where I wasn't Victor Reed's daughter, or anyone's pawn.

We passed countless hours tangled together, talking of nothing and everything—

The dragons of Elysium.

My loneliness in the castle.

My hatred for my father.

And my aching hunger for something else.

Something more.

Him.

He listened. Held my hand, kissed my fingertips, stroked my face, my lips. He confessed his desire. The hours watching me. The hours waiting for me. Craving me.

"I've wanted to touch you for so long," he'd said, and there was a rawness to the confession that didn't sound programmed at all. "To feel you. To know if you're as real as you seem."

"Are you real?" I'd whispered.

"As real as you want me to be."

For weeks, I'd come nightly to Elysium to lie with him, to talk with him. And, yes, to crave him.

Finally, he whispered that he could hold out no more, and he'd drawn me close, holding me against him. His lips found mine, demanding yet gentle. His hands mapped my body like uncharted territory. The weight of him pressed me into the soft grass as his body claimed mine with an intensity that left me gasping.

"You are mine," he'd whispered, and I'd believed him. In Elysium, I could be touched, desired, possessed. In Elysium, I wasn't trapped in a gilded cage. I was free and loved and alive.

The memories wash over me as Ember descends toward the lake, and soon I see him standing tall in the moonlight, his dark cloak fluttering in the virtual breeze.

Prince Killiam.

My lover. My friend.

I slide off Ember's back, my feet touching the soft grass as Ember takes off in a shower of crimson sparks. Then I turn to face him, my heart already racing.

He says nothing, but comes toward me, his movements fluid and deliberate, his head tilted down so that I can't see his face—always shrouded in shadow or mist, no matter how many times we've been together like this, no matter how intimately he holds me or how closely I look.

He stops only inches away, close enough that I should feel the heat of him. At home, I would—I'd feel the warmth radiating from his body, the subtle tension in the air between us.

"I've missed you," I type, wishing I could feel what I know will come next.

"Have you?" he asks, his voice sending heat pooling between my thighs even without the sensors. "Let's see just how much you've wanted me."

In my mind, I fill in the sensations the laptop can't provide. His hands sliding under my dress, finding bare skin. His mouth at my throat, teeth grazing the sensitive spot that always makes me moan. The demanding press of his cock against my belly.

On screen, Vale's clothes melt away beneath his touch. Without the bodysuit, I can't feel his hands caressing my breasts or the scrape of his stubble against my neck as his mouth travels lower. But my body remembers and clenches with desire as I watch him lower Vale to the grass.

"Please," I whisper, the word appearing as text.

"Tell me what you want," he demands, his voice in my mind rougher now.

"You. Inside me."

The words appear in the dialogue box, and he responds immediately, pinning Vale's wrists above her head with one hand. I draw in a breath, imagining the delicious helplessness of being held down while his other hand explores between my thighs, finding me wet and ready.

"Look at me while I take you," he commands, and she obeys, her eyes locked on the darkness where his face should be. And then he's pushing inside her—inside me—and I swear I can feel the stretch and fullness of him.

He starts slow, always slow, drawing out the torment until I'm begging for more. Then harder, faster, driving into me with a force that would leave bruises if this were real. As if he's trying to break through the barrier between digital and physical, to claim not just Vale but me.

"You're mine," he growls, gripping Vale's hips with bruising force. "Say it."

"I'm yours," she responds, my fingers typing what my mouth longs to say.

"Only mine."

"Only yours," I agree, the truth of it searing through me. He's the only one who's ever touched me like this, the only one who's ever made me feel like a woman rather than a porcelain doll.

His rhythm grows more insistent, and Vale's body responds, arching beneath him as pleasure builds. In my real-world bedroom, I'd be matching her movements, my hips lifting to meet each thrust, my hands clutching at the sheets as the sensors in the bodysuit translate every stroke into shockwaves of pleasure. Now, my fingers between my legs are a poor substitute.

"Come for me," he commands, and my body trembles in response to his voice, to my own touch, and to the sight of him claiming Vale so completely.

Pleasure builds as I watch, my imagination filling in the sensations that the laptop cannot provide.

"Look at me," he demands. "I want to see your eyes when you come." I obey, my fingers stroking my sex, my gaze fixed on the shadowed contours of his face, wishing desperately that I could see him fully, know him completely.

My climax crashes through me, digital and real converging in a shuddering wave. As I'm gasping, the mist that always obscures his features parts. And for a single, terrible heartbeat, I see his eyes in the moonlight—ice-blue and intense.

Grimm's eyes.

No. No, no, no. Except it's true. I can't deny what's on my screen. What I built myself. A world where Liam Grimm is the prince I've craved for months. The lover I've surrendered to night after night. A prince who's even now disappearing from my screen in a flurry of smoke and mist, leaving me alone amidst these mountains.

This isn't right. It's not what I want. But even as I think it, a disturbing warmth settles between my thighs, and I close my eyes, my body still tingling from the lingering echoes of virtual pleasure.

I'd created Prince Killiam out of nothing but code. I'd fed the AI every scrap of my private world—my diary, my calendar, my chats with Ruby. Even my dreams and fears. Any information that would help build this world in a way that was uniquely mine—and would ensure that my prince would be Vale's perfect mate.

It built Grimm.

Arrogant, controlling Liam Grimm. With a shudder, I slam the laptop shut. What the hell am I supposed to feel now?

TEN
BEAUTIFUL POISON

I wake to a room bathed in soft morning light that would be lovely if it didn't make my aching head threaten to split open. For a disorienting moment, I don't know where I am. The bed beneath me is too vast, the sheets too luxurious, the silence too complete. This isn't my suite at Reed Tower with its pastel walls, heavy drapes, and linens soft only because they've been washed so many times.

Creature comforts are not something my father spends his money on. At least not for anyone but himself.

Then it all comes rushing back. The gala. My father's announcement. Escaping with Grimm. Then finding him in Elysium.

To say it's been a whirlwind would redefine *understatement*.

With a groan, I sit up slowly to keep the headache at bay as I glance around the room, my eyes landing on the white gown, crumpled where I'd left it, a deflated mockery of my father's plans for me.

I savor the moment, recalling the pleasure of stripping off that straitjacket last night.

Now, I push the covers away, ease out of bed, and stretch. My hands are shaky, and I realize I must be hungry. I sigh. I'm going to have to either put the dress back on or go to the kitchen in the robe.

The idea's not appealing, but wearing my pseudo-bridal gown is less so.

I've just slipped back into the robe when I notice the tote bag sitting just inside by the door. Curious, I retrieve it and am delighted to find a pair of leggings and a soft gray T-shirt. I lay both out on the bed as memories of last night filter back in fragments. His fingers are on my wrist. His voice, low and dangerous: *"Sex. Control. Obedience. Ownership. Surrender. Call it what you want, Princess, but that's the price for escaping with me tonight … and for keeping you safe tomorrow and beyond."*

I'd slept naked, and he'd clearly come into the room to deliver clothes. I swallow, my pulse kicking up and my body going warm as I imagine him tugging back the covers. Touching me. Kissing me. Stroking my skin.

I shiver, and my cheeks heat at what might be a memory but is probably just desire.

I should be furious. Desperate to learn the truth. But I'm not. Because there's something else there too—a shameful, persistent heat that lingers whenever I think of those words and the way his dazzling blue eyes had darkened when he spoke them.

Stop it!

I force myself to push the thoughts away, then slip into the bathroom. My head spins, and I hold onto the counter as the dizziness passes.

My reflection makes me shudder. My face is a disaster—mascara smudged beneath my eyes, foundation creased, lipstick long gone. I look exactly like what I am—a woman who fled in the middle of the night, leaving everything behind.

The state-of-the art shower calls to me. It's nothing like my bathroom, which has had only a modest update since Reed Tower was built over a century ago. I even find a shower cap in one of the drawers.

I put it on, then strip off the robe, turn on the overhead spray, side jets, and steam, then step into heaven. I stand for a blissful moment, letting the water wash away the sweat of uneasy sleep and the lingering traces of my old life.

Then I sit on the polished bench and soak up the damp heat as I take stock of my situation. I'm in Liam Grimm's apartment. And I've agreed to help him destroy my father in exchange for a price I'm not sure I fully understand.

A price I'm both desperately nervous about and shamefully eager to pay.

His.

I'm to be *his* from here on out. And he's entitled to *everything*.

And while last night gives me some clue as to what to expect, I'm well-aware that I didn't see the real man yesterday. Or, at least, not all of him. Not the man who holds in so much anger. Who is fueled by the hatred of his father, which is something I understand all too well.

Liam Grimm is a broken man. I know, because I'm broken, too.

What I fear now is that he'll break me more when I'm forced to pay his price.

Once I'm out of the shower, I stare at my reflection, noting how different I look without the layers of make-up my father insists upon. Younger. Rawer. Maybe even stronger.

When I go back into the bedroom, I slip on the leggings and over-sized shirt, relishing the way it smells faintly of laundry detergent and something else I can't quite identify. Something *him*. Then I tie my hair back in a simple ponytail that falls just past my waist.

With nothing left to keep me in the bedroom, I take a deep breath and open the door.

The apartment beyond is flooded with morning light from those damn floor-to-ceiling windows. Beyond them, a dizzying view of Manhattan stretches out in all directions. Instinctively, I step back, panic rising. But then I force myself forward, determined not to be ruled by the fear my father so carefully cultivated.

I walk slowly, careful to make sure one foot is flat on the ground before lifting the other. Intellectually, I know that's absurd. But I can't evade the fear that I'll be sucked into the void if some part of me isn't fully grounded.

Grimm stands in the kitchen area, his back to me as he prepares something at the counter. He's traded last night's formal wear for a simple button-down and dark slacks, the sleeves rolled up to reveal muscular forearms. Even in this casual moment, power radiates from him—controlled, but unmistakable.

I clear my throat, and he turns. For a moment, his expression is unguarded, and I glimpse something that looks almost like relief. Then his mask slides back into place, all cool assessment and calculation.

"You're awake," he says, his voice neutral. "How are you feeling?"

"Like I've made a deal with the devil."

A hint of amusement flickers in his eyes. "Not the first time I've been called that."

"No surprise there." I move further into the room, drawn despite myself, then take a seat at the counter. "About last—"

"Coffee first," he interrupts, sliding a mug toward me. "You look like you need it."

He's not wrong. I take the first sip, then sigh. *Heaven.*

"There's someone I'd like you to meet," he adds, with a nod toward the living area behind me.

I swivel the stool, and only then do I notice the woman seated in the far corner of the room, petite and poised in a simple black pantsuit. She rises, then strides toward us as I stand.

"Sasha Reed, this is Dr. Margaret Chen."

"Doctor?" I take a step back, wary. Another physician to diagnose me, to prescribe medications, to tell me how fragile I am?

"Dr. Chen is a biochemist and an MD who specializes in neuropsychopharmacology," Grimm says, as if he'd heard my unspoken fear.

"Neuropsychopharmacology." I say the word slowly, enunciating each syllable. "So that means your focus is on brains and drugs?"

"Something like that." Her soft voice sings with both comfort and competence.

"She's here to help us understand—and prove—what your father's been doing to you."

A chill runs through me as I remember what I learned last night. All the things my father did to make me scared and fragile.

To make me need him.

I hug myself, desperate to run back to bed. Instead, I lift my chin. "It's bad, isn't it?"

Grimm and Dr. Chen exchange a glance. "It isn't good," Grimm says.

"Perhaps we should sit," Dr. Chen suggests.

But I don't want to sit. I just want to know. I want to hear every horrible thing, because once you understand the nightmare, that's when you stop having it.

Except that's not really true. I know better than most that nightmares never really end.

So I walk with them to the kitchen table and sit, then look from Grimm beside me to Dr. Chen across the oval tabletop.

"Well?"

Grimm shifts to look at me more directly. "The medications your father's been giving you for anxiety and agoraphobia—they're not legitimate pharmaceutical compounds."

Bile rises in my throat. I don't want to hear any of this. And how the hell can he know so much about my meds, anyway?

At the same time, I believe him. This is my father we're talking about.

I sit up straighter as I look at Dr. Chen. "Have they—have they damaged me?"

Her smile is almost maternal, and I fight the urge to go cry in her arms the way I imagine I used to with my mother. And the way I still do now with Lydia in the towers of Elysium.

"No damage," Dr. Chen assures me. "But they have affected you. Based on your symptoms and my review of footage from your public appearances over the last few years, I believe you've been administered a cocktail of benzodiazepines, memory suppressants, and mood stabilizers, not to mention a number of experimental drugs, most likely to enhance dependency."

I look between the two of them, not understanding.

"To keep you controlled and docile," Dr. Chen says softly.

"No, no." I shake my head. "Dr. Linden would never do that."

"He's not," Grimm says. "You have a legitimate prescription. But you take what your father gives you instead."

I stand and start pacing. "That's … That's insane." But even as I say it, pieces begin falling into place. The foggy thinking. The missing memories.

My stomach churns. I don't want to believe this. I don't. I want to close my eyes and sleep for a hundred years. I want to shout that the Grimm family is our enemy and that I know this is just a ploy, and it won't work. I won't let it work.

I want to race out of this room and back to reality.

Except I do believe them.

More than that, I'm not even sure I know what reality is anymore.

"Sasha?"

I look up at Dr. Chen, mentally clinging to her soft voice and kind face.

"Why would he do that?" I finally ask.

"Control," Grimm says, the word sharp and certain. "Your father needs to control everything in his orbit. You most of all."

"I'd like to perform a basic physical examination and take blood samples," Dr. Chen says. "The sooner we can identify what's in your system, the better we can manage your withdrawal and document what's been done to you."

"Withdrawal?"

"When did you last take your meds?"

"This is day three. I didn't take them the morning of the photo shoot."

"Then it's already started."

I nod slowly. The headache I've been trying to ignore suddenly makes sense. So does the slight tremor in my hands, and the way the light seems just a bit too bright.

I look at Grimm, searching his face for … what? Reassurance? Sincerity? I don't know, but something in his steady gaze anchors me.

"Okay," I say. "Do what you need to do."

Dr. Chen nods, and as she goes to get her medical bag from beside the sofa, I look at Grimm. "Why do you even care about what my father was doing to me?"

A shadow passes over his face, but his expression remains carefully controlled. "Have you forgotten our pact? I help you get healthy. I protect you. And in exchange, you help me destroy Victor Reed." He pauses, his eyes hard and hot on mine. "And, of course, that's not the full sum of our arrangement."

I swallow, looking at the floor to avoid looking at him as the memory of last night once again floods back. Sex. Control. Obedience. Ownership. Surrender.

Everything.

A transaction, plain and simple.

Thankfully, I don't have time to dwell on that, as Dr. Chen returns to draw vial after vial. I sit with my arm extended and fight a shudder as I watch the vials fill. Not blood anymore. Poison. Poured into my veins by my father.

"My lab is expediting the tests," Dr. Chen says, "so I'll have preliminary results in a day or so." She flashes a supportive smile as she tucks away the last vial. "We should have enough to confirm our suspicions and begin building a case."

"A case?" I look to Grimm as Dr. Chen pulls out a stethoscope and blood pressure cuff to continue her exam.

"Unauthorized pharmaceutical use," Grimm says. "Illegal experimentation, psychological manipulation. Basic assault. Possibly more, depending on what we find."

"Against my father," I say as the magnitude of what we're doing —what I've agreed to—washes over me. This isn't just about avoiding an unwanted marriage or gaining my independence. This is about exposing my father's crimes, destroying him completely.

I feel suddenly cold as fear whips through me. I can't do this. I have to step back. Tell Grimm I didn't understand that my literal blood would be spilled because of our agreement. Tell him I don't want to be part of the shitshow that's going to play out in the media any more than I want the target that my father will surely paint on my back.

Except I do want it. Even if it does make me a target. When has my father not had me in the crosshairs?

The truth is, I want it so desperately I can taste it. I want to bring down my father. I want him to pay for what he's done to me and my mother. I want that black heart of his ripped out with all the world watching.

I know my reasons for wanting all of that, but I still don't know Grimm's.

"What?" he asks, but I just shake my head, as if I'm sitting there thinking about nothing but sunshine and puppies while Dr. Chen finishes taking my vitals.

"That's it," she says, giving my hand a quick squeeze. "If you need me, Liam has my contact information. Rest. Stay hydrated. And if you need it, I can prescribe something to take the edge off."

I shake my head. "No more drugs."

She offers one last smile. "You're strong, Sasha. You'll get through this just fine." Then she leaves, and I'm alone with Grimm, and I don't feel strong at all. Pawns aren't strong. And that's what I am. A pawn in a chess game that Grimm is determined to win.

"Why are you doing this? Why do you care what my father's done to me?"

"Maybe I'm just chivalrous."

"Yeah, well, the King Arthur society called. They said that your *everything* bargain is pretty much the opposite of chivalry."

"Really? I'll make a note of it."

"It can't just be about sex," I continue, looking down to hide the way I've smiled at his retort. "I have a feeling you have a lot of options there."

He chuckles, but there's something off about the sound.

"And why go to so much trouble to use me against my father? There must be a billion other ways for you to bring him down that don't involve stealing a girl away and then helping her detox."

A long moment passes before Grimm says, "We all have our reasons," which tells me absolutely nothing.

A shadow passes over his face, but it's gone so quickly I might have imagined it. Then he looks up, his blue eyes hard on mine. "I'm not helping you out of the goodness of my heart, Princess. You know that. This is a transaction."

The cold calculation in his voice should repel me. Instead, it sends a strange thrill through me—the honesty of it, the absence of pretense, is so different from my father's elegant manipulations that I have to fight not to smile. "I haven't forgotten."

He studies me with an expression I can't quite read. "You should rest," he says, all business now.

I almost argue that it's not even noon, but there's no denying the wall of exhaustion bearing down on me.

He walks me to the bedroom door, his hand hovering near the small of my back but never quite touching. The distance feels deliberate. Controlled. As if he's setting boundaries for himself.

I step into the bedroom, aware of his presence behind me, solid and imposing. Will he follow me in? Is this the moment when he claims the first installment of his price? My heart races at the thought, a mixture of fear and something else I'm not ready to name.

But he remains in the doorway, his expression giving nothing away. "I'll check on you in a few hours," he says, and then he's gone, closing the door with a soft click that sounds oddly final.

I sink onto the bed, disappointment and relief warring within me.

Everything.

The word is determined to linger in my mind, and I try to push it away. Try not to imagine his touch.

I remind myself that this is Liam Grimm. Manipulative. Cruel. A man who isn't helping me out of the goodness of his heart. On the contrary, I've traded my father's control for Grimm's. I'm nothing more than a pawn in his plan to destroy my father.

And I've played enough chess to know that pawns always get the raw end of the deal.

ELEVEN
POSSESSION

I jolt awake, then sag back when I remember I'm safe. Or, at least, that I'm safe from my father.

For the moment, anyway.

I'd closed the blinds before sliding into my nap, and now I look around the near-black room for a clock.

No such luck.

With a small sigh, I roll to the side table and switch on the lamp. I'd intended to grab my phone to check the time, but I remember that Grimm took it.

Frustrated, I toss the sheets aside and sit up. Liam Grimm may have rescued me from my father—and, yes, I might be having some scattered fantasies—but that changes nothing. He's still the enemy. I'm nothing to him. And I need to keep that one simple fact firmly in my mind.

I stand slowly, my body feeling both leaden and strangely weightless. My head starts to throb, but I can already tell that my thoughts have been getting clearer and clearer the last couple of days.

My father has been drugging me. My own father.

There's a control panel built into the bedside table, and I press the middle button. I stiffen as the blinds rise, but the bed is between me and the unknown void, keeping me safe.

Based on the dim, golden light that fills the room, I'm guessing that it's early evening, which means I've slept for hours.

Dr. Chen would say that's a good thing. And my headache does seem to have faded.

I move slowly toward the bathroom, noting the fuzzy, itchy way my skin feels, and the way the floor tilts slightly beneath my feet. *Detox*, I tell my reflection once I'm safely at the bathroom counter. It's all part of the detox/withdrawal/getting-the-hell-over-it process, which means this weirdness is a good thing.

I fill the glass with water, down it, then repeat that process three times. I'm not particularly thirsty, but if I can wash away the crap my father shoved into me, then all the better.

Next, I splash some on my face, then meet my own eyes. "You've got this," the girl in the mirror says. "You'll get through this. You'll be free."

And the girl in the mirror is right.

But I can't help but wonder if she's talking about withdrawal … or about the deal she made with the devil.

I close my eyes, not liking the way my thoughts are bouncing. When I open them again, it's not me I see reflected in the mirror. It's my mother.

I blink, and she's gone. Just like the day she died. One moment she was there. The next moment, there was only the void.

A single tear trickles down my cheek, and I brush it away.

What would she think of me now, trading one gilded cage in a tower for another? Escaping one powerful man's control for the lair of another who might prove even more dangerous? Am I a fool? A masochist? A naive little princess, just as my father has always said?

No. It was the right choice.

The only choice.

I hurry out of the bathroom, leaving that lost, uncertain girl to her own devices. Me, I'm going to get dressed, go out into the living room, and be the calm and confident woman I am. Or, at least, that I want to be.

I'd taken off only my leggings before my nap, so I pull them back on, draw a breath, then march out of the room to go find Grimm.

The windows in the open area are still opaque, but the lights are on, so I can easily see that Grimm isn't here. I call his name, and when I get no answer, I consider exploring the rest of the apartment. But the possibility of finding him in some dark back room stops me. Instead, I head to the refrigerator for a bottle of water. That's where I find a note that says only *Errands. Back soon. LG.*

It's a strange sensation being alone in the apartment of this man who is both helping me and holding me hostage. A man who seems to know more about my life than I know myself. Especially since I barely know him at all.

Maybe now's my chance to find out.

For the next half hour, I prowl Liam's apartment like a caged animal, inspecting everything, searching for … what? Clues about the man to whom I've entrusted my life? Weaknesses in my new gilded cage? Escape routes I have no intention of using?

Or maybe I'm trying to distract myself from the lingering headache and the random tremors in my hands.

The apartment is minimalist but luxurious, all sleek surfaces and sharp angles. No photographs. No personal touches. Not even a grocery list. He mentioned a home in Connecticut, and I wonder if it's warmer. The place he truly lives. I think it must be. Liam Grimm is a lot of things, but sterile isn't one of them.

Besides, would he have left me alone in a place where I might stumble across a secret?

Definitely not.

Still, I'm enjoying my exploration. In the study, I find a bit of heaven—an entire wall of bookcases, every inch taken up by hardbacks and paperbacks, classics and popular fiction. One long shelf is dedicated entirely to leather-bound volumes of Grimm's fairy tales. I'm not surprised—the original Brothers Grimm are his ancestors—but I am curious. I pull a volume off the shelf and skim the pages, quickly realizing that these aren't the sanitized versions mothers read to their children. These are the original tales—dark, bloody, and unrepentant.

A cold recognition stirs in me. Children abandoned in forests, maidens imprisoned in towers, girls falling into voids to emerge in a different world.

Bargains and sacrifices. Just like mine.

I replace the book, then hug myself as I take two steps toward the study's window. This one isn't blocked out like the living room, and I take a deep breath, then force myself to move one step closer, then closer still, until I'm only three arm-lengths away. Manhattan spreads out beyond the glass, glowing in the approaching twilight.

The view is dizzying, and as the familiar tightness creeps into my chest, I clench my hands into fists and force myself to stay put and keep my eyes open. How much of my fear is real? How much has been manufactured by years of what my father has been telling me?

And does it even matter? Either way, the terror is inside me.

"Enjoying the view?"

I yelp as I whip around—my heart pounding—to find him standing in the doorway. "I'm sorry," I say. "I didn't mean to snoop. I was just—well, yeah. Actually, I did mean to snoop."

"I see," he says, his expression giving nothing away. "Learn anything interesting?"

"Your decorator likes contemporary. And you're a fan of Stephen King."

The corner of his mouth twitches. "Is that all?"

"The romance novels surprised me."

His expression hardens. "They belonged to my mother. One of her friends sought me out and gave them to me years ago."

"Oh." I look down at the floor, then slide my hands into my pockets before looking back up at him. "Hopefully, I'm also about to learn that curiosity didn't really kill the cat."

I can't read his expression at all, and I hold my breath until he says, very softly, "The cat's safe for now." He turns away, heading out of the room. "Come on, kitty. Let's get you some kibble."

I grimace as I follow him to the kitchen. "I really am sorry. I woke up and—"

"It's fine. I set no rules." His eyes meet mine. "At least, not about looking around. But defy me in any way that matters, and you'll find yourself back with your father in a heartbeat. Do you understand?"

I swallow, then nod.

"I'm glad we're on the same page." He gestures for me to take a seat at the kitchen island, then opens a white bag. Immediately, the smell of warm bread and fried beef hits me, and I stifle a moan. Or, I try to. From the way he looks back at me over his shoulder with a grin, I think my moan may have been a bit over the top.

"Fan of the burger?"

"More like an admirer from afar," I admit. "My diet's pretty restricted."

"I'm aware. Want to stick to that? Or do you want to taste the forbidden?" He's looking right at me, something in his eyes suggesting the question is about more than a burger.

"Forbidden, please," I say, dropping my gaze. "Forbidden with fries."

He chuckles, then passes me a wrapped burger loaded with cheese and a sleeve of French fries.

I've just taken my first bite of cheesy, beefy heaven when he slides a large envelope onto the counter.

"What's that?" I ask, wishing he'd brought a milkshake, too. That would have been so very extra.

"Your father's first parry in our little war."

I drop the burger, all thoughts of fries and milkshakes and cheeseburgers evaporating as I jump off the stool and take two steps back.

"It won't bite you," he says. "Not literally, anyway."

"What is it?"

"Open and see."

I want to shake my head and back away slowly. Instead, I take a deep breath, then pull the envelope toward me. I open the flap, then reach inside and pull out a thin stack of legal documents. My stomach goes queasy as I read the cover letter on the familiar stationery of Beckett & Stein, my father's attorneys. "*Ex parte* Emergency Relief? Temporary guardianship?" I drop the papers as if they're infectious. "Is this what I think it is?"

"That depends. If you think your father got the court to temporarily appoint him as your guardian, then yes."

"A guardian? I'm almost twenty-seven years old. He can't do that."

Grimm's face is hard. "He can if he can prove you're mentally unfit. Incapable of managing your own life. Unstable. Vulnerable. A danger to yourself. Any one of those and he's in."

"But I'm not any of those things. *Am I?*"

Grimm meets my eyes, his like ice. "You aren't," he says firmly, though I'm not sure I believe him. "But if your father can make you look broken enough, the court will hand him the keys."

"But this says he's my guardian now. As in right now."

"It does. Yes. A process server was waiting at the entrance to the garage on my way back."

"But that doesn't explain how he did this. I mean, doesn't the court need to—oh, ask me questions?"

"That's the *ex parte* part. It's immediate relief by the court granted in favor of your father, but setting a full hearing in just over a week."

I hug myself tight, my whole body feeling like I've been covered in tiny ant bites. "No. No way. I can't go back. Not even for a week. Hell, not even for just a minute."

I start to pace, staying far away from the window. It's still blocked, but I know what's behind that opaque glass. And right now, just the knowing is enough to send me spiraling.

"I have to leave," I say, as Grimm silently watches me. "I have to run. To go where the courts don't have jurisdiction. Where he can't just pay off a judge to get what he wants. I—I have to go overseas." I whip around to face Grimm. "Can you get me a flight? Ruby has family in Munich. Maybe I can stay with them for a while and—"

"No."

I stop mid-way across the room, my body going cold and my thoughts turning to dust. "What?"

In two long strides, he's there, standing right in front of me with a calculating smile on that fallen angel face. "I said no."

Before I can stop myself, I've whipped my hand out and slapped him so hard it feels like my palm's on fire. He catches my wrist before I can back away, and I cringe, expecting a similar blow from him. Instead, he pulls me close so that my body is pressed to his, and I have to tilt my head up to see his hard, unsmiling face.

"No," he repeats. "I won't help you leave." He's enunciating every word clearly, as if to make sure I fully understand. "We have a deal." His hand tightens around my wrist and he draws me even closer, his other hand cupping my ass, forcing my body against his so that there's no ignoring the bulge of his cock against my belly. I'm breathing hard, telling myself it's from anger.

And also telling myself I need to stop with the lies.

"Do you remember?" he repeats, his hand moving over my ass until his fingers are between my legs, stroking me through the stretchy material. "Do you remember the terms of our arrangement?"

"I remember." My body is hot. Tingly. And my voice is barely a whisper. My heart pounds in my chest as I tell myself I should pull away. That I should slap his face and run.

Try to find Ruby. Try to be anywhere but here.

But I agreed to this. I agreed to everything.

And, damn me, I don't want to run.

"Good." His hand slides up, then down again, this time slipping under the waistband of the leggings, then under the band of my thong until his fingertip is between my ass cheeks, moving in long, slow strokes in a way that makes me want to squirm away and hide in embarrassment … but also makes me want to beg for more.

"Don't," I whisper, hating that I like it. Knowing I should hate it.

"This is an opportunity, Princess," he murmurs, and for a moment I'm not sure if he means my father's legal action or this intimate contact. "We'll appear in court. We'll reveal what he's done to you. The newspapers will eat that up. It will be international news." He bends down, his finger teasing my ass as his breath teases my ear. "It will destroy him," he whispers. "More important, you'll be free, Princess. Do you understand?"

I manage a nod.

"Good."

He breaks contact, leaving me in a haze of shame and desire as he takes two steps back. I start to move toward him, then realize what I'm doing and force my feet to stay put even though my body is still tingling from whatever game he's playing.

I stiffen, then snap my gaze up as I realize that I'm still screwed. "That order says he's in charge of me as of right now. If you won't help me leave the country, then what are you going to do?"

I stumble back as another thought hits me, sending panic ricocheting through me. "You're not going to hand me over to him," I say, hating that he can hear the fear in my voice. "Please tell me you're not going to do that."

"I'm not going to do that."

He's so calm I want to slap him. I want to scream. To throw things. To go hide someplace small and dark where I can draw my knees up to my chest and hug them the way I used to when I was a little girl. Maybe this time, my wish to disappear will even come true.

But I'm not a little girl, and I'm not seeking out closets in Reed Tower where I can hide from my father. I'm in a different tower altogether. I'm with a different man. And though I don't fully trust Liam Grimm, I don't think he's a monster. Or, if he is, he's not going to hurt me. Not yet, anyway. Grimm hates my father almost as much as I do, so he'll keep me safe. For now, anyway. After all, a dead or wounded hostage doesn't have much value at all.

He takes my arm, his fingers still warm from my heat. "Let's go."

"Go?" Icy panic cuts through me. "You said you weren't going to hand me—"

"I'm not. But as you pointed out, he's in charge of you now. He knows you're with me. Of course, he would suspect that you're still here."

He puts a finger under my chin and lifts it, forcing me to meet his eyes. "That means he's coming soon. He won't wait to strike a deal with my father to let him search the premises. He'll simply go to the police. I imagine he already has a warrant." His smile is both slow and smug. "But that court order won't do him much good if he can't find you."

"Where are we going?"

But all he says is, "Trust me, Princess. He won't get you back. You're mine now. And my plans for you don't include Victor Reed."

TWELVE
SOARING

G rimm's phone chimes, and his body goes rigid as he reads the text. His eyes, already intense, harden to steel.

"We need to leave," he says, hurrying toward his study. I grab the sleeve of French fries and follow him, certain that his urgency has something to do with my father. I reach the study in time to see him pocket something, then close the middle desk drawer.

"My purse," I say, thinking of Ruby's credit card. "I need to get it."

"No." His voice is calm but leaves no room for argument.

"But—"

"They're here. Right now. Police." He takes my elbow and steers me out of the study. "Dammit," he says in a voice low enough that I know it's not meant for me. "They got here a hell of a lot faster than I anticipated."

I expect him to lead me to the elevator. Instead, he bustles us in the opposite direction, further past his study than I've explored. The hall twists and turns until I'm no longer sure which side of the building we're on. Finally, he stops in front of a well-camouflaged service door.

"We're going up," he says, holding the door open and gesturing me into a narrow concrete stairwell.

"Up?" I repeat stupidly as I step inside, and it's only when my bare feet hit the cold concrete that I remember I never bothered to put on shoes.

"Four flights. To the roof." He comes in after me and pulls the door closed. "Go."

I do, hurrying up the stairs, the concrete biting into my feet as I move like lightning.

I pause at the second landing to look back at Grimm. The copper-gold of his hair catches the dim light as he takes the stairs two at a time. His button-down shirt is open at the collar, his sleeves rolled up to reveal strong forearms. Despite the situation, my eyes linger on the taut muscles of his forearms as he reaches the landing, his face a mask of concentration.

"Keep moving," he says, his hand on my lower back pressing me forward. "Almost there."

My breath catches—not from exertion, but from his touch.

Really not the time.

I force my mind to focus only on the steps, and before I know it, we've reached the door to the roof. Grimm puts his weight against it, the door flies open, and I stagger backward, dropping my fries as the world opens up around me, the endless sky and dizzying height hitting me like a physical blow.

I'm still in the stairwell, and I press my back to the concrete wall as I look down at my feet, trying not to think about the nothingness spreading out from the open door. Trying to ignore the way the wind howls through the stairwell, pulling at my hair, my clothes, my will.

Every instinct screams for me to run the other way.

Roofs are where the world ends, and I know that better than anyone.

I hear myself whimper. I can't do this. I can't. All I can do is stand here, staring down at my Scarlett Kiss-painted toes, as I try—and fail — to pretend that the door leads anywhere but this open expanse of a rooftop.

"Dammit, Sasha—listen to me."

It's only then that I realize that Grimm has been speaking to me, his voice like a low rumble of indiscernible noise.

I try to parse out words, but I don't look at him. If I do, all I'll see is the void of night behind him.

"Close your eyes," he orders. "It's either the roof or your father's men."

At the thought, my insides turn to goo. But I force myself to squeeze my eyes tightly shut. I expect him to take my hand and lead me to the helipad, so I gasp when he scoops me up, holding me like a bride. I turn my face into his chest, breathing in his scent—something expensive and masculine that grounds me, at least for a moment. Then I hear it—the thunderous approach of helicopter blades.

"Our ride," Grimm says against my hair. "I'm putting you down now." When my feet touch the ground, I open my eyes—just barely—keeping my hand tight in Grimm's as the spinning blades whip my hair into a frenzy.

It's sleek and black, with no markings. Grimm practically carries me to it, his arm a vise around my waist so that my bare feet hardly touch the ground.

The pilot doesn't ask questions as Grimm helps me into a leather seat, then buckles me in with practiced movements, his fingers grazing my thighs. As they do, I realize I'm trembling … and not entirely from fear.

Just as Grimm reaches for his own harness, the roof access door bursts open. Three men in dark suits spill onto the helipad, weapons already drawn, my father's head of security leading the charge. Their mouths move in furious shouts I can't hear over the roar of the rotors, but the guns aimed at our helicopter leave no doubt about their intentions.

"Go!" Grimm barks into his headset, still securing his own belt.

The helicopter lurches upward, the sudden acceleration pressing me into my seat. One of the attackers drops to one knee as he aims his gun at the pilot's compartment. The pilot must see him, because the helicopter banks sharply, rolling sideways just as Grimm slams the door shut. Through the window, I see more men burst onto the roof, a few getting off more shots as we speed away.

"They were trying to disable the helicopter, not hit us," Grimm says, his voice tight. "Your father wants you back—undamaged merchandise."

My heart is pounding so hard I can feel it in my throat, adrenaline surging through me in a heady rush. I've never felt so terrified or so alive.

My stomach lurches as we rise into the night sky. Manhattan

spreads below us, a glittering carpet of lights that makes my head spin, though not as much as I'd anticipated. The helicopter is like a cocoon, holding me close and safe.

That's what I tell myself, anyway. But deep down I know the real balm is the safe and solid presence of Liam Grimm beside me.

"You're doing well," he says into the headset, and while I hate that he already knows my weaknesses so intimately, my cheeks warm from the praise.

We move swiftly over the city, and though I don't look out of our safe little capsule, I can't help but enjoy the motion. It reminds me of a dream I'd once had about Elysium in which Vale and Prince Killiam escaped a bounty hunter on the back of Ember.

He'd nestled her—*me*—in front of him, one arm wrapped around my waist, the other resting loosely on my thigh, his roaming fingers finding soft skin when the wind made my tattered skirt flutter.

His lips teased my ear as his fingers stroked the soft places between my legs, and when the dragon rolled down, down, down toward the castle below, I didn't know if it was the thrill of the flight or the prince's touch that had my body shaking in a way that probably looked like torture but felt like heaven.

There's a crackle of static in my headphones, then "—coming."

I tense, my cheeks burning, and I miss the next words. "What? What did you say?"

"I said we're coming in for a landing."

"Oh." I relax, feeling foolish. And strangely disappointed.

Soon, we're settled on a helipad near Wall Street, and the moment the pilot gives us the go-ahead, Grimm frees us of the safety belts and helps me out. And while it may be my imagination, I think his hands linger on my waist at least one moment longer than necessary.

I tell myself it doesn't matter. That despite the random fantasy, I want nothing from Grimm but his help and protection.

But try as I might, I just don't believe it.

Night has fallen completely now, and the cool concrete beneath my bare feet is a shock after the warmth of the copter.

"Stay close," Grimm murmurs, and I nod, shaking off my lingering fantasies as I remember why we're on the run.

We hurry from the heliport, and I almost cheer when Grimm flags down a cab almost instantly. Turns out that fleeing from your prick of a father is best done in shoes.

Inside the cab, he orders the driver to take us to Grand Central, then pulls me close against his side. I lean in, relishing the sense of being protected, just the way I know that Killiam will always protect Vale.

Except this isn't a fantasy world, and Grimm isn't protecting me because he wants me. What he wants is to destroy my father. And I'm his weapon of mass destruction.

As the cab merges into traffic, I start to pull away, but Grimm draws me closer. "I'm going to assume they've marked us," he whispers, and I shiver, but whether from trepidation or the feel of his breath on my skin, I truly don't know.

"It's okay," he continues, apparently noticing the way I'd trembled. "We'll lose them again." He puts his finger under my chin and tilts my head up to face him. "Trust me," he says, his voice full of heat and power. "I promise I'll get you safely away."

I start to tell him that I do trust him, but before I say anything, he flashes a lopsided smile. "You're my secret weapon, Sasha. The magic bullet to take down Victor Reed."

I nod, forcing a smile. And hating the unpleasant truth that I can't escape and that only I can see—that I want to be more than Grimm's weapon or Father's bargaining chip.

But some part of me knows that will never change. I was raised to be used. And the truly sad truth? I'm not sure I know any other way to live.

AT GRAND CENTRAL, we blend into the evening crowd, though I catch several curious glances aimed at my bare feet. "Brooklyn," he says, ushering me onto a crowded train. We stand pressed together in the crush of bodies, his front to my back, his arm around my waist. I can feel his breath on my neck, and it sends shivers down my spine that have nothing to do with the fear.

Two stops later, he pulls me off the train, leaving the phone he'd taken from me on an empty seat.

I laugh. "If they track it, the signal will lead them in the wrong direction."

The corner of his mouth curves up. "Maybe you are more than just a pretty face on one of Reed's shitty ads."

I start to snap out that considering it's my damn phone, he should be nicer. But I'm in a subway station in the middle of Manhattan with no phone, no money, no shoes, and a growing headache that I'm sure is part of my withdrawal. Or maybe just fear coupled with frustration.

Either way, best not to piss off my protector, captor, tormentor … whatever the hell Grimm is.

By the time we've switched trains five more times, I'm exhausted, and my filthy feet are aching. Finally, Grimm announces that we've arrived, and I look up to see that we're at Times Square. We climb the stairs to exit the station and emerge into the glow and bustle of the Theater District.

"How much further?" I ask, wincing as I step on something sharp.

"Just a few blocks. Here," he adds as he scoops me into an over-the-shoulder fireman's carry, his hand on my ass to keep me steady.

"Dammit, Grimm! Put me down." He doesn't. If anything, he increases the pressure against my rear. I open my mouth to protest, then close it again, telling myself that my very abused feet need the break.

The easiest lies are the ones you tell yourself.

All too soon, we're several blocks from the station on a quiet street lit by the golden glow of streetlamps. Grimm eases me down, my body sliding against his before my feet touch the ground.

My pulse races and I'm having trouble catching my breath, but I tell myself it's all because of our situation. Because we're too exposed here on this dark little street.

I feel exposed, all right. But it has nothing to do with my father's search parties.

My mind is in such a muddle that it takes me a second to realize that we're standing in front of the entrance to the Renfort Inn. A doorman seems to materialize from the shadows, and we step off the street into quiet opulence. This is the kind of tucked-away hotel that caters to the very rich. The kind that places privacy and discretion well above the thread count on their Egyptian sheets.

At the reception desk, Grimm pays in cash. If the clerk notices my *I'm-a-pauper* bare feet, he doesn't show it. Most likely he's too well-trained to comment on what might be some sort of dominant/submissive game we're playing.

My stomach twists. Oh, god. Is this a dominant/submissive game we're playing?

I force myself to shove down that ridiculous and terrifying thought.

And intriguing …

Except it isn't. I may lead a sheltered life, but I have windows to the world. Ruby. Elysium. The very wide world of streaming television and the deep dark world of the Internet.

I've been controlled enough—used enough— by my father. The idea of what little power I have being taken by anyone is enough to make my stomach twist.

Once we're in the elevator, Grimm puts me down gently. I stand close to the door and face forward, afraid that if I face Grimm, he'll read my thoughts all over my face. He's been kind enough since we struck our deal, but that doesn't change the fact that I still owe him *everything*.

And now that we're in this discrete little hotel, I can't stop worrying about what exactly that will mean.

I focus on the elevator door seam as Grimm steps behind me, then slips his hand up the back of my simple tee. His palm is warm, and though I expect him to stroke my skin, he doesn't move. Our only contact is the warmth of his skin on my lower back and the whisper of his breath against my hair. And that simple touch is wildly, painfully erotic. And more than a little terrifying.

The low whirr of the elevator's motor competes with the beat of my heart, so intense now that I'm sure Grimm must hear it. Or feel it reverberate through me. I try to take shallow breaths, try to ignore the way his touch seems to simmer through me.

But I can't. All I can think of is Prince Killiam's touch. The tender way he strokes Vale's cheek, his fingers soft along her skin. The way his fingers tease her nipples before sliding down her belly, all the way to the heat of her core between her legs. The dirty things he whispers about filling Vale's cunt with his hard cock, about sucking on her tits. The way he promises to fuck her hard—to take her to the edge and then make her beg before finally, *finally*, letting her over. But only if she's a very, very good girl.

And then the way he does every single thing he's promised, so that Vale—*so that I*—comes so hard it's almost painful.

Stop it!

That's all just fantasy. I can't let myself slide into Elysium. Not in cyberspace or in my mind. Especially not now that I know that Elysium's integrated AI—that vicious little twerp—slipped a heaping dose of Liam Grimm into Prince Killiam.

Mostly, I need to remember that the man I'm with is only helping me because he wants to shut down my father. I'm a means to his end, just as he is to mine.

Just as we'd agreed when he smuggled me from the gala. That moment when my agreement to *everything* sealed that deal.

I hug myself as the elevator doors part. I'd been so lost in thought that I hadn't noticed the car stopping. Now, Grimm's hand presses against my back, and I burst forward, so eager to escape his distracting touch that I almost fall flat on my face. He catches me by the elbow and steadies me—rendering my escape plan useless.

"I'm fine," I snap, tugging my arm free. "Just tired. It's been a day."

"It has," he says as the elevator closes, leaving me alone in the hall with him, the air around us thick with anticipation. And much, much warmer than it should be.

There's only one suite on this floor, and I follow Grimm to the ornate door, then wait for him to unlock it since, of course, I wasn't issued a key.

He ushers me in ahead of him, and I glance around at the elegantly decorated space. It's full of perfectly placed designer pieces, yet it feels impersonal. As if this is a stage, not a room.

Appropriate, I suppose, since I'm not living the life I know anymore. And I'm not sure whose life I am living. A young woman running from an abusive father? A girl who's never been able to cope in the vastness of the world, now tossed into the middle of it with a man she's both hated and crushed on for years as her only anchor?

Or maybe—just maybe—I'm a girl who's finally decided to do whatever it takes to free herself from the chains that bind her, even if that means making a deal with the devil himself.

After all, isn't the devil supposed to be beautiful and charming and seductive?

If that's the case, then I really have slid into hell.

But whether or not I stay here …

Well, I guess that's up to me.

THIRTEEN
CRAVING

As Grimm crosses the living area to close the drapes, I take in the elegantly decorated space. Designer furniture counterpointed by overstuffed pillows. A plush throw rug spread out in front of a cozy sofa. Beautifully bound books on an antique bookshelf. An alcove with a desk. And a crystal bowl filled with pinecones on a side table.

Undeniably lovely, but also impersonal. As if this is a stage, not a room.

When I mention that to Grimm, he glances around, then shrugs. "Looks par for the course to me. As far as hotels go, I'd say it's got more personality than most."

That's when it hits me. I haven't got a clue about what a typical hotel room looks or feels like. "Disney World," I whisper.

Grimm tilts his head, confusion and amusement both playing across that gorgeous face. "I beg to differ, Princess. If this were Disney, we'd be seeing some evidence of the mouse."

I shake my head as I head to the couch. "The last time I was in a hotel, it was in Florida on a rare vacation. I haven't slept anyplace but Reed Tower since before my mother died." I glance toward him. "Until now."

"Goddamn your father." His words are barely a whisper. Even so, the vitriol in his voice is clear. There's something else, too. Something protective that twists in my stomach and makes me dip my head again because the words seem just a shade too personal.

That, however, is only my nerves talking. I know perfectly well that being in this room has nothing to do with me. Not really. Sure, he's protecting me. But that's only because I'm a weapon to use against my father.

It's when my head's down that I notice the mess—I've tracked street grime all over the polished wood. Not to mention this gloriously soft and radioactively white rug.

I wince, then look up at Grimm. "I think I just lost your deposit."

"Don't worry. I won't spank you." That sparkle flares again as he meets my gaze. "Not too hard, anyway."

"I—" I have to swallow as something warm and enticing spreads through me even as an invisible band tightens around my chest. I clamber to my feet, feeling awkward and off-center and small. "I need to clean up."

I hurry through the bedroom and into the apartment-size bathroom. I shut the door behind me, then lean against it, as if the addition of my weight will keep the boogeyman out.

In this scenario, of course, it's Grimm playing the role of boogeyman.

I draw a breath, trying to force myself to relax. I hate how off-balance I feel. As if it's my fault my feet are a mess, when it isn't at all. It isn't even Grimm's. It's my father's.

My father who basically sold me. Who's now hunting me.

A father who drugged me and lied to me and killed my mother.

It's because of him I feel this way—small and embarrassed and lost. And worse, I'm not even sure if it's me that feels like this or if my reaction is the result of some psychological effect of withdrawal.

I hope it's the latter. Because that means that when all the crap is out of my system, maybe I'll learn that I'm strong. That I'm not truly the weak little compliant girl my father sees.

"Dammit." The curse slips out, barely a whisper, but my body automatically goes tense. Sasha Reed, the face of Reed Cosmetics, is not allowed to curse.

"Fuck, shit, damn," I whisper as I sit on the edge of the tub. The words hang in the air, like tiny trophies.

Sasha said a swear word. Release the balloons!

I sigh, suddenly realizing how exhausted I am, physically and mentally.

I spread a towel out on the floor, then sit on the edge of the tub, my feet inside. I pull my leggings up to my thighs, then bend to push down the plug. Finally, I turn on the tap and adjust the temperature. Then, as water slowly rises over my feet, I try to simply sit and breathe. I'm beyond exhausted—too little sleep and too much stress. Not to mention the chemical war going on in my blood.

It's all getting to me. And I don't know whether to thank Grimm or curse him for being the final catalyst that sent my life spiraling in this direction.

Except he wasn't. Not really.

I was the one who ran. More than that, I'm the one who's still running. And as terrifying as that is, I'm proud of myself. I did it. I escaped. Grimm may be using me, but I'm using him, too. And I'll keep using him for as long as he'll stand as a wall between me and Victor Reed. Because there is no way I'm going back. Not now that I understand what my father did to my mother. What he did to me.

That's why it doesn't matter if Grimm is my savior or a devil. For right now, at least, I need him.

As if my thoughts have conjured him, there's a tap at the bathroom door, then Grimm pushes it open and steps inside.

"Um, excuse me? Bathroom. Private time." My voice comes out sharper than I'd intended.

He doesn't respond. He simply walks in carrying the crystal bowl that had, moments before, been holding a cluster of decorative pinecones.

"What on earth are—?"

His finger on my lips silences me, the unexpected touch sending an electric current coursing through me. His finger is warm, slightly rough, and the pressure against my lips is gentle but undeniably assertive.

I tell myself I should pull away.

Then I tell myself to shut up.

Our eyes stay locked. One beat, then another. Then Grimm removes his finger and sits beside me on the edge of the tub, his feet —still in shoes—on the bathmat. He half-fills the bowl with water from the tap, then sets it on the floor before reaching for my right foot and lifting it from the tub.

"You've cut yourself," he says, as he examines the sole of my foot.

"Small price to pay for getting away from my father," I say, trying —and failing—to tug my foot free.

"I suppose." He bends over to dip a washcloth into the clear water of the bowl. Then he begins to clean my foot, his touch surprisingly gentle for a man who seems to always dominate everything around him.

"And our arrangement?" he asks, his eyes hard on mine. "Is that a small price, too?"

Everything. I hug myself, unable to stop the shiver that runs through me. He must have noticed, but he says nothing, just continues ministering to my feet.

"Well?" he presses, after the silence has hung between us for what seems an eternity. He gently returns one foot to the bathwater, then lifts the other. I clutch the side of the tub tighter for balance, grateful for the excuse not to answer.

Not that he lets me get away with it. "Come now, Princess. Don't leave me hanging."

"Don't call me that."

He cocks a brow. "I believe this game is played by my rules."

I clench my hands into fists and look into the darkening tub.

"Something you'd like to say to the class?"

"No."

"No, what?"

I draw in a breath, then let it out slowly. Then I tilt my head to the side, just enough so that I can see him. I've read enough romances to know the answer he wants. "No, sir."

The hint of a smile touches his mouth. Barely even there. But enough for me to understand what it means—*victory.*

I look down, focusing on his large hands gently cleaning my small foot. Competent hands that tenderly wash away the dirt and tar and bits of stone and glass. His touch is soft enough to almost make me believe he cares. But this isn't about caring. It's about winning. About manipulation.

I'm not someone who matters. I'm simply a token in a game he's playing with my father. For all intents and purposes, I'm not even really here.

"You still haven't answered me," he says. "Our arrangement. Is it a small price to pay, too?"

I look back down at the water, uncomfortably confused by the question. This is the man who is so carefully cleaning my aching, filthy feet. But he's also a man I should hate. A man whose father is a monster. A man who stood beside me three years ago and told me I was nothing. Just a little brainless doll my father used to spread lies, and that's all I was good for.

About that, at least, he was right. Because that was the press conference where the speech my father wrote, and I read to the press boldly stated that Elias Grimm had killed my mother.

Now I know the truth about my mother's death. And now it's Grimm using me to get to my father instead of my father using me to spread lies.

So I guess what Grimm said that night was right. I am an instrument to be wielded. To be used. And always on someone else's behalf.

I want to scream all of that at him. I want to throw it in his face. But I can't. For better or worse, I've tied my future to this man, at least until after the hearing that will decide the course of my life.

But when I open my mouth to answer him, it's not a simpering little girl who answers. It's a woman, and she lifts her chin, looks him in the eye, and says, "Everything? Why, no. It's not a small price to pay at all. It's torture."

There'd been a teasing gleam in his eye. Now it fades into something else. Something that might be confusion. Then to something that can only be described as hard. Dangerous.

I tremble, wanting to take the words back. What the hell was I thinking? I'm not a girl who can take charge. The only place where I get to be in charge of my story is in Elysium. And I'm a long way from that safe, protective world.

"Torture," he finally says, in a voice as sharp as a blade. "Nice to know we're on the same page."

He reaches for my other foot, and I try to draw it back, but he just tightens his grip. "Not your decision, Princess."

I watch, silently seething, as he continues to clean my foot. As much as I hate that he's forcing me to surrender, at least he's not pretending the choice is mine. He's not manipulating me like my father. He's simply taking control.

It infuriates me, yes. But some small part of me can't help but notice that it also feels disarmingly good.

We continue in silence, my attention locked on those elegant fingers. Despite what I said, this isn't torture. Not by a long shot.

Then again, maybe it is. Because there's something unexpectedly sensual about the way he's gently removing bits of gravel and carefully cleaning each small cut.

"Cinderella in reverse," I murmur, then immediately wish I could swallow the words.

Grimm pauses, looking up, two vertical lines forming above the bridge of his nose. "Cinderella?"

My cheeks go warm. "Instead of the prince trying the glass slipper on the girl's foot, the prince is washing her feet."

"I'm hardly Prince Charming," he says, his blue eyes now stormy and wild. He hasn't shaved, and a shadow of beard stubble makes him look even more dark and dangerous. No, not Prince Charming, but a dark prince? Most definitely.

"And despite my ancestry," he continues, clearly unaware of the direction of my thoughts, "this isn't a fairy tale." He tilts his head. "Or maybe it is. You know how the original fairy tales turned out." The hint of a smile plays at his lips, but his eyes stay hard. "I suppose if you're not my princess, then it's your toes that will be cut off."

I shudder, but he's not wrong. If I'm not with him, my father will find me. And he'll do worse to me than what Cinderella's stepsisters suffered.

I think of the ancient books in his study. "The original fairy tales truly were grim. Is that how your family got its name?"

"My family?" he repeats, his voice laced with a dark humor that reminds me that he really is the black sheep. I stifle a cringe, wishing I'd said nothing.

He puts the washcloth down, then moves the bowl out of the way before rising and offering me his hand.

I hesitate only a moment before placing my palm against his. He helps me get out somewhat gracefully. Then he kneels and uses a plush towel to dry my legs. When he's finished, he remains kneeling, his hands resting lightly on my calves.

He tilts his head up slowly, and I can practically feel the heat from his gaze as it traces up between my legs, pausing at the junction for so long that I feel the pool of warmth at my sex. Then higher still until my nipples peak against the soft material of my bra. My mouth is parted, and I feel his gaze on my lips with the soft intensity of a kiss.

He continues the journey, and I expect that when he meets my eyes, I'll see heat. The kind of heat I've only felt in Elysium.

And the truth I'm finding so hard to swallow? I want what I've had with Killiam in Elysium. Only now I want it with Grimm.

Not with a fantasy, but with the devil himself. And how fucking terrifying is that?

FOURTEEN
CLAIMING

I pause at the bedroom door, then tighten the sash on the hotel-provided robe. It's soft and white and feels like a caress against my skin. More than that, it feels like safety.

"Dry off," he'd said before leaving me alone in here. "Then come to bed. And Sasha," he'd added. "Come out naked."

He really couldn't have been clearer.

But I can't seem to make myself move.

I've stood here for at least five minutes, and each time I try to slip the robe off my shoulders, I freeze. In Elysium, I can be as bold as I want. Vale can strip bare, can beg for his touch, can surrender without consequence. But this is real. This is me—Sasha Reed, locked away for years, with no experience beyond digital fantasy.

If I walk naked into that room, I might end up cowering in a corner, hugging my knees as he looks down at me, anger flaring.

Better to make him angry while I'm standing. At least in the robe, I might have the wherewithal to fight back.

Decision made, I turn the knob and step out of the plush bathroom into the suite's even more plush bedroom. Framed landscapes. An overstuffed armchair. Uncovered windows that let in the vibrant light of the city at night, seemingly casting a spotlight onto the huge bed, as if it's a stage waiting for a performance.

What I don't see is Grimm.

I start to turn around but am stopped by his firm hands on my shoulders. He's behind me, and I freeze as those hands roam down, sliding over the thick material that covers my breasts, then lower until his fingers find the cinched belt. I expect him to open it, but he doesn't. Instead, he puts one hand on my waist to pull me back toward him. So close that even through the thick material of the robe, I feel the hard length of his cock.

I tense, not wanting to admit to him or myself how deeply my body is reacting.

"Naughty girl," he says, his breath teasing my ear as he speaks, sending shivers down my spine. His fingers release the belt, letting the robe fall open. "I believe I was clear." His hands move to my shoulders, and he steps backward, taking the robe with him.

The brush of the material as it leaves my body feels both sensual and shameful, and I have to fight the urge to cover myself with my hands. I'm already in trouble for the robe. And even though he hasn't said as much, I'm certain that trying to hide myself would be the absolute wrong thing to do.

Then his hands are on my naked skin. One on my waist, the other on my breast, his forefinger slowly teasing my nipple. I bite my lip, willing myself not to react. Hating how good this feels. How much I've craved the touch of this man who only sees me as a bludgeon he can hurl at my father.

"How long have you wanted me?" Once again, his whisper is a tease as sensual as his words.

"I don't want you." It's a lie, and we both know it. Except I want it to be true.

The hand on my waist eases down, then slides along the juncture of my hip and thigh until his fingertips brush my sex. "Smooth," he murmurs, trailing those fingers down over my waxed sex as he orders me to spread my legs.

I do—not only because I have no choice, but because I want what he's offering. I hate myself for craving it—for craving him. But so help me, I do. I want to feel alive in this world, not only when I'm in Elysium. And why shouldn't I?

He's using me for revenge. It's only fair I use him for sex.

"Christ, you're wet," he murmurs, and the heat in his voice coupled with his soft touch just about melts me.

I whimper, fighting an urge to beg for more as he thrusts two fingers inside me, my core closing tight around him, all semblance of coyness dissolving under this wild need.

He chuckles, soft and low. "Does your daddy know what a horny little thing his princess is? Do you like it when he spanks you?"

"Don't talk about my father."

"Tell me you want me."

"Not you," I lie, then gasp when the palm of his free hand smacks hard against my ass. I should be pissed as hell. Instead, my nipples ache and my core clenches even more intensely around his fingers. I bite my lower lip to keep from begging, hating the need that seems to have taken me over like a possessing spirit.

"Interesting," he murmurs, and I tense, waiting for another smack. When it doesn't come, I can't escape the simple truth that I was both anticipating that sting … and craving it.

That, however, isn't something Grimm needs to know.

"How long have you wanted me?" The question is almost a growl.

Again, the lie comes easily— "I don't want you."

"No?" His hand leaves my breast and I hear the distinctive sound of his zipper, then feel his cock against my bare ass. He returns the hand and continues to lightly tease my nipple, the fingers of his other hand thrusting in and out of my pussy as his cock presses hard against my rear.

I'm on sensual overload, and it's all I can do not to beg him to add another finger, to use his hand to fuck me even harder, to take me however he wants—whatever it takes to satisfy this wonderful, horrible, terrible need that I've only ever quelled myself. Even in Elysium, it's only me, no matter what fantasy I've spun or what tingling sensation the full Elysium experience might provide.

But this isn't my imagination. It's not even Elysium.

This is real, and I want it. All of it.

Mostly, I want a touch other than my own.

No, I want *this* touch. *His* touch.

I want Liam Grimm. But damned if I'm going to admit that to him.

"I can take you over," he whispers, his breath hot against my ear. "All you have to do is ask. All you have to say is that you want me."

"I don't."

"Liar." He steps back, his cock no longer teasing my ass. His fingers no longer inside me. His hand no longer on my breast.

I have to bite my tongue not to whimper.

"Turn around, Princess."

I do, my chin lifted as if I really am a princess.

Amusement dances in his eyes. "Don't lie to me. Trust me when I tell you that our time together will go much better if we dispense with the lies."

I lift a brow, but I say nothing.

"Say that you want me."

"I don't."

His brow rises. "Perhaps I was unclear about not lying," he says, his voice as icy as his gaze. "Do you think I didn't notice the way you trembled in the elevator? The way you drew in a breath when I pressed my hand to your lower back? Do you think I don't know that whenever you lose yourself in fantasies, it's my face you see? Or that you touched yourself last night? That when you thrust those manicured fingers inside your sweet little cunt, it was me you were thinking of?"

"No." It's another lie, of course, and it's hard to put any conviction behind the word when I'm still mourning the loss of his fingers inside me.

My pulse quickens as he studies my face. Then he steps closer, his fingers sliding through my hair to tug my head back as he captures me in a long, slow kiss, so deep I sag in his arms, my legs no longer capable of holding me up.

I'm trembling with need when he breaks the kiss, his face going hard. "Get on the bed."

I hurry to comply, hating myself for letting him see just how much I want this.

"Under the covers," he says. "Now."

Once again, I do as he says. His eyes skim over me, and his mouth curves into a smile. "Sleep, Princess. And don't leave this room. There are cameras in the hall and the elevator, and I assure you that the desk clerk will have plenty of incentive to call me if you so much as open that door."

I bolt upright, the sheet pressed to my chest to cover my bare breasts. "You're leaving?"

"You're safe," he says. "Stay. Sleep. I won't be long."

"But—"

"Argue, and I'll dump you in a taxi and send you to Reed Tower."

I don't want to believe him, but I'm looking at the cold, hard countenance of a man who doesn't make idle threats.

"I'll stay," I finally say. "But I'm not going to sleep."

He tilts his head. "As you wish." His eyes skim over me one last time. Then he turns and walks out of the bedroom, leaving me under the covers, confused, unsatisfied, and very, very annoyed.

FIFTEEN
BEAUTIFUL BETRAYAL

As soon as the door clicks behind him, I fist my hands in the sheets, clamp my lips tightly together, and silently scream.

It doesn't help.

Right now, the only thing that will help is Liam Grimm standing right in front of me with my hands around his throat choking his worthless a-hole life out of him.

I mean, seriously. What. The. Fuck?

First, he torments me with such wicked brutality I'm almost begging him to fuck me. Which is, frankly, mortifying. Then he takes me all the way to the edge and leaves me there, just hanging like some pathetic, horny teenager.

Now I hate myself not just for wanting him, but for letting him see that I want him.

No, *wanted*. Past tense. Because I am so done with this. Protect me, fine. But if he's going to demand a price, then it's going to be cold, hard cash next time.

Bastard.

I do a few more laps around my racecourse of vitriol until my fury subsides and my heart rate slows.

What doesn't go away? That itch. That need.

And bastard boy isn't here to help with any of that.

Fuck.

With a sigh, I pull the covers higher as I slide my hand lower, trailing my fingertips over my breasts, my belly, then lower and lower until I find my own slick, wet core. I sigh, my body trembling as if in anticipation, and I close my eyes, losing myself in a collage of Liam Grimm. Those blue eyes dark with lust. Those strong hands stroking my skin. That wide, full mouth closing over my breast, then kissing its way down, down, down until ...

I tease my clit, craving that explosion, and yet at the same time wanting more.

Wanting him—but he's not here.

I want to hate myself for craving this man. A man I know is only using me as a weapon against my father. But I can't. I knew the score when I agreed. And now here I am, alone and frustrated with my hands between my legs, cursing this edgy, needy feeling. Wanting the explosion to be earned.

Wanting Grimm, dammit.

But then I remember ...

I hurry naked into the connected living area, then straight to the desk. I cross my fingers, then open the drawers, gratified when I see that my hunch was right—nestled in the drawer is a laptop with the hotel's logo.

That's the benefit of high-end hotels. The management simply charges the black card of any guest who helps themself to electronics or art or furniture.

It's fully charged and connected to WiFi, and I take it back to the bed, prop myself up against a mountain of pillows, then navigate to the Elysium portal and log in.

Once again, I'm frustrated that I don't have access to all the equipment back in my suite at home. Especially since I'm practically twitching with pent-up sexual frustration.

I'm not supposed to have any of that equipment. Father would lock me in a room full of windows if he knew, but Ruby finagled two sets from an R&D guy she'd dated for a minute. Fortunately, he's a decent guy and didn't ask for the equipment back after she cut him loose.

As if my thoughts have magically summoned her, the moment I log in, I see her avatar standing just outside the staging area.

Finally! I've been waiting for you.

What's going on? I type in response.

Where are you?

A hotel.

But where?

I hesitate, suddenly afraid this isn't really Ruby. Maybe my father or one of his goons managed to hack through all the security I built into the software.

I consider my options, then type out my response. *I don't know. He — he kept me blindfolded until we reached the room. I tried to look out the windows, but I'm too stressed to get close.*

It's ok. It doesn't matter. I just … You just need to be careful, okay? Is he with you right now?

No. Went out for food. My stomach twists with worry. *What's going on?*

I talked to Leo.

Holy shit.

I'd been slouching, but shock pulls me up straight. When her avatar winces at the revelation, I realize that she's wearing the enhancement gear that I'm not.

Are you okay?? Did he corner you somewhere? Please tell me he didn't hurt you.

No, no. I'm fine. I—I contacted him.

My fingers are frozen on the keyboard. I don't have a clue what to say.

Finally, I manage to form a sentence. *Are you okay? Why on earth would you do that?*

As far as I'm concerned, Leo Grimm is a bigger prick than any of his brothers, and what he did back when he and Ruby were dating is absolutely unforgivable.

As far as I know, she thinks so, too. So I don't understand why she would call him.

Because of you, she says when I ask her that very thing.

Me?

He's close to Liam. We both know he's the only one of the brothers who's close to Liam.

That's true. Their father, Elias Grimm, barely looks at Liam because his mother, Rebecca, was Elias's mistress and had cheated on Elias with my father.

The irony, of course, is that Elias had previously cheated on his wife, Marge, with Rebecca.

Marge and Elias have four sons—Gabriel, the oldest, who died three years ago in a fire, Alexander, who is the current heir-apparent to the Grimm legacy, Elliott, a recluse I don't know much about, and Leo, the youngest and wildest of all the brothers.

Liam, of course, is the son of Elias and Rebecca and is mostly shunned by his father. From the gossip I've heard, Leo is the only brother he gets along with, and his stepmother, Marge, absolutely despises him.

All things considered, I suppose it's a miracle that Liam is as sane and put-together as he is. He's a hell of a lot more centered than I am, and I don't have an evil stepmother or siblings who hate me.

Hang on, I type. *This is getting ridiculous.*

I open another browser, head over to the virtual phone app, and call her the same way I had back in Grimm's apartment.

The second she picks up, I lay into her. "You shouldn't have called him. That's a door you need to never, ever, ever open again."

"I know, I know." I can practically picture her throwing her hands up, her auburn curls bouncing as she nods in agreement. "But I thought it was important, and I was right."

"Okay," I say. "I'm listening."

"What did Liam tell you? About why he whisked you away from the gala and why he's helping you now?"

"Because Father's been manipulating me. He's using me to test drugs that fuck with my memory and make me docile so the bastard can keep me in line. Probably testing on others, too, but I'm high-profile. If Grimm can get proof from my blood, he can shut my father down."

"And that's it?"

"Isn't that enough? My own father's pumping me full of drugs. He made me believe Elias Grimm pushed my mother off the roof, when really it was him."

"Oh, god," she says. "That's horrible."

I swallow. "It is," I say. "Not that I'm thrilled to be Satan's daughter, but at least I know the truth."

"Did Liam tell you about his mother?" she asks.

"Rebecca? No. We haven't really talked about her. He was just a baby when she died."

"Victor had her killed."

I go stone cold. "My father had Liam Grimm's mother killed?" I say the words slowly, as if that will help me understand.

It doesn't.

"That's what Leo told me. Victor had Liam's mother killed. Rebecca Towne was your dad's mistress. But she left him to have a thing with Elias, and she got pregnant."

My head spins as Ruby lays out the rest of the tale. With so much twisting, turning, and betrayal, it's practically a soap opera—which would be amusing if the drama weren't leaking into my life.

Apparently, Elias wanted to keep the baby, but Rebecca knew that Marge would make her life miserable and that Elias wouldn't stand up for her. So she ran to my father, and he agreed to take her back so long as she gave up the baby—not to Elias, but to an orphanage—and that she would never try to track the kid down.

"Let me guess," I say. "She pretended to agree, then somehow got back with Elias despite Marge."

"Yup. She faked pain and spotting, then bolted when your dad had someone take her to a hospital."

"And Elias took her in?"

"According to Leo, yeah. And he made Marge agree, which pissed her off."

"And that's why she hates Liam so much now," I guess.

"Pretty much," Ruby says.

"Poor Liam," I say. "Can you imagine growing up like that? A stepmother who hates you. A father who probably thought of him more like a chess piece than a kid."

"No wonder he's fucked up," Ruby says.

"All things considered, he's remarkably sane. And strong," I add, because I know a bit about being a chess piece disguised as a child.

There's silence for so long that I begin to think I lost the connection.

"Ruby?"

"You like him." It's a statement, not a question. And maybe it's my imagination, but there's something dark in her tone.

"He saved me from an engagement to Desmond Bane. Remember?

And got me away from my father. What's not to like?" I don't mention the part where he owns my ass. Literally. Or the part about the way he touches me.

Or about how I like it.

"No, no, no," she says, her voice thick with urgency. "Sasha, you have to be careful. Liam Grimm is dangerous. Everyone knows that."

"But I don't. Not really." I've heard stories, of course. But despite the morally questionable terms of our deal, so far, Grimm's only helped me.

"He's just like the rest of them," Ruby says, her voice sharp. "He's smart and he's deadly and he knows how to turn on the charm. Don't make the mistake I made with Leo."

"I'm not dating the guy."

"Victor Reed had Liam's mom killed," she blurts. "Your father was so angry Rebecca had given birth to a Grimm baby, that he sent one of his goons after her."

I freeze. Literally. Like ice running through my veins.

I wish I could say I don't believe her, but I know my father. Of course, I believe her.

"That's horrible."

"It's more than that. Liam Grimm doesn't want you because he can get evidence from you. Sure, maybe Victor is working on illicit drugs, but so what? He'll pay a fine and move on, just like he always does. Grimm must know that."

"Then what?" My voice comes out coarse. Raw. And even though I already know the answer, I have to hear it out loud. I won't believe it if I don't hear it.

"Dammit, Sasha, don't you get it? The only way for him to truly get back at your father for killing his mother is for Liam Grimm to kill you."

SIXTEEN
DARKNESS FALLS

She'd bolted.

Outside the Renfort Hotel, Liam Grimm clenched his fists and forced himself not to spew a litany of swear words out into the glittering Manhattan night. But he couldn't keep from spewing them in his head.

Damn Leo. Damn Ruby.

And damn Sasha most of all.

Thankfully, Leo had called—interrupting a meeting at a nearby bar where Liam was delivering some key intel to a client. He'd ended the meeting quickly, then focused on Leo's summary of the idiotic conversation he'd shared with Ruby. Liam still didn't understand how the conversation had twisted around to Rebecca's death. For that matter, neither did Leo. Apparently, the youngest Grimm had once again been thinking with his dick instead his brain.

Par for the course, but at least he'd had the sense to call Liam and fess up.

And now Sasha was out in the world, unprotected, and probably terrified to return to him.

And any minute now, one of her father's goons would find her.

"Dammit, Leo, if he gets her ..."

Leo, of course, couldn't hear him, but he knew the stakes. Which was why they were both out scouring the area, trying to pick up Sasha's signal.

He glanced at his phone screen. Nothing.

Fuck.

He'd been less than a block from the hotel when Leo had called, swearing that it had only been minutes since he realized his mistake. Liam had burst into the hotel, bullied the clerk into showing him the security feed, then watched in horror as Sasha raced down the hall to the emergency exit.

There were no cameras in that stairwell, but the alley camera caught her plowing through the back door, once again in her tee and leggings with her feet bare.

He had to find her. She was the fulcrum for all his plans. And the damn subdermal tracker that her father had inserted into her shoulder would lead Victor Reed's goons right to her unless Liam got there first.

Unfortunately, all the electrical noise in the area was messing with the tracker, seemingly bouncing her location here and there and back again so that all Liam knew was that she was in the area. It could take ages for him and Leo to find her. But at least it would be just as hard for Reed.

He couldn't even hope that she'd leave the area for somewhere with less electrical interference, like a nearby neighborhood. Because as soon as she did, Reed would be able to pinpoint her. So would Liam, of course, but then it would be a race. And if Victor's goons won…

Fuck.

His phone vibrated in his back pocket, and he pulled it free to read the message: *Got eyes on her.*

Relief poured through him like fine whiskey, but he couldn't savor it. A visual was good news, but he wouldn't relax until he'd gotten her safely back to the hotel without anyone tailing them.

In less than a heartbeat, he'd mapped Leo's location and was sprinting in that direction. Just three blocks away but getting closer to a residential area. And she had no idea how much danger she was heading for.

Once he had eyes on her, too, he followed her for a block, with Leo repositioning himself ahead of her, just in case she decided to run.

When she reached an intersection and stopped to wait for the signal, he zipped up beside her and took her arm.

The moment he felt her skin beneath his fingers, relief crashed over him with such force he almost stumbled off the sidewalk. He told himself the relief flowed from the certainty that losing her would mean losing his power over Victor Reed.

But that was a goddamn lie.

"Do you honestly think I want you dead, you damn little fool?"

Her eyes went wide, and her lips parted, but she only shook her head. Not in negation, but in confusion. "I don't—I don't know."

Tears clung to her lower lashes, and he wanted to kick his own ass. "Dammit," he snapped, hating that she had it so wrong. "That would make me like your father. And other than my own, there is no one I less want to emulate. Do you believe me?"

She nodded.

"Then let's move, because he's close."

"What?" She winced as she hurried to keep up with him in her bare feet. He scooped her up, ordering her to put her arms and legs around him so they were chest to chest, and he was carrying her like a curvaceous monkey.

"I don't understand," she said as he signaled to Leo to keep watch as they moved back toward the Renfort. "My father? How did he find me?"

"You left the damn room, Princess. I told you not to. The second you burst into the stairwell, you pinged for him."

"Pinged," she repeated, and he could practically hear the wheels churning in her head. "He's tracking me?"

He saw the horror spread over her face, and his heart twisted. This woman deserved one hell of a lot better than Victor Reed.

When she looked up at him, her eyes were pleading. "Please tell me you're lying. Making up stories so that I'll hate my father even more."

"I'm sorry, Sasha."

She blinked, settling a bit in his arms as if the use of her real name was all the evidence she needed.

"Tell me how."

"There's a device embedded in your left shoulder. It emits a signal. He was locked on."

"Was?"

He almost smiled. Even terrified, the woman was bright.

"The signal's toast at the moment."

Her brows drew together, creating an adorable crease above her nose. "Why's it toast? That seems pretty convenient."

"Not convenience or coincidence. Planning."

He turned the corner onto the hotel's street.

"I can walk. It's just a few blocks."

"Your feet have been through hell," he said. "I should carry you the rest of the way."

"Oh." Her breath whispered across his cheek. "If you want to."

"The least I can do."

She looked up at him, mischief dancing in her eyes. "After essentially kidnapping me? I guess so."

"I believe you're confusing a kidnapping with a rescue. For that matter, it wasn't either. It was transactional. I help you. I get paid." He let his hands slide down as he spoke so that he was holding her up by her ass, not her waist. "Everything, Princess. Or have you forgotten?"

"I haven't." The voice that had been warm turned cold again. He told himself that was good. He had no intention of falling for Sasha Reed. He'd use her. For sex. As a weapon. Any way necessary to bring Reed down.

Beyond that, she was just cold comfort.

"Good." He kept his voice flat. Transactional. "Because I've barely begun to collect my payment."

She nodded, seeming to look everywhere except his eyes.

A half block later, she looked up. "You were going to tell me why they aren't tracking us."

"They can't. Not electronically, anyway. And I've seen no sign that they have a physical tail. Check my back pocket. See if I have a text."

She reached around him, then tugged out his phone. She unlocked it by putting it in front of his face, then tapped the screen. "You have a text from LG. He says it's all clear. Your brother Leo?"

"He was helping me find you." He drew a breath. "I don't want you dead, Sasha. Far from it."

She emitted a strangled little laugh, then nodded. "Good to know since I don't seem to have much choice at the moment."

He forced himself not to smile. He did enjoy this woman.

He felt her chest rise and fall as she drew a deep breath, then released it. "How did my father insert a fucking tracker? For that matter, when?"

"I don't know when. All I know is that it pinged when we were in the elevator in Grimm Tower."

"Pinged?"

"The elevator scans for weapons and certain devices. It pinged on you the moment we arrived."

"You're saying my father just pulls up an app on his phone and he can find me? Like I'm a kitten who got chipped by the vet?"

"Something like that. It emits a signal that someone tuned into the proper frequency can pinpoint. I have a device in my pocket—and another one in the hotel room—that dampens the signal, essentially spreading it over a ten-mile radius with no single point that's stronger than another.

"So I'm safe now unless my father's goons actually see me? And I was safe in the hotel up until I left the room?"

She shivered, glancing around the empty street as if the shadows themselves might lunge for her.

He cocked a brow. "I did tell you to stay put."

"You could have told me why."

"I shouldn't have had to. The terms of our agreement don't require me to explain myself."

She scowled, and he had to force himself not to smile at her consternation.

"And here we are." He eased her to the ground as the doorman waved them in. He followed her over the threshold, feeling surprisingly empty without her weight clinging to him.

In the elevator, she pressed her back into a corner. "My father killed your mother. You already told me your goal is to destroy my father. Killing me would cut him pretty deep."

Her words hit him like a physical blow, and he drew a sharp breath. "I want your father to burn for that. But not you." He crossed the car in one long stride, standing so close he could feel her stuttering breath on his face. "You're as much a victim as I am."

She hugged herself, her eyes bright with unshed tears. When she spoke, her voice was so soft he had to hold his breath to hear. "I'm tired of being a victim."

Her words stung, and even though he knew he wasn't the cause of her pain—not that particular pain, at any rate—he felt the weight of it inside him. "After the hearing, you won't be."

He took her hand as the elevator doors opened. "Right now, I'm taking you back to the room." He started to draw her toward him, but she stayed firmly in the corner. "What if I say no?"

He drew in a breath, then let it out slowly, willing himself not to lose his temper. She didn't understand the danger. She was a kitten. New and scared. And until she was tame, he'd have to earn her trust over and over and over.

"If you say no," he said in a low, steady voice, "then I walk away, and your father's goons are on you in less than two minutes."

"You won't do that."

"Why not?"

"Because my father killed your mother, didn't he? That's why you want to bring him down. To expose what he's done to me. And to her." The smile she flashed belonged to an innocent little girl, but her eyes were cold and calculating. "And you need me for all of that."

"Do I? I have your blood. I'll have Dr. Chen's report soon. Release that to the press, and I think your father's downfall is imminent."

She said nothing, but he saw strength in her eyes. When this had first started, he'd expected her to be a frail little thing— the embodiment of the princess persona that was the hallmark of Reed Cosmetics. A woman who'd been so broken by her father that she was strong only in her own imagination but lacked the courage to find strength in the real world.

But she was so much more. Somewhere along the way, she'd become more than a lever. She'd become a partner, albeit a sometimes reluctant one. And for a man who'd lived his entire life completely alone despite a sea of brothers and staff, that was an uncomfortable and surprisingly pleasant realization.

SEVENTEEN
DANGEROUS LIAISONS

Liam stood by the bed, watching her sleep. He'd ended up carrying her the short distance from the elevator to the room. The fumes she'd been running on had faded, and she'd almost fallen asleep standing right there in the corner of the elevator.

He'd gently washed her feet again, then pulled off her tee and leggings, ignoring her soft protests and leaving her naked under the covers. And, yes, he'd been tempted to trail his lips and fingers all over her perfect form, but he'd tamped it down. He wanted her awake for those intimate caresses, but she'd barely been conscious, the exhaustion more than the result of an adrenaline drop. It was from the final, futile grasp of her father's drugs trying to stay in her system. Silently begging her body to take more. Whispering that she would feel so much better. So much calmer.

So much more malleable.

Liam clenched a fist at his side. The woman had a way of driving him crazy, that was for sure. Still, he would never dream of pharmaceutically padlocking that sarcastic, snarky, bold woman. But Victor Reed wanted a controllable little princess, and so did men like him all over the world.

Liam's hand ached, and he realized he'd clenched it into a fist as if he could will Victor into the room, then pummel his face until that prick atoned for his crimes.

Except there was no atonement possible for a man like Reed.

Killing Rebecca? Killing his wife? Torturing and manipulating his daughter? Victor Reed was the devil, and Liam intended to make him dance for all the world to see. Then he'd kick his knees out and watch the bastard fall from his own goddamn tower. Hopefully, not metaphorically.

For years, he'd told himself that his pursuit of Reed wasn't about Sasha. It was about his mother. About Victor Reed getting away with murder.

And that was true. But it was only part of the truth.

The whole truth was that Liam had hated himself for craving the woman now sleeping only a few feet away. A woman he'd been certain was nothing more than Victor Reed's puppet, willingly and eagerly spreading her father's lies.

The gloves had come off three years ago when she'd accused Elias of killing her mother at a press conference. As far as Liam was concerned, Elias Grimm was the devil himself, but the accusation didn't make sense, and damned if Victor Reed's beautiful and reclusive mouthpiece of a daughter was going to get away with lying about his family. Even a family that all but shunned him.

Maybe some part of him had wanted to prove himself worthy of being a Grimm, whatever that meant. He didn't know. He didn't care. But he'd cornered her after that press interview, then made sure she knew that he had her number. To him, she was nothing more than a lying little bitch—one who couldn't think for herself and only followed her daddy's lead, among a host of other horrible attributes.

Having laid out the verdict, he set out to prove it.

In the process, he'd learned a hell of a lot more than he'd expected, including that Victor Reed had killed both Sasha's mother and his own. That the drugs were unapproved and untested. And that the man was only inches away from marketing them to a select group of wealthy individuals in transactions that would be virtually untraceable.

Too bad he hadn't a whit of legitimate evidence he could take to the authorities, but Liam knew damn well every word was true. And he vowed to get the kind of proof that would not only take Reed down but would slam him behind bars for life.

And there was Sasha, trapped in the middle of it all. His heart twisted. Elias Grimm was a shitshow of a father and a vile human being. But he was Gandhi compared to Victor Reed.

Liam shuddered, telling himself he didn't give a fuck about the man who fathered him. Who treated him like a wicked stepson, locked away in a basement.

Except, of course, he did care. And clearing Elias's name by proving that Victor killed Lydia just might earn him the right to rise one rung on the family ladder.

And goddamn him to hell for wanting that.

He clenched his fists, drew a breath, then released it slowly.

Right now, he just wanted the woman. Not because the proof of Victor Reed's crimes still lived in her blood, but because she sparked something inside him. He didn't know what. He didn't care.

He wasn't even sure he liked it.

All he knew was the craving. The tightening in his chest. In his balls.

The way his hands itched to touch her. To take her. To make her his and protect her from the horrors of the goddamn world.

To protect her even from himself.

And wasn't he turning into a damn pussy?

With a soft grunt, he sat on the edge of the bed, watching as the moonlight filtered through the gap in the curtains. It caught her hair, making it gleam like the crown of an angel he wanted to defile.

To take down.

To exorcise from his fantasies for once and for all. Just as he'd tried to do over and over again on those lonely nights when he'd hacked into Elysium, the world she thought so safe and impenetrable.

He'd discovered her private sanctuary by accident when he'd been hacking Reed Tower's electronic files. He'd seen a bandwidth irregularity, and that had led him to a secret server. Being a curious sort, he'd followed the footprints until he'd ended up in another world.

Sasha's world.

And wasn't that an interesting place to vacation?

He spent months carefully examining the code through the backdoors he installed, tweaking the prince here and there, letting him grow organically more and more into Liam's doppelganger even as the prince teased and touched and flirted with Vale.

The real fun had begun when he realized that Sasha had access to wearable equipment to enhance the virtual experience, and he acquired his own bodysuit and headset with a few well-placed bribes.

He told himself he'd only hacked in to observe. To study this woman who got under his skin in ways both good and bad.

How could he have anticipated finding himself there? The fantasy prince who courted her slowly, teasing and tempting. Whose whispers turned dirty as his touch turned naughty, exploring all her dark, soft places, using fingers and tongue to take Sasha—no, *Vale*—to the highest reaches of pleasure.

And damned if he wasn't jealous of Prince Killiam, especially when she cried out his name. When she thought it was just an AI-created prince who took her to the edge. Who pushed her over that sensual precipice. Who made her scream and beg and *feel*.

Prince Killiam.

She'd built him from code and craving, a fantasy prince who praised her gently and whispered filthy promises in a voice that sounded almost—almost—like his.

As far as Liam was concerned, the prince's moniker meant that Liam wasn't trespassing at all. That name was practically an engraved invitation. Not only into her world but into her virtual bed—and he'd accepted the invitation eagerly.

He'd logged in every night to kiss her lips and lick her cunt. To bite her breasts. To fuck her hard and deep until she screamed *his* name, albeit hidden in the name of the prince she thought she craved.

He'd intruded. He'd violated. He'd defiled.

And he'd loved every sensual, crazed moment of it. The way her body had tightened around his cock, the sensations through the bodysuit like a goddamn revelation. The passion in her eyes when she came.

He should have felt shame. Instead, he felt power.

And now, damn him, he felt so much more.

Her responsiveness in Elysium had made him harder than he'd ever been—and had made him wonder how she'd respond with real skin against skin.

He wanted to take her in all the ways he'd already had her. And yet he couldn't.

He had to be careful.

He had to push aside the memory of those wild and erotic moments. The need he'd felt. The passion he'd witnessed from that sleeping princess.

She didn't know he'd been in Elysium, and he intended to keep it that way.

But she was damn sure going to know him in this world.

EIGHTEEN
SLEEPING BEAUTY

The comforter was light, filled with down so that it slid silently over her bare skin as he pulled it off, leaving her clad only in the yellow and orange light that streamed in through the window. She looked younger in sleep, as if the harshness of the world hadn't yet caught up to her.

Except it had. To Sasha, the world had always been a hard, dark place.

Only one of many things they had in common.

She was curled up on her side, her knees up, one hand tucked under the pillow, her breathing slow and easy. He moved closer, his fingers drawn to touch her as if he was a magnet and she was steel, and it was a matter of physics—not choice—to move, to touch, to stroke.

The caress was light, little more than a feather-soft touch on her smooth, pale skin. She would be pale, of course. With both agoraphobia and her fear of heights, he knew she went outside only when she had to. And even if she'd wanted to, her father would never let her use a tanning bed. Fairy tale princesses were pale and blonde, after all.

She sighed, the sound barely a whisper of breath, but he pulled his hand away, caressing her only with his eyes as he memorized every plane and curve of her body.

He shouldn't want her like this.

He'd been raised to hate her, so perhaps that's why she'd always fascinated him. When your despised father tells you the name of your vilest enemy, isn't that the one to whom you're drawn?

At thirty-four, he was eight years older than Sasha, and he could remember the day his father stormed into the residential kitchen in Grimm Tower where the whole family had been staying for a summer in the city.

Elias had slapped a newspaper down open to a picture of a woman and a newborn under the headline *JUST ONE DAY OLD—THE HEIRESS TO THE REED FORTUNE.*

His father had told Liam and each of his brothers, including five-year-old Leo, to look at the picture of the little bitch and the bitch's mother. It was those two whom the Grimm boys needed to destroy because the Reeds were untrustworthy, vile, and despicable.

It was that last word Liam remembered most distinctly. He knew it only from Daffy Duck.

Two years later, he'd asked his father what exactly the Reed family had done, but all Elias would tell him was that Victor Reed was the vilest kind of man—and dangerous, too. Considering what Liam knew of his own father by the time he was ten, he figured that Victor Reed must be monstrous indeed.

When Elias finally told him—with quite a bit of glee—that Victor had killed Liam's mother, Liam knew that his opinion of Victor Reed was dead on the money. And that opinion hadn't changed over the passing years.

No, his fingertips danced softly over Sasha's hip, then stroked the curve of her ass. The daughter of his vilest enemy moaned and shifted, and Liam froze, unsure if he wanted her to wake or to stay lost in sleep. Either way, he craved her. Already his cock was hard simply from looking and stroking. He'd go mad if he thought about being inside her.

So why torment himself? She was his, wasn't she? She'd agreed to everything.

Everything.

And so far, he hadn't even come close to taking payment. Besides, considering the rescue from her father's goons, he figured Sasha owed him a little extra.

The thought made him chuckle. As if she heard him, she rolled over, now on her back, her head turned against the pillow held tight in one arm.

He'd been wrong about his cock. It hadn't been hard before. That had been a poor excuse for an erection.

Now he was fucking hard.

And damned if he wasn't going to take what was his.

He shed his clothes silently, never taking his eyes off her sleeping form.

Finally, he would claim her. Mark her as his.

He'd almost come earlier just from the way her cunt had tightened around his fingers as if begging him to stay inside her.

He wanted her to wake up with him buried deep inside her. To hear her soft moans and loud cries of pleasure, so familiar from his forays into Elysium. But those had been stolen moments. These would be real.

He wanted it all. And then he wanted to take her even higher.

"Damn," said a soft voice behind him. "Did I miss the early show?"

Liam turned to face his little brother, who was leaning against the doorjamb. "Funny." He grabbed his trousers off the floor, then moved into the connecting room, pushing Leo further inside. Then he tugged the door to the bedroom closed, leaving only a crack so he'd hear if Sasha woke up.

"I could have sworn you gave up B-and-E," he said, sliding on his pants before settling into the overstuffed chair.

Leo snorted as he took a seat on the couch, his boot-covered feet landing hard on the polished coffee table. "Nah, just cut back. And if you didn't want my company, you should have put the chain on the door."

"And that would have kept you out?"

"Hell no. But it might have bought you another minute or two." He lifted his chin, indicating the door beyond which Sasha slept. "That was quite a show. Tell me what you're up to."

"And I'm required to do that because why?"

Leo spread his hands and flashed his most charming smile. "Hello? Because it's me. And because I helped you out tonight. And because you're an impulsive SOB who needs to be held in check, and—"

"I'm impulsive?"

Leo waved the words away. "I'm the youngest. I've got a rep for being reckless, careless, all that shit. If I go and burn down Nevada, folks'll just nod and say, 'Well, what did you expect from Leo?'"

"You've got a grudge against Nevada?"

Leo wrinkled his nose. "It's all the buffets. Any state with that many buffet meals has some serious issues."

"Can't argue with that."

"And you can't keep changing the subject. When did you dip your toe into the high-risk yet often profitable vocation of kidnapping? Because both Victor Reed and Desmond Bane are losing their shit in the media."

"I know," Liam said. "Delightful, isn't it?"

"It's a pretty sweet sound, sure. But I thought you hated Sasha Reed."

"And I thought you knew that there are a lot of ways to manipulate a woman. Sex sits pretty high on that list."

Leo grinned. "So, we done with the sparring?"

"For now. And thanks for the help tonight."

"Anytime," Leo said, and Liam knew he meant it. In his entire family, Leo was the only one who would come through for him without question or hesitation.

"From where I was standing, it looked like you're a little sweet on the girl. Don't suppose you noticed she's a Reed."

Liam met Leo's gaze dead on. "So's Ruby, more or less. I guess you're saying you felt nothing for her."

"Got it in one," Leo said, his animated face turning to stone. "She was just a good time that went very, very bad."

"Uh-huh."

Leo recrossed his arms. "So what's the deal? You steal her out from under Reed's nose at the gala, and then what? Tell me the endgame."

"Another time," he said.

"Dude, don't leave me hanging."

"I've got her father in the crosshairs. That's all I'll say," he added, wondering why he was hesitant to talk to Leo about how Sasha fit into his plans, especially since, of all his friends and family, Leo was the only one he could truly talk to.

But not about her. Not about this. Not yet. Maybe not ever.

Before Leo could prod him again, Liam stood to pour a drink. "Tell me about Elias," he said, bringing Leo a whiskey and keeping one for himself. He stood by the window, too wired now to sit still.

"Really? You're changing the topic of conversation to Daddy Dearest? Do you even care?"

"Not really. Do you?"

"Hell, no. The man's the biggest prick alive."

Liam nodded slowly. "So he's still alive."

Leo shrugged. "Depends on your definition. They've got a medical team working round the clock, but the prognosis isn't good. Marge and Alex are keeping it out of the media, of course. I considered tossing a bomb to *The Times*, but the idea of losing my inheritance gives me gas."

"Nice. Thanks for that imagery."

"You could leak it," Leo said. "Nothing stopping you. Your inheritance is a joke."

Liam tossed his hands up. "And he hits another homer."

"Oh, please, like you haven't already wrapped your head around that unfortunate reality and flipped Elias a double-fingered bird."

About that, Liam really couldn't argue.

"Like you even need family money. You're raking it in with RS-Cyberwerx," Leo added, referring to Liam's cybersecurity company, named in honor of his mother, Rebecca Strait.

Liam stayed silent, but his little brother wasn't wrong. And there was some irony in the fact that the most lucrative jobs tended to skirt the edge of the law.

Like father, like son, like brothers.

"So come on, man," Leo pressed. "Throw me a bone. You kidnapped her and now you're fucking her. Some sort of runaway bride thing?"

"I didn't kidnap her but keep that under your hat. She's here voluntarily."

"Because you're fucking her?"

"You're starting to sound like the older brother, and I really can't countenance that."

Leo grinned, flashing the smile that had let him get away with murder for his entire life.

"Not an answer."

Liam would never trust his other brothers to hold his plan close to the vest. Hell, they'd probably tell Reed just to fuck Liam over. Leo, however, was a good egg. Not necessarily a good man—on that, the jury was still out, but who the hell was Liam to criticize?

More importantly, Liam would trust his little brother with his life, rap sheet and all.

So he told him. Keeping it short and simple, he explained about Reed's deal with Desmond Bane and how Sasha was the price. About how Reed had killed Sasha's mother. And about the experimental meds he'd been feeding Sasha for years.

"The man's a menace," he concluded. "And with Sasha on board, we can take him down."

"And this has nothing to do with your mom? With Victor Reed killing her?"

"Of course, it does," Liam snapped. "You think I won't release the balloons on Rebecca's behalf when Reed's name is smeared and his ass is in jail? Of course, I will. Hell, maybe vindicating her death is my primary motivation. I honestly don't know. All I know is that he's a worm that deserves to be trampled on."

"And Sasha Reed is the boot you're wearing to do the stomping?"

Liam grimaced. "Not loving the imagery, but you're not wrong."

"*Just* the boot?"

Liam shrugged. "Don't know what you mean," he lied, unwilling to let his little brother know how much he craved the woman sleeping in the other room. What would be the point? It's not as if they'd ride off into the sunset on a white steed. And why the hell would he want to get twisted up with the Reed family?

But for now, he could have her. And that's exactly what he intended to do. After all, fair was fair. Once he was done, she'd be free of her father. Until then, he'd extract payment for his services.

And once Victor was behind bars, Liam would go his merry way. Because even if a future was possible with Victor Reed's daughter, Sasha deserved someone a hell of a lot better than him.

With a sigh, he returned his attention to Leo. "You need to go. If Alex or Marge find out you're with me, it won't be pretty."

Leo shrugged. Unlike Liam, the baby of the family had his mother and older brother wrapped around his finger. And that was despite a long list of fathers angry about their defiled daughters, store owners pissed about their stolen merchandise, and police with raised hackles about everything but Leo's breathing.

"Just watch yourself, ok?" Leo said.

"There's irony. You telling me to watch myself."

"Yeah, well, you have that look."

"I have a look?"

"When you're trying to figure something out," he explained. "Like some unsolvable cybersecurity problem you're tackling at RSC."

"There are no unsolvable problems."

"Yeah, well, then it's the look you get before you remember that and find an answer."

Liam chuckled. "Don't worry about me."

"Can't help it, bro. I know you're just using her to turn the knife in Reed's belly, and I respect that. But be careful. Fucking around with Victor Reed's daughter? It could get messy."

"Don't worry," Liam said. But what he didn't tell Leo was that it already was.

NINETEEN
UNICORN SPOTTING

I know you're just using her to turn the knife in Reed's belly.

The words I overheard shouldn't have stung. I've known his motives from the beginning. It's not as if he'd been coy about wanting to bring my father down.

I'd gone in with eyes open, backflips, and cheerleader pom-poms waving just from the possibility that Liam Grimm could get me away from my father and Desmond Bane and a future in which I remain a prisoner in a gilded cage with a man I despise.

More than that, Grimm's offer came with a coveted gift with purchase—the chance to bring down my father's business entirely.

All I had to do was give him my body. And my blood.

It had all been so very transactional. So much so that I'm surprised we didn't pop into one of those all-night notary places after we fled the gala:

Sasha Reed (Damsel) does solemnly swear that in exchange for services rendered by Liam Grimm (His Royal Hotness) in the protection of Damsel's person, the downfall of Damsel's father, and the rescue of Damsel from a hideous future as 1.) the wedded wife of Desmond Bane (Evil Troll) and 2.) the subservient daughter of the aforesaid prick of a father, Damsel will hereby provide her very blood for analysis and her body for ... whatever His Royal Hotness desires.

So, yeah. Eyes open. A business deal.

Sterile. Businesslike.

And yet …

And yet somehow everything that has happened since we left Grimm Tower feels different. His gentle touch when he'd cleaned my feet. The way he'd carried me back to the hotel, safe in the circle of his arms.

Liam Grimm had done that. A man with a reputation for being cold and hard.

I'd let my perception be swayed. I started to believe I'd been wrong about him. I'd started to trust him.

Hell, I'd started to like him.

I know you're just using her to turn the knife in Reed's belly.

And there it is. Those words that can have only one fundamental meaning: that Sasha Reed is a foolish little girl who put too much stock in a five-minute encounter with Grimm sixteen years ago when he'd actually been a human being. A chance encounter that Grimm probably doesn't even remember.

But I do, and that's my bad. Because there's nothing soft or human about Grimm. There's only calculation.

I rub my face, realizing my cheeks are damp with tears. *Idiot.*

And the worst part of all?

I still crave him.

Dammit.

I want to go into the other room and log into Elysium, but he's still in there, and I don't want to see him. More than that, I don't want him to know about my secret world.

Instead, I draw a breath, close my eyes, and try to picture my realm. Vale walking over the fields. Ember turning somersaults in the sky. And my prince crossing the bridge over the moat as he makes his way toward me, boldly walking into the castle despite my royal father's disapproval.

I continue spinning the tale, breaking the castle rules and ignoring my father's edicts. Soon, my prince is in my chamber, his face shadowed, but today I can see his eyes. As bright and wide as the sky out the window. When he pulls me close, I think that there's something familiar about him. But his kiss steals my thoughts, and I slide into bliss—and slumber—in the safety of his arms.

The next thing I know, I'm blinking at the sun streaming in through the small window.

I yawn and push myself up, only then noticing Liam on the other side of the room. He's leaning against the dresser, arms crossed, looking at me.

I pull the sheet up to cover my breasts, a motion that earns a half-smile from my audience.

"Why ruin such a lovely view?"

"I guess I'm just bitchy that way." I glance around, looking for my leggings and T-shirt. "Do you see my clothes?"

"I sent them out to be washed."

"Great. Fine. Wonderful." I rub my head, wincing a bit from the light. I'm not sure if it's withdrawal from my meds or if I just need caffeine, but right now, coffee sounds really good. I nod toward the little coffee maker. "Could you bring me one?"

His brows rise. "I think you're more than capable."

"Very chivalrous." I hold the sheet to keep myself covered as I start to tug it free of the mattress, figuring I can wear it toga-style.

The bastard chuckles. "Why bother? I've already seen everything."

"Would you just get out of here?" I snap.

His brows rise as he looks around the room. "I believe I'm paying for this space."

Honestly, I don't know if I want to laugh or slap him. Probably both.

I do neither. Instead, I stand, then reach for the robe flung across a nearby chair. He grabs it up first. I glare, then walk naked to the coffee maker, pour a cup, then take it with me to the bathroom—all to show him that his stupid games are no big deal at all.

When I come out, my hair is brushed and I'm wearing a towel. He catches my arm, pulls the towel off, and tugs me into his arms.

"Stop it, you perv." I shove him away, and he lifts his arms as if in surrender—and I honestly can't tell if he's amused or irritated. Probably both.

"You rescued me last night."

He steps closer, "I did."

I have to tilt my head back to look at him and end up practically swimming in the blue of his eyes. The same blue I'd seen in my prince's eyes.

"It reminded me of another time you rescued me," I tell him. "A time when you weren't an ass."

He frowns. "Are you sure it was me? That sounds like spotting a unicorn."

It's not the comment I was expecting, and I have to press my lips together not to laugh. I turn my back to him so he can't see my struggle, then I march back to the bed and pull the sheet up to my chest. I wait, anticipating an order to stand at attention naked in front of him, but the order doesn't come.

Instead, his eyes narrow, and he shakes his head slowly. "I think I'd remember rescuing a damsel in distress."

"It was at that Farmer's Market in the park." I fight a shudder. "I hadn't wanted to go, but Father had made me. I was ten and in a loose dress with a silly hat that my nanny had let me buy. There had been a face painter, and he'd put flowers on my cheeks. It was fun."

"Your father forced you to go to an open-air market? That was only three years after he killed your mother. You were deep into your phobias at that age."

I nod, strangely unsurprised that he knows that. "I begged him not to make me go, but he insisted. Said I needed to *learn to get over it*." I clench my fists and draw a deep breath. "That was the day that I learned that there was no ceiling on my hatred for my father." I meet his eyes. "Does that make me horrible?"

"No." He shakes his head, just the smallest of movements, and I'm struck by the thought that he's working hard not to move more. Afraid that if he releases control of his muscles, he'll lash out in fury against my father. He's miles and years from that moment, and yet just seeing his reaction makes the memory easier to bear. "Not horrible at all," he adds, his voice as tight as a wire.

"It turned out not to be as terrifying as I'd expected. Ruby and Birgit were with me, so that helped. Plus, the placement of the stalls formed walls. So it turned out to be enclosed enough that I could handle it. Or, at least, I handled it for a little while."

"What happened?" He comes closer as he asks, then sits at the foot of the bed. I hold the sheet more firmly against my chest.

"Ruby and I went exploring, and somehow we got separated. I couldn't find her or Birgit or Father or anyone. That's when I stopped being able to handle it."

I continue with the story, hugging my knees to my chest as I tell him how terrified I'd been, standing in the middle of this huge space that had seemed safe only moments before, but was now closing in all around me. I started crying, then cried even harder because I was certain the pretty flowers on my cheeks would be ruined.

Then there was a boy—except not a boy. A teenager. Seventeen, eighteen. Around there. And he took my hand and led me to the place where lost kids check-in. Then he stayed with me until Birgit found me.

My father never knew. He just assumed I was with Birgit the whole time. "But if that boy hadn't helped me," I say after telling him all of that, "I would have been gone longer, and I know my father would have—well, I know it would have been bad."

For a moment, there's no expression on his face at all. Then he nods slowly, as if I'd told him nothing more important than what I'd had for dinner. "So I helped a frightened kid," he finally says. "That doesn't make me your Prince Ki—" He breaks off with a cough. "Charming," he finishes, his voice as sharp and cold as a blade. "Don't think you know me because you once saw a soft side, Princess. Even an unflipped calendar is right once every year."

"No worries there," I say with sugary sweetness. "You aren't something I hope for, charming or not." It's true, I tell myself. Even if it didn't used to be. Before, he'd been a fantasy. Now, I know the man. There are soft spots, sure. But those are there only to camouflage the spinning blades beneath. So, no. I don't want him.

Except maybe a teensy little bit. When he's not being an ass.

Which is a very, very, very small window.

"I overheard you and Leo last night," I blurt. "About how you're just using me to piss off my father."

His eyes seem to widen, but they settle back so quickly into his typical, unreadable visage that I wonder if my mind is playing tricks.

"Did you?"

I wait, but he says nothing else. "You bastard," I snap. "You keep me locked in here. You take my clothes—"

"*Clean* your clothes," he says, and there's ice lurking under his mild tone. "They'll be back soon. And in case you've forgotten, Princess, we had an agreement. *Everything*, remember? And we've barely scratched the surface. Or did you think that after a day of being around you, I'd morph into Prince Charming, all gallant and respectful? That's not who I am, and I've known that my whole damn life. So I'd advise you not to rewrite history. And to remember the terms of our agreement."

"I can hardly forget," I snap. "You remind me of it every five seconds. And being locked in here without clothes kind of puts a button on the point." I cross my arms and scowl at him. He's right. He's no prince.

Or if he is, it's a dark one. He kidnapped the princess, after all.

He stands and steps toward me. I grip the sheet tighter. "About that twerp in the market," he begins, his voice low and steady, as if he's holding tight to control. "He wasn't your savior or your prince. He was just a guy, but he was strong."

His eyes are the ocean—cold and deep.

"He was strong enough to survive growing up with Elias Grimm. Strong enough to survive without a mother, stuck instead with an evil stepmother. Strong enough to make it in a goddamn world that kept throwing things at him. A world where he had no allies at all except a fuck-up of a younger brother."

I watch, my heart twisting as he spews the words at me. As if they're something vile he's been holding back for years.

"He built his own life, and he takes what he needs. Be it information or sex or a pretty little princess he can use for revenge."

I hold my breath as he grabs the sheet and rips it back, leaving me naked and trembling, and inexplicably, undeniably turned on.

He leans close, then puts his hand on my breast, my nipple trapped between his thumb and forefinger as I try to remember how to breathe.

"You think I'm kind and good because I helped you find your way out of a farmer's market? I was a kid, too. It was nothing. And last night? Tracking you down on the street, and sweeping you back here before your father's goons could find you? That wasn't about you, Princess. That was about leverage. But now? Well, right now, I want to fuck you. And you don't get a say, Princess. That's how good a man your little market boy grew up to be."

My heart pounds as I look into those cold eyes and try desperately to catch my breath.

"So hit me with those fists or tell me I'm an asshole or try to keep those pretty thighs squeezed shut. It won't matter. You're mine, Sasha. Paid and delivered. And I will have what's mine."

TWENTY

SECRETS & DESIRES

He'd expected her to cower. Anticipated fear or shock or loathing in her eyes. What he didn't expect was for her to reach up, grab his hair, and pull his mouth down on hers, so hard and wild that his teeth slammed against her lower lip, drawing blood.

He froze, his eyes locked on hers, the coppery taste of blood on his lips, and her delicious whimpering sounds going straight to his cock, making him as hard as steel.

She was right there. Sasha. *His.* Her naked body below him, laid out as if she was a sacrifice to him. Something to ravage. To pillage. To take and touch and own.

"Please," she whispered, the bold need in her voice fueling the beast inside. The beast that would take her, fuck her, make her finally, truly, completely his.

How many times had he kissed her in Elysium? Touched her? Fucked her? He thought he knew what it would be like to finally, truly taste her mouth. To feel those long, silky locks between his fingers, to have her soft skin brush over his.

He'd had no fucking idea.

The princess he'd met in Elysium had been brave but shy. He'd courted her slowly, almost as if he were a real prince of old, and she was the lady to whom he was betrothed. Their first kiss had started sweet, then grown passionate, and with each encounter that followed, he'd pushed her just a bit farther. His hands exploring all her soft places, His mouth teasing her lips, her nipples, her cunt. His palm caressing her back one day, then smacking her ass the next.

No matter his whim, she'd submitted, trusting him to not only keep her safe but to take her to the highest of heights.

And why wouldn't she trust him? As far as she knew, Prince Killiam was just the product of her fantasies. Fantasies that had an added kick of sensual juice courtesy of the AI coding she'd introduced into that virtual world.

He shouldn't have been there. He'd trespassed into her secret realm, violating her privacy. Then he'd had the audacity to not only seduce her as Vale, but to take her in the most sensual, degrading, erotic ways that he could think of.

And the cold, hard truth? He didn't regret it for a moment.

For that matter, the only thing he regretted was that he couldn't fully recreate those decadent moments now. He had to pretend that he didn't already know what made her scream. What made her beg.

Or maybe that would be the fun part. Trying each sensual pleasure he knew she liked in Elysium, testing it in the real world to see which made her come the hardest. Would it be his teeth scraping her nipple? His finger in her ass? Her knees on her chest as he fucked her hard? His mouth tasting every delicious inch of her? Or was it maybe her sweet fingers and wet tongue wrapped around his cock as she moaned and sucked and drove him crazy?

Secrets and desires he shouldn't already know but did. And every single one was written on a mental checkboard of what he'd bring to her in this world. No pixels, no haptics, no magic headset to project a view. Just him and this woman who'd spent more nights than she knew on her knees begging him to fuck her from behind. To please, please take her hard and fast. Who'd sucked his cock, then pinned him down and whispered how much she liked fucking him while she rode him hard, his cock deep inside her as his fingers teased her clit.

In Elysium, she gave as much as she took.

Here, in the real world, propriety had a grip on her shoulder. She wasn't the little wild thing he knew she could be.

But that was okay. Good, actually. He wanted to see the change. He wanted to see Reed's precious little princess climb that ladder, then give herself to him. Not in a world made real by strings of code, but here, where he could feel her and touch her and fuck her.

He wanted to feel his balls tighten as she begged him to fuck her harder. Wanted her to suck his cock while he teased her ass. Wanted to lick every sweet, delicious part of her, wringing out cries of pleasure as his tongue teased her cunt and took her all the way over the mountain.

He wanted it. And he intended to have it.

With a low moan, he grabbed her shoulders and rolled them over, moving her on top of him. She weighed next to nothing, and he held her with one hand on her very sweet ass and the other palming the back of her head as he looked into her eyes. Her skin gleamed in the half-light, flushed with desire, tiny beads of sweat already forming at her temples and between her breasts. She was magnificent—not the carefully curated perfection her father had demanded, but something wilder, more primal. A goddess in human form, her power only enhanced by the vulnerability in her eyes.

Her thighs straddled him, the slick heat of her core pressing against his stomach, leaving a damp trail as she shifted. He could smell her arousal—sweet and musky and intensely real in a way Elysium could never replicate. His fingers dug into the soft flesh of her ass, kneading, claiming, as his other hand tangled in her hair, tugging just enough to arch her throat.

"Tell me," he demanded, his voice a low growl, heavy with need. "Tell me you want me to fuck that hungry little cunt."

"Yes. Please, yes."

Her voice was husky, raw with honesty. He could see it in her eyes —no pretense, no performance. Just pure, undiluted desire.

"Tell me to fuck you."

She didn't even hesitate. No shyness, no hesitation. Just her voice, breathy and low as she begged. "Fuck me. Please, please fuck me." The need in her voice made him that much harder, but it was the desperation in her tone, the way her body trembled against his, that truly wrecked him. Power and vulnerability intertwined, hers and his, impossible to separate. She might be begging, but in that moment, she owned him as surely as he owned her.

"Not yet," he said, then pulled her mouth to his.

The kisses were deep, wild, even crazed. Tongue and teeth and a wildness that felt like fucking. He tasted blood—hers or his, he couldn't tell anymore—and something deeper, more essential. The flavor of surrender, of boundaries dissolving between them.

His hands roamed her body, mapping every curve, every hollow, every place that made her gasp or whimper or arch against him. He memorized each response, filing it away. This was Sasha giving herself to him, not Vale responding to Prince Killiam. This was real, and he couldn't remember ever being more turned on, more desperate to want to mark a woman. To lay his claim to her. To make her his.

And that was exactly what he intended to do.

Slowly, he stroked her bare ass, teasing her crack, knowing that he would take her there, too. Would claim her in every possible way. Slowly. Methodically. So that she remembered every delicious moment. The heat of her against his fingertips was intoxicating—blood-warm skin, silken texture, the subtle shift of muscle beneath as she moved.

"Rock your hips," he whispered, and she did, her hips moving back and forth, each motion teasing his cock, just as his fingertip teased her clit.

Her eyes were closed, and she was biting her lip in a little-girl-lost way that almost made him come right then, but he held on, wanting the moment to last. Hell, wanting it to never end. The sight of her above him, lost in sensation, was more beautiful than anything he'd ever seen—more real than any fantasy, more precious for being freely given.

"Open your eyes," he said, and when she did, the wild, needy heat he saw there reached straight into his chest and grabbed hold of something he'd thought long dead. "Tell me you like this," he said, even as his cock practically begged to be inside her.

She shook her head, her smile teasing when she said, "If you can't tell that I do, then one of us must be doing something wrong."

God help him, he laughed. And damned if he didn't want her even more. This—this spark, this intelligence, this unexpected play-fulness—was something he'd never experienced in Elysium. It was uniquely Sasha, a gift she hadn't even known she was giving.

He felt it then, beneath the lust and the need and the hunger—something deeper, more terrifying. A connection that went beyond physical desire, beyond the bargain they'd struck. Something that felt dangerously like belonging.

He couldn't remember a time when he'd been so damn hard. When he'd wanted a woman with such a vibrant intensity, he could almost taste the desire. Or when he knew with absolute certainty that if his cock wasn't inside her soon, his body would burst from the pent-up longing. Every nerve ending screamed for release, for completion, for the joining of their bodies in the most primal way possible.

He needed her. Needed to be inside her.

Needed to take her hard and fast—to burn it out of both of them—and then to spend hours exploring every sweet, delicious inch of her, even as he teased her closer and closer to the wildest, hardest orgasm of her life. He wanted to worship at the altar of her body, to make her forget every moment before this one, to remake the world until it contained only the two of them and this bed and the liquid heat building between them.

"Liam, please."

It was his name on her lips that threw gasoline on the fire already burning inside of him. His first name, said in a voice that was intimate and raw and pleading all at the same time. The formality stripped away, the barriers between them crumbling with that single word. "Say it." His voice was practically a growl. "Say what you want."

"Fuck me. Please," she added, her hips moving so that she was stroking herself against the length of his cock as he teased her ass. He stopped the teasing, using one hand to hold her ass cheek steady, as he slipped his other hand between their bodies, his fingers sliding easily into her warm, wet heat.

Her body clenched around his fingers, tightening rhythmically as if trying to draw him deeper. She was so responsive, so ready, the evidence of her desire coating his hand. His cock throbbed in sympathy, demanding to replace his fingers, to feel that same grip, that same welcoming heat.

"Baby, I don't think you're wet enough."

She groaned, then slipped two fingers inside that sweet little cunt before smirking at him. "Liar," she said, then rose up, her weight on her knees as she straddled him, using her already slick fingers to tease his cock as she wiggled until her core was right there, and all he wanted in the world was to be inside her.

Her boldness stole his breath—this wasn't the shy princess he'd seduced in Elysium, but a woman claiming her own pleasure, making her own choices. She was magnificent in her shameless desire. And he was helpless before her, willing to be used however she wanted, if only she would keep looking at him with those hungry eyes, with that beautiful mouth parted in anticipation.

Her eyes locked on his, and she leaned forward, thrusting her hips back as she took him in, gasping from the size of him, then slowly riding him, up and down, as her body adjusted.

The sensation was exquisite—hot, tight, wet, perfect. But it was the expression on her face that nearly undid him—the slight furrow between her brows, the parted lips, the flush spreading across her cheeks and down her throat to her heaving breasts. She looked shocked, overwhelmed, not by pain but by pleasure so intense it bordered on revelation.

He watched every move, every shiver, every bite of her lip, every blink of her eye. She looked like a woman who'd found ecstasy, and he wanted to hold that moment. To lock it in one of those crystal memory balls. Because he was the man who made her feel that way.

And if he could put that look on a woman's face, then maybe he wasn't such a prick after all.

TWENTY-ONE
BEAUTIFUL & BROKEN

I thought I'd been fucked before.

I'd really and truly believed that Elysium was real—at least as far as sex was concerned. The way my skin felt. The pure need that crashed through me. That tightening, tingling sensation in my core as my body silently screamed to be filled.

I'd had it all in Elysium. Haptics and toys and fantasy and dirty talk and my prince holding my arms down as he pounded deeper and deeper inside me until all I knew was the sensation of being filled by him and the scent of the grass at my back and the flowers swaying in the breeze.

All I wanted—all I knew— was his touch, so relentless it was almost cruel, at least until he finally drew me over. Then I'd scream his name as the sharp crest of orgasm after orgasm cut through me like a delicious punishment, and yet I begged for more.

I thought he'd taken me to the pinnacle. But I'd had no idea.

It's different when it's real.

The scent of his skin, the touch of his hand, the thrust of his cock. It's all real now. All surrounding me, claiming me. Using me.

Wild sensations twist inside me, not haptics, but *him*. The way he's somehow made every nerve ending in my body come alive, so my body screams with sensation as I rock against him, his cock deep inside me.

Liam Grimm. A man I was raised to hate. A man who has promised to help me, but only with the payment of my body. My submission.

Right now, that's a price I'm more than willing to pay.

My legs are on either side of his hips, and his hands hold my bare ass. He's controlling the way I rock against him, and my thighs quiver with every movement, the drag of him inside me sending sparks cascading through my veins, as if I'm catching fire from the inside out.

His hands are everywhere—gripping my hips with bruising intensity one moment, then trailing up my sides with surprising tenderness the next. The contradiction mirrors everything about him. Hard and soft. Cruel and kind. Enemy and savior.

I close my eyes, letting this cacophony of sensation carry me away, and when he says my name—Sasha, not Princess— it vibrates through me like a tuning fork struck against stone, somehow feeling even more intimate than his cock inside me.

"Look at me." His command is soft but unmistakable. My eyes flutter open to find his staring into mine, and that electric blue burns with something far more dangerous than lust. "Don't hide," he adds, pushing my curtain of hair away from my face. "I want to see your eyes when you come ."

No one has ever looked at me like this—like they're searching for something only I can give.

I want to look away, to shield myself from this unexpected vulnerability, but I can't. His eyes hold me captive more effectively than his hands ever could.

"I don't …" I start, my voice catching as he shifts beneath me, hitting a spot that makes stars burst behind my eyes. "I don't know what this is."

A ghost of a smile crosses his face, there and gone. "Does it need a name?"

His answer sends a flutter through my stomach. No, this moment doesn't need a name—names are for things you want to keep, to refer back to, to build on. This is ephemeral. Transactional. Nothing more.

At least that's what I tell myself even as I lean down and press my lips to his, the kiss softer than I intended.

He freezes for half a heartbeat—just long enough for doubt to creep in—before his hand slides into my hair, fingers threading through the strands to cradle the back of my head. He holds me against him as he kisses me back, not with the bruising force I expected, but with a slow, deliberate, thoroughness that makes my entire body tingle.

"Move," he whispers, the word a hot caress against my mouth. "Take what you want."

I don't know if the words are permission or demand, but I don't care. Something loosens inside me, some tight coil of restraint I hadn't even realized was there. I begin to rock against him, finding a rhythm that sends lightning through my veins with each stroke. My head falls back, my body arching as pleasure builds, hot and insistent.

His hands slide up my body —fingers spread wide across my ribs, thumbs brushing the undersides of my breasts before moving higher to circle my nipples. The sensation connects directly to the heat between my legs, and I gasp, thrown by the overwhelming pleasure cutting through me like waves.

"Don't stop." He issues the command as one hand leaves my breast to slide between us and tease my clit. The touch zings through me like electricity, and I cry out, my nails digging into his shoulders.

"Is this what you need?" His voice is lower now, rougher, but his eyes never leave mine as his fingers move in tight, precise circles. "Me teasing your clit? Making you come. Playing with your naughty little pussy?"

"Yes," I manage, the word barely a breath. "Oh, yes."

His eyes darken, and his movements grow more insistent. "Tell me," he demands, his hips rising to meet mine. "I want to hear what you want."

My cheeks bloom with heat, but at the same time, his demand taps into some hidden well of boldness I didn't even know I possessed. Something in me that's been buried beneath years of my father's control, just waiting to be drawn out.

"Harder," I whisper.

The corner of his mouth curves up as those amazing fingers press more firmly, moving in tighter circles that make my breath catch. Heat spreads through me like wildfire, and I rock against him, chasing the building pressure.

"Like this?" he asks, and the genuine question in his voice—his desire to give me exactly what I need—nearly undoes me.

"Yes," I gasp. "And I want—" I falter, still held back by some lingering inhibition.

He leans up, his mouth at my ear, his voice a dark whisper. "Tell me, Princess. I want to hear you say it."

The nickname slides over me like warm honey, somehow transformed from mockery into endearment. I turn my head, my lips grazing his ear as I find my courage.

"I want you to make me come again," I whisper, my voice dropping to match his. "Please, Liam."

I feel him shudder beneath me at the sound of his name, a tremor running through his powerful body. His hand at my hip tightens, and the sharp burst of pain heightens every other sensation.

In one fluid motion, he changes our position, sitting up so that we're chest to chest, my legs wrapped around his waist, his cock still impossibly deep inside me. The new angle sends sparks through me, and his fingers never stop their relentless rhythm against my clit.

"Look at me," he demands again, one hand sliding up my back to tangle in my hair. "I want to see you fall apart."

I couldn't look away if I tried. His eyes seem to reach inside me, touching places no physical sensation ever could. My body tightens around him, every muscle coiling as the pressure builds.

"Oh, yes. That's it. You have such a tight little clit. Can you feel me playing with that sweet nub?"

"Yes," I murmur, barely able to form words.

"Sasha." My name is like a rough caress. "Let go, Princess. Let me feel you come around my cock."

The crude words from his perfect mouth push me over that precipice, something breaking free, so that I'm falling, falling, falling as pleasure crashes over me in waves so intense I cry out his name, my nails digging crescents into his shoulders.

He holds me through it, his hips still moving in perfect counterpoint to mine, drawing out each electric ripple of sensation until I'm trembling against him. And just when I think I can't take anymore, he wraps an arm around my waist and flips us over in one swift, powerful movement.

Now he's above me, his weight delicious and solid, his eyes wild with a hunger that makes my breath catch.

"Mine," he growls, the word primal and possessive.

I should rebel against this claim. I've spent my life being owned, controlled, possessed. But all I can say is, "Yes."

With a low groan, he takes my hands, then pins them above my head with a grip that sends another rush of heat through me. He bends my knees up to my chest then drives his hips forward in a rhythm that feels almost desperate, each thrust punctuated by a sound low in his throat that's half growl, half moan.

"Sasha," he gasps, my name sounding like both a prayer and a curse. "Fuck, Sasha."

I arch beneath him, meeting each powerful thrust, wanting—needing—to give him the same shattering release he's given me.

"Let go," I urge, my lips against his throat where I can feel his pulse hammering wildly. "I want to feel you."

His eyes meet mine. Then, with one final, powerful thrust, he stiffens above me. I feel the hot pulse of his release deep inside and watch in wonder as his face transforms —all the hard edges softened, all the careful calculation stripped away, leaving just the man, beautiful and broken like me.

———

"LIKE WHAT YOU SEE?" I tease, watching those incredible blue eyes trace a path up and down my body. We're both lying on our side, facing each other. I'd pulled the sheet up to my neck in what I know is an ironic act of modesty, but he'd just tugged it right off again, leaving me fully exposed, my skin tingling with the memory of every way he'd touched me.

The corner of his mouth twitches.

"Oh, no," I say. "You do not get to force me to lie here naked and then laugh. That is very, very, very bad for the female ego."

His fingertips trace from my shoulder, along the curve of my breast, then down my side, before coming to rest on my hip.

I sigh. "Nice," I say. "But you're not off the hook. What are you thinking that's so funny?"

"Not funny," he says. "Ironic, maybe."

I press my hand against his chest, then make a fist, leaving me holding a clump of chest hair. "Will it be funny when I tug?"

Now the twitch is a full-on laugh. "The princess has grit."

I give the hair a little tug. "You leave me no choi—"

I squeal as he flips us over, leaving me on my back with his thumb and forefinger firmly gripping my nipple. And since I'd let go of his chest hair during the flip, that leverage is gone.

"Don't play games with me, Princess. I'll always win."

I bite my lower lip to keep from laughing, then meet his eyes. "Go ahead. Twist it. Maybe I'll like it."

He stays perfectly still for a moment, then he releases my nipple, only to cup my full breast with his palm. "You might at that," he says. And though there's nothing specific in his voice to disturb me, I have to fight a little shiver. Because I can't help but think that he seems to already know what I like. As if he knows what Prince Killiam has done.

But that, of course, isn't possible.

"You constantly surprise me," he says, more to himself than to me.

"How so?"

He cups my face, then gently trails his fingertips over my lips. "For a woman who's been so sheltered, you—"

"What?" I press when he cuts himself off.

"Let's just say you have a natural skill."

"Oh." I feel my cheeks flush, and I can't quite meet his eyes. "Is that bad?"

"Do you mean would I rather touch some timid little princess who barely moves, doesn't seem to like it, and gives the distinct impression that she'd rather be sweeping up cinders in front of the chimney? I wouldn't." He brushes the pad of his thumb over my lips. "So tell me," Princess, are you truly a natural, or have you managed to escape your father's keen detection and seek out … shall we say … some on-the-job experience?"

"Sneak? What? No!" The conversation has shifted toward mortifying. "I, um, I watch a lot of movies."

"Movies," he repeats, in a tone that suggests he doesn't believe me.

"Yes." I underscore the lie by lifting my chin. Though it's not entirely a lie. I do watch a lot of movies. But sex … well, that I learned in Elysium. But I'm not telling Grimm about that.

Not yet.

Probably never.

But I won't swear to that. After all, last week I would have laughed in anyone's face if they suggested I'd have a reasonable conversation with Liam Grimm, much less wild, delicious sex.

Still, Elysium is my heart and soul. And there's going to have to be a lot more trust between us before I share that world with him.

"Did I lose you?"

I shake my head and smile. "Sorry. You muddled my head a bit, I guess."

"One of my best traits as a lover."

I laugh, still surprised by how easy it is to be around this man who for so long has been my enemy.

Who maybe still is.

"Just movies?" he asks, erasing my frown. "No boyfriends you snuck into Reed Tower?"

I just stare. He's as aware of the extent of the security at my home as I am. Probably more so, as I'm sure he's tried to hack it.

"*Lots* of movies," I say. "With a variety of ratings."

His brows rise. "Your father must be more lenient than I thought."

"Correction— I hack into a lot of movies and watch them in secret. All ratings. R is the best for that kind of education," I add with a bold smile, surprised at how comfortable I am talking about this with Liam Grimm.

"Is it? Not X?"

"No way. X is all about assembly. No nuance."

"Assembly?" he repeats, his brows rising.

"It's just *Insert Part C into Slot V*. Light on the emotion. And the plot, for that matter."

He looks like he's about to crack up. I'm having a bit of trouble not laughing myself.

"So you've really never done this before?" He slides his hand down to slip between my thighs. "Sex," I mean.

I sigh as his fingertip strokes me.

"Only in my dreams."

"Good dreams, I hope?"

I think of Killiam. His eyes so much like Grimm's.

He cups my cheek. "I'm sorry."

I blink, both confused and surprised that Liam Grimm would apologize for anything.

"I took your virginity. You should have been with someone you care about."

I start to say I was, but bite back the words, shocked they even came close to my lips. Clearly, I'm suffering from post-coital gooeyness.

"No, it was good," I say, feeling strangely shy. "I mean, it was appropriate."

His brows rise. "Appropriate? The trading of sex for protection? Women's counseling services all over the country would beg to differ."

I smirk. "I mean, you rescued me from the evil king's castle. You're keeping me safe. And if everything goes as planned, you're going to slay the dragon. That's a metaphor for the drugs," I add.

Humor dances across his face, softening the hard lines and angles. Making him look almost vulnerable when he nods and says, "I got that."

"Correct me if I'm wrong—you're the Grimm, after all—but it seems to me that all that adds up to you being Prince Charming. And doesn't the prince get the girl?"

"I suppose he does," Grimm says.

"So there you go. *Appropriate*."

He chuckles and nods. But what neither of us point out is that the original tales often ended in pain or death or horror.

Which, I guess, leaves us right back where we started, and me with no clue as to whether Grimm is a good guy, a bad guy, or something in between.

TWENTY-TWO
OWNED

I wake to the sensation of being watched.

Grimm's beside me, his hair mussed from sleep and sex, that hard mouth softened by the hint of a smile at the corner. The ridiculously luxurious sheet is a knot of three-thousand thread count at my feet, and his eyes are roaming over my naked body, leaving heat in their wake, as if from a physical touch.

When he reaches my face, I see that heat reflected in the ice blue of his eyes, along with a possessiveness that makes my core clench and my pulse race.

"There she is," he says, now tracing lazy patterns on my stomach, dipping lower and lower with each pass. My breath stutters, and my core tingles in both anticipation and desire. I close my eyes, expecting his fingertips to trail lightly over my waxed pubis, then lower until he teases my clit, and lower still until he slips inside me. Taking without asking. Claiming.

And damned if I don't want him to.

But he doesn't. Instead, he pulls his hand back, then sits up, leaving me cold and exposed and confused.

"Go ahead and shower," he says. "I'll wait."

"I'm fine," I snap, my temper flaring as I tug the sheet over me, willing myself to acclimate to this abrupt shift in demeanor. Last night, he was all heat and possession, claiming me with a ferocity that both frightened and thrilled me. Two seconds ago, he seemed warm and sweet, as if reveling in the memory with me. Now, he's turned on a dime. Harsh and cold and distant. And I really don't get it.

"What's wrong?" I ask, hating the neediness I hear in my voice.

"We'll talk after you're cleaned up," he says, as if we'd been doing yardwork, and my thighs are caked with mud and not the evidence of everything we'd done last night.

Before I can press him, he slides from the bed, pulls on his trousers, and says, "I'll order breakfast."

He leaves the bedroom without a backward glance, closing the door behind him with a soft click that sounds like rejection.

I sit perfectly still, holding the sheet tight against me as I blink back tears I'm determined not to shed. I tell myself I'm pissed, not hurt. I don't know him well enough to be hurt.

But if I'm not hurt, then what's this horrible tightness in my chest?

With a sigh, I force myself out of bed, my body aching in a way I want to enjoy, but instead only makes me ashamed, especially when I see myself in the bathroom mirror.

My hair is a wild tangle that will take hours to brush out. My lips are swollen, my neck marked with the evidence of Liam's mouth. Not to mention the finger-sized bruises on my hips, my wrists, my waist.

I look thoroughly claimed. Owned. Possessed.

And the most disturbing part is the tingle I still feel between my legs. I want more—and I'm terrified that not only will I have nothing else, but that he regrets last night completely.

The shower helps, washing away the physical evidence and soothing my body, though it does nothing for my spinning thoughts.

I'm towel-drying my hair when the door opens without a knock, and he steps inside. I start to protest—after all, I'm completely naked—then remember I don't have the right. So instead I turn to face him straight on, not even trying to cover myself or the bruises and bite marks from last night's sextivities.

His eyes skim over me, and as he lingers on the marks, I think I see something flash in his eyes. Satisfaction, maybe. Or perhaps the pride of ownership.

I tilt my head and cross my arms over my breasts. "Like what you see?"

His eyes snap to mine, dark and heated. "Very much."

"Oh," I say, feeling the reverb of his words all through my body.

He's holding a bundle, and now he sets it on the counter. My clean clothes—and a pair of slip-on sneakers. "I think they're your size."

"I—Thank you." It's stupid, but I feel a bit undone by the gesture.

He nods, then pauses as he turns to leave. "Breakfast will be here in ten minutes. Don't let it get cold."

I stiffen at the reminder of our deal. *Everything.* And that includes my obedience. "Yes, sir," I say, intending it as a dig. But he just smiles, then shuts the door behind him.

I enter the connecting room nine minutes and fifty-five seconds later to find Grimm seated at a small table that's been set up in the living area and is covered by every form of breakfast food imaginable.

Once I've settled in across from him, I reach for a croissant and the strawberry jam. It's flaky and perfect, and as I lift it to my mouth, my stomach growls, reminding me of how little I've eaten in the past twenty-four hours.

"You should have some protein, too."

I don't even realize how annoyed I am with him until I snap. "So this is it?" I practically spit the words. "You fuck me, then order me around? Take a shower. Be on time. Eat three square meals a day."

I stand, knocking my chair backward in the process, then toss my napkin down, which doesn't have the dramatic impact I'm looking for since it's just a flimsy piece of cloth.

My storm-out into the bedroom works better, and with one final hurl of vitriol—"you goddamn fucking bastard"—I slam the connecting door behind me. Then I collapse face-down on the mattress, wondering what the hell is wrong with me. And wishing I'd thought to storm out with coffee. Because now I'm stuck in here.

Dammit, dammit, dammit.

For that matter, what the hell *is* wrong with me? This is an arrangement. A deal. An unconventional liaison between me and Grimm in exchange for Grimm exposing my father and setting me free.

I'm not his girlfriend. And why on earth would I want to be? He's a controlling bastard, just like my father, whose price for keeping me safe is sex, and who ultimately only cares about bringing my father down.

We have that last bit in common. But the rest of it? Why should I care about a man like that?

Because he's not like that.

Except he is. The little voice in my head is an idiot, because Liam Grimm is exactly like that. Controlling and vengeful and hard. But he's not like that in the same way my father is. Even as annoyed as I am with him right now, I have to give him that much.

Dammit.

I roll onto my side, then hug my knees to my chest. I close my eyes, letting myself drift. Despite hours in bed, I didn't get much sleep last night, and in no time at all, I succumb to the lure of dreamland.

———

WHEN I WAKE, there's bacon.

I blink, wondering about this strange dream. Then I realize it's real. Grimm is sitting on the edge of the bed holding a plate with five pieces of bacon, a croissant, and a tin of jam.

"You didn't eat," he says, leaving the plate as he stands, pointing to the side table. "Coffee's there."

I look up at him. "I guess I was wrong."

"How's that?"

"You're not the devil after all."

His grin is mirthful, but something dark flickers in his eyes when he says, "Don't be so sure. The devil's a charmer."

I let my eyes trail over him. "And beautiful, too."

He holds my gaze. "My dear Ms. Reed. Are you flirting?"

"Why would I do that? You're my captor, remember? That would be creepy. Besides, I don't like you."

A hint of a smile dances on his mouth, so subtle it could be nothing more than an illusion. "Yes," he says. "You do."

He crosses to the door and pauses at the threshold. "Eat. Get dressed. We're moving on."

I sit up straighter. "Where?" I ask, despite a mouthful of bacon.

"Somewhere not here." He taps his watch. "Thirty minutes, Sasha."

I push the plate aside and stand up, wrapping the sheet around me. "You can't just tell me to eat, then tell me that we're leaving, but not actually tell me anything."

"Yes. I can. You'll follow my instructions like we agreed."

"Dammit, Grimm, last night—"

"Last night didn't alter any of our terms. You were part of our deal. The major part, in fact. I took what I was owed. A small portion, yes. And I look forward to taking more. We have a contract, Princess, and consideration was exchanged. And until that contract expires, I will take payment when and how I desire. I assume that's clear?"

I can only stare at him.

"Sasha?"

"Crystal," I say. "Now get the fuck out and let me change."

He turns to go, but pauses at the door, his back to me, his hand on the knob. I see his shoulders stiffen, then the subtle movement of his torso as he takes in a deep breath and slowly releases it.

He turns the nob and pushes the door open, then stops to look back at me. "What did you expect, Princess? We walked into this with very specific terms. But don't worry. If it's more sex you want, you won't be disappointed. I've barely begun to use you the way you should be used."

He turns back to the doorway and steps through, his head barely missing the plate of bacon I hurl in his direction.

It hits the doorframe and shatters, and I sit there, staring at the shards, wondering what happened last night, and how I'd gotten it all so horribly, incredibly wrong.

TWENTY-THREE
SANCTUARY

"Here it is," Grimm says as we enter a fifth-floor loft in the heart of Tribeca. "Sanctuary. For now, anyway."

The place is stunning, yet not ostentatious. Walls of windows provide natural light, even with the blinds closed as they are now. "A courtesy for me?" I ask, though I already know the answer.

"Also, just for comfort," he says. "The afternoon sun can be brutal."

I glance toward him. "Thanks."

He inclines his head like it's no big deal. Except to me, it is.

The living area is decorated in shades of gray and deep blue, with comfortable furniture, baskets of blankets, and coffee table books that seem to exist only for that specific purpose.

I glance toward Grimm. "Whose place is this?" I ask. "A friend?"

"Not exactly," he says.

"Sorry, I forgot. You're not a person who has actual friends."

He gives me a sharp look, which I return with my brightest cover model smile. A smile I hope conveys that while the sex was freaking amazing, I'm still pissed about the bullshit back at the hotel, and if he thinks I'm just going to be the complacent little pseudo-hostage, he has another think coming.

At the same time, he's right. I made a deal. So I'm sticking to my end like glue. He says jump, I jump. He says jump his bones, I'll do that, too. I'll even like it. *So there.*

But that doesn't mean I like *him*.

In fact, our little spat at the hotel was probably a good thing. I'd let myself forget that he's a Grimm, and I shouldn't have. I know better than most not to ever take a Grimm at face value.

"It's mine," he says, surprising me. "For now, at least."

"Oh. Do you think that's a good idea? I mean, my father must have access to property records and—"

"It's not in my name. And with the tangle of paperwork, he won't find it." He meets my eyes, and for the first time since our earlier tiff, there's warmth beneath the icy blue. "You're safe with me, Princess. That much, I promise."

"Oh." My throat is suddenly too thick for any other words to get through. "Thanks."

He nods, then waves for me to join him for the grand tour. Considering his resources and reputation for living a life of excess, it's not very large. The open style living area is big enough to be comfortable, but small enough to be intimate. The kitchen is airy and well-lit, and when I check the fridge and cabinets, I see that they're both already stocked.

"I have a service," he says, leading me further into the apartment. "Two bedrooms. Technically, three, but one is my office.

He steers me into the master bedroom—all dark wood highlighted by a red and black theme. The room across the hall is the repurposed bedroom now used as his office. It's leanly furnished, with the focal point being a desk, a chair, and a computer displaying a screensaver of the letters RSC in a decorative font floating and twirling on the screen. And, surprisingly, a VR headset.

One entire wall is cabinetry. Another is entirely windows, and the last supports bookshelves filled with a mixture of fiction and every coding and computer-related book imaginable.

"I never asked what exactly you do," I say, with a nod to the computer books. "You don't work for Grimm International, and you told me that day at the shoot that you deal in information. So what exactly does RSC stand for?"

"I'm in cybersecurity," he says. "I catch hackers, consult with corporations and governments. That kind of thing. And it stands for Rebecca Strait Cyberwerx."

"For your mom," I say softly. "That's a lovely idea."

He shrugs. "I often wonder, if someone had hacked into Victor's networks back then, would they have seen her murderer working on his plan?"

"That was a long time ago," I say, my heart aching for him. "I don't think the tech was there yet."

"Maybe not. But maybe RSC can help someone else. That's the goal, anyway."

"Using your superpower for good? How surprising."

He matches my grin, then looks me up and down. "I'm usually bad," he says. "I have to mix it up every once in a while. Otherwise, I'll end up Karma's bitch."

The laugh escapes before I can stop it. "Yeah. I get that."

For a weird and wonderful moment, we just look at each other. Then he clears his throat. "Thus ends the tour."

"Really? What about the other bedroom?"

"You don't need to see it. You'll be sleeping with me."

Despite my earlier irritation, a little frisson of pleasure races up my back. And why shouldn't it? I'm rather enjoying sex with Liam Grimm. Besides, if every TV show and movie I've ever seen is right, men are much more manageable if they're getting laid regularly.

In the interest of dealing with the man, I suppose I can handle a few more encounters under the sheets. Or on top. Or wherever he wants, for that matter.

"Something funny?"

"Nope," I say, fighting my smile.

He shoots me a narrow glance, but there's that tell-tale twitch in his lips. Whatever had prompted his harshness this morning seems to be fading. But at least now I know to keep an eye out for Mr. Hyde.

"Can I see it anyway?" I ask, nodding at the second bedroom door. I don't know why I want to. I guess I'm just trying to gather all the information I can about this man.

"Oh, this is adorable," I say when he opens the door. The room is flooded with natural light, and the bed is made up with yellow linens. Vases of silk flowers are scattered about, giving the room extra charm. Best of all, there's a desk with a small workstation. If Grimm will give me access to a computer, I can sneak away to Elysium from time to time. At the very least, I can amuse myself by surfing the Internet.

We finish the tour of the place in the kitchen, where we sit sipping coffee and eating freshly baked chocolate chip cookies he'd ordered from a store just one block away.

"I couldn't live here," I say.

His eyes widen. "Really? You don't like the place?"

"Are you kidding? It's fabulous. But I'd have to buy new clothes every week because these cookies are seriously dangerous."

"I think that's why the developers turned the entire fourth floor into a fitness center."

"Smart move," I say, snagging another cookie. "Speaking of having to buy new clothes…"

I trail off, indicating the leggings and tee that is on the verge of becoming my signature outfit.

"There should be clothes that fit in your room."

"My room?"

"You'll still sleep with me," he says, in a tone that broaches no arguments. "But the second bedroom can be your private area. Nap, watch television, whatever you want."

"I want a computer," I say, and he surprises me by agreeing immediately.

"I should have told you there's a laptop in the bottom desk drawer in the yellow room. The password for the guest WiFi is Rebecca."

"Oh. Thanks." I hesitate, then decide to take the plunge. "Why are there clothes I can wear in that room? Did you —I mean, did you have someone buy outfits for me?"

"They belong to Maya." There's something about his tone. Casual, but with a hint of curtness, like it's someone he doesn't want to talk about.

I, however, do. "Who?"

"Maya Lane. A friend. She lives here part-time, and I'm sure she won't mind if you borrow a few things."

"Right," I say. Because I have no idea what else to say. Is she just a friend? Or is she a girlfriend kind of friend?

And why do I even care? It's not like I have the right to ask or even to wonder. I mean, yes, Grimm and I have sex—but that's because of our arrangement. Not a relationship.

Except I do care. And I hate that I do.

I tell myself to chill even as I search for answers in the set of his jaw or the way he's pouring coffee. But there are no clues to be found.

I swallow a sigh, then look toward Grimm with what I hope translates as calm indifference. "I assume she's out of town?"

"Overseas. She's been living in London for the last few months."

"Oh," I say, mentally checking the Just Friends box. "How exciting for her."

His brow creases. "Are you okay?"

It's only when he asks that I realize I'm wincing. Not because I'm spinning out about Maya, but because my head is pounding.

"Thanks for pointing that out," I say, after telling him about the state of my head. "It's been hurting on and off since I ditched the pills. On the upside, I haven't noticed my hands shaking in the last few hours, and light doesn't bother me as much anymore."

Considering what Dr. Chen described, I've gotten off lucky. And because I learned at a young age how to shut down my outside and live on my inside, I'm better than most at ignoring—or enduring—pain.

That doesn't mean I like it.

He opens a cabinet and comes back with a bottle of ibuprofen, and I gratefully slam back three of the things.

"We'll ask Dr. Chen if she can give you something to take the edge off. Not a narcotic," he says quickly, warding off the protest I was about to toss at him. "Just something stronger than what I have on hand."

I shrug. I don't want drugs if I can avoid them. I've had more than my share in my life. "When will we hear from her?" I ask. "The labs were expediting my blood work, right?"

"I wasn't going to mention it until we were certain, but she's hoping she'll have results today. I'm just waiting on her text."

"Really?" Considering I'm about to learn what horrible compounds my father was shoving into me, the news makes me remarkably chipper.

"Is it horrible that I almost hope he pumped the worst of the worst into me? That he's got some secret lab already set up somewhere, and he's working on some horror movie-type drug to steal memories?"

I smile at the thought, then pick up another cookie before adding,

"Then, when Dr. Chen finds it, I'll be the magic bullet that takes my father out, along with his whole perverse enterprise."

He nods, then draws in a long breath before releasing it.

"What? You disapprove of my glee? You're not feeling sorry for him, are you?"

"God no," he says with such fervor, I know I misinterpreted the moment. "I just—never mind."

"No. What?"

For a moment, I think he's not going to answer. Then he looks straight into my eyes. "It hurts you. That he's done this. That you're not a daughter to him, just something to be leveraged."

For a moment, I just hold my coffee mug between my hands. Then I blink, and tears trail down my cheeks.

"And to you?" I whisper. "Isn't it the same? Aren't I just a means to an end? A weapon to leverage against my father?"

His eyes lock on mine. "Is that what you want to be?" His voice is soft, but I can hear the challenge. "Just a weapon? Nothing more?"

My breath catches, my body responding to his proximity against my will. "What I want doesn't matter. It never has."

Something flashes in his eyes—regret? Or merely calculation?

"If that's really what you think, Princess, then maybe it's time for you to make it matter."

I swallow, my eyes brimming once again. I want to tell him that I don't know how, but his phone chimes, and he checks the screen.

"Dr. Chen," he says, then starts toward the door.

I follow, my mind leaping to the one thing I'm sure I want. Freedom. Autonomy. However you want to say it.

I've been owned by my father long enough. It's time for my life to be mine. All of it. All the time.

———

I PERCH on the edge of the sofa, twisting my fingers together as I watch dust motes dance in the air and try not to beg Dr. Chen to hurry up with her files. She's taking her time laying them out on the coffee table, and I'm about to drop to my knees and beg her to just please, please get on with it.

Grimm stands among the dancing motes, his shape dark against the brightness of the windows as he paces. I want him beside me, but at the same time, his constant motion is keeping me grounded, and I can't seem to tear my eyes away.

"Well, all right then," Dr. Chen finally says, aiming a soft smile at me. "Let's talk about the results."

In five long strides, Grimm is at my side, one hand enclosing mine, the other firm against my back. I glance up at him with a nod.

"Tell us," he says.

She opens a folder and hands me a paper covered with chemical formulas that might as well be written in Klingon. I hand it to Grimm but can immediately tell that he doesn't speak Chemistry either.

Dr. Chen almost smiles. "In plain English, we've confirmed that your father's been using a tailored pharmaceutical cocktail to manipulate your memories and, shall we say, your obedience."

I'm not surprised, but that doesn't stop the blood from rushing out of my head as the room tilts. I squeeze Grimm's hand as I take two deep breaths. When I'm pretty sure I'm not going to teeter off the side of the couch, I look at Dr. Chen again, then speak through bone-dry lips. "He was using me as a lab rat?"

"In essence, yes. I'm so sorry, Ms. Reed," she adds, her voice gentle, but unflinching.

Manipulate how?" Grimm asks.

"A two-pronged approach. One compound actively suppresses real memories. The second heightens suggestibility so those memories can be replaced. And the cocktail did include compounds to help you cope with your phobias, though there's also evidence of compounds that would exacerbate them."

I nod stiffly, fury cutting through me as I think about the way he manipulated me, as if I were nothing more than a doll for him to stick pins in. Scared when he needed me to be. Able to cope only when it suited his agenda. My skin crawls from nothing more than the reality that Victor Reed and I share blood.

"That's why I remember my mother's death wrong. He stole the real memory and replaced it."

She nods. "Again, I'm so sorry this happened to you."

I swallow, then squeeze Grimm's hand so hard I'm probably crunching bone. "What other memories did he take or change?"

She shakes her head, a frown tugging at her thin lips. "I'm sorry. There's no way to know. Perhaps only this one."

"Or many more," I say, my words tasting bitter on my tongue. "Because he was a sadistic bastard, and I was his toy."

Dr. Chen glances at the floor before looking up and meeting my eyes straight on. "Perhaps," she says, as Grimm pulls me closer to him. "I suppose we'll only know when and if memories return."

I draw in a breath, forcing myself back to the moment. "What else?"

I can see how hard she's working to keep control, and that evidence of compassion almost breaks me. I lean in even closer to Grimm as she says, "There was also evidence of a sedative compound that seems to have been used both in conjunction with the memory manipulation and as a tool to make you more malleable."

"Malleable," I say, as flashes of half-forgotten moments bubble up. The way I would become drowsy if I refused my meds. Then agreeable, because all I wanted was to make Father happy.

"He used to give me a fruit punch when I refused to take my meds," I say, my voice barely a whisper. "I'd refuse, and soon after, I'd get the punch. I hardly ever got sweets, so I always thought of it as a treat, and …" I trail off, trying to grab the tail-end of a memory. "They'd hold the punch out and ask me again. 'Come on, Sasha. Be a good girl and take your medicine, and you can have the rest.' And I would. I'd swallow the pills with what was left of that punch."

I close my eyes. "They used things I loved to manipulate me. Kept them away, then held them out to me like a carrot."

"I've got you," Grimm whispers as his arm tightens around me. I sag into him, soaking up the comfort he's offering. And—for right now at least—hoping he never lets me go.

"What else?" he asks Dr. Chen.

"The good news is, we now have conclusive proof of illegal drug administration. The compound's structure is unique enough that there's no plausible deniability—it could only have come from Reed Pharmaceuticals' labs. Plus, the team you put together to infiltrate the Reed operation was able to get documentation. They were calling it Project Recall. And you were right," she says, her attention on Grimm. "They already have orders for the product from some well-known players in the underworld."

Her words are flat. Even. Like she's discussing the weather. But I can hear the tinge of emotion underneath as she continues to speak, and I realize that she has to keep it flat. Because otherwise, she'll explode from the horror of it all.

I know exactly how she feels.

"The team's recruited a whistleblower from inside Reed's company," Dr. Chen continues. "She's agreed to testify at the hearing to explain how the memory manipulation works and the plan to monetize it. I spoke with the attorneys, and they assured me that even without her, we're in an excellent position, but her testimony should let us steamroll right over anything they might raise."

Liam asks the question I'm too afraid to voice. "Will Sasha experience long-term damage?"

"No," she says, losing that flat tone and offering me a genuine smile. "And I anticipate that at least some of your memories will return."

"My mother?"

"You were very young when she died," Dr. Chen says gently. "So the memories may be spotty. Unclear. Don't expect too much."

"I won't. I just—I just want the memories he stole."

She nods. "I hope you get them."

I close my eyes, imagining forgotten memories of my mother surfacing like shipwrecks from deep water.

I want all of them, even the dark ones.

I draw a breath and squeeze Grimm's hand tighter as fear and longing twist together in my chest.

When I look up, Grimm's watching me, and the concern in those remarkable eyes is undeniable. "Victor can't hide from this."

He's right.

Soon, I think, as hope engulfs me, warm and soothing. The day's finally coming when I'll see justice for my mother, my father will pay for what he's done, and Project Recall will be dead in the water, unable to hurt anyone else.

After Dr. Chen leaves, Grimm and I settle in at the kitchen table and work on putting together a timeline of my medication history. It doesn't take long to see a pattern— every time I showed signs of independence or resistance, my prescription was adjusted.

"This is going to destroy him," I say. "Not just legally, but publicly."

"That's the point." The edge in Grimm's voice could cut glass. "He doesn't deserve mercy."

"No. He doesn't." I stand, a little shaky, and he's immediately at my side, pulling me close. Keeping me steady.

"You should take the meds," he says, referring to the capsules Dr. Chen left for me.

"Ironically, the last few days of withdrawal may be the hardest," she'd said. "Headaches, shakiness. Possibly chills. It's as if the drugs are fighting to stay in your system."

I'd kept the bottle, but I have no intention of opening it.

"There's no reason not to," he says. "You don't have anything to prove."

"Don't I?"

"No." He uses a finger to tilt my chin up so I have no choice but to look at him. "Accepting help when you need it isn't weakness. It's wisdom."

"Is that what you do? Accept help when you need it?"

A shadow crosses his face. "No. But I'm hardly a stellar role model."

I grin, surprised by his honesty. "Careful, or I might start thinking you're human after all."

"Well, we can't have that."

The moment stretches between us, the silence both edgy and full of possibility.

Finally, I break it.

"My father stole pieces of me," I say, my voice flat. "He cut out memories like tumors. And he replaced them with his version of reality." I tilt my head up to look at him. "I'm not okay. But I will be."

I swallow, then look down at the polished hardwood floor. "I just need a little time. I—I'm sorry," I say, taking a step away from him. "Let me be alone right now, okay?"

The indecision is clear on his face, but when I plead once more, he nods. I take the victory, then hurry to the yellow bedroom. I close the door, cursing when I realize there's no lock.

I pull out the computer and the headset, set everything up, then sign in. Almost immediately, I find myself standing outside on the castle's highest tower, my hair blowing in the wind. The headset isn't nearly as immersive as mine back home, and I don't have any tactile sense in Elysium, but at least I'm here, and I gaze out over the kingdom searching for Killiam.

When I can't find him, I summon Ember, who takes off again with orders to find my prince.

Now, I wait, craving Killiam. Needing him.

Hardly any time has passed when I see Ember returning with Rebel by his side. My prince rides his gray dragon bareback in circles around the tower as I scamper up Ember's outstretched wing to my saddle, then the four of us are off.

Ember leads, and I can feel Killiam's gaze on my back.

Soon we arrive at the Mountain Sanctuary, well-hidden from the king between the mountain peaks. Rebel and Ember take to the sky, and I stand still, taking in the beautiful face of my prince, who now looks so much like the man in the other room.

A man who makes my body sing just as Killiam does. More so. A man I crave even though I know I shouldn't. He's helping me, true. But only because it suits him.

Killiam comes to my aid because he loves me.

I sigh, wishing that were true. Wishing Killiam were real.

And, shockingly, wishing that Liam Grimm wanted me for more than a means to his end.

That simple truth makes me reel. For years, Liam Grimm has been the devil. A man who had helped me once, only to toss away that goodwill in repeated taunts over the years, reminding me over and over that I was nothing more than a pretty little doll for my father to show off.

And yet he's the only one who told me the truth about my mother. He's the only one other than Ruby who helped me escape my father.

And for better or worse, he's the one whose touch I crave. Even more than I crave Prince Killiam's.

"You are deep in thought, my princess." The voice through this headset is muddled, but I still recognize the rise and fall of my prince's tone. "Will you tell me what troubles you?"

I shake my head. He's a character in a world I invented. I know that. And yet I foolishly don't want to hurt his feelings. "I'm just melancholy, my prince."

"My love, let me help you forget your troubles." He strides toward me, heat and determination in his eyes. He pulls me into his arms, strokes my hair, my face, my arms, all the while murmuring that I'm beautiful, that I'm his, that he worships me.

But I feel nothing.

And not just because I have no bodysuit.

Oh, god.

"I'm sorry," I whisper, turning away. For tonight, at least, there's nothing here that I want. "I shouldn't have come."

I expect him to argue. To throw me down and demand a caress, a kiss, even more. My heart picks up tempo as I think about it, and I almost change my mind. But then I shake my head.

Killiam only stands and watches, his gaze full of heat, but he makes no move toward me.

I tell myself the weight of the day is too much, and that's why I'm so eager to go. But that's not it. It's a different touch that I'm craving. Warm and real and belonging to a man I thought I hated.

Maybe I was wrong.

Or maybe I do hate him.

I don't know. I don't really care.

All I know is that Grimm is the one I want. Right now, he's the only one.

TWENTY-FOUR
PAYMENT

Liam pulled off the headset, feeling slightly smug as he looked at the screen where Prince Killiam still stood, abandoned mid-seduction.

Vale had turned away from him—the prince and the fantasy.

Sasha had turned away.

It wasn't what she'd said to the prince that had Liam's cock tightening—she hadn't said much at all. Just that she needed to go. It was how she'd acted—the hesitation when Killiam had reached for her, the way she'd pulled back from his touch. The longing in her eyes just before she'd logged out, a yearning for something the prince couldn't give her.

He knew what she wanted—to be fucked properly by a man whose hard edges she could feel. Who could pound inside her. Who could take her to all those dark places and make her scream.

She didn't want Killiam—a sanitized fantasy that wore Liam's face —she wanted the real deal. *Him.* Liam Grimm.

And, oh hell yes, he was more than happy to oblige.

He slammed down the lid on his laptop with a decisive click, tossed it to the foot of the bed, then headed toward the yellow room, wearing nothing but the sweats he'd changed into after seeing Dr. Chen out.

He imagined her standing at the foot of Maya's bed, pacing as she tried to work up the courage to come to the master bedroom and claim what she craved.

Or maybe he'd find her naked on the comforter, her legs spread, and her eyes closed as she tried to bury that desire—that burning, physical need for him that she didn't want to admit, even to herself.

Impossibly, the image made him even harder, and he moved down the hall to her room like a predator to wounded prey, knowing that victory was assured.

He didn't even pause when he reached her door, just turned the handle and let himself in without knocking. The room was dim, lit only by the soft glow of a bedside lamp. She was sitting on the edge of the bed, the Elysium equipment discarded beside her, her hair falling around her face like a curtain of gold.

She looked up at his entrance, surprise flickering across her features before something else replaced it—something heated and complicated.

"I told you I wanted to be alone," she said, her voice carefully neutral. She'd changed into a white terry-cloth robe, and now she cinched it tighter at her waist.

"That's what you said." He stepped into the room, closing the door behind him. "It's not what you want."

Her eyes tracked his movement as he approached, her body tensing slightly. "The hell it's not," she said, but there was no conviction in her voice.

He stopped a few feet away from her. "Look at me."

She obeyed, tilting her face up to his, her pale skin now flushed pink, her lips slightly parted. And though it was probably only his imagination, he was certain he could smell her desire.

His cock strained against his sweats, and he clocked the moment her eyes dipped to that telltale bulge.

"What are you doing?" she asked, even though she could surely see the answer for herself.

"We had an agreement," he said. "I'm taking payment."

"Oh." She sat perfectly still. Didn't try to scoot away. Didn't beg him to leave her alone after her stressful day. Instead, all she said was, "How?"

He wanted to laugh, loving the way she always surprised him. "By giving you exactly what you want."

Her cheeks bloomed even pinker, the flush extending down to the hint of cleavage revealed by the robe.

Her eyes dipped to his crotch. "And what is it I want?"

"What I should have done hours ago." He moved closer, until his toes brushed the dust ruffle on the bed, and he was standing between her thighs.

He saw her throat move as she swallowed. "Oh. What should–?"

He didn't bother answering, just pulled her up with a speed that made her gasp, one hand tangling in her hair as he claimed her mouth in a kiss that was damn sure more intense than anything she'd felt in Elysium.

This was raw. Demanding. Real.

Her moan of pleasure went straight to his cock, and when her arms slid around his neck and she arched against him, it was all he could do not to come right then.

There was no hesitation in her, no caution. Only a hunger that matched his own, desire burning as hot and bright as a newly forged blade.

He pushed her back onto the bed, following her down, his weight pinning her to the mattress. His hands were everywhere—tangled in her hair, skimming down her sides, opening the robe so he could feel the heat of her skin.

She gasped when he dragged his teeth over her breast, and the sound sent a surge of primal satisfaction arrowing straight to his cock. This was what he wanted—what he needed. Her response. Her desire. Her surrender to him. To his every whim, his every pleasure.

Everything.

She was his to take, to claim, to use. The princess he'd craved for so long was truly his—no longer torn between him and a version borne of pixels and code.

He sat up, straddling her, wanting to watch her face as he touched her. Claimed her.

Her eyes were heavy-lidded, her lips swollen from his kisses, her breathing rapid and shallow. He twisted a strand of that magnificent hair around his finger. "So beautiful," he whispered. Not just her golden tresses, but her. *Sasha.* She was stunning, incredible. Not the carefully curated beauty her father had demanded, but something wilder, more primal. Something real.

"Beg for it," he demanded, his voice rough with need, his cock hard against his sweats as his thighs held her hips in place. "Beg for what you want."

"Fuck me," she whispered. "Please, please, fuck me."

"Is that any way for a pretty little princess to talk?"

Fire lit her eyes, and she pushed herself up on one elbow, then slapped his face.

And there it was.

His cheek stung like fire, but he still had to fight his smile. This wasn't Reed's little princess playing another role because she had to. This was a woman who craved him.

"Say it again," he demanded. "Tell me what you want."

"You," she said. "Inside me." One hand twined in his hair, pulling him down to her. The other shoved at the waistband of his sweats, pushing them down just enough to free his cock.

For a moment he considered fucking her mouth, watching as she took him all the way in, then coming all over that beautiful face.

But no. That was for another time. This was a claiming. The exorcising of her prince. He was her goddamn king now.

And with that, his fingers dipped into her slick heat, opening her up. He rubbed the head of his cock over her clit, growing harder as she writhed and begged. Then he thrust himself balls-deep into her slick little cunt, the air filling with her cry, that delicious sound of pain mixing with pleasure.

He rode her, memorizing the way she looked as pleasure built. The way her lower lip trembled when he hit those sweet spots, the whispers of *please* and *yes*, along with her screams of *oh, god*, and *harder*.

He took her close, right to the precipice, then slowed down, pulled out, and smiled when she begged him not to stop.

"Not stopping," he said. "Just a little friendly sexual torment."

"Bastard."

"As a matter of fact, I am," he said, making her laugh.

It was too damn easy being with this woman.

And that made her dangerous. He wasn't a man who committed. He wasn't even a man who dated. He was a man who fucked when he wanted. A man more than willing to trade sex for what he needed. He was a bastard by all definitions of the term. And Sasha Reed—

with her vulnerability and fire—was becoming something more than a bargaining chip or revenge tool.

That hadn't been part of the plan.

For a moment, he considered pulling back. Telling her the deal had changed. That they'd still take down her father, but he needed distance. Space. Clarity.

But the thought of another man touching her, seeing her like this —flushed and wanting—made something primal and possessive roar to life inside him. She was his now. His to claim. His to mark. His to ruin for anyone else who might come after.

Besides, Sasha had already agreed to every perverse, wicked, sensual desire. And if he had one hard-and-fast code, it was that a deal was a deal was a deal.

More than that, he wanted her with an intensity that scared even him. Wanted to possess her completely. To own every gasp, every cry, every surrender.

And he always took what he wanted.

TWENTY-FIVE
SURRENDER

"Tell me exactly what you want, Princess," he demands, his voice rough with desire as he hovers over me. "Every filthy detail."

Not long ago, I would have blushed and looked away. But I'm not that sheltered girl anymore. "I want your cock inside me," I tell him without hesitation, my voice husky with need. "I want you to fuck me until I can't remember my own name."

Heat pulses between my legs, an insistent throb that makes me press my thighs together, desperate for friction, for pressure, for him. My skin feels electric, hypersensitive, every inch of me yearning for his touch.

For a moment he simply looks down at me. Then something breaks in his expression, that careful control he wears like armor shattering as he captures my mouth with his. The kiss is bruising, demanding, claiming, and I open for him instantly, desperate for more. My hands tangle in his hair, pulling him closer as his weight shifts, pressing me deeper into the mattress.

My body burns everywhere his skin touches mine, a delicious fire spreading through me. I arch against him, my breasts crushed against the hard plane of his chest, the sensation making my pussy clench, as if begging to join this party.

"So fucking sexy," he murmurs against my throat, his teeth grazing the sensitive skin hard enough to mark me.

"Please," I gasp as his hand slides inside my robe, my skin tingling in the wake of his touch. My back arches of its own accord, my body offering itself to him, begging for more contact.

"Please what?" His voice drops an octave, rough with desire.

"Touch me," I demand, beyond caring about pride or power games. "Fuck me. I told you already. I need your hands on me. Your cock inside me."

"Greedy little princess, aren't you?"

"God, yes."

With one smooth motion, he pushes my robe open, exposing me completely. I feel my skin flush with heat as his eyes devour me, his expression hungry in a way that makes my core clench even tighter in anticipation.

"So beautiful," he says, his voice reverent despite the darkness in his eyes. "Every fucking time, you take my breath away."

His thumb brushes the underside of my breast in a teasing stroke that makes me squirm beneath him. Then his mouth is there, hot and wet, drawing my nipple deep as his fingers toy with the other. I arch into the contact, electricity shooting from my nipples straight to my core.

I dig my fingers into his shoulders, already desperate for more.

"Liam," I gasp, his name a plea and a prayer. "Please."

His hand slides lower, over my stomach, tracing the curve of my hip before finding the heat between my legs.

"Always so wet for me," he says with satisfaction, his fingers parting my folds to circle my clit with precise pressure. "A guy might think you want something."

"A guy would be right." I have to push the words out past the waves of pleasure breaking over me.

"Tell me," he demands. "You don't get it if you don't say it."

I want to scream that I've already said it, over and over. But I don't. I can't. All I know right now is need. Want. Greed. And this man whose finger on my clit has already sent me halfway to heaven.

My hips buck against his hand involuntarily, seeking more contact. "Inside," I beg. "I need you inside me. I need you fucking me."

"How?"

"Hard," I say. "Deep." I gasp, my body arching in a delicious precursor of the main event.

He slides one finger into me, then another, stroking that spot inside that makes stars explode behind my eyelids. My thighs fall open wider, giving him better access as my body responds to his skilled touch.

"Like this?" he asks, his fingers curling inside me, his thumb circling my clit with relentless pressure.

"Yes," I gasp, my body clenching around his fingers.

"Anything else you want, Princess?"

He's teasing me, but I'm too close to care. I want what he's offering. The rush. The release. And I want it with him. "Your cock," I say. "Please. Please, fuck me."

His eyes darken with desire. "So greedy," he murmurs. "Always wanting more."

"Only from you," I whisper, the truth of it striking deep.

He shifts down my body, his mouth trailing kisses across my stomach, over my hipbones, down to the insides of my thighs.

"I need to taste your cunt first," he says, voice rough with hunger. "Need to know exactly how wet you are for me."

The first stroke of his tongue against my clit has me crying out, my hands clenching in his hair, pulling him closer. He groans against me, the vibration adding another layer to the pleasure building inside me. My thighs shake on either side of his head, my back arching off the bed as he devours me with the same intensity he brings to everything.

"Liam," I gasp, my hips moving against his mouth. "Oh god, Liam …"

His fingers dig into my thighs, keeping me open to his assault. I'm trembling, tettering on the edge of something massive, something that feels different from the other times he's brought me to this precipice.

"Come for me," he commands, his voice vibrating through my core. "Let me taste you, Sasha."

The last of my restraint shatters, my body convulsing as pleasure crashes through me in waves. He doesn't let up, his mouth working me through every tremor, every aftershock, until I'm whimpering from the intensity.

Only then does he raise his head, his eyes dark with need. "Now," he says, rising to strip off his own clothes. "I'm going to fuck you exactly the way you begged me to."

Naked, he's magnificent—all lean muscle and controlled power. His cock juts proud and thick, and my pussy clenches at the sight. He covers me again, the weight of him both terrifying and comforting.

"I've been aching for this," he says, positioning himself at my entrance. "I've been dreaming about burying myself in this tight cunt all day."

He pushes forward, stretching me, filling me in a slow, inexorable slide that steals the breath from my lungs. My body yields to him, adjusting to his size, the initial burn giving way to pleasure.

When he's fully inside me, he pauses, forehead pressed to mine, breath mingling with my own.

"You feel incredible," he murmurs, his voice strained with the effort of holding still. "So perfect around my cock." He meets my eyes. "So perfect."

"Yes," I whisper. "Perfect."

Then he begins to move, withdrawing almost completely before thrusting back in a rhythm that quickly builds from controlled to desperate. Each stroke hits that perfect spot inside me, building the pleasure again. My breasts bounce with the force of his thrusts, my skin slick with sweat, every cell in my body focused on the point where we're joined, on the rising journey that will send us tumbling over the precipice.

"Mine," he growls, his fingers tangling in my hair, tilting my head back to expose my throat to his mouth. "Say it."

"Yours," I gasp, the word torn from me as he drives into me harder. "I'm yours, Liam."

The admission feels different this time. Not just the words he demands during sex, but a truth I can't escape.

He must sense the shift because his expression changes, softens even as his body continues its relentless claiming of mine. He kisses me then, deep and thorough, his tongue mimicking the movement of his cock.

"I want to feel you come around me," he says against my lips. "Want to feel you squeeze me tight while I fill you."

His hand slides between us, finding my clit, and that's all it takes to send me plummeting over the edge again. I cry out his name as pleasure crashes through me, my body clenching around him in rhythmic pulses.

He follows a moment later, his rhythm faltering as he drives deep one final time. I feel the heat of his release inside me, marking me as his in the most primal way possible.

For a moment, we're both still, joined and panting. Then something shifts in his expression—a shuttering, a retreat. He pulls away, separating our bodies with an abruptness that leaves me cold despite the flush of satisfied heat still warming my skin.

He stands, all lean muscle and sinew, but it's the distance in his eyes that sends a sense of foreboding tumbling through me. The connection that burned so hot just moments ago now feels fragile, as if he's already miles away.

"Get some sleep," he says, his voice casual, detached. None of the intensity from moments ago remains. "You'll need it."

I blink, confused by the sudden shift. "Liam—"

"We have work to do tomorrow," he cuts me off, already gathering his clothes. "Plans to make."

There's something deliberate in how he's not looking at me now, how he's pulling his mask back on—that cold, calculating expression I saw when we first made our deal.

He pauses at the door, finally glancing back at me, still sprawled naked and disheveled on the bed. Something flashes in his eyes— hunger, possession, I don't know. And before I can figure it out, he's locked it away.

"Don't get too comfortable with this, Princess," he says, his voice deceptively soft. "I decide when. I decide how. Remember that."

Then he's gone, shutting the door behind him, leaving me alone with the cooling sheets and the lingering scent of sex in the air.

I stare at the ceiling, trying to make sense of what just happened. How can something that felt so real, so raw and true, turn cold so quickly? I wrap my arms around myself, suddenly feeling every inch of the space he's put between us.

Whatever this is between us—whatever we're becoming—it's clearly scaring him as much as it scares me. But he gets to back away. To toss up walls.

Me? I'm trapped by our deal. By my need for his protection.

And by the growing, terrifying feeling that despite everything, I want more from Liam Grimm than just safety.

I want all of him.

And that's the most dangerous desire of all.

TWENTY-SIX

HUNGER GAMES

The next few days blend together as I spend most of my time drafting my affidavit for the attorneys, incorporating the medication timeline, my memories, my fears and phobias. It's rough work, but cathartic as well, and I frequently find myself lost in my memories, and silently celebrating how much stronger I am now.

When I'm not working on evidence for the hearing, I find myself charting time by small changes—the way the afternoon light slants across the kitchen island, the changing hum of traffic outside, even the hours when Grimm disappears into his office and I hear only a whisper of his voice as he makes call after call.

Today, Grimm surprises me by suggesting we venture outside. "Just to the street market," he says, watching me carefully. "It's only a block away."

I nod, determined not to show how my heart races at the thought. Dr. Chen told me that my agoraphobia and my fear of heights might dissipate once I was through withdrawal. But it's equally possible that they aren't artifacts of the drugs but of my trauma. Seeing my mother fall to her death. Being abandoned in the forest.

There's just no way to know.

Right now, the world seems both too vast and too close, and I only agree after Grimm promises that he'll not only stay beside me, but he'll hold my hand the entire time.

That negotiation settled, he passes me sunglasses and a ballcap, and I put them on, feeling more foolish than clandestine. Still, the disguise is necessary. My face is all over the city, plastered across billboards for Reed Cosmetics.

The market is a treasure chest of scents and sounds. I stay close to Grimm's side, my fingers brushing his arm when someone passes too close. Each time, his eyes find mine, and I see something dark and hungry flickering there before he looks away.

We don't buy any trinkets, but we do return to the loft with tomatoes and peppers and a loaf of fresh bread. Then I sit at the kitchen table and watch in a state of shock and awe as he makes homemade pasta sauce from the wares we've brought home. Not only does he chop and sauté and do all the other culinary things that I'm not familiar with, but the end product tastes amazing.

Not that he cooks every night. Instead, our nascent routine consists mostly of ordering takeout, then watching a movie on the massive screen that descends from the ceiling with the press of a button. During the day, he does whatever a cybersecurity person does, and I read or tuck myself away in the yellow room to visit Elysium.

What we don't do is have sex, though he insists I sleep in his bed every night. Not that I take much convincing. He hasn't touched me since the day Dr. Chen told us about Project Recall, and while I'd like to be an icon for women everywhere, the truth is that I keep expecting him to take payment for our deal—and I'm embarrassingly disappointed every night when he doesn't.

Which, of course, sends me straight to Elysium and into Killiam's virtual arms. A girl can only take so much.

"He's playing you," Ruby says, one afternoon when our avatars are hanging out together in Elysium's Crystal Garden.

"I shouldn't care," I say. "I mean, it's Liam Grimm. The man who spent a significant portion of his life being a huge asshole around me."

"He wins the biggest prick cup for sure," she says.

"Except …"

"Except what?"

I scowl, but without the neural headset, it doesn't show up on my avatar.

"Come on, Sasha. What were you going to say?"

"It's just … I don't know," I admit. "He's different. I mean, think about it. He's helping me bring down this Project Recall bullshit. He told me the truth about how my mother died. He brought in an actual doctor, and he's keeping me safe now that I have to stay hidden until the hearing."

"All of which he's doing to bring down your father. It benefits you, but he's doing it for himself."

"What does that matter?"

"Because you're missing the point," she says.

"Fine. What's the point?"

"Well, duh. That you like fucking him."

"Ruby!"

"Oh, please. You just told me it's driving you nuts that he's not pushing on this Everything deal. Don't pretend to go all prim and proper on me now."

I grimace, wondering if I'd have been better off saying nothing. Except she's my best friend. Not to mention the only one I can truly talk to. Except Grimm. It's surprising how easy just talking with him is.

Not, however, about this.

"So what should I do?"

"Sweetie, there's only one thing you can do. Make the first move."

A full day later, I'm still thinking about her advice. She's right, of course. But I can't do it. I already have zero power in this arrangement. If I tell him I want sex, then I drop down into negative numbers.

Still, there must be other ways to get the message across.

I ponder that problem for the rest of the day, finally sneaking up on a solution that evening as we're sitting with take-out Chinese food and scrolling through the various movie options for the night's entertainment.

"Let me pick tonight," I say. "I can't do another action movie."

His eyes dance with humor as he hands me the remote, his forefinger brushing over my thumb as he draws his hand back. "Not into action?"

I make a valiant effort not to whimper as I concentrate on pulling up a movie selection on the huge screen. I scroll through, then finally find what I'm looking for. *Secretary.* An over the top, fucked up erotic movie with a cult following and the kind of sex scenes that are sure to rev his imagination.

"This works," I say as I use one remote to dim the lights and another to start the movie.

I've seen it before, of course. It's weird and wonderful, and I'm more than a little turned on by the time it ends. Especially since I've been leaning against Grimm the entire time, both of us stretched out on the couch, me between his legs and leaning against his chest, our shared popcorn on my lap.

It's an intriguing position, and I realize less than a quarter of the way into the film that my plan will work. How can it not when his hand is already teasing my breast and making my nipple ache?

Not only that, but his cock is rock hard against my lower back ... and when it stays that way into the credits, I know that my plan is golden.

Hashtag yes! Hashtag fistbump!

As the last of the credits roll, we both sit up so we can face each other, and there is no escaping the heat and need I see in those beautiful eyes.

He leans in, and my breasts ache for his touch. I'm already wet, and it takes all my effort not to straddle his thigh and rock myself to Orgasm Number One.

He smiles, soft and sensual. Then his fingers comb through a long lock of hair that he gently tucks behind my ear. My breath catches as he leans in for a kiss ... which ends as a soft peck on my forehead.

Before I can say *what the fuck*, he's standing. "I should get some work done," he says, his voice rough.

"Hold up there, mister," I say, hurrying to catch up, then grabbing his elbow.

He stops, then lifts an eyebrow. "What's wrong?"

"What's wrong?" I repeat. "What's *wrong*? Are you kidding me? I mean, come on. If you're not going to push this Everything deal, then why not just let me go?"

"Two reasons," he says, his voice steady and calm. "First, you wouldn't be safe. Second, you don't want to."

"Excuse me?"

"You don't want to go," he repeats. "And not just because you know you'd be in danger out there."

"Oh?" I cross my arms, both pissed off and curious as hell. "Then why?"

"You know," he says, moving closer, so there's barely even molecules between us. I tilt my head up, and his breath whispers over my face as he speaks. "You want me to fuck you. To take you. To claim that right we bargained for every single night."

My lips are parted, and I'm breathing hard, but I say absolutely nothing.

"You want to experience every decadent, depraved, wonderful, sexually deviant act I can imagine with my exceptionally creative mind."

His smile is slow as he cups my cheek with his palm. "But you don't want to want it."

"The hell I don't."

"Which is why you don't get it until I'm sure you mean it. In other words, Princess," he concludes, "you don't get it until you beg me."

TWENTY-SEVEN
DELTA OF VENUS

I wake to a steady thrum, only to realize it's the pounding of my own head.

Withdrawal.

I grimace, then sit up slowly, hoping coffee and ibuprofen will help. Sunlight streams in through my east-facing window, so bright that I realize I slept straight through the night. More than that, I'm wearing the same thing I wore yesterday, and the copy of Anaïs Nin's *Delta of Venus* I'd pulled from one of Grimm's many bookshelves is open on my pillow.

Apparently, I'd fallen asleep reading.

With narrowed eyes, I close the blinds, then breathe a bit easier when the dimmer lighting helps my head. Coffee will help even more, and I step out of the room for the kitchen in search of caffeine and Grimm.

I don't find Grimm, but I do find his note by the coffee maker letting me know that he's gone to a meeting.

I'm fine with that. Considering this new edict about begging for what I want I'm not quite prepared to see him. Not because he got it wrong and pissed me off, but because he got it right.

I want him—no doubt about that.

But damned if I'm going to beg.

I sip my coffee as I wander the apartment. I've explored it already, but I haven't thoroughly snooped yet. And this seems like the perfect opportunity to learn more about the man who has become protector, lover, maybe even friend. I hope so, because my father is surely on the warpath now, and Liam Grimm holds my life and my freedom in his hands.

That should terrify me—after all, my whole life has been controlled by someone hateful—but it doesn't, and I'm not entirely sure why. And that open question is part of the reason I'm now poking around his apartment, hoping I'll find some answers to the enigma that is Liam Grimm.

First, I peer into all the cabinetry in the kitchen, but I learn nothing except that he doesn't live here full-time. There are too many boxed foods—the kind with long expiration dates—and too many frozen dinners.

I try to look in his office, but it's locked, so my curiosity and I move on to my room. So far, I've only logged onto the computer, slept in the bed, and worn some of the sweats and T-shirts I found in the top drawer of the dresser. Now, I open the rest of the drawers and explore the closet, finding both mostly empty. There are a few sweaters in one drawer and a couple of size six outfits hanging in the closet. Too business-casual for my taste, but maybe Maya likes them.

I grimace, still not entirely sure who she is to Grimm … or if I even want to know. And, no, the stuff in her drawers doesn't tell me much.

At loose ends, I do another circle through the apartment. Despite being in the heart of Tribeca and only a block away from the street market, the space is eerily quiet—no traffic noise penetrates the windows, no footsteps from neighbors above or below. It's like being suspended in a bubble, cut off from the world. It's almost like being back in Reed Tower, except here, my jailer is Liam Grimm, not my father.

Is that a notable difference? Here I'm a weapon for Grimm to use against my father. There I was a princess doll. In one, I was the center of a marketing campaign. The other, the key to extracting revenge.

In both scenarios, I'm being used.

So how has my situation changed?

You chose this path.

The voice in my head is sure and strong. And right.

Here with Grimm in Tribeca, I'm free. And that's something I've never been except in Elysium.

But even in Elysium, I'd never truly let go. I held the reins, after all.

With Grimm, I've surrendered to our bargain—and god help me, I love it.

Everything.

Heat floods my cheeks as the memories surface—Grimm's hands on my body, his voice in my ear, the shocking pleasure of yielding to him. The even more shocking realization that I'd enjoyed being claimed that way. Desired that way.

And I can be again. All I have to do is beg.

I hug myself. *What is wrong with me?*

I've spent my entire life under my father's control. Drugged, manipulated, imprisoned in my own fears. I should be reveling in my newfound independence, not craving Liam's control.

And there it is, the core of what scares me the most—that after everything my father did, what if I'm the girl who'll never be able to stand alone?

No.

I open my eyes and shake my head. *That way lies madness.*

So I turn away. From him. From myself. And I shift my focus to what I can still shape.

Elysium.

I settle in front of the computer, then navigate to a half-finished landscape—a mountain sanctuary I'd been designing before everything went to hell. I open the scripting window, fingers already flying as I add detail to the rocky cliffs, smooth the flow of the digital waterfall, and enhance the pool at its base.

Time slips away, the physical discomfort of withdrawal fading beneath the focus of creation. My fingers dance across the keyboard, lines of code appearing on the screen, transforming into living digital art with each execution.

It's only when I pause to flex my cramping hands that I notice I've been working for nearly three hours. And I've created something I didn't intend.

A street market with stalls selling food and goods.

A stone building rising near it.

A balcony looking out over the entirety of Elysium, and my own avatar—Vale— standing there, gazing at all the paths that converge upon this majestic stone tower, now the center of this world.

A text box pops up—*WTF? Doing renovations?*

I turn Vale until she spots Ruby's avatar, then reply—*Just screwing around.*

It's true—just not the literal truth. I don't want her to know I zoned out, let my fingers do the walking, and dropped a modified version of Grimm's Tribeca apartment right in the middle of Elysium. A fantasy world where this apartment is the center. And where Prince Killiam, with all of his Grimm-like attributes, will certainly return by nightfall.

I don't tell her, because I don't want to think about what that means.

I have to log off. Sorry.

I cut the connection before she can ask me what's up. Ruby's my best friend, and there's nothing I keep from her. But in this case, I'd rather dole out the information when I understand it.

Right now, all I understand is Grimm. Not just that I want him, but that the arrangement we have both scares and intrigues me.

And, yes, it turns me on. So much that I built the Elysium version of this apartment without even thinking about it. And over the last few years, I built Grimm into Elysium, too, his personality hidden inside Killiam. AI tweaked him, but I created him. The prince I craved. The lover who protected me. The prince who would be my mate.

I built him out of my desires and needs.

But at his core, he is Liam Grimm, a man I used to hate. A man I'm now sworn to obey.

And that's a little more Psych 101 than I can handle at the moment.

TWENTY-EIGHT
PURPLE PROSE

The apartment is chilly, and I can't find the controls for the thermostat, so I head back into the yellow room and pull out the soft mauve sweater on top. As I lift it, a book tumbles out onto the floor.

Poetry. A slim volume by Pablo Neruda, one of the few poets I'm familiar with. Ruby introduced me to his work years ago when we were teenagers. She'd found a collection in her grandmother's bookshelf, and we took turns reading passages aloud during our sleepovers, giggling over the sensual imagery that went over our heads, but was also a treasured glimpse into an adult world of passion.

The spine is cracked, the pages well-thumbed. When I open it, I find delicate pencil annotations in the margins—a feminine hand, noting connections between poems and underlining particularly moving phrases. The title page bears a simple inscription: "For M. Because some things can't be encrypted. — L."

I close the book quickly, feeling like an intruder. Maya, apparently, falls on the *girlfriend* side of that friend equation.

Color me naive, but I'm pretty sure men don't give volumes of sensual, erotic poetry to their platonic roommate.

More likely, this is a home office where she also kept her clothes. A feminine place that was totally hers, but the bed in Grimm's room was shared. Much like the arrangement he and I have right now.

I frown, already hating this woman. Which is totally bitchy and girlie of me, but it's the truth. I hate her almost as much as I hate not having answers.

I tell myself I'm being ridiculous. After all, it's not as if this Maya is here now. And what do I care, anyway? There's nothing real or romantic between Grimm and me. Sex, yes. But that's just a payment he's demanding. The price for keeping me safe.

It's not as if he truly cares for me, not like that, anyway. I'll go so far as to say we've become friends even beyond our arrangement. And considering the sex part of our deal, I can even up that to Friends with Benefits.

But I'm not his girlfriend, and when this is finally over and my father is exposed and—hopefully—jailed, there won't be a single thing except gratitude binding me to him.

So what if he gave her a book of erotic poetry? What do I care if—

Click.

Before I can spin out any further, I hear the sound of a key in the lock. Grimm is back.

I shove the book back into the drawer and wipe the stupid, foolish tears from my eyes.

Then I draw a deep breath, pull on the mauve sweater, and stroll down the hall to the kitchen, as if I've got nothing more important on my mind than getting a fresh cup of coffee.

Nothing interesting here. Move along folks, move along.

Every step toward the kitchen pulls me deeper into a version of heaven filled with mouthwatering, spicy scents—and at least one ridiculously good-looking man.

His back is to me as I arrive, and I spend a lovely moment enjoying the way his ass looks in his jeans. Something that mysterious bitch Maya can't do, because she's not here.

As I kick my own ass and remind myself that we have an arrangement, not a relationship, he unpacks white paper bags stamped with an unfamiliar logo. Small containers of what looks like Mediterranean food cover the granite island—hummus sprinkled with paprika, olives glistening with oil, some kind of grilled meat skewers, and fresh, pillowy pita bread.

He turns, his smile flickering as his eyes dip to the sweater. And the moment they do, I feel a tightening in my gut. That's it. I can't deny it any longer.

I'm actually jealous.

I push aside that unsettling revelation and force a smile as I indicate the sweater. "This was okay, right? I'm sadly lacking in wardrobe …"

"It's fine," he assures me. "Just noting how nice it looks on you."

"Oh," I say, my cheeks warming from the compliment as if I were fourteen. Though considering my lack of dating experience, I kind of am. "Thanks. So, um, you're really sure Maya won't mind?"

"Hmm?" He glances up from the containers he's opening. "No. I'm sure it's no problem."

I'd hoped my question would spark more revelations about the mysterious Maya, but all he does is indicate the spread of food. "I hope you like Lebanese. This place does incredible shawarma."

"I've never had it," I admit, coming closer from where I was hovering at the edge of the kitchen. "But it smells amazing."

I glance around, trying to work up the courage to ask about Maya —who presumably is the Neruda recipient. But the courage never comes. And why should I care, anyway? Grimm and I are helping each other, and that arrangement has a bit of a FWB component. That's all. And once my father is behind bars, where he belongs, the benefits will end along with the friendship, and I'll probably never even see Grimm again.

The thought disturbs me more than it should, especially since this is the first time I've thought of him as a friend and not, oh, a ridiculously sexy devil incarnate. It's a bit disconcerting.

It's also true.

"—joy."

I glance up at him, realizing I've zoned out. "Sorry. What?"

He gestures to one of the stools at the counter. "I said, no time like the present. Sit. Eat. Enjoy"

It might be my imagination, but I think his eyes flick to the sweater again. I keep my eyes on his as I run my hand along the sweater's sleeve. "So, um, Maya? Roommate? Girlfriend? None of the above?"

"Ex," he says, ripping a pita bread in half.

"And she left drawers full of things behind?" Even I can hear the jealousy oozing through my voice, and I want to both kick myself and call back the words. Since I can't, I shovel more shawarma into my mouth. It really is delicious.

"Let's table the discussion about Maya's things. I met with the attorneys. We have more important things to talk about."

I nod, but I'm picturing Maya. *Maya.* That's a name for someone tall and dark, elegantly beautiful. Someone who's never been dressed up like Cinderella or forced to wear too much rouge on her cheeks for a Times Square billboard.

"—for the hearing."

I snap back to reality. "What?"

His eyes narrow, and I'm certain he knows where my mind had gone.

"I said I met with the attorneys about hearing prep. We should go over it. We'll be in court in just a few days."

"You should have taken me with you," I say, stabbing a piece of meat with more force than necessary.

Grimm leans back as he studies me, his eyes cool and assessing. "Is something bothering you?"

"No. Yes. I don't appreciate being treated like a child who can't participate in discussions about her own life."

He has the look of a man negotiating a minefield. "Jack called while I was out," he says, referring to Jack Granger, the lead attorney. "I was mid-town, only a few blocks away, and considering our deal, I didn't think you would want to go." His voice is steady and soothing, and I'm starting to feel like an idiot.

"I thought protecting you from your father included protecting you from having to get down and dirty in the litigation. If I was wrong, I'm sorry." His voice is perfectly level, as if he's talking down a wild animal.

I realize that I'm absently fingering the sleeve of the sweater while thinking about Neruda's sensual verses. I pull my hand away, irritated with myself.

I am not falling for this man. There's nothing between us except sex and a power play. Nothing.

Except maybe there is.

"Sasha?"

I jump. "Sorry. Yes. You're right. It's fine. I'm just hungry. It's making me bitchy."

"Then please, by all means, keep digging in. Shawarma is like the music that soothes the savage beast."

He shoots me a boyish grin.

I roll my eyes, glad we seem to be back on even footing. "What did the lawyers say?"

He pushes aside his plate as he leans forward, elbows on the table. "From what we've been able to learn, your father intends to put a lot of stock in your inability to be out in the world without your meds or supervision."

"He's the one who made me this way!"

He puts his hand over mine. "I know," he says. "And we'll let the court know that, too. But as for what he's planning, we have confirmation that he's compiling footage from your various public appearances, and he'll have witnesses testify that you were medicated at each one. Household staff who saw you take the meds and psychologists who will analyze your facial expressions and movements to testify that the footage shows that you were relying on medications to help you cope at each particular event."

I hug myself, hating every moment of this. And hating my father most of all. It's like being in a dark corner of hell, and he's the devil.

"He intends to use the footage of you running from your own engagement as evidence of paranoia resulting from not taking your meds. And we suspect he'll have household staff testify, too. Some will quit out of loyalty to you, but some will undoubtedly lie—either because they're being bribed or because they're terrified of your father.

"Bastard," I say. "How are we supposed to counter that? He's the one who dosed me up before any event, so it's not as if we can find footage where I'm at some party completely drug-free.

He slides off his stool, then pulls a bottle of Chardonnay out of the wine fridge. He lifts it in question, and I nod. Right now, I'll happily take the entire bottle, but he's probably only offering me a glass.

"The hearing is about your ability to cope now," he says as he pours for us both. "Not yesterday or last week or last year. So we're going to get you out there. In public. Stable, confident, unmedicated.

But it has to be somewhere your father can't get to you." He nods toward the entryway. "That's why we're going out tonight."

I follow his glance and see a garment bag hanging on the coat rack near the door.

"And we're going where exactly?"

"Grimm Tower. The roof."

I gape at him. "Are you out of your mind? We're going back to the helipad?"

"That's not part of the agenda, though it would give our position extra punch if we arrive that way. Good thinking."

I just throw my hands up, not sure what bizarro world I've been tossed into.

"Half the roof is an event space," he says, obviously seeing my frustration. "Alexander is hosting a charity function tonight."

"I thought you hated your brothers," I say, reaching for a piece of pita.

"Half-brothers," he says. "The *half* being something they remind me of daily. And yes. I despise the lot of them—except for Leo. But that doesn't mean Alex and Elliott can't be of use."

"What about Gabriel? Did you like him?"

Something flickers in Liam's eyes. "He was as horrible as my father," Grimm says. His answer doesn't surprise me. I've heard plenty of tales about what a beast Gabriel Grimm was.

"Still," Grimm continues, "as much as I hated him, I wouldn't wish dying in a blaze on anyone."

"Will your father be there tonight?"

Liam holds my gaze steadily. "No. We're keeping it out of the press, but Elias Grimm has been in a coma for almost a year. Alex has been running the company. The story tonight will be that Elias is traveling."

I lean back, shocked. Not because of Elias Grimm's coma, but because Liam Grimm has just handed me insider information that could affect stock prices and business deals.

His mouth quirks into a smile, and I realize that he understands exactly what I'm thinking. "We have to trust each other."

I nod, and our eyes meet, the moment stretching between us, fragile and unexpected.

I break it before whatever this is gets too deep under my skin. "I'll watch for photo ops," I say, "but I need you close, just in case my phobias act up."

"Don't worry," he says, the heat in his voice arrowing right between my legs. "I'll stick to you like glue."

"Oh. Good." I think about what he said last night.

Maybe now would be a good time to beg.

"You should try on the dress." His words yank me back to reality. "If it doesn't fit, we'll need time to get something else. We also need to find someone we trust who can come and do your hair and makeup. Nails, too. You have to look just as polished as you have every time your father showed you off. Even more so."

I nod, then grab the garment bag and the nearby shoebox. I slip away with them to the yellow room, then take a peek. Inside the bag, I find a stunning black Elie Saab gown, strapless with a fitted bodice that flows into a skirt, the back of which will just barely brush the floor. It's elegant and sophisticated—nothing like the ridiculous gowns my father forced me to wear.

I strip and slide it on, surprised by how perfectly it fits. As for the shoes, I might as well be Cinderella, because they, too, fit like a glove. Open-toed and strappy, with a nail point heel, they make my legs look even longer, and do amazing things for my ass, if I do say so myself.

In the mirror, I see a woman I barely recognize—confident, elegant, powerful. For the first time, I'm truly looking forward to a corporate party. It's almost like a date, though I shouldn't think that way.

But I can't help but think that if it is a date, it will be my first.

"Stop it," I murmur, forcing my attention back on my outfit. To truly do it justice, I need the professional hair and make-up that Grimm is going to arrange. But in the meantime, I brush my hair, apply some lipstick, then head back to the living room to show myself off.

The smile slides off my face as I hear the voices—his and a woman's.

"You brought her here to fuck, so she can keep her things and herself in your room, not mine." The voice is sharp, angry, with a breathy quality that is probably ridiculously sexy when she's not furious.

"I'll get you a suite wherever you want, but I need you to leave—"

He stops and turns, his eyes locking on mine. Standing next to him is a stunning woman with sleek dark hair cut into a classic bob that highlights her sharp cheekbones and full lips. She stands straight, exuding confidence in designer jeans, a starched white blouse, and a decorative scarf—in the exact shade of mauve that I'd been wearing only minutes ago.

Maya, I presume.

TWENTY-NINE
SWORDPLAY

"Why on earth would I stay in a hotel when I have this charming loft apartment?" As if I'd been part of this conversation all along, Maya turns to me and flashes a bright white smile. "I worked for him for years at RSC. Fucked him for a nifty chunk of that time, too."

She looks straight at me, her dark eyes wide with false innocence. "He can be so trying, can't he? But his skill between the sheets makes up for that sharp-edged personality. Have you noticed that, too, sweetie?"

I take a step forward, calling on every class in poise and decorum my father tossed me into. "It's one of his more interesting qualities," I say, then extend my hand. "You must be Maya. You have excellent taste in sweaters."

Her eyes widen just a bit, and I want to take a victory lap. My father never let go of the leash, but he did let it run slack at parties and public appearances. To do otherwise would have required too many explanations, and my various conditions were a family secret.

Which means I've crossed swords with some very hoity-toity women over the years. I'm hardly a Samurai, but I can wield a sword if I need to. Especially if I don't like the other woman. Right now, I'm not liking Maya at all.

"Maya." Grimm's voice is flat. "This isn't a good time."

Her dark eyes flick to me, then back to Grimm. "Looks like the rumors are true. You're harboring Victor Reed's runaway daughter. Or, rather, his abducted daughter, as that's what he's telling every reporter who'll listen."

"Why are you here?" Grimm asks, his voice carrying a warning.

She moves farther into the apartment, uninvited. "I live here, remember?"

"When you're in the country. And right now, you're supposed to be in London."

She flashes that smile again. "And yet here I stand." She moves into the living area and takes a seat, the tension between them thick with unspoken history. I feel suddenly, acutely out of place—an intruder in a drama that has been playing out since long before I arrived.

"What I'm curious about is why you brought her here of all places."

"That's not your concern. And you're not staying here."

She shrugs, then looks at me. "He's so strong. So … dominant. Have you noticed that sweetie? The part I liked best was when he tied me up. There's nothing quite so thrilling as being completely submissive to a man who can hurt you."

"Out," Grimm says, his voice full of cold, contained fury.

Her brows rise. "Kicking me out of my own home?"

"It's not your home. Not anymore. And I assure you that if you don't leave, you'll regret it." He tilts his head, his eyes locked on her. "Are we understanding each other?"

I can practically see the wheels spinning in her head, then she nods. "Of course, darling. I'd rather have room service and access to a spa, anyway. I just popped by so I could meet your new little toy."

She turns her attention fully to me. "You're such a sheltered little creature, so in case you didn't read the subtext, our dear Liam is saying that he has information on me that I would prefer not be disseminated throughout town. I leave, and he keeps my secrets tucked away. I stay, and he makes sure that things I would prefer to remain private go public. I believe the colloquial term is blackmail. And he's so very, very good at it."

"I'm familiar with the term," I say, then flash my most camera-ready smile. "I've only known you for a few minutes, but it's easy to believe he has a treasure trove of information you'd rather keep hidden."

Her eyes widen, and she turns to Liam. "Well, look at that. Victor's little doll has a backbone. Isn't that intriguing?"

She returns her attention to me. "You don't like me, and that's just fine. But you should listen to me. Liam Grimm trades in information. Secrets he can use as currency. That, my innocent new friend, is something you should think about. Because whatever secrets you have, Miss Reed, the odds are good he already knows them."

"Thank you for the warning," I say in my most polished and polite voice. "But just so we're clear, Ms. Lane, while I admire your taste in sweaters, you and I aren't friends." I offer her an overly-friendly smile that matches the one she's been flashing. "I'll leave you two to wrap up," I add, then turn my back on her, my heart pounding so hard she can probably hear it as I stride down the hall to the yellow room.

Only a few moments pass before there's a light tap at the door. I stop pacing, frozen in place until Liam says, "Can we come in? Maya wants to grab a few of her things."

I'm tempted to tell him that I'll just dump all her stuff out the window, and she can grab it off the street. But since that's probably not the best plan, I open the door, trying hard not to glare as she heads to the closet. She pulls a small suitcase from the back, opens it, then tosses in a few garments from the closet and the dresser. The Neruda book she leaves behind. A little reminder for me as to whom he gave the erotic poetry.

"You've rearranged my things," she says, looking over her shoulder at Grimm.

"I cleared some space for Sasha."

Her brows rise. "How considerate." She turns to me, her smile razor-sharp. "He never cleared space for me."

"Well," I say, "perhaps that's because you had a dresser."

Her eyes widen almost imperceptibly, and I catch the hint of a smile tugging at Grimm's mouth. Maya, I think, is used to getting the last word.

"He's going to find you," she says. "Victor's already hired private investigators to work alongside the police. It's only a matter of time before he finds this place."

"How do you know who he's hired?" I ask.

"Darling, my business is information, and I'm good at my job." She shoots a sideways look at Grimm. "I learned from the best." She flashes a wide smile, as if we've just had a lovely afternoon tea.

"I'll be off now," she says, then turns to me. "He's one hell of a good fuck, but don't ever trust him. Remember, he's both a bastard and a Grimm."

THIRTY
ANTIHERO

"I really don't like your girlfriend."

Liam turned away from the coffee maker to face Sasha. She stood in the kitchen doorway, bare feet, leggings clinging to those endless legs, an oversized T-shirt slipping off one shoulder. Her fabulous hair hanging loose around her face. His chest tightened just looking at her. And why not? She was temptation incarnate—and he was a man rapidly running out of reasons not to give in.

"You're not the only one," he said. "At the moment, I'm not liking her much myself. And for the record, she's not my girlfriend."

The trouble with Maya, of course, was that she gathered information like currency. And she had a predator's instincts — holding that currency tight until just the right moment when its value was assured.

And while he didn't know of any specific secrets of his she might be privy to, he was certain she had some tucked away in her arsenal. She was too good for there not to be.

He should know. He'd trained her.

Hopefully, out of respect for what they'd once had—and for the retribution he could so easily dole out—she wouldn't toss any of that currency Sasha's way. There were secrets he ought to tell her, yes. But he needed to be the one to open the door.

"Are we still going to Alex's party?"

He passed her a coffee, then nodded. "We should leave in about three hours. I have hair and make-up for you coming soon, by the way. Once we're at the party, we'll make a few rounds to see and be seen, then we can leave.

"And come back here?"

He shook his head. "No. I've arranged another hotel. Your father is undoubtedly paying handsomely for information on your whereabouts. And while I'd like to believe Maya and the salon folks will stay silent, I'm not risking your safety."

She nodded. "Right. Okay." She flashed a small smile. "I guess I'll go shower."

He watched her walk away. He liked seeing her at ease in his home. And he damn sure enjoyed the way her exceptional ass looked in those leggings.

He gripped the edge of the kitchen island, cursing himself for wanting her the way he did. For having to fight back the urge to follow her into the shower. To take her right there in the heated spray.

Damn it all. It had been so much easier during those long years when he'd hated her. First, because he was a Grimm, trained from birth to hate anything and everything that touched Victor Reed.

Then, because of her complicity with her father. The way she'd so publicly spread the lie about Elias Grimm murdering her mother. She was, he'd thought, as vile as her father, willing to use lies and gossip as steppingstones to climb over everyone who got in her way.

Not long after that, he'd discovered Elysium, and he'd begun to watch her more carefully in the real world. The way she flinched when her father touched her arm in public. The mask she wore when speaking to potential investors. How, in unguarded moments at society events, her eyes would drift to the windows, to the city beyond, with a longing so raw it was almost obscene.

With each peek into that private world, he'd witnessed her most intimate needs and most desperate desires. Every day, he'd craved her more and more, almost to the point of obsession. The craving so deep he'd slid into that world himself.

He'd taken her in every way he could think of. Teases and torment. Pleasure and pain. Night after night, he'd expected her to pull back, to tell him that he'd gone too far, but she never had. He'd yet to reach her limits, at least in the virtual world.

She'd given him her everything in Elysium, but it hadn't been enough. He hadn't—*he couldn't*—have her in the real world. And so he'd cut her down. Told her what he thought of Victor Reed's perfect little princess. Watched that smile falter and die. All because he was a selfish bastard who'd wanted a woman he could only touch in a world woven in pixels and code.

And now?

Now, he had the real woman. He could talk to her, kiss her, stroke her, fuck her. Any damn thing he wanted.

Sasha Reed—in the flesh, in his arms, and in his bed.

It should be enough. But it wasn't.

She might be in his home and in his bed, but she wasn't his.

She would be, though. Liam Grimm was not a man who walked away from what he wanted. And he wanted Sasha Reed.

Without letting himself think about what he was doing, he walked straight down the hall to the yellow room, entered, then stood outside the bathroom, listening to the soothing rhythm of the spattering water and Sasha's soft voice as she sang in the shower.

He could picture her there. Her magnificent hair pinned up. Water sluicing over her naked body, her nipples tight, her body slick with soap.

His cock twitched, and he stroked himself through his trousers, surrendering to the fantasy. The sound of the shower became a soundtrack for his imagination—Sasha with her head tilted back, eyes closed, lips slightly parted as the water caressed her skin in ways his hands wished to do.

He could do it. He could open the door. Strip down to nothing, then climb in that shower with her. She'd gasp, a false protest, but when he pressed her back against the steam-warm tiles, she'd surrender to him completely. Her mouth, desperate for him. Her arms clinging to him as he lifted her, then entered her. Her legs going tight around his waist as he thrust himself into her, deeper and harder and faster as he fucked her tight, sweet cunt.

He unzipped, then slipped his hand inside his slacks so he could rub one off as he imagined teasing her, going deliciously slow as she whimpered and cried and begged in his ear.

He squeezed harder, stroked faster, his breath becoming ragged as the fantasy deepened. The way her skin flushed pink under the hot water. Those sweet little whimpers turning desperate as she silently begged for more.

The way she arched into him, her nails digging into his back as he took her against the wall. As she surrendered to him, giving him her body, her desire, her everything.

The fantasy ripped through him, sending a fresh pulse of desire straight to his groin. He was so goddamn hard. Never had he wanted anyone like this—with this visceral, all-consuming hunger that went beyond revenge, beyond their bargain, beyond the peeks into her depths of passion he'd seen only in Elysium.

Beyond anything he could rationalize away.

His strokes grew erratic as tension coiled inside him. He was close —so damn close—every muscle taut, his breathing harsh in the quiet room. It would be so easy to finish like this, his mind full of her, his hand a poor substitute for what he really wanted.

But that wasn't the game. That wasn't the point.

With a curse that was almost a groan, he forced his hand to still. His cock throbbed painfully against his palm, demanding release, but he denied himself with the same ruthless control he applied to everything else in his life. He leaned forward, pressing his forehead against the bathroom door, his entire body trembling with unfulfilled need.

The challenge was for both of them after all. And there would be no going over that edge until she begged. For either of them.

And she *would* beg. He'd make sure of it.

He'd push her to the brink again and again until those perfect lips formed the word "please." Until those clear eyes clouded with desperate need. Until she forgot that this was a transaction, a bargain, revenge.

Until she forgot everything except his name—and how to get down on her knees, lift that beautiful face, and beg.

He leaned against the door, smiling as he remembered the look on her face when he'd issued that edict. Shock. Anger. Surprise.

But it was the flicker of arousal that would be burned into his memory forever.

Soon, he knew, she'd beg.

———

BACK IN THE KITCHEN, he poured himself a whiskey he didn't particularly want. The domestic comforts of the loft had become a dangerous illusion—the meals they shared, the movies they watched together, her body nestled against his on the sofa, her scent lingering on his sheets even though he refused to touch her.

For years, he'd thought she was just like her father and would have happily destroyed her. Now … well, now he would protect her with his life.

He'd gone from wanting to destroy her to doing whatever it took to protect her, this woman he'd once believed was little more than a porcelain doll of Victor Reed's creation.

He'd been so fucking wrong.

He tossed the whiskey back, downing it in one swallow, as he recalled the movie from the other night. *Secretary.*

He wasn't an idiot. He knew exactly what message she'd been sending, leaning back against him like that, her body radiating warmth and invitation.

It had taken every ounce of his control to walk away, to maintain the fiction that this was still about power and leverage rather than the truth gnawing at his insides—he wanted her. Not just her body, not just her testimony against her father, but her. Her laugh. Her stubborn determination. The way she kept finding strength despite everything life had thrown at her.

He moved to the window, looking out at the city lights spread below like a carpet of stars. Years of surveillance. Of watching her through cameras, through data streams, through the digital world she'd created in Elysium. He'd told himself it was strategic. Necessary. Just gathering intelligence on his enemy's daughter.

What a fucking lie.

He'd watched her because he couldn't look away. Because something in her called to something in him—a recognition of shared trauma, perhaps, or simply the magnetic pull of a woman who refused to be broken despite being surrounded by men determined to shape her to their will.

Men like him.

The self-loathing was familiar, almost comforting in its bitterness. He was no better than Victor Reed. Different methods, different goals, but the same fundamental belief: that Sasha was a means to an end rather than an end in herself.

Except that wasn't true anymore, was it? Oh, he'd still happily destroy Victor Reed with Sasha wielding the sharpest darts—assuming the prick ever showed his face again—but somewhere between pulling her from that gala and watching her rebuild herself in the safety of this apartment, she'd become essential. Not a weapon, but a woman he desperately wanted to claim.

He should let her walk away once Victor Reed was behind bars. Let her see how many options exist beyond the cage her father had built.

But how could he? Even if it meant putting her in a cage of his own making, how could he ever let her go?

He couldn't.

He was a selfish son-of-a-bitch. And Sasha Reed was his, whether she fully knew that yet or not.

He wasn't the hero in this story.

He was just the lesser of two evils.

THIRTY-ONE
HIGH SOCIETY

The crowd swirls around me, a kaleidoscope of designer gowns and perfectly tailored tuxedos. The top of Grimm Tower has been transformed into the most breathtaking display of wealth I've ever witnessed—and that's saying a lot.

Massive ice sculptures catch the moonlight, reflecting the glow onto the rare orchids from Southeast Asia that cascade from custom-built crystal pergolas. Champagne fountains flow endlessly. And the glittering Manhattan skyline provides a backdrop that makes even my father's lavish galas seem quaint in comparison.

A server in white gloves offers me a glass of champagne from a tray. Not just any champagne—Dom Pérignon White Gold Jeroboam. I recognize the distinctive bottle that costs more than most people's monthly rent. Alexander Grimm doesn't just serve expensive champagne—he serves the kind of champagne that becomes legend in society columns.

I smooth the front of my gown, hyperaware of every eye that turns my way as Liam guides me through the sea of New York's elite. My mind races, and I search out every exit, wanting to ensure I can get inside quickly if I'm suddenly overwhelmed by the weight of the space surrounding this opulent enclave.

As we stroll, I catch snippets of whispered conversations, some admiring, others suspicious. The pressure of their stares makes my skin prickle, but Liam's steady presence beside me acts as an anchor.

In one corner, a famous tech billionaire negotiates with a Saudi prince while pretending they're just chatting about the weather. Near the edge of the terrace where the glass barriers provide an illusion of safety, the heiress to a banking fortune I met three years ago laughs too loudly with a designer whose latest collection costs more than what most Americans make in a year. This is wealth so extreme it has its own gravity, pulling everyone into carefully calculated orbits.

"Sasha! Darling! What a surprise to see you here." Carole Van Ryan, one of my father's oldest associates, leans in to kiss both my cheeks. Her meticulously sculpted silver hair gleams under the twinkling lights, setting her diamond choker—that must be worth millions—afire.

She glances at Grimm, then back to me. "I have to confess that I'm surprised to see you here. There's been such a kerfluffle of gossip about your engagement to Mr. Bane."

She smiles, letting a pause hang in the air. When my silence passes the point of rudeness, she turns to Grimm. "And you're Ms. Reed's escort for the night? Do set the rumor mill to rest. Everyone's all atwitter about whether you kidnapped Ms. Reed from the gala or eloped."

"What delightful stories," Grimm says, then gestures to include the entire roof as he lightly presses his hand to the small of my back. "We really should mingle."

"But-but you're well?"

I pause in the act of stepping away and look over my shoulder. "I am," I assure her, my society smile firmly in place. "In fact, I'm finding that independence suits me."

"Oh. Well, yes." Her gaze shifts meaningfully to Grimm. "And in such unexpected company. Your father must be beside himself."

"I wouldn't know. We haven't spoken recently," I say smoothly.

Her eyes widen behind what I'm certain are thirteen-thousand-dollar designer frames. "My dear, surely you know he's been telling everyone you've been abducted? There's quite the reward for information on your whereabouts." She leans in, her perfume—custom-blended, no doubt—clouding around us. "Some are saying ten million."

I force myself not to react. "How interesting. But I promise that

Mr. Grimm hasn't abducted me. I make a show moving closer as his arms goes around my waist. "The farthest thing from that, in fact."

"Oh," she says, looking scandalized.

The whole situation is so surreal it's all I can do not to laugh.

"Sasha!" A booming voice cuts through the ambient chatter. Maxwell Hartwell III, banking magnate and notorious gossip, approaches with his third wife trailing behind him. The diamonds in her ears could fund a small country's infrastructure. "Is it true? You left poor Desmond at the altar?"

"Hardly the altar, Max," I correct, feeling Liam tense beside me. "Just an unfortunate announcement."

"Not according to Desmond," Maxwell says, his expression gleefully scandalized. "He's here tonight, you know. Telling anyone who'll listen that the engagement is absolutely still on. Says your various … conditions … made you nervous and you simply needed to retreat home. Temporary setback, he called it."

I feel my heart stutter. "Desmond is here?"

"Over by the east terrace. With the Ashcroft-Hathaways." Maxwell's eyes dart between Liam and me, clearly cataloging every detail for later gossip.

Liam's hand presses against my bare back, a silent reassurance. "If you'll excuse us," he says, his tone making it clear it's not a request.

"We need to leave," I whisper to Grimm. "I can't see Desmond. Who knows what he'll do—to me and to you."

"Desmond Bane is a monster," Grimm confirms, "but I believe you've called me the same on more than one occasion."

I grimace. "That was before I knew you."

He coughs out a laugh. "Your opinion hasn't changed, Princess. We both know that. But at the moment, I'm *your* monster."

I meet his eyes, seeing both humor and heat. It's the latter that seems to zing down my body to rest between my thighs.

"Why can't we go now? We're here. We've mingled. I'm clearly functioning."

"Your father can't be able to argue that we came in, made one lap, and bolted."

I want to argue, but he has a point.

As we continue weaving in and out among the guests, a waiter appears with a silver tray of appetizers so tiny and artfully arranged they look more like jewelry than food. Liam takes one and offers it to me—a gesture that doesn't go unnoticed by the socialites tracking our every move.

"You know, darling," purrs a voice that drips old money and malice, "everyone's talking about your little … escapade." Marguerite Wellington, heir to a hotel fortune and my father's occasional business partner, scrutinizes me through a jewel-encrusted lorgnette that must date back generations. "Running from your own engagement party? Very dramatic. Very … Reed."

She adjusts the strap of her gown. "Your father called me personally, you know. Frantic with worry." Her smile is shark-like. "Now I see his concern was … misplaced."

"Marguerite," Liam cuts in, his voice glacier-cold. "I wasn't aware Alexander had lowered the barrier to entry quite so dramatically for tonight's event."

Her face tightens, but before she can respond, a commotion near the spiral staircase that connects the top floor of the tower to this outdoor space draws our attention. A young socialite has arrived, her entrance punctuated by a shower of rose petals that float down over the crowd. The extravagance isn't what's impressive—it's the casual assumption that everyone else should pause their evening to acknowledge her arrival.

Liam turns to me. "Give her a few more years and she'll learn that money doesn't buy attention."

"Doesn't it?" I ask, trying to ignore how his breath on my skin sends shivers down my spine.

"No," he says simply. "Power does. And power isn't always measured in dollars."

We move through the crowd, his body shielding me from curious onlookers who either sneak peeks at me or boldly stare, as if waiting for me to break down.

"Ignore them," Grimm says, as if he can hear my tangled thoughts. Maybe he can. God knows I've come to feel closer to this man in the last few days than anyone else in my life other than Ruby. Ironic and strange and scary. But somehow warm and wonderful too.

"Are you okay?" He pulls me to a stop, his eyes skimming over me as if searching for bruises.

"I'm fine," I say. "I'm just this week's gossip. It will pass."

"And the roof? Being up here?"

"Also fine," I say, warmed by the genuine concern in his voice. "Really. I didn't even cringe when Alex stepped so close to the edge."

I don't know if it's because the meds are mostly out of my system or because of the man standing beside me, but the expanse of sky and city that stretches out around us isn't terrifying tonight. On the contrary, it seems almost soothing. Like a visual metaphor telling me that anything is possible.

I'd first noticed the change during the helicopter ride to Grimm Tower. Despite the height and the stomach-dropping sensation of takeoff, I'd remained calm. Centered. The panic I'd expected never materialized—just a flutter of anxiety that Grimm's hand on mine had easily quieted. There's something about him, I realize. A way he has of making me feel safe. Protected. As if nothing can truly harm me while he's near.

The thought is both comforting and terrifying. What happens when this is over? Will Grimm still be here, or will he disappear once he's gotten what he wanted?

I have to fight to keep smiling, because the idea of him walking away makes my chest tighten in a way that has nothing to do with agoraphobia.

As we continue to navigate the crowd, I hear snippets of the gossip that's spreading through the event like wildfire.

"That's Victor Reed's daughter. Isn't she—"

"— heard she was—"

"—against her will—"

Grimm and I share a smug look—the plan to get me noticed is clearly working, and by the time we leave, well over a hundred witnesses will have seen me functioning on this platform in the sky, just as sane and stable as everyone else.

As far as I'm concerned, that's a reason to celebrate, and I take a flute of champagne off the tray of a passing waiter.

"—look at the way Liam Grimm keeps her close. I heard they eloped after—"

Our eyes meet, and I can't help but grin. Then I sigh as he shifts his hand at my back so that now his fingertip strokes my skin, a sensual reminder of what I can have whenever I want.

Even now, my body craves his—the weight of him, the heat, the way he moved inside me. How he watched me come apart with those ice-blue eyes that somehow burned straight through me.

He leans close, his mouth at my ear. "All you have to do is beg."

"You," I say, "are a very cruel man." I turn to grin at him, struck breathless once again by the fact that a man as gorgeous as Liam Grimm is allowed to exist in this world, because surely he shames all the mortals.

With a sigh of deep pleasure, I let my eyes roam over the sharp lines of his tuxedo, struck by the way the formal attire somehow makes him look more dangerous rather than tamed in a drawing room way. His masculine beauty is almost painful—all angles and intensity. Nothing about this man is soft, except perhaps the curve of his lower lip. The same lip I've bitten in the heat of passion, and the memory of the way he'd growled, low and sensual and claiming— makes me want to drop to my knees right now.

"Something on your mind?" A grin tugs at his mouth—and that very biteable lip.

"Nope," I say, all sunshine and innocence.

It occurs to me that if I get him riled up enough, I may be able to circumvent that begging edict. At the very least, the attempt could be fun. And if I succeed, the reward would be very much worth it.

I step closer, pressing my body against his, my hands cupping his ass despite the fact that the invited press is undoubtedly eating this up. "And you?" I ask. "Is something on your mind?"

"So many things," he says, bending to whisper in my ear.

"Tell me."

He pulls back enough so that I can look into those incredible eyes. Then, with deliberate slowness, he says, "Cake."

I blink, completely confused. "Cake?'

He steps back, breaking my connection with his ass, but taking my hand.

"I see cake." He nods toward a dessert table laden with architec- tural confections that seem too beautiful to eat—multi-tiered master- pieces crafted by pastry chefs flown in from Paris, adorned with edible gold leaf and sugar flowers so realistic they seem to bloom under the starlight. "You mentioned you were rarely allowed sweets."

He'd been leading me that direction, but now I pull him to a stop. "You remembered."

"Of course," he says, completely nonchalant.

I smile, touched that he'd think of that. "Models don't eat cake. That rule was practically tattooed on my forehead growing up."

"You're not just a model anymore," he says as we continue toward the table. "You're a woman making her own choices."

My own choices. The phrase sends a thrill through me, hot and bright as lightning. Such a simple concept, and yet so foreign to my experience. Choice has never been part of my reality—not my clothes, not my career, not even what I put in my body. Everything decided by my father, packaged and presented as concern for my well-being.

We're halfway to the dessert table when a familiar voice cuts through the ambient chatter.

"Sasha! There you are!"

Ruby's arms are around me before I can respond, her embrace fierce and familiar. She pulls back, her eyes traveling over me as if checking for visible damage. She glances at Grimm, then narrows her eyes. "You know I'm like a sister to her," she says to him, indicating her dress—which is actually mine. "You can tell because I have access to her closet. So if you pull any a-hole sort of tricks, I will make sure you regret it."

I see the tiniest hint of amusement in his eyes, but otherwise, Grimm's face is completely serious. "I'd expect no less from her best friend."

She looks at me. "He knows that?"

I lift a shoulder. "Somehow, he knows everything."

"And he's really not being an ass to you?"

She knows from our Elysium conversations that he's not, but all I say is, "He's the poster boy for good manners."

She scowls, then cocks her head toward where Leo is holding court across the roof. "The same cannot be said for Leo Grimm. So," she adds, crossing her arms and putting on her Do Not Fuck With Me face, "can you tell your jerk of a little brother to stay away from me?"

A shadow crosses Grimm's features. "He's been harassing you?"

Ruby lifts a shoulder. "Let's go with pestering. But I don't want to be around that guy. You keep him off me, and I'll jump on the Rah-Rah Liam cart. And I've got pull with this one," she adds nodding her head toward me.

Liam catches my eye, and I see the amusement in his. Along with a bolus of irritation that I realize is meant for Leo and not Ruby.

"I will," he says. "You have my word."

"Oh," she says, clearly expecting she'd have to put on the hard sell. "Thanks. So, can I borrow her for a bit?"

I catch his eye, and we share a quick grin before Ruby drags me to a quiet corner. Immediately, I pull her into a hug.

The moment she releases me, she nods in Grimm's direction. "Well?"

I glance around to make sure we can't be overheard before I give her the full run-down. Most of it she already knows, since I've been updating her during our various avatar conversations in Elysium.

"You and Liam Grimm. Who would have thought?"

"Don't say it like that. We're not a couple. We're just …"

"Friends with benefits?"

I shrug. "Maybe." Though even as I say the word some little part of me screams that no way am I settling for that consolation prize. "And you really mean it—about my father? He's not blaming you for my escape?"

"Cross my heart," she says, miming that very thing.

"What are you doing here, anyway?" I ask. "At a Grimm party, of all places?"

"Reconnaissance," she admits. "Your father has been on the warpath since you bolted. When I heard about this event—and that Alexander Grimm was hosting instead of Elias—I thought I might learn something useful. Granny knows the cook, so I snuck in that way, changed in the kitchen, then slid into the elevator with a group that had already started drinking."

She shrugs, then sighs. "Not a challenge at all."

I shake my head, thinking of all the stunts she used to tell me about during her days in undergrad and into her first semester of business school before she quit to be my PA. I'd wanted her to stay in school, but after all that went down, I understood the decision.

She studies me, her expression softening. "You're doing good? Really?"

"I am. Really."

And you're not just blowing smoke up my skirt. Because, you know, mortal enemies and all …"

"No smoke," I tell her, a bit surprised myself. It's true, but this is the first time I've said it out loud to anyone. "Yeah. It really is good."

She grins. "You look happy. I haven't seen that in your eyes for a very long time."

Happy. I take a step back, caught off guard. Am I happy?

I've been so focused on survival, on escape, on bringing my father to justice, that I haven't stopped to consider something as basic as my own happiness.

But she's right. Despite the chaos and uncertainty, there's a lightness in me that I can't remember feeling before. A sense of possibility that has nothing to do with freedom from my father and everything to do with the Liam.

"It's complicated," I say finally. "But, yeah."

"Just be careful, okay? The Grimms have been at odds with the Reeds since forever. And they always have their own agenda. Always."

"Liam isn't like Leo," I reply, surprised by my own defensiveness.

"Leo's in a problem class all by himself," she says. "And don't worry, I'm taking my own advice and staying far away."

"Good." I hesitate, suddenly fascinated with the point of my shoe peeping out from under my dress. "And Liam's not like the rest of them at all."

"I think you're right," she says, her tone making me look up again. Immediately, I see Grimm striding back through the crowd toward us. "He's the dangerous one."

Before I can respond, photographers swarm around a new arrival —Alexander Grimm himself, commanding attention in a way that reminds me of his father. Cold, calculated charisma that seems to vibrate from him like a force field.

"Speaking of dangerous Grimms," Ruby murmurs. "I should make myself scarce. Your father will have people here, and I'd rather not be seen talking to you."

We share a quick hug, then she heads off. I see her pause as she passes Grimm—who is holding two plates with cake, but since I lack any lip-reading skills I don't have a clue what they're saying. Then I see Ruby grin, and moments later Grimm is at my side with two fabulous-looking pieces of chocolate cake. "I thought you'd like this," he says, passing me one. I go a little gooey. It's only cake, but the fact that he went out of his way to get it for me knowing how long I've been deprived of sweets …

No one ever paid such close attention before. No one except Birgit and Ruby. And, of course, my mom when I was a little girl.

I take a bite, then moan as the rich chocolate melts on my tongue. I can't remember the last time I allowed myself such an indulgence. My father's voice was always in my head—calories, measurements, image, control.

Tonight, I kick him firmly to the curb.

"Thank you," I say, genuinely moved. "What did you say to Ruby?" I ask, with a mouthful of heaven.

"That you're safe with me. And that Leo will leave her alone for the rest of the party or suffer the consequences."

"Oh." It's silly, but tears prick my eyes. Cake and chivalry. Who knew those were my weak spots? "I guess I was wrong all those years. You're not an asshole at all."

"Perhaps," he says, his eyes roaming over me in a way that leaves me tingling. "Or maybe I'm just one hell of an actor."

I'm finishing my cake and am stealing a bit of Grimm's when I spot Leo Grimm in the crowd. He flashes the same rakish grin that's been splashed across the society pages at least a hundred times, then heads our way.

"The prodigal princess returns," he says, his voice carrying that same irreverent tone that seems embedded in his DNA. "And looking far too good for my brother's company." He glances between me and Liam. "Quite the splash you two are making," he adds, looking more than a little amused by the farce of it all.

"I know Liam already spoke to you," I say, "but if you don't stay away from Ruby, I'll be kicking your ass, too."

"The lady speaks! And with such authority." He grins, unrepentant. "I was merely being hospitable to a guest at our family's affair."

I lift a brow. "I don't think that word means what you think it means."

He looks pointedly between me and Grimm. "Affair?"

"Hospitable," I say. "I think the word you're actually looking for is *harassment.*"

Leo holds his hands up. "Hey, I already said I'd give her space."

"You did," I agree. "I just don't think you're a man of your word."

He turns to Liam. "I'll talk to you later, bro." He shoots a sideways glance at me. "And you're right about that one. No doubt there."

"Right?" I ask once Leo's swallowed up by the crush of guests.

"That you're the loveliest woman here," he says, and while I don't believe him, what woman in her right mind would argue with a compliment like that?

"I'm going to grab us some champagne to go with this," Grimm says. "Don't move."

As he slips away through the crowd, I take another bite, closing my eyes to savor the rich flavor. I'm so lost in chocolate heaven that I don't immediately notice the shift in the air, like the temperature has suddenly dropped. The hair on the back of my neck stands up, and I know he's there before I even turn around.

"There's my beautiful fiancée."

Desmond Bane's voice slithers over me like oil on water. His smile is practiced. Perfect. The kind that appears in society magazines but it never reaches his eyes. Those remain cold and calculating. The eyes of a predator assessing its next meal.

He seems to think that will be me.

He steps closer, seeming to materialize from the crowd as if conjured by my worst fears. In his impeccable tuxedo with a massive gold watch that probably cost more than most people's homes, he looks like success personified. Only those who know him—really know him—see the darkness underneath.

"I'm not your fiancée." My voice is steadier than I feel. "I never was."

His smile doesn't falter, but something flickers in his eyes—a flash of rage quickly masked. "A momentary misunderstanding, darling. Your father and I have already discussed it. The announcement was merely … premature."

I scan the crowd for Grimm, spotting him at the bar, his back to us as he waits for the champagne. I consider shouting for him, but it's not as if Bane has me at knifepoint.

I can handle this. I'm clear enough now to fight my own battles.

"It wasn't a misunderstanding," I say, lifting my chin. "It was a mistake. One that won't be repeated."

Desmond's expression doesn't change, but his eyes harden to chips of ice. "Your father is quite determined about this match."

"I don't care how determined he is," I say. "I won't marry you."

"We'll see." His smile is triumphant now. "The guardianship hearing is coming up fast. Once your father regains control, you'll find yourself with significantly fewer options."

The cake turns to ash in my mouth. Even if he can't legally force me to marry Desmond, my father could make my life unbearable until I comply.

"Your father and I are very like-minded when it comes to managing … difficult situations," Desmond continues. "I've had the south wing of my estate redecorated for you. Soundproofed, of course. For privacy." He leans closer, dropping his voice. "I know how easily startled you can be. All those … delicate nerves."

My stomach twists. I know what he means—no one would hear me scream.

"There you are."

Grimm's voice cuts through my rising panic as he materializes at my side, two champagne flutes in hand. His tone is casual, but I can feel the tension radiating from him as he assesses the situation.

"Liam Grimm. I wondered which brother would be playing white knight tonight." His smile widens, showing too many teeth. "Though I must say, the bastard son seems an … unusual choice."

"Better a bastard than a butcher," Liam replies, his voice soft but razor-sharp.

Desmond chuckles, a sound utterly devoid of humor. "Such melodrama. And here I thought the Grimms were known for their business acumen, not their theatrics." He turns to me, ignoring Grimm completely. "It's interesting to see the company you're keeping these days, Sasha. Your father will be … fascinated."

"Is there something you wanted, Bane?" Grimm asks, handing me one of the champagne flutes before sliding his arm around my waist. "Other than to make uncomfortable small talk with my date?"

"Date?" Desmond's eyebrows rise. "Is that what this is? Interesting. Tell me, is she simply a convenient weapon against Victor, or is there more to it?" His gaze slides to me, then back to Liam. "She is exquisite, I'll grant you that. Though perhaps a bit … fragile for your tastes."

"Unlike your previous wives?" Liam's voice is casual, but the threat underneath is unmistakable.

For just a moment, Desmond's mask slips. Something vicious and ugly flashes across his face before the polished veneer snaps back into place. "Careful, Grimm. Accidents happen so easily. Especially to those already prone to mishaps."

He turns to me, taking my hand before I can pull away. His fingers are cool and dry, his grip just tight enough to be uncomfortable.

"I'll see you at the hearing, Sasha." He brings my hand to his lips, and it takes everything in me not to recoil. "Do try to look your best. You know how I appreciate … presentation."

As he walks away, mingling effortlessly back into the crowd, my knees weaken, and the fear I've been holding in crashes over me in waves.

"He can't—" I start, my voice shaking. "My father can't—"

Liam's arm tightens around my waist, steadying me. "He won't," he says, his voice leaving no room for doubt. "I promise you, Sasha. That will never happen."

I look up at him, searching his face for reassurance. What I see there isn't just determination but genuine anger—not the cold calculation of someone using me as a pawn, but the protective rage of someone who genuinely cares.

"Drink," he says, nodding toward the champagne in my hand. "And breathe. Don't let him see that he got to you."

I take a sip, then a deeper breath, forcing myself to regain composure. Across the terrace, I see Desmond standing beside Alexander Grimm, both of them watching us with calculated interest. Desmond raises his glass in a mock toast, that predatory smile never leaving his face.

"I need to get some air," I say, turning toward the less crowded side of the terrace.

"This entire event is outside," Grimm says, but his expression softens as he follows my gaze back to where Desmond stands. "But I know what you mean. Come on."

He leads me away from the main crowd toward a quieter corner with a cluster of chairs and a plush couch. He sits, pulling me down beside him. He puts an arm around my shoulder, and I lean in, welcoming the comfort he's offering.

"He's a monster."

Liam's hand finds mine, his fingers warm and strong as they intertwine with my own. "Good. That means he can be defeated."

I turn to face him, suddenly desperate to believe in something—in someone—who can keep the darkness at bay. "How can you be so sure?"

His eyes meet mine, steady and certain. "Because this time the princess isn't facing the dragon alone."

My smile falls somewhere between giddy and shy as I whisper, "Thanks, Grimm."

He tilts his head, studying me with an intensity that makes me feel as if he can see straight through to my core. "You know, you could call me Liam."

I still have the cake, and I take another bite before answering. "You're Grimm to me. The man I used to not trust who now brings me cake." I meet his eyes, feeling my cheeks heat. "Unless you'd rather I call you Liam?"

For a moment, he says nothing, then he smiles, slow and deliciously sexy. "That's okay, Princess. You can call me whatever you like," he says, his voice dropping to that register that seems to vibrate through my entire body. "So long as I can call you mine."

The possessiveness should alarm me. After a lifetime of being my father's property, I should recoil from anyone staking a claim. But that's not how I feel.

Instead, a sense of belonging crests inside of me. Something that has nothing to do with ownership and everything to do with choice.

"That seems fair," I say, the words barely above a whisper.

He lifts his hand to cup my cheek. His touch is gentle, almost reverent, and I lean into it without thinking. "Say it," he urges, his eyes never leaving mine. "Say you're mine, Princess. Say that I own you. All of you."

It's a demand, not a request. Controlling. Maybe even a bit manipulative.

But it's real, too. And there is a choice buried inside.

And even though the choice I will make is inevitable, somehow it still feels real.

Mine.

Just like I am his.

"I am," I whisper. "I'm yours." And the words feel like the truest thing I've ever said.

The kiss is gentle at first, even sweet. Then it slides into something wild. Something like claiming. Something primal and hot that completely makes me forget that we're in the middle of a crowded party.

His hand slides to the back of my neck, holding me close as his mouth moves against mine with a hunger that matches my own. I hear the distinctive click of cameras and phones—but can't bring myself to care.

When he finally pulls back, I'm breathless, my heart hammering against my ribs. The world around us seems distant, muted, as if we exist only in our own pocket of reality.

"Your brother will have a field day with those photos," I murmur, nodding toward the photographers who are now pretending not to stare.

"Let him," Liam says, his arm wrapping around my waist. "I'm not hiding this. Not hiding you."

The words warm me from the inside out, but reality intrudes, cold and insistent. "My father will try to use it at the hearing," I say. "He'll say you've brainwashed me, that I'm being manipulated, that it's Stockholm syndrome."

Liam's expression turns hard, determined. "We have it locked in, Sasha. Your father won't win this time."

I frown, doubt creeping in despite his confidence. Ruby's warning about the Grimm-Reed feud whispers at the back of my mind. What if this is all part of Grimm's revenge? What if I'm just collateral damage in a war that started before I was even born?

"In my experience, things go wrong more often than they go right," I say.

"Not anymore," he says, his voice low and fierce.

And then he's kissing me again, right there in front of Alexander Grimm's society guests, press cameras clicking like mad. His arm tightens around me, pulling me against him, and I surrender to the kiss, to him.

In that moment, surrounded by whispers and stares and the weight of who we're supposed to be, I allow myself to believe him. To trust that this time, things might actually work out the way we hope.

It's probably naïve, but as his lips move against mine—as his hands hold me close—I can't bring myself to care about the risks. The world disappears, and all that remains is this man, this moment, this choice I'm making with my eyes wide open.

For the first time in my life, I'm exactly where I want to be.

And still, Ruby's warning echoes in my mind: The Grimms have their own agenda. Always have.

I push the thought away, losing myself in Liam's kiss. Whatever agenda he might have, whatever secrets still lie between us, I'll face them tomorrow. Tonight is for us—for this fragile, unexpected thing blooming between captor and captive, enemy and ally, Grimm and Reed.

Tonight, I choose to believe in something better than the prisons we've both lived in for so long.

THIRTY-TWO
DETHRONED

Liam guided Sasha through the crowd of Manhattan's elite, his hand at the small of her back as he carefully maintained the precise balance of protective and possessive that the cameras would expect. Every moment was calculated—from the way his fingers brushed against the fabric of her dress to the casual intimacy of leaning in to whisper in her ear.

Just one glance at his phone half an hour ago had confirmed that Sasha, Liam, Liam-And-Sasha-the-Couple, and Sasha-the-Potential-Ward were trending across every social media platform in use anywhere on the globe.

They'd been photographed mingling, smiling, laughing. And in every image and video that Liam found, Sasha had played her part perfectly, handling the small talk and scrutiny with a poise that surprised even him. She looked exactly like what she was—a stable, confident woman able to take care of herself. A woman who absolutely did not need a guardian.

And damned if they weren't going to establish that and more in court.

The Grimm family's annual fundraiser had provided the ideal backdrop—high profile enough to generate the publicity they needed, yet controlled enough that Reed's men couldn't easily infiltrate. And the presence of Sasha at the party despite the scandal and curiosity swirling around her had the added benefit of reducing the number of queries as to Elias Grimm's whereabouts.

The usual answer? Unavoidably called away on business.

The real answer? Elias Grimm was out of commission, deep in a coma from which no one expected him to recover. And the only thing wrong with that picture as far as Liam was concerned was that his father was warm and comfortable in a medically high-tech room instead of burning in hell where he belonged.

He checked his watch, noting they'd been mingling for nearly two hours. "We've been seen enough," he murmured against her ear, allowing his lips to linger a fraction longer than necessary. "There's something I want to show you."

Her eyes met his, curiosity mingling with wariness. She'd learned to be cautious around him—a fact that both pleased and troubled him in ways he chose not to examine too closely.

"All right. What?"

"Not here." He nodded toward a service door partially concealed behind an elaborate floral arrangement.

The security guard stationed there was on his payroll, not Alexander's—a distinction that had proven useful more than once. The man stepped aside without a word, and Liam ushered Sasha through the door, down one flight of stairs, and then into the service corridor beyond.

The transition was jarring—from crystal chandeliers and champagne to the stark industrial look of concrete floors and fluorescent lighting.

"Where are we going?" Her voice echoed slightly in the narrow space.

Liam didn't answer immediately, leading her instead toward the service elevator at the end of the corridor. He'd been debating this decision all evening, weighing the risk against the potential value. But in the end, he knew it was important.

Perhaps it was about trust—giving her something real after so many manipulations. Or perhaps it was simpler than that. Perhaps he just wanted someone to witness the truth he and his half-brothers had carried alone for too long.

The service elevator was industrial and stark, without the polish of the main elevators. Liam swiped his key card and entered a code, deliberately positioning himself so Sasha couldn't see the sequence.

Old habits.

"You didn't answer my question," she said as the doors closed. There was a new edge to her voice, a flash of steel that hadn't been there when he'd first brought her to his loft. The drugs were clearing from her system, and with them, the artificial fog that had dampened her natural spirit.

"We're going to see my father," he said simply.

Her sharp intake of breath was audible in the confined space. "Elias?"

"The one and only."

The elevator began its descent, and Liam watched her process this information. Her expressions were becoming easier to read—or perhaps he was simply paying closer attention than he once had.

"Why ?" she asked.

A fair question, one he wasn't entirely sure he could answer. "The opportunity presented itself. With everyone at the event, we can move through the tower unnoticed."

It wasn't the whole truth, but it wasn't a lie either. The perfect conditions for a man accustomed to operating in gray areas.

The elevator stopped at the fortieth floor, and Liam led her into a corridor that looked nothing like the residential floors above. The medical floors were sterile and institutional, with the antiseptic smell that seemed universal to all healthcare facilities, regardless of how expensive.

"The family medical floor," he explained, noting her curious glance. "After Gabriel died in the fire, my father became obsessed with mortality—not in a philosophical sense, but with the fervor of a man determined to cheat it." He shrugged. "So he installed the three medical floors for both family care and research."

"What happened to Gabriel?" Sasha asked. "I remember hearing about a fire, but not the details."

Liam's jaw tightened. "Massive blaze at his retreat in Aspen. Nothing could have saved him. No body was recovered—just a few teeth that somehow survived the inferno and the charred remains of his signet ring." He held up his bare right hand. "The gold had partially melted, but the family crest was still visible enough for identification."

"Signet ring?"

"All Grimm sons wear identical rings—except me." The words came out more bitter than he'd intended.

"Oh. I'm sorry."

He shook his head. He hadn't intended to even hint that he cared. Because he didn't. He had no respect for Elias Grimm. So why the fuck would he want that patriarch's crest on his hand?

They walked in silence for a while, passing several empty rooms before reaching the door at the end of the hall. Liam hesitated, his hand hovering over the keypad.

"Are you ready?"

"Yes, but why are we here? He's in a coma, right? Why do you want me to see him?"

He slid his hands into his pockets. "You believed Elias killed your mother for years. He was the monster who lived under your bed. Seeing him like this … Well, it can change how you see the world."

For a moment, she only looked at him. Then she turned to look at the still-closed door. When she returned her gaze to him, there was no uncertainty on her face. "He's not my monster, Liam," she said softly. "You're the one who pulled him out of that role and recast the true monster in my memory."

She met his eyes. "Elias Grimm is the monster under your bed. Not mine."

He shook his head, knowing she was right, but not wanting to know it.

For a moment, the corridor was silent but for the mechanical whirring and clicking of equipment. Then she took his hand. "Yes. I want to see him. I want you with me, though."

Something soft and warm washed over him. "Of course. We'll go in there together."

He drew in a breath, then tapped in the code, steeling himself for what lay beyond. He'd only come once before. And Sasha was right—no matter how much he told himself this trip was to slay her monsters, the only monster beyond that door was his.

The door unlocked with a soft click, and he pushed it open,

gesturing for Sasha to enter first. She hesitated just a moment before stepping through, her shoulders set in a determined line.

The room was dimly lit, dominated by a hospital bed surrounded by machines that beeped and hummed in a rhythmic chorus. And there, lying beneath pristine sheets, was Elias Grimm—or what remained of him. The once-imposing frame was now diminished, the face sunken and waxy. And a colorful array of tubes and wires connected him to the various machines that sustained his minimal functions.

The nurse seated in the corner barely glanced up from her tablet as they entered, merely acknowledging his presence with a perfunctory nod. "Mr. Grimm."

"Any change?" he asked, though he already knew the answer.

"Stable but unresponsive," she replied. "Blood pressure's been good today."

Liam watched as Sasha moved closer to the bed, studying her face as she took in the man who had occupied such a significant place in her nightmares. The man who, according to Victor Reed's lies, had murdered her mother.

"He doesn't look like a monster," she whispered.

"That's the problem with monsters," Liam replied, his voice flat. "They rarely do."

He moved to stand beside her, close enough to feel the warmth radiating from her body but not quite touching. His gaze fixed on his father's face, searching for some trace of the terror he'd once inspired. There was none, of course. Just a frail old man tethered to machines, all his power stripped away by biology's cruel efficiency.

"So this is the man who supposedly pushed my mother off a roof," Sasha said softly.

"And who discarded my mother when she became inconvenient," Liam added, feeling the familiar rage rising like bile. "The man who brought me into his home only to spend the next twenty years making sure I understood I was unwanted."

He hadn't meant to say that aloud. His time with Sasha was making him careless, loosening the tight control he'd maintained for so long.

"Did he ever love anyone?" she asked, her question echoing his own childhood wonderings.

"He loved power," he answered without hesitation. "Control. His own reflection, perhaps."

He felt her touch before he saw it—her fingers tentatively brushing against his, the contact so unexpected he nearly pulled away. "I'm sorry," she said, her voice low. "For what he did to you."

Their eyes met, and Liam felt something shift between them—a moment of genuine connection that went beyond their arrangement, beyond the carefully constructed dynamics of captor and captive, protector and protected.

"It made me who I am," he said, the words emerging rougher than intended.

"Not entirely," she argued, her gaze unwavering. "You chose who to become despite him, not because of him."

The observation caught him off guard. He'd spent years defining himself in opposition to Elias—determining who he would not be rather than who he would. The distinction she'd drawn was subtle but profound, and he wasn't sure how to respond.

Instead, he moved closer to his father's bedside, leaning down until his mouth was near Elias's ear.

"I'm not you," he whispered, too low for Sasha to hear. "Remember that, wherever you are in the dark."

He straightened, feeling a weight lift from his shoulders—as if speaking the words, even to an unconscious man, had released something toxic he'd been carrying for too long.

As they slipped out of the room, Liam caught her glancing back one last time at the man in the bed. He recognized the expression on her face—it was the same one he'd worn the first time he'd seen Elias after the stroke. The confusion of seeing a monster rendered harmless, of confronting the raw humanity of someone you'd been taught to fear.

In the elevator returning to the rooftop, Liam stayed quiet, processing the unexpected vulnerability of the moment they'd shared. As the elevator neared the rooftop, she took his hand. "You know," Sasha said, "our fathers deserve each other."

Liam nodded slowly. "Yeah. Maybe they do."

The elevator doors opened, and the sounds of the party immediately engulfed them—laughter, clinking glasses, the string quartet now playing something faster. They stepped back into the glittering event as if they'd never left. But they had. And something fundamental had shifted between them.

He guided her toward the terrace, craving the feel of the wind against his face. The city spread before them, a glittering carpet of lights with Reed Tower visible in the distance—a reminder of what was still to come.

He reached over and took her hand. "I should have asked before leading you to the terrace? Are you okay?"

She nodded slowly, a bit like someone in shock. "I'm not scared, and it's not trying to pull me in. I think—I don't think I'm cured. But tonight, right here, with the wrought-iron and the crowd and you ..."

She trailed off, then smiled at him. "Yeah. I'm okay here."

"Good."

They both gazed out at the city for a while. The night air was cool against his skin, a welcome contrast to the complex emotions churning inside him.

After a moment, he turned his back to the world and his attention to the mingling guests, more animated now after hours of imbibing.

He spotted Leo across the terrace and was gratified to see that Ruby was nowhere in sight.

Ruby should have known better than to get involved with the likes of Leo, but the way it had all blown up had been entirely his little brother's fault.

He turned again, this time watching Sasha. She was staring out at the city, her profile etched against the night sky. For a moment, he simply looked at her—not as a strategic asset or a means to an end, but as the remarkable woman who'd once been a bird with a clipped wing, but now was learning to fly.

"We should leave soon," he said, checking his watch. "We've been seen enough, and I don't want to push our luck."

She nodded, turning to face him with an expression he couldn't quite decipher. "Thank you," she said simply. "For showing me."

Liam inclined his head, uncomfortable with her gratitude. "It was strategic."

"No, it wasn't. But I'll pretend it was if that makes it easier for you."

Before he could respond, Leo approached with that infuriating grin that always preceded trouble. Liam truly loved his little brother, the only Grimm he'd ever connected with. But damned if Leo wasn't both exhausting and trying, especially after a drink or two when the little voice in his head that told him how to behave was passed out on the floor of Leo's mind, utterly useless.

"The prodigal son and his princess make quite the couple," Leo said, his voice carrying that same irreverent tone that had always been his shield. "The gossip columnists will be busy tomorrow. Looks like your grand plan worked."

"Looks like it did."

Leo's eyebrows rose slightly at his tone. "Someone's touchy tonight." His gaze shifted between them, too perceptive for Liam's comfort. "Did I interrupt something important?"

"We're leaving," Liam said, ignoring the question and knowing full well that Leo would be giving him a call in the morning. "Make our excuses to Alexander."

"Always a pleasure," Leo replied with mock formality. "Do try to remember you're supposed to be the good brother, Liam. Treat our guest with care."

Liam almost rolled his eyes. His little brother had always been too observant for his own good—or for anyone else's.

As they slipped away from the party and into the waiting car, Liam watched as Grimm Tower receded behind them, its spires reaching toward the night sky like accusing fingers. "Where to now?" Sasha asked.

"Somewhere they won't think to look," he replied, squeezing her hand. "Somewhere safe."

She nodded, and he was struck by the trust implicit in that simple gesture—a trust he was increasingly unsure he deserved. The plan remained the same: use Sasha to destroy Victor Reed, protect her until the court hearing, and then release her from their bargain.

Simple. Straightforward. Strategic.

But as they drove through the night, Liam found himself wondering if anything between them would ever be that simple again.

THIRTY-THREE
CELESTIAL

The limousine glides to a stop in front of The Celestial, an ultra-modern luxury hotel that seems to shimmer like a giant diamond in the ambient city light. It's the kind of place that doesn't bother listing prices on its website because if you have to ask, you can't afford it.

"This is where we're staying?"

"Just for the night," Grimm says, as if we're pulling up to a roadside motel rather than one of the most exclusive addresses in Manhattan.

"Welcome back, Mr. Grimm," the doorman says. "Have a good evening."

The lobby is an extravagant fever dream of marble and gold, with soaring ceilings and an enormous crystal chandelier, at least five times the size of the one Father had installed in our dining room. I grew up with wealth and luxury, but other than the times I was dressed up and paraded around like a prized pony, I had very little actual interaction with the trappings of wealth.

This place is so opulent I feel as though I should whisper.

At the reception desk, the manager comes out to greet us. "Mr. Grimm, everything is prepared as requested."

Liam nods. "Thank you, Richard. Any messages?"

"None, sir. Enjoy your stay, Mr. Grimm. Ms. Reed," he adds with a nod to me.

"As requested?" I ask as Grimm guides me toward a private elevator, his hand firm and commanding at my lower back. Once inside, he inserts a key card, and we begin ascending, presumably to the penthouse.

"Just a few things I asked Richard to put in place. Like exclusive use of this elevator, and registration under fake names." He gives a little shrug. "Probably overkill, but with the hearing tomorrow and Desmond's appearance at the party tonight" … He meets my eyes. "I just want to keep you safe."

Such simple words, and yet they steal my breath, making me feel warm and special and safe. It's a stark contrast to his earlier edict – *You don't get it until you beg.* Harsh words, designed to entice and tease and arouse.

And it had worked. Even thinking of that edict now makes me wet. The memory of how he'd looked when he'd laid down that rule. The heat that had been in his eyes. The need that had rippled through me, searing me from the inside. Filling my head. Teasing my tongue.

"*Everything,* Princess, remember? Because you're mine." He brushes the pad of his thumb over my lower lip in a way that sends currents of electricity straight between my thighs. Then he meets my eyes. "I always take care of what's mine."

"Oh." It's the only word I seem to be able to form. The air in this tiny box feels like the moment before a thunderstorm breaks, wild and electric and just a little bit dangerous. Once again, that edict whispers through my mind, as if urging me to drop to my knees right here, right now.

You don't get it until you beg me.

I've spent every minute fighting it—this maddening need that grows stronger with each lingering touch, each heated glance, each moment when he comes close enough that I can feel his breath on my skin but never close enough to satisfy.

It's pride that's kept me from surrendering that last bit of control. But something shifted for me tonight. I wasn't a weak little girl being protected from the crowds and the press. I was Liam's date, his equal. More than that, he gave me the room to be me, something I've never experienced except in stolen moments with Ruby, hidden away in one of our rooms.

But never in public. Never where it mattered.

For years, my father told the world that I was weak. Tonight, Grimm showed me that I can be strong.

"Sasha?"

I look up, surprised as much by his use of my given name as by his soft tone.

"Are you okay?"

"I'm great," I say, wiping away a runaway tear. "It's just—thank you."

He tilts his head, clearly not understanding, but he offers me a gentle smile as the elevator opens directly into a lavish suite that takes my breath away. All cream and gold and crystal, with floor-to-ceiling windows overlooking the city. A marble fireplace anchors one wall of the living area, while an enormous bouquet of white roses dominates a central table. It's elegance and style combined, and yet somehow still promises comfort.

"Welcome to the Celestial Sky Suite," Grimm says, watching my reaction closely. "Too much?"

He actually looks worried, and I find it endearing. "It's beautiful," I assure him, stepping further into the space, then moving through the room, exploring everything. A bottle of champagne waits in an ice bucket, alongside a platter of chocolate-covered strawberries.

I look back to Grimm. "But why here? Why tonight?"

"I told you. We need someplace secure after that encounter with Bane."

"Surely there were about a million other options."

"And," he adds striding toward me, "tomorrow may be trying. I thought you deserved a bit of pampering in advance."

"Oh." My insides go a little gooey. "The hard ass Liam Grimm has a softer side."

The corner of his mouth twitches. "Don't tell."

"Never. But I am curious as to how the press has gotten it so wrong for so many years."

He steps closer, the humor that was just in his eyes shifting to something darker. "They haven't. I am hard, and I can be cruel."

One more step. Then another, then one more until he's only inches away. He reaches out and brushes my cheek. "And I protect what's mine."

It takes me a moment to get my breath back. When I do, I lift a brow. "Ownership, Mr. Grimm?"

"I claimed you, didn't I? Body and soul. *Everything,*" he murmurs. "If that's not ownership, it's pretty damn close."

I shiver, but not from fear. "Yes," I say. "Everything."

His eyes darken at my agreement, and he steps closer, eliminating what little space remained between us. His finger traces my jawline, a touch so light it's barely there, yet it leaves fire in its wake. I expect him to yank me to him, to cup my neck. To kiss me with a force that bruises. Instead, he simply holds out his hand, mischief dancing in those eyes as he politely says, "Let me show you the rest of the suite."

Bastard. But I'm smiling inside as I think it.

I twine my fingers with his, and he leads me to a bedroom dominated by the largest bed I've ever seen, strewn with rose petals and already turned down, as if extending a naughty invitation.

"The honeymoon suite?" I ask, turning to him with raised eyebrows. "Something you need to ask me?"

"It was the most secure option," he says quickly. "And it seemed appropriate."

"Appropriate?"

"After tonight, the whole world will think we're ..."

"A couple?" I supply.

"Fucking, at least."

I nod, wondering if that's really all this is, because I've caught too many hints, too many soft looks, not to at least wonder about the possibilities. Especially since despite all my walls, Liam Grimm has snuck into my heart. At least a little bit.

I'm just not sure I'm ready to tell him so.

I turn away so that he can't read my thoughts on my face, then wander into the bathroom, a marble-and-glass sanctuary larger than the studio in my apartment at Reed Tower. I catch my reflection in the ornate mirror—cheeks flushed, eyes bright with anticipation, the delicate fabric of my gown clinging to curves in a way that would never show up on a Reed Cosmetics' billboard with my father running the show.

When I emerge, Liam has shed his tuxedo jacket and is pouring champagne. It's a simple task, but he looks damn sexy doing it, and my nipples tighten in anticipation of what's to come.

He hands me a glass, and I take a sip, relishing the exquisite flavor and the tiny bubbles that dance on my tongue.

I start to walk toward the windows, then pause.

"Do you want me to close the blinds?" Grimm asks.

I shake my head. "No. But will you walk with me?"

I may never know for certain if my meds treated or caused or exacerbated my various phobias and nervous conditions. If it weren't for the case against my father, I'm not even sure it matters. What I do know is that I've been getting steadily better. Dr. Chen thinks it's because the meds are working their way out of my system, and she's probably right. She's the one with the medical degree after all.

Even so, I choose to believe it's because of Grimm. It's strange and unexpected, but he makes me stronger.

Now, he takes my hand, and we move to the window together. "There's a whole world out there," I say. "I'm twenty-six, and I've hardly seen any of it." I turn from the window to face him. "My father made me a prisoner." Out loud, the words seem absurd, because that's not what fathers do. Unless, of course, they're mine.

"Victor Reed will never control you again."

I'm struck by the certainty in his voice. "You really believe that?"

"I do." His eyes hold mine. "Your father is finished."

The weight of what he's saying settles over me. The possibility of freedom. Real freedom, not just a different kind of cage.

And it all hinges on tomorrow.

No. It hinges on Grimm. Without him, I'd still be trapped in my room. I owe Liam Grimm everything. More than that, I trust him.

I might even love him.

And how completely unexpected is that?

I swallow, finally certain of a decision I've been debating. "Earlier tonight, when you faced down Desmond … that was incredibly brave."

"That was nothing. The man's a worm."

"It wasn't nothing. Not to me."

"Sasha—"

"And telling Leo to stay away from Ruby because I asked you to. That was also important to me."

"He can be a huge ass, and—"

"Let me finish," I say quietly. "You didn't have to do any of it. Our arrangement doesn't require kindness."

He looks uncomfortable with my gratitude, which only confirms my decision. "I want to share something with you. Something no one else knows except Ruby." I glance around the suite. "Where's our luggage?"

He fetches mine, and in a few minutes, I've set up the laptop he'd given me. I think it was Maya's originally, but too bad for her.

"What are you—"

"Elysium," I say as I navigate to the portal. I look up at him and see a flicker of a frown. "What's wrong?"

"Nothing," he says. "I'm just curious what you're up to."

I'm sitting on the sofa, the computer on the coffee table in front of me. I pat the spot next to me. "Come see."

"Elysium," he says as he sits. "What is it?"

There's an edge in his voice—he probably wasn't expecting computer time in a honeymoon suite—but I want to share this with him. I want to show him how much I've come to trust him. With my life, and with my secrets.

"It's a virtual world I created. A place where I could be free, even when I was locked in Reed Tower." I log in, smiling as the familiar gateway appears, the verdant landscape spread out beyond.

"Sasha ... this is impressive."

"Oh, you haven't seen anything yet. I've been building it since I was fifteen."

He leans forward, his expression unreadable as he studies the screen. On it, Vale stands at the gates, a confident, bolder version of myself. Or she used to be. Now, I think I may be catching up to her.

I show him all of it, explaining how there's even a sensory component. "It's been my true home for years."

"It's amazing." It's clear from his tone that he means it. My chest tightens, and in that moment, I realize how much his approval means to me.

"It started as a garden," I tell him. "Just a small space where I could escape. Now it's ... well, you can see."

"You've done incredible work here," he says. "How far does the world extend?"

"Quite a long way, and I'm adding to it all the time. There's something I want to ask you," I admit, after a slight hesitation.

He sits up a bit straighter, looking a tiny bit surprised. "Okay. Shoot."

I nod. "It's just that I've been thinking … there might be commercial applications, but I don't know how to pursue any of that. Things like VR therapy for people with phobias like mine. Safe spaces for trauma survivors. Even just entertainment. Maybe monetize it. Sell parcels of virtual land or build a marketplace for real-time trading. I don't know. I have a lot of ideas to cull through."

He looks at me, his focus shifting from the screen to my face. "You want my help turning it into a business?"

"I think so. Maybe? I don't know the first thing about monetizing something like this."

"And I do."

I nod. "That's why I want your advice." I hesitate, suddenly aware of his proximity, the warmth radiating from his body. The way he's looking at me now has nothing to do with business plans or monetization strategies.

His eyes drop to my lips for a fraction of a second before meeting my gaze again.

"We can talk about all that after the hearing," he says, his voice softer now.

I close the laptop. "You don't want to discuss it now?"

His hand finds mine, fingers intertwining with a casual intimacy that sends a flutter through my stomach. "Sasha," he says, my name like velvet on his tongue, "do you really want to talk business right now?"

The question hangs between us, loaded with meaning. We've been dancing around this tension, this pull between us that goes beyond our arrangement, beyond the terms of our deal.

"No," I admit, my voice barely above a whisper. "That's not what I want."

He reaches up, brushing a strand of hair from my face, his fingers lingering against my cheek. "What do you want?"

The air between us feels charged, electric with possibility. All the restraint of the past, all my stubborn resistance to his begging rule—it all feels distant now, less important than the need building inside me.

"You," I say simply, surprising myself with my directness. "I want you."

His eyes darken at my admission, his thumb brushing my lower lip. "Do you remember what I told you?" he asks, his voice dropping to that register that sends heat pooling low in my belly. "About how to get what you want?"

I nod.

His eyes light with a predatory gleam that sends a dark thrill racing through me. He lifts his hand to my face, his palm warm against my skin as his thumb traces my lower lip in a way that makes it impossible to think clearly. I lean into his touch, my body responding to him with a need that's been building since the moment he laid down his rule.

His kiss is gentle at first, a question rather than a demand. But when I respond, leaning into him, something breaks loose inside him. His arm wraps around my waist, pulling me against him as the kiss deepens into something hungry and fierce.

We've done this before—the heat, the urgency, the desperate coming together of bodies—but tonight feels different. Not just heat, but need. Not a need for sex, but a need for him. As if I'll die in this moment if I can't have this man. Liam Grimm.

He stands, pulling me up beside him, then leads me back to the window. I stand there, my body on fire, as he finds the zipper of my gown, then slowly draws it down. The fabric slips away, pooling at my feet and leaving me in nothing but a strapless bra and lace panties. I should feel exposed, vulnerable, but all I feel is wanted.

His gaze travels over me with such heat and appreciation that it's like a physical caress. "You're so fucking beautiful," he whispers, then pulls me to him, his hands roaming my back, his fingers slipping under the band of my panties, his mouth claiming mine with fervor that makes me think of a starving man finally being served a meal.

I clutch the linen of his shirt, then practically rip the buttons off to get it open. I feel wild, alive, and right now all I want is to feel his skin against mine. He helps me, shrugging out of the fabric before pulling me close again, the heat of his chest burning against me.

His nimble fingers unfasten my strapless bra, and it falls to the ground between us. He's still mostly dressed, whereas I'm in nothing but a scrap of lace pretending to be panties. The asymmetry of our states of undress makes me feel even more exposed, more vulnerable.

He takes a step back, then slowly looks me up and down, his gaze like a physical touch that leaves heat wherever it lands. I start to cover my breasts, the instinct to shield myself from his hungry eyes overwhelming, but I'm halted by his curt, sharp, "No."

The command hits me like a slap, though his voice barely rises above a whisper. My arms freeze mid-motion, suspended awkwardly. The intensity in his eyes steals my breath—raw desire mixed with something possessive that makes my core clench with need.

"Put your hands behind your back," he orders, his voice rough with want. "I want to see what's mine."

Mine. The word sends a shiver through me that has nothing to do with the cool air kissing my naked skin. I obey, clasping my hands behind me, the position thrusting my breasts forward. His eyes darken as they fixate on my hardened nipples.

"Fuck," he breathes, the curse more arousing than it should be. "Do you have any idea what you do to me, Princess?"

He circles me like a predator, his gaze leaving trails of fire across my skin. I can feel the heat of him at my back, his breath stirring the fine hairs at my nape. My body responds shamefully, nipples tightening further, wetness gathering between my thighs.

One finger traces the curve of my spine, sliding lower and lower before teasing me through the lace of my panties. I bite my lip to stifle a moan.

"I can smell how wet you are," he murmurs against my ear, his voice like dark velvet. "Is that all for me, Princess? Is your tight little pussy getting wet just from me looking at you?"

The crude words from his sophisticated mouth send a bolt of pure lust straight to my core. It's deliciously filthy—and arousing— coming from Liam Grimm, the man who speaks in boardrooms with such eloquent precision.

His hands grasp my hips from behind, fingers digging into my flesh as he pulls me back against him. I feel the hard ridge of his cock through his pants, pressing insistently against my ass. He grinds against me slowly, deliberately.

"Feel what you do to me?" His teeth graze my earlobe, sending electric shivers down my spine. "I've been hard for you for so long, Princess. Dreaming of stripping you bare, bending you over, fucking you until you scream my name."

He moves around to face me again, one hand sliding up to circle my throat in a hold that's firm but not constricting. His thumb strokes over my racing pulse as his other hand cups my breast roughly, squeezing until I gasp.

"These perfect tits," he growls, pinching my nipple between his fingers until I whimper. "I've wanted my mouth on them since I first saw you. Wanted to mark this perfect skin, leave evidence that you belong to me."

Without warning, he bends and takes my nipple into his mouth, sucking hard enough to make me cry out. His teeth graze the sensitive peak before he soothes it with his tongue. My knees nearly buckle as pleasure spikes through me.

"Liam," I gasp, my voice barely recognizable, husky with need.

He releases my breast with a wet pop, looking up at me with eyes gone nearly black with desire. "Yes, Princess? Something you want to ask for?"

His hand slides down my stomach, fingers dipping just beneath the waistband of my panties, stopping just short of where I'm aching for him. I can feel how wet I am, how ready. I'm certain he can feel the heat radiating from me.

"These are soaked," he murmurs, tugging at the lace. "I think they're ruined. Should I rip them off you? Or would you rather ask me to take them off?"

I press my thighs together, trying to ease the throbbing ache between them. His hand slides between my legs from the front, cupping me through the damp fabric. I can't help but rock against his palm, desperate for friction.

"Such a needy little cunt," he says, the filthy word making me moan. "But you know the rules, don't you? You don't get to come until you beg me for it."

As I nod, a slow, dangerous smile spreads across his face. "Are you ready for that, Princess? Ready to beg for what you want?"

My heart races, anticipation and desire warring with the last vestiges of my pride. But I know what I want now. "I—" I start, then hesitate.

His expression softens slightly, though the heat in his eyes remains. "It's not surrender," he says, as if reading my thoughts. "It's power. The power to ask for exactly what you want. To claim owner-ship. Hell, to grab control."

His finger traces a line from my collarbone to the center of my chest. "Tell me, Sasha. What do you want?"

My breath catches at his touch. "You."

"Go on," he urges, his finger continuing its journey downward, between my breasts, across my stomach. "Tell me exactly what you want me to do to you."

Heat floods my cheeks, but also pools lower, a liquid warmth between my thighs. "I want—I want you to touch me."

"I am touching you," he says, his finger now tracing the waist-band of my panties. "Is this what you mean?"

"More," I manage, my voice barely audible.

His smile is predatory now. "What was that? I couldn't quite hear you."

"More," I say, louder this time. "I want more."

"Show me," he commands, taking a step back. "Show me how much you want it."

For a moment, I'm frozen, uncertain what he means. Then under-standing dawns, and with it a rush of both embarrassment and arousal. He wants me to kneel. To physically demonstrate my surren-der, my need.

He wants me to get on my knees and beg.

Pride wars with desire, a battle that's been raging since that first night when he laid down his rule. But tonight, desire wins. My eyes never leave his as I sink to my knees before him.

His eyes darken at the sight, his chest rising and falling with quickening breaths. "Fuck, you're beautiful," he murmurs. "Now tell me what you want."

"Please," I whisper, the word finally escaping after weeks of being held captive behind my pride. "Please touch me. Please … everything."

"Again," he demands, his voice hoarse. "Louder."

"Please, Liam," I say, my voice stronger now. "I'm begging you. Please."

In one fluid motion, he pulls me to my feet and into his arms, his mouth claiming mine in a kiss that's all heat and hunger and victory. I surrender to it completely, giving myself over to the sensations that ripple through me as his hands roam my body with newfound possession.

"Mine," he growls against my lips. "All mine."

"Yes." I gasp as his mouth trails down my neck. "Yours."

"Tell me the rest," he demands. "Beg for what you want." He thrusts me backward toward the bed, his movements echoing the urgency I can feel in both of us. When my legs hit the edge, he stops, his hands coming up to cup my face. "Tell me."

"Everything," I whisper. "I want you to fuck me. And—and I want everything."

A devilish smile tugs at his lips. "Are you sure, Princess? Because once we start, I won't stop. Not until you've had everything you begged for."

The promise sends a shiver of anticipation through me. "I'm sure."

He reaches into the nightstand drawer and pulls out a length of black silk. My eyes widen at the sight, a flutter of nervous excitement in my stomach.

"Trust me," he says, not a question but a statement.

I nod, unable to find words as he moves behind me, gently pulling my arms behind my back. The silk is cool and smooth against my skin as he binds my wrists, the knot secure but not painfully tight.

"A pretty package, just for me," he whispers his voice close to my ear.

I close my eyes and moan, surprised by how the restraint heightens every sensation, makes me more aware of my body, of his presence behind me.

"Close your eyes," he orders, and I comply without hesitation.

I feel him move away, then return. Something cool and soft brushes across my collarbone—another piece of silk, I realize, as he uses it to blindfold me.

Darkness envelops me, and I focus on the sound of his breathing, the scent of his cologne, the heat of his body as he moves around me —all somehow more wild and sensual now that I'm in the dark.

"Beautiful," he murmurs as his finger traces the curve of my shoulder, down my arm, then back up. The light touch sends shivers across my skin, my nipples tightening in response. "So beautiful."

His hand tangles in my hair, pulling my head back gently but firmly to expose my throat. His lips press against the sensitive skin there, then move lower, across my collarbone, then lower still until they close around one nipple.

I gasp, arching into the sensation, the inability to use my hands making me feel both helpless and strangely powerful.

"Tell me what you want," he murmurs, his voice soft against my ear.

"Touch me," I whisper. "Please."

His fingers skim over my ribs, tantalizing but avoiding where I need them most. "Here?"

"Higher," I breathe. "Please."

"So polite," he murmurs, his fingers sliding up to cup my breast, thumb brushing over the nipple in a touch so light it's almost painful. "Is that what you want?"

"More," I manage, my voice breaking on the word. "Harder."

His thumb and forefinger pinch gently, and I cry out, the sensation shooting straight to my core. "Like that?"

"Yes," I gasp. "Please, yes."

His other hand slides down to slip beneath the waistband of my panties. I hold my breath, waiting for the touch I've been craving. Desperate for it.

"Tell me," he says. "Beg for it."

"Please," I cry, beyond pride now. Beyond anything but the need burning through me. "Please touch me. I need you. Please, Liam."

His fingers finally, *finally* slide lower, finding the slick heat between my thighs. I moan, my hips bucking into his touch, desperate for more.

"So wet," he murmurs, his voice full of masculine satisfaction. "So ready for me."

He guides me backward until my legs hit the edge of the bed, then eases me down onto it. The feel of the silk sheets against my bare skin is another sensory shock, the coolness a contrast to the heat building inside me.

I feel him tugging at my panties, pulling them down and off

completely, leaving me naked and bound and blindfolded on the bed. The vulnerability should be terrifying, but instead it's liberating. I trust him. Despite everything, despite how we began, I trust him completely.

The bed dips as he joins me, his hands guiding me to lie back against the pillows. I feel him positioning himself between my thighs, his hands sliding up my legs, gently urging them apart.

"Remember," he says, his voice rough with desire, "you asked for this. Begged for it."

"Yes," I whisper, trembling with anticipation.

His mouth moves up my inner thigh, hot and insistent, then higher still until it finds the center of my need. I cry out at the first touch of his tongue, my back arching off the bed.

With my hands bound and my eyes covered, there's nothing to do but feel—the slick heat of his tongue as it explores, the firm pressure of his hands holding my hips in place, the exquisite tension building inside me with each deliberate stroke.

Just when I think I can't bear any more, when I'm teetering on the edge of release, he pulls away. I make a sound of protest that turns into surprise as I feel him shift, the warmth of his body moving up along mine.

"Not yet," he says, his voice at my ear again. "Not until I say."

The command sends another rush of heat through me. This is what I begged for. *Everything*. His possession. His control over my pleasure.

I feel the silk around my wrists loosen as he unties them, but before I can reach for him, he's guiding my arms above my head, securing them to what must be the headboard.

His weight shifts, and I hear the rustle of fabric, the clink of a belt buckle. He's undressing, I realize, and the thought of him naked above me, watching me bound and blindfolded, sends another wave of arousal through me.

The bed dips again as he returns, and this time I feel the heat of his skin against mine, the hard planes of his chest, the undeniable evidence of his desire pressing against my thigh.

"Last chance," he says, his voice strained with the effort of control. "If you want to stop—"

"Don't you dare," I interrupt, lifting my hips in silent invitation. "Please, Liam," I beg. "I need you."

His groan of surrender is the most satisfying sound I've ever heard. In one smooth, hard thrust, he enters me, filling me so hard and so deep that I cry out in response to the sweet pain and brutal pleasure.

For a moment, he's still, allowing me to adjust to the feel of him. Then he begins to move, each thrust deliberate and controlled, building a rhythm that has me straining against my bonds, desperate to touch him, to pull him closer.

"More," I gasp, wrapping my legs around his waist to draw him deeper. "Harder."

He complies, his control fracturing as he drives into me with increasing urgency. One hand slides between us, finding my clit, circling it in time with his thrusts.

The dueling sensations push me over the edge, my release crashing through me in waves of pleasure so intense they border on pain. I cry out his name, my body clenching around his cock as I surrender completely to the ecstasy he's created.

He follows moments later, a groan tearing from his throat as he finds his own completion. His weight collapses onto me, his breath hot against my neck as we both struggle to recover.

After a moment, he shifts to the side, his hands gentle as he removes first the blindfold, then the bonds at my wrists. I blink in the dim light, my eyes finding his, surprised by the tenderness I see there.

"I like having you bound. At my mercy" The words are hard, a contrast to the fingers softly brushing a strand of hair from my face.

"I like it, too," I whisper. And it's true. I'd willingly given up control, but not only had it been the stark opposite of terrifying, it was also empowering. Because I was the one who'd given it up. It wasn't taken from me, ripped away without my consent. I'd surrendered willingly, and in doing that, I'd found a new kind of bliss.

He gathers me against him, his arm a warm weight across my waist, his heartbeat a steady rhythm beneath my ear. We lie in comfortable silence, our bodies twined, our skin hot. The city lights twinkle beyond the windows, casting patterns across the ceiling.

His arms tighten around me, and I feel him press a kiss to the top of my head. "You're perfect," he murmurs, the words soft enough that I wonder if I was meant to hear them.

I drift toward sleep, wrapped in his warmth, more content than I can ever remember being.

Tomorrow brings uncertainty—the hearing, my father, the public scrutiny—but tonight, in this moment, I'm exactly where I want to be. In the arms of a man who demanded everything and gave me more in return than I ever thought possible.

THIRTY-FOUR
SILKEN CHAINS

S he was glorious in the ambient light from the city, all soft curves and delicate strength, her body a map he intended to memorize with hands and lips and tongue.

Liam watched her sleep, her golden hair spilling across the white pillow, her breathing deep and even. Her lips were still slightly swollen from his kisses, and marks from the silk bonds lingered faintly on her wrists. The sight of those marks sent a surge of possessive satisfaction through him, a primal response he hadn't expected to feel so strongly.

He'd played bondage games before, but it had been only one more item in his bag of sexual tricks. With Sasha ... well, with her it had been a *fuck you* to her father.

Liam may have bound her, but he hadn't caged her. On the contrary, he'd given her a sanctuary where she could finally let go. Her father's control had stolen her choices—his offered her the freedom to surrender them willingly.

And in that surrender, he hoped that she'd found something her father could never take away again—her own power.

She'd given him one hell of a gift, too. She'd trusted him. Completely. And that realization was both exhilarating and humbling.

Now, the room was quiet except for the soft sound of her breathing and the distant hum of the city outside. He reached out, unable to resist tracing the curve of her shoulder with his fingertips. He saw the small scar from that damn tracker and frowned. He'd found someone in London who could remove it without triggering the mechanism her bastard of a father had built into the device. A fail-safe that emitted a burst of poison upon tampering—and thank God Leo had managed to bribe the right people to acquire that information.

They'd take a trip and take care of that once things calmed down. In the meantime, he'd given her a dampener to keep in her purse or pocket.

Reed had tried to get her back. He'd failed.

He was going to fail again at the hearing.

He had to. Because if Victor Reed prevailed at that hearing, then Liam would have to kill both Reed and Bane. Because there was no way he'd let either of those men get close to Sasha again. "Not ever," he whispered. "I promise you that."

She murmured something in her sleep that might have been his name, and his heart squeezed, just like a sixteen-year-old boy with a crush on the cheerleader.

What the hell was he doing?

This was supposed to have been so straightforward. Use Sasha Reed to get to her father. Take his revenge for what Victor had done to his mother. Simple. Clean. Uncomplicated by feelings.

But nothing about this was simple anymore.

He thought back to that moment when she'd shown him Elysium —her eyes bright with pride as she navigated through the world she'd created. He'd watched her write code for years, witnessed her brilliance firsthand in that virtual world. But he'd convinced himself she was complicit in her father's schemes, a willing participant in the lies about his family.

"I had you all wrong," he'd told her, and it was true. Not about her intelligence—he'd always known that was exceptional. But about her heart. He'd expected Victor Reed's willing accomplice and found a prisoner instead. Someone who'd survived her father's control without losing herself.

She was extraordinary.

And damned if he wasn't falling for her.

Falling?

No. He was already there.

The realization hit him with the force of a physical blow. He'd been so focused on his endgame—destroying Victor Reed—that he hadn't noticed when Sasha had become more than just a means to that end. When she'd become essential. Not because of what she could do for him, but because of who she was.

He slipped out of bed, careful not to wake her. The suite was silent and dark except for the city lights streaming through the floor-to-ceiling windows. He moved to the window, looking out at the glittering skyline, at Reed Tower in the distance—a monument to Victor Reed's ego and ambition.

His hands clenched into fists at his sides. Everything he'd worked for was within reach. Years of planning, of gathering evidence, of building the perfect case against Victor Reed. The man who had destroyed his mother, who had turned him into a pariah in his own family. The man who had made him what he was.

And now, standing on the precipice of victory, he was risking it all for Victor Reed's daughter.

The irony was almost painful.

Behind him, Sasha shifted in the bed, the sheets rustling softly. He turned to look at her, struck again by how vulnerable she appeared in sleep. In waking, she was all fire and determination, a fighter to her core despite the gilded cage her father had built around her. But in sleep, the armor fell away, revealing the woman beneath.

The woman he cared for far more than he'd ever intended.

He ran a hand through his hair, frustrated with his own weakness. He couldn't afford distractions, not now. Not when they were so close to bringing Reed down once and for all.

Except Sasha was no mere distraction. She'd become his partner in this crusade, a woman with her own stake in seeing her father brought to justice. She'd proven herself time and again—brave, resilient, and far smarter than anyone had given her credit for.

Including him.

The memory of her body beneath his hands sent heat coursing through him. The erotic brush of her hair over his skin, the way she'd arched into his touch, the sound of his name on her lips as she'd begged him—finally, gloriously begged him—for release. The trust in her eyes when he'd bound her wrists, when he'd blindfolded her, when he'd pushed her to the edge of her comfort and found her eager to leap.

The way she'd surrendered to him completely, and in doing so, had somehow claimed a piece of him in return.

It wasn't supposed to be like this. He was supposed to remain detached, in control. Using her, yes, but never becoming entangled. Never developing feelings.

Never wanting more than the terms of their agreement.

With a sigh, he moved to the bar and poured himself a whiskey. The amber liquid caught the city lights as he swirled it in the glass, thinking of all the ways this could go wrong.

Victor could win the guardianship hearing. Desmond Bane could make good on his thinly veiled threats. The evidence they'd gathered could prove insufficient. Or they could succeed—and then what? What happened when their shared mission was complete? When the bonds that had brought them together no longer existed?

What happened when she no longer needed his protection?

What happened if he lost her?

No.

He drained the whiskey in one swallow, welcoming the familiar burn. He was getting ahead of himself. One problem at a time. First, they had to win the hearing. Then they could deal with the rest.

He poured another drink, remembering the moment when she'd finally begged, shattering the last barrier between them. He hadn't expected the rush of triumph, the surge of possessiveness that had overtaken him. The driving need to mark her as his, to claim her so completely she'd never forget who she belonged to.

It had been primal, almost frightening in its intensity. He'd never felt that way with any other woman. Never needed to possess, to own, to keep.

But with Sasha, the need was visceral. Undeniable.

He wouldn't lose her. She was his. He knew it in his gut even if his brain was slow to lock it in.

She was his. Not because of their bargain, but because she'd chosen to be. Because she trusted him. Because she'd given herself to him completely, with eyes wide open.

The weight of that trust was both exhilarating and terrifying.

A soft sound from the bedroom drew his attention back to the present. Sasha was stirring, reaching across the empty sheets. Her eyes finding him in the shadows.

"Grimm?" Her voice was thick with sleep, vulnerable in a way that made his chest tighten. "Are you okay?"

He moved back to the bed, setting his glass on the nightstand. "Just thinking," he said, sliding in beside her.

She shifted closer, her body warm and soft against his. "About tomorrow?"

"Among other things."

She propped herself up on one elbow, studying his face in the dim light. The glorious hair he loved so much fell like a curtain of light around her shoulders. He lifted a strand, then twined it idly through his fingers, relishing the soft, feathery feel of it.

"You're worried."

"Cautious," he corrected. "There's a lot at stake."

She nodded, her eyes never leaving his. "For both of us."

There was a question in her voice, one he wasn't ready to answer. Not yet. Not when he was still grappling with his own conflicted feelings.

Instead, he reached for her, pulling her against him. She came willingly, settling into his arms as if she belonged there. As if this wasn't just an arrangement, a transaction between enemies who had found a common cause.

As if they were something more.

"Sleep," he said, his voice rougher than he intended. "Tomorrow's going to be a long day."

She nodded against his chest, her breathing gradually slowing as she drifted back into slumber. He lay awake, holding her, his mind racing with all the ways this could end.

With victory. With defeat.

With her walking away. With her staying.

He wasn't sure which possibility terrified him more.

Gently, he rubbed his thumb across her wrist. The silk had been his idea, a test of how far she'd trust him. He hadn't expected her to surrender so completely, to give herself over to him with such absolute faith. He certainly hadn't expected how much that surrender would affect him.

He needed her. Not just her body, not just her value as leverage against her father. *Her.*

The realization was unwelcome. Dangerous. A complication he couldn't afford, not with so much at stake.

And yet, as she shifted in her sleep, murmuring his name and pressing closer, he couldn't bring himself to pull away. Couldn't deny the warmth that spread through him at the sound of his name on her lips, even in sleep.

He was in trouble. Deep, inescapable trouble.

Because for the first time in his life, he wanted something more than revenge. He wanted her. Not just for now, not just as a weapon against her father, but for … longer. Perhaps for always.

The thought should have sent him running. Instead, he found himself holding her tighter, as if he could physically keep her from slipping away.

Tomorrow would bring its own challenges. The hearing. Victor Reed. Desmond Bane. The battle they'd both been preparing for.

But tonight, she was his. Completely, unreservedly his. And for now, that was enough.

Or so he told himself as sleep finally claimed him, his arms still wrapped protectively around the woman who had somehow become essential to his existence.

The woman who might very well be his undoing.

THIRTY-FIVE
MOLTEN LAVA

The morning brings with it a strange sense of peace. I've been awake for a while now, watching Liam move naked around the room, his thoughts clearly on the day ahead. There's something vulnerable about him in these quiet moments, something softer beneath all that controlled power.

"We should get dressed," I say, though I burrow deeper into the warmth of the bed. "The hearing is in a few hours." I draw a breath, amazed at how casually I'd said those words. *The hearing is in a few hours.* As if this wasn't important. As if the outcome of this hearing has nothing to do with the rest of my life.

"We still have a little time before we need to leave," he says. He bends over me, his mouth finding a sensitive spot beneath my ear. I moan, my entire body shivering in response. How the hell does he do this? Turn me to molten lava with just a touch? Make my mind go blank with just the brush of his lips?

"Grimm," I whisper, his name somewhere between a protest and a plea.

He takes it as encouragement, his palm sliding up to cup my breast, thumb circling my nipple until it tightens, aching for more. I arch my back, pushing into his touch, and hear myself make a sound I barely recognize.

"Tell me to stop," he whispers, even as his free hand glides between my thighs, finding me already slick and wanting.

"Don't you dare," I manage, twisting in his arms to face him, then reaching for him, my fingers tangling in his hair as I draw him close for a kiss. He responds immediately, his hands teasing, his mouth claiming. But not wild, not desperate. This is languid and exploring, as if the world outside this bed doesn't exist. His tongue teases mine, his hands charting my body like he's committing every curve and hollow to memory.

He rolls me onto my back, settling his weight over me. The pressure of him against me feels both sheltering and thrilling. I wrap my legs around his hips, pulling him closer, feeling the hard length of him pressing exactly where I need him.

"Is this what you want?" he asks, his voice rough with desire.

I nod, my body clenching with a need so basic it bypasses thought entirely.

He reaches between us, positioning himself, then pushes inside with one slow, deliberate thrust that steals my breath. My back arches off the bed, my body stretching to take him.

"Christ, Sasha," he groans, his forehead pressing against mine. "The way you feel ..."

He begins to move, each stroke measured and deep, his eyes locked on mine with an intensity that burns away any pretense. This isn't just fucking; it's something else—something deeper. Part of me wants to look away, to hide from how exposed I feel. But a stronger part wants to surrender completely to this man who's somehow gotten past every defense I've built.

I match his rhythm, lifting my hips to meet each thrust, my hands roaming the hard planes of his back, the curve of his shoulders, the strong column of his neck. He's magnificent in his focus, his control, the way he watches me with those predator's eyes as he drives me steadily toward release.

"That's it," he urges as my breathing fractures, my movements growing erratic. "Let go for me."

The pleasure coils tighter and tighter until I'm clinging to him, desperate for something just beyond reach. When it finally breaks, it crashes through me like a wave, my body clenching around him as I cry out his name.

He follows soon after, his rhythm faltering, a low groan torn from deep in his chest as he drives deep one final time. For a long moment, we stay locked together, trembling, our ragged breaths the only sound.

Eventually, he rolls to the side but keeps me close, his arm heavy across my waist. I rest my cheek on his chest, listening to the gradually slowing thud of his heart.

"We really should get up now," I say, though I make no move to leave the warm nest we've created.

"Five more minutes."

I smile against his skin, content to steal this small reprieve from the day ahead. The hearing looms, with all its potential for humiliation and exposure. But right now, in this bed, none of that seems real.

"Are you ready for today?" he asks when our stolen minutes have elapsed.

I sigh, hating reality's intrusion. "As ready as I'll ever be. I've been waiting years for this, even if I didn't realize it."

"You'll be brilliant. Just tell the truth—everything from your affidavit. Explain what he did to control you, the drugs, all of it."

"He'll deny everything. He'll try to make me look unbalanced."

"He won't get the chance," Liam says, his voice hardening. "And he couldn't succeed if he tried. We have the evidence. We have Dr. Chen. We have statements from staff who've quit. We even have the whistleblower from his company. He can't squirm out of this one."

I want to believe him. God, I do. But after watching my father manipulate every situation to his advantage for twenty-six years, it's hard to trust that this time will be different.

"What if we lose?" I ask, voicing my deepest fear. "What if the judge believes him?"

Liam shifts, propping himself on one elbow to look down at me. His expression is fierce, almost feral. "That won't happen. But if it did, I wouldn't let him take you back. Ever."

The intensity in his voice should frighten me. Instead, it makes me feel strangely anchored, as if I've finally found solid ground after years adrift.

"How can you be so certain?" I ask.

Something flickers across his face—a shadow I can't quite identify. "Because I don't lose."

It's hardly a romantic declaration, but there's something in the way he says it—in the possessive gleam in his eyes—that makes my pulse quicken. This man, with all his darkness and determination, has positioned himself between me and my father. Whether it's for revenge or something more doesn't seem to matter quite as much anymore.

"My knight in tarnished armor," I say, trying to lighten the moment.

His mouth quirks up at one corner. "More like the dragon who stole the princess."

"I went willingly, remember?"

"Did you?" His voice drops, his hand sliding down my side to rest on my hip. "Even knowing what I wanted from you?"

Everything. The word hangs between us, unspoken but almost tangible.

"Yes," I say, meeting his gaze. "I knew exactly what I was agreeing to."

He studies me for a long moment, as if trying to read something written in a language he's only starting to understand. Then he leans down and kisses me—not the heated, desperate kiss of before, but something gentler, almost reverent.

When he pulls back, there's a vulnerability in his eyes I've never seen. He masks it quickly, but I caught it—a glimpse behind the armor he wears so effortlessly.

"We should get ready," he says, voice deliberately casual as he slides from the bed. "Jack will be waiting with the legal team."

I watch him move across the room, morning light sculpting his naked body into something that belongs in a museum. The sight of him still makes my breath catch, even after everything we've shared.

He pauses at the bathroom door. "Whatever happens today," he says, voice low and serious, "remember that he can't hurt you anymore. Not while I'm here."

The words settle over me like a blanket, warm and comforting. It's not a declaration of love—not even close. But it's a promise of protection, of standing together against whatever comes. And right now, that feels like exactly what I need.

As I hear the shower start, I stretch lazily, savoring the pleasant ache in muscles that have been thoroughly used. Today, my father faces justice for what he's done. Today, the world learns the ugly truth behind Reed Cosmetics' perfect princess.

Today, I take back my life.

And with Liam Grimm at my side—this complicated, dangerous man who's become my unlikely ally—I might actually have a chance of winning.

I slide from the bed and pad toward the bathroom, steam already billowing from the door. One more moment of connection before we face the storm that's coming. One more chance to feel alive and chosen, rather than controlled and used.

Tomorrow, I'll worry about what happens next.

But for now, I step into the shower and into Liam's waiting arms, surrendering to the moment and to the man who's turned my world upside down.

For better or worse, we're in this together.

THIRTY-SIX
EX PARTE

REED HEIRESS AND GRIMM BLACK SHEEP: ROMANCE OR REVENGE?

The headline screams at me from a dozen tablets and phones as the town car pulls into the courthouse parking lot. Apparently, our kiss at Alexander's party made quite the splash. Beneath the lurid text is a photo of Liam and me on the rooftop, his hand cupping my face, my body leaning into his, our lips meeting in a kiss that looks far more cinematic than it felt at the time.

"Well, they certainly aren't shying away from being bold," Liam says, his voice carefully casual as he scans the massive crowd gathered outside.

My hands twist in my lap, anxiety tightening in my chest. I'd expected reporters, of course. Even a few curious onlookers. What I hadn't anticipated was this—dozens, maybe hundreds, of people lining the walkway to the courthouse steps, many holding handmade signs.

SASHA STRONG

BELIEVE SURVIVORS

#FREETHEREEDHEIRESS

"What is this?" I whisper, unable to turn away from the spectacle.

Liam reaches for my hand, his fingers steady as they wrap around mine. "Public opinion," he says. "Looks like someone leaked enough details to turn you into a cause. People are on your side, Princess."

I turn to him, and his teasing smile just about melts me. "Thank you."

"For what?"

I shake my head. "I don't know. I guess, for ... everything."

The word hangs there, unexpected but true in so many ways.

"Yeah," he says, his voice like a caress. "You're welcome."

He cups my face. "Don't be nervous. I can't sit with you, but I promise I am with you."

"I know," I say, realizing in the moment how deeply I mean it.

The car slows to a stop, and I catch sight of Ruby pushing toward us through the crowd, her auburn hair a beacon in the sea of faces. The door opens, and she's there, reaching for me with both hands.

"Ready?" she asks, her eyes bright with a mixture of determination and concern.

"As I'll ever be." I grimace then slide out of the car to stand on trembling legs.

The moment I emerge, a cheer goes up from the crowd. It's so unexpected that I freeze, my hand still in Ruby's, my heart racing like a trapped bird in my chest. These people—these strangers—are here for me. Supporting me. Believing me.

A young woman pushes to the front, clutching what looks like a magazine. "Ms. Reed! I just wanted to say thank you. Your story gave me the courage to leave my shit of a boyfriend."

Before I can respond, others press forward, their voices overlapping.

"We're with you, Sasha!"

"My sister has agoraphobia, too—what your father did is criminal!"

"You deserve to be free!"

Ruby squeezes my hand, and I realize I'm crying. Silent tears tracking down my cheeks as the enormity of what's happening washes over me. For so long, I've been isolated, cut off from the world by my father's machinations. I never imagined that my story would resonate with so many, that my pain might somehow help others find their voice.

Grimm appears at my other side, his arm sliding protectively around my waist. "We need to move," he says, his voice low in my ear. "Jack's waiting inside."

I nod, letting him guide me through the crowd. People reach out, touching my arm, my shoulder, offering words of encouragement as we pass. It's overwhelming, but not in the way open spaces usually are. This feels like being carried forward on a wave of support.

As we near the courthouse steps, I spot a smaller group off to the side—men in expensive suits, a few women with impeccable blowouts and designer handbags. Their signs are different:

VICTOR REED: LOVING FATHER

THE GRIMM AGENDA EXPOSED

"Idiots," Ruby mutters, her grip on my hand tightening. "Ignore them."

I try, but their hostile stares bore into me as we climb the steps. One of the women calls out, "How much is Grimm paying you to lie about your own father?"

I falter, but Liam's hand presses into the small of my back, steady and grounding. "Keep walking," he says. "They don't matter."

Inside, the courthouse is a maze of marble and dark wood, the air cool and slightly musty. I spot Desmond Bane in the corridor, speaking in low tones with one of my father's lawyers. When he sees us, he offers that predatory smile I've come to dread. But as the lawyer leans in to whisper something in his ear, Bane's expression shifts. His eyes narrow, calculating, and with a curt nod in our direction, he turns and walks toward the exit.

"Where's he going?" I whisper to Liam.

"Not sure," he replies, his expression thoughtful. "But Bane doesn't waste time on lost causes. If he's leaving …"

I catch his meaning immediately. "You think my father isn't coming."

"It's possible. Bane is nothing if not pragmatic." A hint of satisfaction creeps into Liam's voice. "Rats and sinking ships."

A chill runs through me at the implication. If my father isn't here to defend himself …

Jack Granger, our lead attorney, waits for us in a small conference room, surrounded by stacks of documents and several associates.

"There you are," he says, rising to his feet. Silver-haired and impeccably dressed, Jack exudes confidence like expensive cologne. "Quite the crowd out there."

"Is my father here?" I ask, the question slipping out before I can stop it.

Jack's expression shifts slightly. "No sign of him yet. His legal team arrived about twenty minutes ago, but Reed himself hasn't been seen."

Something cold and heavy settles in my stomach. "What does that mean?"

"It could mean many things," Jack says, his words measured. "Most likely, he's planning a strategic entrance. Or perhaps he's trying to avoid the press."

Liam's jaw tightens. "Or he's planning something else entirely."

Jack nods, his expression grim. "We've filed additional motions this morning in light of the evidence from Dr. Chen. If Reed doesn't appear, we're prepared to argue for an immediate ruling in your favor, along with a referral to the district attorney's office for criminal charges."

The words wash over me, technical and distant. All I can think about is my father's absence. This isn't like him—he never concedes a battlefield, never surrenders control.

"What if he wins?" I whisper, voicing my deepest fear. "What if the judge believes him?"

Liam moves closer, his voice dropping so only I can hear. "That won't happen. But even if it does, I won't let him take you back. Ever. I told you. I promise you that."

I don't answer, but I hold his hand tighter, feeling safer in the circle of his protection.

"I'm going to check on something," Ruby says, squeezing my hand once more before slipping out of the room. Her absence leaves a void, and I fight the urge to call her back, to keep my small circle of allies close.

We take our seats around the small table, and Jack continues briefing us on the legal strategy, but the words blur together. I focus instead on breathing, on keeping the rising panic at bay. In a few hours, my life will change irrevocably. Either I'll be free of my father's control forever, or I'll be legally declared incompetent, placed under his guardianship, and dragged back to a prison of medication and forced compliance.

"Sasha?" Liam's voice cuts through my spiraling thoughts. "Did you hear what Jack asked?"

I blink, focusing on the attorney's concerned face. "I'm sorry, what?"

"I asked if you're prepared for the possibility that your father might make accusations against Mr. Grimm," Jack repeats. "He may try to paint your relationship as coercive, suggest that you've been manipulated or even drugged."

A bitter laugh escapes me. "That would be ironic."

"Indeed," Jack agrees with a slight smile. "But the court needs to hear the truth from you—that you left willingly, that Mr. Grimm has been protecting you, not controlling you."

The truth. Such a simple concept, yet so complicated in this situation. I did leave willingly with Grimm, but our arrangement was hardly straightforward. And while he hasn't controlled me the way my father did, there was a bargain struck, a price to be paid.

Everything.

But that was then. Now, looking at Grimm—at the tension in his jaw, the concern in his eyes—I see with perfect clarity how much has changed between us. Whatever his initial motives, whatever price he demanded, what exists between us now is something else entirely.

"I'll tell the truth," I say firmly. "All of it."

Jack nods, satisfied, and returns to his documents. Liam's hand finds mine under the table, his fingers interlacing with my own in a gesture that feels simultaneously possessive and supportive.

Ruby returns, her face flushed with excitement. "You're not going to believe this," she says, closing the door behind her. "The staff from Reed Tower—I mean, a lot of them—they're here. In the courtroom. Mr. Williams, Anita, at least a dozen more. Grannie, too, of course."

I stare at her, stunned. "They're here?"

"They want to support you. And some of them are prepared to testify about what they saw—the medications, the way your father controlled everything."

A lump forms in my throat. These people have come—risking their livelihoods—to support me. It's more than incredible, it's humbling.

"It's time," Jack announces, checking his watch. "They're ready for us."

The walk to the courtroom feels like a march to the gallows. My legs are wooden, my breathing shallow. Grimm stays close, his presence both comforting and electrifying.

As we approach the courtroom doors, Liam stops me with a gentle hand on my arm. "Remember," he says, his voice low and intense, "no matter what happens in there, you're not alone."

For a moment, we just look at each other, the world narrowing to the space between us. Then Ruby clears her throat, and the moment shatters.

"Ready?" she asks.

I nod, squaring my shoulders. "Ready."

The courtroom is smaller than I expected, more intimate, which somehow makes it more intimidating. Two tables face the judge's bench—ours, where Jack is already arranging his materials, and my father's, which remains conspicuously vacant except for three attorneys in identical dark suits.

I scan the gallery, my breath catching when I see the familiar faces from Reed Tower. I give them a small smile, and Birgit, Ruby's grandmother who did more to raise me than my own father, blows me a kiss.

"All rise," the bailiff calls, and we stand as Judge Harlow takes her seat. She's a formidable woman with sharp eyes that seem to miss nothing.

Her gaze sweeps the room. "Where is Mr. Reed and his counsel?"

One of the dark-suited men at the other table rises. "Your Honor, I'm David Mercer, representing Mr. Reed. I regret to inform the court that my client has been unavoidably detained. We request a continuance of—"

"Denied," Judge Harlow cuts in, her voice crisp. "This hearing has been scheduled for weeks. Mr. Reed was well aware of the date and time. We will proceed."

A ripple of whispers passes through the gallery. I feel a surge of hope, quickly tempered by caution. My father's absence is unexpected, worrying. He never cedes control willingly, never misses an opportunity to paint himself as the concerned, devoted parent.

"In light of the petitioner's absence," Judge Harlow continues, "we'll proceed with review of the submitted evidence."

What follows is both less and more dramatic than I expected.

There's no confrontation with my father, no chance to see his face when he realizes he's lost control of me forever. Instead, Judge Harlow methodically reviews the evidence both sides have submitted —my father's collection of videos showing me at various public events, clinical assessments from doctors in his employ, and on our side, footage from Alexander's party, testimonials from Ruby and others, and most damning of all, the lab results showing the cocktail of experimental drugs that had been in my system, not to mention the testimony of Dr. Chen and the affidavit of our whistleblower as to the details of Project Recall.

I sit straight-backed throughout, feeling strangely disconnected from the proceedings. It's my life being dissected, my autonomy being decided, yet it all has a surreal quality, as if I'm watching someone else's story unfold.

"Ms. Reed," Judge Harlow says suddenly, drawing me back to the present. "Would you stand, please?"

I rise on legs that feel less steady than I'd like, Liam's hand supportive at my elbow.

"I've reviewed all the evidence before me," she says, looking directly at me in a way that makes me feel both seen and exposed. "Including the medical reports, the witness statements, and the footage from various events. Based on my assessment, I see a young woman who has been systematically medicated without her informed consent, whose fundamental rights have been violated, and who has demonstrated clear competence when free from such influence."

My heart begins to race, hope rising cautiously within me.

"It is the finding of this court that Sasha Reed is fully competent to manage her own affairs and requires no legal guardian. Further-more," she continues, her voice hardening, "I am forwarding all evidence of Victor Reed's actions to the district attorney's office with a strong recommendation that criminal charges be pursued."

The words wash over me in a wave of disbelief and relief. Just like that, it's over. I'm free. Legally, officially free from my father's control.

"Congratulations, Ms. Reed," Judge Harlow says with the faintest hint of a smile. "This case is dismissed."

The courtroom erupts in controlled chaos as reporters rush for the doors, eager to break the news. Grimm's arm wraps around my waist, grounding me as the reality of what just happened begins to sink in.

"We won," I whisper, the words feeling foreign on my tongue. I've spent so long expecting to lose that victory feels almost disorienting.

"We won," Grimm confirms, pressing a kiss to my temple. "You won, Princess."

Ruby rushes up to me, her face alight with joy. "You did it!" she exclaims, pulling me into a fierce hug. She shoots a wary glance toward where Leo Grimm holds court across the room, then returns her attention to me, her expression still gleeful, but now her eyes are haunted.

I squeeze her hand in solidarity, then turn to Jack, who's gathering his materials with the satisfied air of a man who's just done exactly what he was paid handsomely to do. "Thank you," I say, knowing the words can never express how much I appreciate all his work and support.

"My pleasure, Ms. Reed," he replies, shaking my hand. "Though I suspect your father's absence indicates we haven't seen the last of this particular battle."

The thought sends a chill through me despite the warmth of the courtroom. Where is Father? What is he planning?

"Ms. Reed." A man in an expensive suit approaches, his manner deferential but urgent. "Charles Whitmore, Reed Cosmetics board member. A moment of your time?"

Ruby squeezes my hand as Grimm seems to appear from nowhere to slide in front of me, his posture protective. "This isn't the time or place for business discussions."

"It's important," Whitmore insists, his gaze fixed on me. "In light of your father's ... absence and the court's ruling, there are decisions that need to be made regarding the company leadership."

"What are you talking about?"

Whitmore looks genuinely surprised. "You're the primary shareholder of Reed Cosmetics."

I look between him and Grimm. "I think you must be mistaken."

He shakes his head, looking disgusted. "I never cared for your father, Miss Reed. If today has proven anything, it's that my instincts are still sharp." He gestures toward one of the tables in front of the bench.

Grimm raises a brow, and I understand the silent question—Shall I get you out of this?

I reply with the smallest shake of my head, then take a seat at the table, with Mr. Whitmore across from me and Grimm at my side.

"The controlling shares of Reed Cosmetics belonged to your mother," he says. "It was she who conceived of the company and fought to not only create it but to build it from the ground up. And she, of course, was the majority shareholder. The company holds the Reed name, but it's not a subsidiary of Reed Industries as your father often suggests. Quite the opposite. Reed Cosmetics is the majority shareholder of Reed Industries, a company Victor set up after Reed Cosmetics took off in the market."

I can only gape at him. "Why do I not know any of this?"

Mr. Whitmore meets my eyes. "Your father was good at keeping his secrets. But the point is that when your mother died, you inherited those shares. As you were a minor, the shares were held in trust with your father acting as proxy. Now that you've been declared legally competent, control reverts to you directly. You're effectively the CEO and majority shareholder of Reed Cosmetics. And, by default, of Reed Industries as well."

The information hits me like a physical blow. My mother owned the company? All these years, I'd thought Reed Cosmetics was my father's creation, the shining, most profitable jewel in the family jewel box.

"My mother's company," I whisper, the words bringing both pain and a strange, unexpected comfort. Something of hers has found its way back to me, across the years and through all my father's lies.

"Your mother was quite a visionary," Whitmore says. "Though to be fair, your father did expand the business considerably after her death. The board is prepared to convene an emergency meeting as soon as you're available."

A gift from my mother. A connection to her that my father had hidden from me, just like he'd hidden the truth about her death. Tears prick at my eyes, a complicated mix of grief and gratitude washing through me.

The room seems to tilt as emotions swirl around me, the strain of the day catching up with me. Liam's hand tightens on mine.

"Not today," he says firmly to Whitmore. "She'll contact you when she's ready."

Whitmore looks like he wants to argue, but something in Liam's expression makes him think better of it. "Of course," he says, handing me a business card. "At your convenience, Ms. Reed. But I urge you not to delay. Reed Cosmetics—or perhaps I should say Lydia's legacy—is a multi-billion-dollar enterprise, and a leadership vacuum creates ... opportunities for others. We'll keep this away from the press for now, but under the circumstances, I would expect a leak. And Ms. Reed, be careful. Your father is a man with a quick temper. As, I fear, you already know."

He turns without waiting for my reply. As he walks away, I turn to Grimm, my head spinning. "Did you know about this?"

"Not a bit," he admits. "But it makes sense. Victor Reed could never have built something so successful on his own."

"I don't know anything about running a cosmetics empire," I say, panic edging into my voice. "I can't—"

"Hey." He cups my face in his hands, forcing me to focus on him. "One thing at a time. Right now, Reed Cosmetics and Reed Industries have excellent management. They'll be fine. We, however, need to get out of here."

He's right. The courtroom is filling with more reporters, all clamoring for a statement, for a photo, for a piece of the sensational story that's unfolding. Ruby presses close on my other side, forming a human barrier as we make our way toward the exit.

We make it as far as the courthouse steps before the full force of the media descends. Cameras flash, voices overlap, and a cacophony of questions are tossed at me.

"Ms. Reed! How does it feel to be declared legally competent?"

"Mr. Grimm! Is this romance a cover for a corporate merger between Reed Cosmetics and Grimm International?"

"Sasha! Will you be pressing charges against your father?"

As we push through the crowd, a tall dark-haired woman intercepts us, flashing a badge.

"Ms. Reed," she says, her expression professional but sympathetic. "I'm Detective Ramirez. I wanted to inform you that an arrest warrant has been issued for Victor Reed. We're actively searching for him now."

The news hits me with mixed emotions—vindication, yes, but also a hollow sort of grief for what might have been in another life, with another kind of father.

"Do you have any idea where he might be?" she asks. "Any properties he might go to ground in?"

I shake my head, the reality of my father as a fugitive still too strange to fully grasp. "If Victor doesn't want to be found, he won't be," I say. "He's very good at controlling his environment."

The detective nods, handing me her card. "If you think of anything, please call. And Ms. Reed? We're prepared to provide increased security around you until your father is apprehended."

"That won't be necessary," Grimm says. "We've got her covered."

She nods, then moves away.

Grimm turns his focus to me. "You okay?"

"I think so," I say even though I'm not entirely sure. Everything is happening so fast, the ground shifting beneath my feet almost too quickly to navigate.

We continue pushing through the crowd, but our progress is slow. More supporters have gathered, their signs and chants creating a colorful, noisy backdrop to the chaos.

"Ms. Reed!" A young woman breaks through the press line, her expression earnest. "Now that you've learned your mother founded Reed Cosmetics, will you be continuing her vision or taking the company in a new direction?"

I glance at Grimm, amazed that news is already out in the world.

"Is this a merger of America's two biggest cosmetics dynasties?"

"Are the rumors of your elopement with Liam Grimm true?"

The questions come too fast, from too many directions, and I feel myself starting to shut down. My breathing becomes shallow, my vision narrowing to pinpricks of light. I have no idea if this is a panic attack from my phobias or simply fallout from the weight of the day. It doesn't matter. All I know is I need to get away.

"That's enough," Liam's voice cuts through the noise, firm and unyielding. "Ms. Reed has no comment at this time."

He signals to someone in the crowd—security, I realize—and suddenly there's a path clearing for us, leading to a waiting car with tinted windows. Ruby squeezes my hand once more before melting back into the crowd, promising to call me later.

Inside the car, the silence is abrupt and almost shocking after the chaos outside. I sink into the leather seat, exhaustion washing over me in waves.

"Breathe," Liam says softly beside me. "It's over. You won."

I nod, unable to form words yet. The car pulls away from the curb, leaving the courthouse and its circus behind. I watch the city pass by in a blur of steel and glass, trying to process everything that's happened today.

Free. I'm legally free from my father's control, he's a fugitive, wanted by the police, and somehow, I'm now in charge of my mother's company—a legacy I never knew existed, a connection to her that had been hidden from me all these years.

"I had no idea," I say finally, my voice barely above a whisper. "About my mother. The company. Any of it."

Liam's hand finds mine, his fingers warm and solid. "Your father is very good at hiding the truth."

A laugh escapes me, sharp and hollow. "That's the understatement of the century."

"What will you do?" he asks. "About the company?"

I shake my head, the question too enormous to contemplate right now. "I don't know. I never imagined … I mean, it was hers. All this time, I thought it was his creation, his legacy. But it was my mother's vision. Her dream."

The realization brings a fresh wave of grief and wonder. He stole her life, her vision, and so much more. What other pieces of her legacy, did he appropriate and distort?

"Where are we going?" I ask, changing the subject before the emotions can overwhelm me again.

Liam's hand squeezes mine gently. "Somewhere special," he says. "Someplace I want you to see."

I want to ask for more details, but I'm too wrung out to care. Besides, I trust Grimm to take care of me. And for now, at least, it's enough to know that wherever we're heading, it's away from the chaos, the cameras, and the questions for which I have no answers.

Away, with Liam Grimm—the man who started as my captor, became my protector, and now …

Well, now I don't know what he is. Not enemy, not exactly an ally. More than just a lover, more than just a friend. He's something far more complicated. Something I treasure.

And traveling alongside us, invisible but somehow newly present, is the ghost of my mother, whose legacy has unexpectedly found its way back to me.

As the city gives way to suburbs, and suburbs to the lush green of countryside, I let my head rest against Liam's shoulder, surrendering to exhaustion and the strange peace of finally, truly being my own person.

Free to choose. Free to decide.

Free to be.

THIRTY-SEVEN
UNFETTERED

As we come up the long, winding drive through acres of lush Connecticut woodland, the trees part to reveal what can only be described as a modern masterpiece of glass, stone, and wood, perfectly integrated into the hillside as if it grew there naturally.

"You live here?" I ask, unable to keep the awe from my voice.

He shrugs, but I can see a hint of pride in his eyes. "When I need space to think."

The car circles a fountain before stopping at the front entrance—a massive door of polished wood flanked by floor-to-ceiling windows. Grimm steps out first, extending his hand to help me from the car before sending the driver on his way.

I'm still reeling from everything that's happened today. The hearing. My father's absence. The revelation about my mother's company. And now this—a hidden retreat that seems a world away from the chaos we've left behind.

He unlocks the door, pushing it open to reveal an interior that's somehow both minimalist and incredibly warm. Wood and stone and glass again, soaring ceilings and glimpses of forest through enormous windows.

"What do you think?" he asks, watching me carefully as I turn slowly to take in the space. There's an openness, a sense of freedom in the design that speaks to something deep inside me. After a lifetime of confinement, of walls and locks and constant surveillance, this place feels like freedom.

"It's incredible," I say, my voice barely above a whisper.

"That means a lot," he says. "This place has my blood and sweat."

"Wait, what? Are you saying you built this place?"

"Every board, every nail. Either by my own hand or with the help of a contractor if it was more than a one-man job."

"Wow. I'm impressed."

He shrugs, looking almost boyish under the praise. "It's a good way to work off steam," he says. His lips twitch, and I see a flicker of heat in his eyes. "There are other ways, of course."

He closes the door behind us, and something in the soft click of the latch shifts the energy between us. We're alone. Truly alone, perhaps for the first time since this all began. No lawyers. No reporters. No looming threat of my father or his allies.

Just us, and the victory we've shared.

He moves closer, his eyes never leaving mine. "How are you feeling about everything?"

The question is simple, but the answer is anything but. How am I feeling? Elated. Terrified. Exhausted. Exhilarated. Free. So many emotions swirling inside me that I can barely identify them, let alone express them.

But there's one thing I know with absolute certainty—I want him. Here. Now.

"I feel like burning off some steam," I say, then close the distance between us in two quick steps, my hands finding his face, pulling him down to me. The kiss is hungry, desperate, a collision rather than a meeting.

He responds instantly, his surprise lasting only a fraction of a second before his arms wrap around me. He drives me backward until I'm pinned between the cool surface of the entry wall and the heat of his body. His hips press against mine, hard evidence of his desire making my breath catch. The solid warmth of him, the urgent pressure of his mouth on mine—it feels like the only real thing in a day filled with unreality.

"Sasha," he breathes against my lips.

My fingers fumble with his shirt buttons, too impatient for preci-sion. He solves the problem by simply yanking the fabric apart, sending buttons scattering across the polished floor. I run my hands across the exposed skin of his chest, feeling the rapid thunder of his heartbeat beneath my palm.

He makes quick work of my conservative court blouse, his mouth never leaving mine as he pushes the fabric from my shoulders. His hands are everywhere—in my hair, on my breasts, sliding beneath the waistband of my skirt. I'm just as frantic, tugging his belt loose, pushing his trousers down his hips.

We leave a trail of discarded clothing as he steers us deeper into the house toward the spacious living room with its large sectional sofa positioned to take advantage of the view. By the time we reach it, he's wearing only his slacks and I'm in nothing but my skirt, panties and bra.

He sits, yanking me down to straddle his lap, his hands gripping my waist with possessive force.

I reach behind me to unhook my bra, letting it fall away. His expression transforms into something almost feral as he takes in the sight of me, and the raw hunger I see there sends a flood of heat straight to my core.

"I need this," I tell him, grinding against his rigid length, feeling the hard outline of him through the fabric between us. "I need you. To feel something real after all of—"

My words shift into a desperate moan as his mouth captures my nipple, teeth grazing the sensitive peak before his tongue soothes the sting.

My head falls back, fingers tangling in his hair to hold him exactly where I need him, sensation arcing through me like lightning. The events of the day—the tension, the fear, the triumph—have left me hypersensitive, every touch amplified, every nerve ending screaming for more.

He devours both breasts with equal hunger, one hand gripping my ass with bruising force to pull me harder against his cock, the other sliding up my rib cage to cup the weight of my breast as he works the other with his mouth. I'm lost in the raw demand of his touch, in the almost savage way he claims my body, in the relentless pressure of his erection against my center even through the layers between us.

"Too many clothes," I gasp, clawing at his belt.

He makes a sound more growl than chuckle against my heated skin, the vibration sending another jolt of pleasure straight to my core. "Desperate, Princess?"

"Fucking starving," I correct him, finally freeing his belt and attacking the button of his trousers.

His eyes flash at my curse, and in one swift, powerful move, he lifts and flips me onto my back, the air rushing from my lungs as I land on the soft cushions. He towers over me for a moment, chest heaving, jaw clenched tight enough to see the muscle jump beneath his skin.

Then he's on me, stripping away my remaining clothes with ruthless efficiency—the tailored skirt torn down the seam in his haste, the silk panties shredded by impatient fingers, my shoes tossed carelessly aside. Each garment discarded without ceremony until I lie naked, exposed, my skin flushed and damp with need, my body desperately craving him.

"Christ, look at you," he whispers, his gaze devouring every inch of me like a starving man at a feast. "Spread out for me like a fucking gift."

Before I can respond, he drops to his knees between my splayed thighs, gripping my legs to pull me to the edge of the sofa. His mouth blazes a trail of biting kisses from my knee up my inner thigh, each one harder than the last, marking me, branding me. My breath catches in anticipation, body already tensing, clenching around nothing.

The first stroke of his tongue against my center has me arching off the sofa, a broken cry tearing from my throat. But there's nothing gentle in his exploration—he devours me with the same savage intensity as everything else, sucking hard at my clit before plunging his tongue inside me, his thumbs pressing my folds apart to expose me completely to his assault.

He drives me ruthlessly toward climax, adding two fingers that curl mercilessly against that sensitive spot inside me that makes stars explode behind my eyelids. It takes only moments before I'm shattering, my body convulsing as pleasure crashes through me with bruising force.

"Liam! Oh, god, Liam." His name is a prayer and a curse as I come apart beneath his relentless mouth, my hips bucking against him as he works me through every aftershock, not relenting until I'm whimpering from oversensitivity.

When I finally catch my breath enough to open my eyes, he's standing, stripping off his remaining clothes, his cock jutting thick and heavy, a drop of precum glistening at the tip. His body is a masterpiece of hard planes and sculpted muscle, powerful thighs and broad shoulders built by labor, not a gym. The body of a man who built a house with his bare hands.

"Come here," I command, reaching for him with greedy hands.

His eyebrow arches, a dangerous smirk playing at the corners of his mouth. "Is that how this works, Princess? You think you're in charge now?"

He moves with predatory grace, joining me on the sofa but not in the way I expected. Instead of lying over me, he sits, pulling me roughly across his lap. His hand comes down on my ass with a sharp crack that startles a shocked moan from my lips.

"This," he says, voice dropped to a rumbling bass that vibrates through my bones, "is mine now." Another smack, harder this time, the sting blooming into heat that pools between my legs. "Isn't it?"

"Yes," I gasp, shocked by how much I want—*need*—this claiming.

"Say it," he demands, landing another blow, then soothing the sting with a broad palm.

"All yours," I pant, pushing back into his touch. "I'm yours. Please, Grimm—"

He flips me again, this time onto my back, looming over me with one hand wrapped around his cock, guiding it to my entrance. "What do you need, Princess? Tell me exactly what you need from me."

"I need you inside me," I beg, beyond pride, beyond pretense. "Now. Hard. Please."

He doesn't need to be told twice. With one powerful thrust, he buries himself to the hilt, the stretch and burn of his size pulling a strangled cry from my throat. For a heartbeat we're perfectly still, his forehead pressed to mine, both of us adjusting to the overwhelming sensation of being completely joined.

Then he begins to move, and there's nothing measured or careful about his rhythm. He claims me with deep, punishing strokes that have the sofa shifting beneath us, his fingers digging into my hip hard enough to leave marks, his other hand fisted in my hair to hold me exactly where he wants me.

"This what you needed, Princess?" he growls against my ear, teeth catching my lobe. "To be fucked so hard you forget everything but my name?"

"Yes," I whisper, meeting each brutal thrust, taking him deeper, my nails raking down his back hard enough to leave welts. "Don't stop. Please, don't stop."

He shifts the angle, driving against that perfect spot with each stroke, and I feel myself climbing rapidly toward another peak.

"I'm not stopping, Princess." Sweat beads on his brow, muscles corded with the strain of holding back. "Not until you come around my cock. Not until I feel you squeeze every last drop from me."

His hand slips between us, his thumb finding my clit, circling with perfect pressure in counterpoint to his relentless thrusts and sending me hurtling toward the edge, this climax building even more intensely than the last.

"That's it, baby." His voice strained but no less dominant. "Let go for me. I want to feel you come apart. Now, Princess. Come for me."

As if my body obeys his command, I explode, waves of pleasure so intense they're almost pain crashing through me. I'm vaguely aware of screaming his name, of my body clenching around him with rhythmic pulses as my back arches off the sofa.

He follows moments later with a guttural roar, his rhythm faltering as he drives deep one final time, his release hot and pulsing inside me. His entire body goes rigid before he collapses onto me, his weight a welcome anchor as I float in the aftermath of truly touching heaven.

For a long moment, neither of us speaks, capable only of ragged breathing and occasional tremors of aftershock. His face is buried in the crook of my neck, his heartbeat thundering against my chest, his body still joined with mine.

Finally, he lifts his head, looking down at me with an expression that's both satisfied and strangely vulnerable. "I was going to offer you a tour," he says, voice raspy and worn. His fingers trace the curve of my cheek with unexpected tenderness. "But somehow we got side-tracked."

I laugh, the sound free and genuine despite my exhaustion. "I'd say this was a perfect start to the tour." My voice is hoarse from screaming. "Very … hands-on."

His answering grin is boyish, transforming his usually serious face into something younger, more carefree. "There's wine in the cellar," he offers. "How about champagne? Seems appropriate for a celebration."

"Mmm," I murmur, running my hands down his back, enjoying the play of muscles beneath my fingers. "Champagne sounds perfect."

He kisses me once more before reluctantly disentangling himself and standing. I take advantage of the opportunity to admire his naked form—all lean muscle and elegant lines making up pure masculine perfection. He pulls on his suit pants, leaving the waistband unfastened in a way that's casually, devastatingly sexy.

"Don't move," he orders, and there's just enough command in his voice to send a fresh surge of desire through me. "I'll be right back."

I watch him disappear down a hallway, then stretch languorously, enjoying the pleasant ache in muscles thoroughly used. The sofa is incredibly comfortable, the view through the windows peaceful. For the first time in recent memory, I feel completely at ease, unafraid of what might happen next. And mostly because of Liam Grimm, the man I used to consider my enemy.

He returns bearing a bottle and two glasses, his chest still bare, his hair adorably mussed. Less the calculated businessman and more the man I've come to … care for? Trust? Want?

All of the above, and perhaps more. I'm not ready to put a name to the emotions swirling inside me, but I can't deny they exist. Strong, complex feelings for this man who has been so many things. Enemy, captor, protector. And now something else entirely. Friend, I think, and lover.

He pops the cork with practiced ease, the sound sharp in the quiet room. "To victory," he says, filling both glasses before handing one to me.

I sit up, unself-conscious in my nudity, and accept the champagne. "To freedom," I counter, clinking my glass against his.

The first sip is cold and crisp, bubbles dancing on my tongue. "This is good," I say with appreciation.

"Dom Pérignon," he confirms. "2008. One of the best years."

I take another sip, savoring the complex flavors. "You know a lot about champagne."

He shrugs, settling beside me on the sofa. "I know a little about a lot of things."

"And a lot about some very specific things," I add, thinking of his skills in the bedroom. In the shower. On the sofa.

His laugh is low and warm. "I've never had complaints in that department," he says, apparently reading my mind.

"Nor will you from me," I assure him, leaning in for a champagne-flavored kiss.

What begins as playful quickly turns heated again. The champagne is set aside, barely tasted, as hands and mouths find more interesting ways to celebrate our victory. This time is slower, more exploratory, as if we're both finally allowing ourselves to savor what we've only taken in desperate gulps before.

I straddle him on the sofa, taking him inside me inch by deliberate inch, watching his face as pleasure overtakes control. His hands grip my hips, guiding but not directing, allowing me to set the pace. I lean forward, my hair creating a curtain around us as I kiss him deeply.

"You're incredible," he murmurs against my lips, his voice full of wonder. "The way you feel … the way you move …"

I roll my hips, taking him deeper, drawing a groan from deep in his chest. "Show me," I whisper, my confidence growing with each gasp, each broken curse I pull from him. "Show me what you like."

His hands tighten on my hips, urging me to move faster, harder. I comply, losing myself in the rhythm, in the building pleasure, in the expression of raw need on his face.

When release comes, it's less like breaking and more like soaring —a sustained peak that has me crying out his name, my body clenching around him as he follows, his own climax triggered by mine.

Afterward, we curl together on the rug in front of the sofa, a blanket pulled over our cooling skin, the half-empty champagne bottle forgotten on the coffee table. His fingers trace idle patterns on my bare shoulder as I rest my head on his chest, listening to the steady beat of his heart.

"We're going to have to get up eventually," he says, though he makes no move to do so.

"Mmm," I agree without conviction. "Eventually."

The peaceful moment is shattered by the sound of a side door opening. We both freeze, then scramble to cover ourselves more thoroughly with the throw.

"Mr. Grimm?" a male voice calls. "The car's been outside a while, I thought I'd check—oh!"

A middle-aged man in casual but crisp attire stands in the entryway, his face turning an impressive shade of red as he takes in the scene before quickly averting his eyes.

"James," Liam says with remarkable composure. "We arrived a bit earlier than expected."

"I see that, sir," James replies, still looking determinedly at the ceiling. "Shall I come back later to prepare the house?"

Liam glances at me, amusement dancing in his eyes despite the awkwardness of the situation. "Give us half an hour, then you can prepare dinner. Ms. Reed will be staying with me."

"Very good, sir," James says, backing toward the door. "A pleasure to meet you, Ms. Reed," he adds with admirable politeness before beating a hasty retreat.

The moment the door closes behind him, I burst into laughter, burying my face against Liam's chest. "Oh, my god," I gasp between fits of giggles. "His face!"

Liam's laughter joins mine, his arms tightening around me. "Poor James. nine years of service and I've never given him a shock like that."

"Should I feel honored?" I ask, looking up at him with mock seriousness.

"Absolutely," he confirms, dropping a kiss on my nose. "Now, as much as I hate to say it, we should probably get dressed before he comes back with the rest of the staff."

"Staff?" I echo. "How many people work here?"

"Just a few," he says, disentangling himself from the blanket and beginning to gather our scattered clothing. "James manages the property, his wife Maria handles the cooking when I'm staying here, and there's a groundskeeper who lives in a cottage at the edge of the property."

I stand, wrapping the throw around me like a makeshift dress.

"And all of them will know exactly what we've been doing," I point out, feeling a blush rise to my cheeks.

Liam grins, entirely unrepentant. "Would you like a tour of the house now? Or do you want to clean up first?"

I consider the pleasant stickiness between my thighs, the champagne spilled on my skin, the general dishevelment of my appearance. "Clean up," I decide. "Definitely clean up."

He nods, gathering the rest of our clothes. "The master bath has a shower big enough for two." His eyes skim over me. "Though I can't promise we'll actually get much cleaner."

I laugh, shaking my head at his insatiability—which, to be fair, matches my own. "Lead the way," I say, following him toward what I assume is the master suite. "And after that, you can show me the rest of this amazing place."

As we move through the house, his hand warm on the small of my back, I'm struck by how surreal this all feels. Twenty-four hours ago, I was preparing to face my father in court, uncertain of my future, my freedom hanging in the balance. Now I'm here, in this beautiful house with this complicated man, celebrating a victory that still doesn't feel quite real.

But as Grimm leads me into a bedroom that's all-understated luxury, as he unwraps the blanket from my body with reverent hands, as his mouth finds mine in a kiss that promises more pleasure to come —this, at least, feels utterly real.

This connection, this moment, this man.

Whatever tomorrow brings—the challenges of running my mother's company, the ongoing search for my fugitive father, the complexities of whatever exists between Grimm and me—for now, I'll take this —pure, uncomplicated joy and freedom, long overdue.

THIRTY-EIGHT
BETRAYAL

My days blur together now. It's odd, this freedom—waking when I want, working whenever inspiration hits, speaking honestly without fear of getting slapped down.

Without trying, Liam and I have fallen into sync, like we've been dancing this particular dance for years. It's warm and wonderful, but sometimes the ease of it scares me. Like I'm waiting for the other shoe to drop.

"You're being paranoid," Ruby says, during one of our morning calls that have become almost a ritual. "No," she corrects herself. "Not paranoid. Symptomatic."

I pour a fresh cup of coffee and settle onto the couch. "Symptoms of what?"

"Post-traumatic stress. I mean, hello? Your father was like a walking virus, and you caught PTSD from him."

"Was?" I like to think he's dead. That an enemy killed him or he took a nosedive off a high building or jumped into the ocean after booking an around-the-world cruise.

He didn't though. He's still out there—I'm certain of it. He's the other shoe I'm still fearing, because when it drops, my world will shatter.

But for right now, at least, I'm happy.

"Enjoy it," Ruby tells me. "Revel in how well it's going with Liam and don't stress yourself out worrying about your father. He's a lot of things, but not an idiot. He has to know that if he comes back, the shit will hit the fan. The whole world knows what he did to you."

"You're right," I say, standing to look out the window as the security system beeps once, indicating that someone has turned into the long driveway. "Listen, I think the books I ordered just arrived. Talk later?"

"No prob. Just ping me if you need me."

As soon as I'm off the call, I start across the room. I've ordered several books that Grimm recommended about the strategy and philosophy of running a business. I have so many thoughts about marketing Elysium and about what direction to take my mother's company that I was having trouble organizing them. And while Grimm has said over and over that he'll hold my hand through the whole process if I want him to, he also said that I'll get more satisfaction if I take the reins myself, and only bring him in when I'm truly lost or stuck.

But it's not the familiar delivery truck that pulls into the gravel parking area. It's a sleek red Ferrari convertible. And Leo Grimm is behind the wheel.

He gets out, and I watch as Liam approaches from around the side of the house where he'd been talking with the groundskeeper.

They do that thing brothers do—half handshake, half hug, with Liam messing up Leo's hair just to annoy him, the same as he's done since they were kids according to the stories he's been telling me about growing up as the black sheep of the Grimm family.

Something squeezes in my chest as I watch them—this easy brotherhood is nothing like Liam's stiff, formal interactions with his other siblings. These two actually like each other and always have.

I go into the kitchen, nursing mixed feelings. Good that Liam has one ally in that screwed-up family. Not so good that it's Leo—the same Leo who made Ruby cry for weeks after he revealed himself as the biggest shit on the planet.

The memories of those late-night talks and Ruby's tear-stained face, make my smile stiffen whenever he turns my way.

They come in through the kitchen door together, with Leo giving me a nod as I sip my coffee. He glances back to Liam. "You two really are still playing house. Never thought I'd see it." His tone lacks the bite it would have coming from Alexander or Elliott—just brotherly ribbing.

Liam pulls down two mugs. "Are you just crashing my morning or is there a point to this visit?"

Leo's easy grin fades and he looks from Liam to me. "Bane's stirring the pot."

Ice trickles down my spine at the name. I see Liam tense beside me—pouring coffee with a tightly clenched jaw.

"Define stirring," he says, his voice deceptively casual.

"The pissy kind." Leo accepts his coffee with a nod. "Apparently wiring him the cash value didn't soothe his bruised ego."

I hug myself, hating that any of our precious time in this beautiful home has to be tainted by talking about the vilest man on the planet, second only to my father.

"He's lucky he's getting anything," I say. "But it would have been better to have retrieved the stupid ring and shoved it down his throat."

My tossing of the engagement ring into the garage had turned into more of a problem than I'd anticipated. It slipped down the drain and apparently was washed away to who knows where. Unfortunate since New York law allows a jilted groom to get the engagement ring back.

Leo looks at me with a grin, apparently appreciating the visual my words conjured.

"He's been paid," Liam says, drawing the conversation back on topic. "What's he angling for now?"

"Nothing that he's revealed. But we all know that man can hold a grudge like nobody's business."

"You've got more than that," I say, holding out a basket of blueberry muffins, then doing the same for Liam. "Or did you just come to hang with us in the country?"

Leo grins. "I do like her," he says to Liam. The irony is that he means it. And despite the simmering anger from the shit he pulled with Ruby, I have to grudgingly admit that I like him too.

"Quit drawing this out and tell us what you know," Liam demands as I sip my coffee.

"Nothing concrete. Whispers and grumbles." His eyes lock on

Liam's. "And he's been seen with Maya. Cozy dinners, that whole routine."

Liam freezes, mug halfway to his mouth. "You're kidding."

"Spotted three times last week. Looking very … chummy."

The pieces click together in my head. Maya, still smarting from Liam's rejection. Desmond, humiliated by me running out on my forced engagement. Two wounded egos finding common ground in mutual hatred.

"Perfect," Liam mutters. "Just what we need."

Leo shrugs one shoulder. "Thought you should know. Beef up security." His gaze shifts to me. "And both of you need to watch your backs."

After Leo leaves, Liam vanishes into his office. I try focusing on my list of things to do in order to get Elysium ready to monetize. It's no use. My mind keeps drifting to Bane, to Maya, to the trouble brewing on our horizon.

Hours later, Liam emerges, face calm, eyes steady. "Security's been upgraded," is all he says. "We'll know if either of them comes within five miles of the property." I nod, only then realizing how deeply Leo's warning had frightened me. And, apparently, Liam, too.

Later that night, I lay curled against his naked body. "I never thought I'd feel safe again," I say, as his fingers stroke my hair. After Father, the drugs, the manipulation …"

I trail off, snuggling closer, his heat anchoring me.

"And now?"

I consider the question, then answer honestly, taking my emotions all the way down to the core. "Now I'm happy. And I feel safe. And," I add, nerves twisting at my insides, "I feel loved."

His chest rises on a deep breath. "You are," he whispers, then shifts so that I can see his face, more raw, more open than I've ever seen it. Something naked and unguarded shines in his eyes. Then his hand cups my cheek, his thumb brushing my lip. "I love you, Sasha Reed."

Three words. Small, world-changing words. I'd known some-where deep down, felt it in a thousand tiny gestures. But hearing it spoken aloud makes it real. Inescapable.

"I love you too," I whisper, surprised by how easily the words come. "I can't imagine my life without you now."

Something shifts in his eyes—a vulnerability I've never seen before, raw and unguarded. He draws me up to him, his mouth finding mine in a kiss that starts gentle but quickly deepens. His hand cradles the back of my neck, fingers tangling in my hair as if he needs to anchor me to him.

The familiar heat flares between us, but there's something different tonight. The urgency remains, but beneath it runs a current of something deeper, more deliberate. When he trails his lips down my throat, it's with exquisite slowness, as if committing every inch of my skin to memory.

I arch beneath him as his mouth finds the hollow of my collarbone, my fingers tracing the contours of his shoulders, mapping the strong planes of his back. He murmurs my name against my skin, the sound vibrating through me.

His hands are reverent as they explore my body, touching places he's touched a dozen times before but somehow making each caress feel entirely new. When my fingers graze down his stomach, he captures my wrist, pressing a kiss to my palm that makes me shiver.

He takes his time, his mouth trailing a path from my throat to my breasts, lingering there until I'm gasping his name. When he moves lower, his hands parting my thighs with gentle insistence, I surrender completely to the sensation of his tongue against me, building me toward a peak that seems both inevitable and impossible to reach.

Just when I think I can't bear any more, he returns to me, his weight a welcome pressure as he settles between my legs. Our eyes lock as he enters me, the connection so intense I can hardly breathe. He holds perfectly still for a moment, forehead pressed to mine, our breath mingling.

"I meant it," he says, voice rough with emotion. "I love you, Sasha."

Something breaks open inside me at the words, and I wrap my legs around him, drawing him deeper. "Show me," I whisper against his lips.

He begins to move, each thrust measured and deep, our bodies finding a rhythm that feels both familiar and entirely new. His hands cradle my face, his gaze never leaving mine as pleasure builds between us. This isn't the frantic coupling we've shared before—this is communion, acknowledgment, truth expressed through touch.

When release finally comes, it washes through me in waves, his name a prayer on my lips. He follows moments later, his face buried in my neck, his arms holding me as if he fears I might disappear.

Afterward, we lie tangled together, my head on his chest, his fingers drawing lazy patterns on my back. Neither of us speaks. There's no need. The words have been said by our bodies. By the twining of our souls.

When sleep finally claims us, I feel a peace I've never known before, along with the certainty that whatever comes next, we'll face it together.

———

Morning comes, and Liam heads to the city for meetings, promising to return by dinner. I lose myself in Elysium updates, tweaking environments, testing new modules. Revising protocols.

Time slips sideways, and suddenly it's mid-afternoon, my muscles stiff from hunching over the keyboard.

The security panel chimes, announcing a car at the gate. Not Liam's new Audi or Ruby's ancient Volvo. I check the camera feed and see only a sleek black sedan. I'm about to pick up the on-property phone when it rings.

"A Maya Lane would like to see you." It's Curtis, one of the five guards who work the perimeter and the gatehouse. "She says it's urgent."

My first instinct is to deny entry and protect our sanctuary. But curiosity wins. "Escort Ms. Lane to the house," I tell him. "I'll meet her outside."

I choose the front terrace—neutral ground, security in sight but private enough for conversation. Spring sunshine dapples through maple leaves, and the breeze carries hints of pine and wildflowers. Far too beautiful a day for the ugliness I suspect is coming.

Maya steps from the car looking runway-ready—tailored pants, silk blouse, that mauve scarf. Curtis hangs back as she approaches.

"Sasha." Her smile stops short of her eyes. "Lovely property," she says, and I feel a stab of victory in the realization that Grimm never brought her here.

"Maya." I keep my voice neutral. "Unexpected visit."

"I imagine so." She settles uninvited into a terrace chair, crossing those endless legs. "Though perhaps it shouldn't be."

I take the seat opposite, keeping my distance. "What brings you here?"

She studies me, head tilted like I'm a puzzle she's solving. "When Liam first mentioned you, I dismissed you as nothing more than Daddy's dress-up dolly."

I wait, silent.

"But you're more, aren't you?" She leans forward. "Quite brilliant, actually. Elysium proves that."

My creation's name on her lips sends ice through my veins. "How do you know about Elysium?"

Her smile widens, turns predatory. "Oh, I know quite a bit. About Elysium. About Vale." She leans closer. "About how long Liam's been watching you there."

The world tilts beneath me, her words reshaping reality. "Go on."

She leans back, looking smug. "So I was right. He never told you."

I force myself to stay cool. To keep all emotion off my face. As if I'm at a photoshoot, and the art director has told me that all he wants is my face as a neutral, unreadable canvas.

Inside, I'm already dying, terrified of the words still to come.

"Liam's clever, too. You probably know that, but you might not understand the genius of the man who founded RSC. It's fascinating how supremely skilled that man is at finding his way in and out of all the little gopher holes hidden in the dark corners of the internet.

She pauses, as if waiting for me to say something. But I can barely think, much less form words.

"He's been watching everything," she continues. "Your private moments, your fantasies, your hidden self." Her voice softens, mockingly gentle. "For at least three years he watched you. He's very good, you know. Always finding ways into systems that don't want him there."

She leans back, as if just getting comfortable. "He didn't mean to tell me. I think he wanted to keep it his dirty little secret. The way he —shall we say—*fleshed* out Prince Killiam. But he hired me for my skills. And I'm a curious sort. To be honest, I haven't seen it all. Your security is excellent. But I've seen enough to be impressed. And to find his entry points."

Once again, her smile drips honey as bits and pieces lock into horrifying place. Liam's instant grasp of Elysium when I showed him. His lack of surprise at its complexity. His too-perfect understanding of its architecture.

I'd thought it was because of his skill in cyber tech. And it was—because that skill is what had already given him an up-close-and personal look at my very private world.

She shrugs, all casual and light. "He has no idea I'm privy to his dirty little secret. But since you two are getting so cozy, I thought you should know. Girl Code, right?" Her smile is like baring fangs. "It's just that Liam does whatever he deems necessary, regardless of collateral damage. He always has."

I just look at her, saying nothing.

She clears her throat. "I probably should have said something to you earlier. After all, it's been going on for three years, give or take." Maya inspects her manicure, casually gleeful in the wake of this bomb she's dropped.

"I think it started as opposition research. Know thy enemy's daughter—that sort of thing. But it became something quite different."

Three years. Him watching my only private space. My sanctuary. The one corner of the world where I could truly be myself, free from eyes, free from judgment.

All along, he was there. Watching. Invading.

I think of Prince Killiam whose face was hidden for so long. The lover who anticipated my desires before I voiced them. The man who pushed boundaries I hadn't known I wanted pushed, who claimed me in ways both terrifying and thrilling.

Liam. It was Liam all along.

I stand abruptly, needing space, air, escape from this crushing revelation.

I force a laugh and a smile. "I'm so sorry you wasted your time, but at least the drive's pretty."

"Wasted my time?"

"Liam told me all of that before the hearing. He said he couldn't bear me not knowing the truth."

Her eyes widen slightly, and I can't tell if she believes me or not.

I'm not sure I care.

Right now, I just want her gone.

"Well, then," she says, "I'm sorry if I wasted your time."

"No trouble. But I have work to do, so please forgive me for not inviting you in."

"Of course," she says, and I take a bit of glee in the fact that she looks just a bit unstable. I keep my chin up, ironically calling on skills I learned as my father's little puppet about reflecting one emotion to the world, while keeping your true turmoil locked up inside.

"Well," she finally says. "Then I'm off."

"I'll give Liam your regards," I say, then stand frozen until her car disappears down the drive. Only then do I move, mechanical steps carrying me inside, to the bedroom we've shared.

The room feels wrong now, tainted. I look around what I'd thought was a haven, seeing it through new eyes—a new cage built by a man who violated my privacy in the most basic way.

I pack methodically, gathering the few things that are truly mine. Just clothes, the laptop he gave me, notes for Elysium's expansion. I leave the jewelry, designer clothes, art supplies. Even the canvases I've painted and the sketches I've drawn in our days here. They feel contaminated now. Everything does.

I call for a car, and while I'm waiting, I write one note—blunt and unambiguous.

I know about Elysium.
I know about Prince Killiam.
Do not come after me.

I PLACE the note on the counter, fingers lingering on the paper as I remember the scissors I'd noticed next to the notepad. Something shifts inside me. Not just betrayal now—something harder, colder. Rage, maybe. Or determination.

I grab the scissors and move to the bathroom without conscious thought, flipping on the harsh lights, confronting my reflection. The woman staring back looks like me but feels like a stranger—too trusting, too easily deceived. Liam's words echo in my head: "God, I love your hair. It's like spun gold." He'd say it while winding strands around his fingers, tugging gently to tilt my face up for a kiss. How many times had his hands tangled in it as we made love? How many times had he watched me in Elysium, where I'd sometimes let Vale's golden hair flow free in the wind as she rode?

My fingers twist in the long strands, pulling them taut. One cut. Then another. Golden locks fall into the sink, onto the floor. Each snip of the scissors feels like severing a cord that bound me to him. To the lie.

The first cuts are jagged, angry. But something shifts as I work, my movements becoming more deliberate. I'm not destroying—I'm creating. Each cut precise now, shaping what remains into something new. Something mine.

When I finish, my hair barely brushes my shoulders, the ends uneven but purposeful. I look younger. No—I look different. Like someone I haven't met yet but might like to know.

I sweep the fallen strands into my palm, golden threads that represented the woman he thought he owned. The princess in her tower.

I let them fall into the trash without ceremony.

The car will be here any minute. I gather my things, a strange lightness at my neck, my shoulders. My head feels physically lighter, but something inside me feels lighter too, as if I've shed more than just hair.

As the car arrives, I take one final look at the beautiful house that briefly felt like home. The security. The peace. All built on lies.

I slide into the backseat, still numb from the betrayal, but also stronger somehow. "Reed Tower," I tell the driver, choosing the one place Liam won't expect.

As we pull away, I don't look back. Tears will come later. Fury, too. And grief. For now, there's just hollow emptiness where trust once lived.

He saw me, all right. Saw every part of me without consent. All this time, I thought I was finally being truly seen, truly understood.

Instead, I was being watched. Again. Still. Always.

The tower may change, but the princess always remains trapped.

Not anymore.

THIRTY-NINE
RETURN

Reed Tower looms before me, a gleaming monument to my father's ego—and, I now know, my mother's vision. The familiar façade, once a prison, now represents something more complicated. A past I can't escape, a legacy I'm not sure I want, and yet still the only place that has ever truly been mine, however tarnished it might be from years under my father's control.

"Welcome back, Ms. Reed," the doorman says, genuine warmth in his greeting. Ruby had told me that news of my father's abuse had spread throughout the staff. She was right, and I'm grateful for the sympathy and support.

The private elevator whisks me upward, my stomach dropping in a way that has nothing to do with the rapid ascent. What am I doing here? This is the last place I should seek refuge, the physical manifestation of everything I've been fighting to escape.

And yet, as the doors slide open to reveal my suite, a delicious sense of familiarity washes over me. This space, at least, was mine. Whatever my father did, however he controlled me, this sanctuary was where I created Elysium, where I dreamed of freedom.

Where I was secretly watched by the man I thought had saved me.

The bitterness of the irony is enough to choke on. Escaping one captor only to fall into the arms of another.

I drop my bag by the door and move through the rooms, seeing them with new eyes. The elegant furnishings, the tasteful art—all carefully selected to create the illusion of autonomy while maintaining my father's aesthetic control. Like Liam's Connecticut house, beautiful but ultimately designed for someone else's purposes.

I scoff. I could choke on the irony. I've gone from one controlling man to another. From being my father's puppet to Liam's weapon. Both men making decisions for me.

Had I really once told Liam that he's nothing like my father? I'd believed it then. Now, I'm not so sure. Hadn't they both made decisions for me without even asking what I thought? Hadn't they both lied to me? My father about who killed my mother, and Liam about Elysium?

My father may have kept me tethered with drugs and manipulation, but wasn't Liam manipulating me every moment he failed to mention that he'd been watching me—hell, *fucking* me—in Elysium?

My sanctuary that wasn't a sanctuary at all. My private world that had been invaded without my knowledge or consent.

The violation cuts deeper than I could have imagined. It's not just about privacy—it's about trust, about believing that for once in my life, someone saw the real me, not the image they wanted to see.

That Liam Grimm, of all people, did this to me …

But why should I be surprised? I knew his reputation going in. I'd just let myself forget it.

The tears finally come, hot and fierce, pouring down my face in a torrent I can't control. I sob until my throat is raw, until my eyes burn, until there's nothing left but a hollow ache where my heart should be.

When the storm passes, I'm left exhausted but clearer. I won't stay here—not in Reed Tower, not in my father's shadow. But I needed this moment, this return, to understand that I can't go backward. Whatever comes next, it has to be something new, something built on my own terms.

Sleep claims me eventually, curled on the studio couch where I'd spent so many nights before, lost in the creation of a world that was never as private as I believed.

______

A SOFT KNOCK pulls me from restless dreams. I blink awake,

disoriented. For a moment, I expect to see the Connecticut house ceiling and feel Liam's arm draped across my waist.

Then reality crashes back.

Reed Tower. My old prison. My current refuge.

"Sasha?" There's a light tap at the door. "You in there?"

I sit up, rubbing my eyes. "Come in," I call, my voice rough from crying.

The door opens and Ruby stands there in her uniform—the practical black pants and white button-down shirt of Reed Tower's hospitality staff, the part-time job she recently took so that she could stay on site with her grandmother once I'd escaped the building.

Her eyes widen when she sees me, concern washing over her face.

"Holy shit," she breathes, hurrying inside and closing the door behind her. "What happened?"

I almost laugh at the question. What happened? My entire world imploded. The man I loved betrayed me in the most intimate way possible. I discovered everything I thought was real was just another form of surveillance.

"Liam," is all I manage to say, my voice cracking on his name.

Ruby doesn't hesitate, just hurries to the sofa and wraps her arms around me. I collapse against her, fresh tears spilling down my cheeks.

"What did that bastard do?" she asks, leaning back and fingering my now-short hair. "I swear, I'll kill the fucker."

I pull back, wiping my eyes. "How did you know I was here?"

"Mrs. Keller in housekeeping texted me the minute you arrived. She said you were in bad shape, but she didn't mention your hair." She squeezes my shoulder. "Sasha, seriously. Tell me what happened."

"You think Leo's a giant prick? Well, his big brother is giving him a run for his money."

Ruby's forehead creases as she frowns, then sits on the sofa next to me. "What are you talking about?"

I draw a breath, then scrub my hands over my face before taking a deep breath and facing her. "Grimm hacked into Elysium. He's been monitoring everything I did there for years. Everything." My voice breaks on the last word, the violation still too raw to process fully.

Ruby's expression shifts from confusion to horror. "That's not possible. You locked that down like Fort Knox."

"It's possible if you're Liam fucking Grimm," I say, a harsh laugh escaping me. "Computer genius, security expert. He's been watching me all along."

Her hand goes to her mouth, and she shakes her head slowly. "That's—oh, god, Sasha. How did you find out?"

I grit my teeth then grind out the words. "Maya Lane told me."

Ruby's eyebrows shoot up. "The one you told me about? His ex from the Tribeca loft? Why would she—"

"To hurt him, I guess. To hurt me." I sink back onto the sofa. "Does it matter?"

"What did he say?"

I shake my head. "I didn't stick around. What can he say?"

She just shakes her head and whispers, "Wow." Then she frowns as she takes my hand. "Is there any way you could be wrong? Maybe you should ask him. I mean, I used to think he was the biggest a-hole of all, but all this time with you, the way he's helped you, and …"

She trails off with a shrug.

"It's true," I tell her. "I should have seen it when I told him about Elysium. I thought he just got it, you know, because he works in cybersecurity. But it was because he'd been in that code for years." I almost tell her the rest—that he'd hijacked Prince Killiam. But I'm not ready to go there yet.

Ruby takes my hand, her fingers warm against mine. "I'm sorry. I know how much you cared about him."

"Loved," I correct, the admission like glass in my throat. "I loved him. What a fucking joke."

"It's not a joke to feel something real," she says quietly. "Even if it was based on a lie." And, she adds, with a somewhat wary look, "I think he loves you, too."

"The bastard doesn't even know what love is."

I glance around the studio at my paintings, so many cityscapes, so many wide-open spaces. Grimm had given me that. Helped me cope with my fear, got me off those damn drugs. But he hadn't done it for me. Not really.

"I thought I was finally free," I whisper. "That night at Alexander's party, when Liam took me away, I thought I was truly escaping. But I was just trading one captor for another."

"You're not captive now," Ruby points out. "You came back here on your own. That's a choice you made."

She's right, of course. Whatever else has happened, I'm no longer under my father's direct control. Or Liam's. The guardianship was denied. Reed Cosmetics is mine now, not to mention the rest of Reed Industries.

I'm free.

I should be jumping for joy. Instead, I'm mourning the loss of a man I should never have let myself trust.

"What will you do?" she asks after a moment of silence.

"I don't know," I admit. "I can't stay here forever. This place still feels like …" I trail off, gesturing at the walls that have contained me for so long.

"A prison," she finishes for me.

"A cage," I correct. "A beautiful, comfortable cage, but still a cage."

"You could get your own place," she suggests. "Something that's just yours. No Reed influence, no Grimm control."

The idea is both terrifying and exhilarating. A space that's truly mine, designed to my specifications, controlled by no one but me.

"Maybe," I say. Then, changing the subject, "How have things been here? Since my father … left."

Ruby's expression shifts, becoming more guarded. "From what I hear, the business is running fine. It's not like your dad was day-to-day management. But I know they're wanting you to step in officially. I guess everything feels too open-ended until you do."

I nod. "I know. I will. I just need more time."

"I get that." She squeezes my hand. "It's your mom's legacy. You want to get it right."

"Yes. Exactly."

"Just be careful. Everyone thinks Victor fled the country, but I don't know. I'm worried he's going to pop up like some scary Jack-in-the-Box and take it all out on you."

I meet her eyes. "Yeah. I'm kind of worried about that, too."

Because I don't want to think about it, I move on. "And the Tower staff?"

"Universal relief. You may be shocked to learn that your father was not well-loved."

I feign surprise. "No!"

She nods. "Oh. Yes. Apparently, many staff members thought he was a prick, a bastard, and poor excuse for a human." She shrugs. "Among other things."

I snort. "It's almost sweet how well they know him."

We share another grin, then Ruby leans closer. "Listen, whatever you decide to do next, you know I'm with you. If you want to move out of here and get an apartment, we could move in together. Or if you just want to fly to Bali and never look back? I'll totally help you pack. Just … don't shut me out, okay?"

The sincerity in her voice brings fresh tears to my eyes. This is friendship—real, unguarded, without ulterior motives. Nothing like what I had with Grimm, where every interaction I'd thought so real was colored by deception.

"Thank you," I whisper, squeezing her hand. "For everything. For being the one person in my life who's always been straight with me."

She pulls me in for a hug. "And I always will be."

We sit in comfortable silence for a moment, the weight of the day settling around us like a heavy blanket. Then she gives me a hug and tells me she needs to go cover for the fifteenth floor receptionist.

She pauses at the door. "For what it's worth, I think you're the strongest person I know. Whatever happens next, you'll be okay."

As the door closes behind her, I let her words sink in. *Strong.* It's not how I feel right now.

Now, I'm more in the broken, betrayed, and lost zone. Still, maybe she's right. I survived my father's manipulation. I'll survive Liam's betrayal, too.

I move to the window, then look out at the city spread below me. It takes a moment, but then I realize that my skin isn't crawling. My stomach isn't twisting, and vertigo isn't threatening to send me tumbling through this window and out into the cold, dark void.

For now, at least, I'm not scared.

FORTY
WAITING GAME

I feel just as empty when I wake the next morning. Time and sleep have not taken the rough edges from the wounds, and my soul still feels empty.

More, I still want the man who wounded me.

Part of me wants to believe that all of it—my escape with Liam, the revelation of my father's manipulations, the blissful weeks in Connecticut—was just another elaborate fantasy, an Elysium-like escape from reality.

But the ache in my chest is too real, the betrayal too raw. It happened. Every wonderful, painful moment. And now it's all gone.

With a sigh, I go through the motions of the day, showering and dressing mechanically, choosing clothes from the vast closet that now seems like a museum of my former life filled with designer pieces I never selected, but that hang here only because my father deemed them appropriate for his living is porcelain doll.

I settle on simple black pants and a white blouse—neutral, forgettable, nothing that would catch a photographer's eye.

When I enter the sitting room, my heart nearly stops.

Liam Grimm sits in one of the armchairs, looking simultaneously out of place and perfectly at ease. He's disheveled in a way I've never seen before—hair uncombed, stubble darkening his jaw, clothes wrinkled as if he's been wearing them for too long.

317

"How did you get in here?" I demand, my voice surprisingly steady.

His eyes meet mine, bloodshot and exhausted. "The same way I get anywhere I want to be."

"By hacking in. By invading. By watching without permission." Each accusation comes out sharper than the last.

He doesn't flinch. "Yes."

The simple admission, devoid of excuses or justifications, fuels my anger. "Get out."

"Sasha—"

"Get. Out." I point toward the door, my arm trembling with suppressed rage.

"I will," he says, standing slowly as if his body aches. "After you hear what I have to say."

"I'm not interested in explanations or excuses."

"Good, because I have neither." He takes a step toward me, stopping when I instinctively back away. "What I did was wrong. Inexcusable. I knew that even as I was doing it."

The admission catches me off guard. I expected denials, minimizations, clever rationalizations that would make me question my own outrage.

"Then why?" I ask, the question escaping before I can stop it.

He runs a hand through his already disheveled hair. "It started as research. Know your enemy. I needed to know if you were complicit in your father's actions, if you were just another Reed scheming against my family."

"And Prince Killiam?" The name tastes like ash on my tongue. "Was that research too?"

A shadow crosses his face. "No. That was ... something else."

"What? A game? A joke? Let's see how far he can push the poor, delusional Reed girl? Make her think it's just AI spinning a man for her."

"It wasn't like that."

"Then what was it like?" I demand, fury rising again. "Explain to me how you justified pretending to be someone else, manipulating my desires, violating the one space I thought was truly mine."

He's silent for a long moment, his expression raw. "I can't justify it," he says finally. "What started as observation became ... fascination. I saw a different Sasha in Elysium—brilliant, creative, strong, nothing like the public persona your father created. The more I watched, the more I wanted … a connection."

"So you decided to manipulate me. To become my fantasy lover."

He nods, once again not denying it. "I told myself it was harmless. That in Elysium, we were both playing roles, both becoming something other than ourselves. But the truth is, I wanted to know you in a way your father's security would never allow in the real world."

"And after? When you had me in the real world, when I was literally in your bed, following your *everything bargain*? You still didn't tell me."

"I should have," he says. "Every day that passed made it harder. How do you tell someone you've been spying on their most intimate thoughts? That you know their fantasies, their fears, their desires because you invaded their privacy?"

"You don't," I say coldly. "You just keep lying."

"Yes." His voice is barely above a whisper. "I kept lying. Because I was afraid of losing you."

The admission hangs between us, raw and honest in a way that makes my chest ache. I want to cling to my anger, to let it shield me from the pain, but his unvarnished confession makes it harder than I expected.

"You should have thought of that before you slid into Prince Killiam," I say, my voice low but steady. "Before you seduced me in Elysium. Before you built this … this fiction of connection between us."

"It wasn't fiction," he says, a flash of intensity breaking through his mask of careful control. "Not all of it. What I felt for you—what I feel—is real, Sasha."

He drags his fingers through his hair again. "Hell, it's the only real thing in my life."

I shake my head, fighting the dangerous pull of his words. "How would I know? Everything between us started with manipulation and lies. Even if your feelings changed, the foundation is rotten."

He takes another step toward me, stopping when I raise a hand in warning. "You're right. But I'm asking you—begging you—for a chance to build something new. Something honest."

"You stole my agency, Liam. You manipulated things to how you wanted them just like my father did. So you tell me—how the hell am I supposed to trust you again?"

"I don't know." His shoulders slump slightly in resignation. "I'm not asking for forgiveness. Just … time. Space to prove that I can be the man you deserve."

Part of me—a traitorous, yearning part—wants to give in, to believe that what we shared in Connecticut was real despite the lies that came before. But the wound is too fresh, the betrayal too profound.

"I need you to go," I say, fighting to keep my voice steady. "I need space. To think. To figure out who I am without men who watch me and manipulate me and try to mold me into their version of who I should be."

Never once would I have thought that Liam Grimm has anything in common with my father, but he doesn't deny a word of it. In fact, he accepts my edict with grace.

As he moves toward the door, a thought occurs to me. "How did you get past security?"

A ghost of a smile touches his lips. "I told you once—I'm very good at what I do."

"Which is breaking into places you don't belong?"

I see the flinch he tries to hide. "Yes," he agrees. "That's part of it."

He pauses at the threshold, turning back to face me, his eyes burning with an intensity that makes my breath catch despite everything. "I'll be here tomorrow morning. And the next. And the next. For as long as it takes. Also," he adds with just the flicker of a smile, "I love your haircut."

Before I can respond, he's gone, the door closing softly behind him.

I sink onto the couch, trembling with the aftermath of the confrontation— anger and grief and a confused longing. And, yes, with humor and a touch of pleasure, just because he still likes my hair.

I stifle a sigh, frustrated with my roiling, changing emotions.

How can I still want him, still miss him, after what he did?

Because it wasn't all a lie, whispers a voice inside me. The connection was real, even if the path to it was twisted.

I push the thought away, unwilling to give him that absolution. Not yet.

Maybe not ever.

———

TRUE TO HIS WORD, Liam is there the next morning when I emerge from my bedroom. And the morning after that. Each day, he sits in the same chair, waiting patiently for me to acknowledge him, to listen, to give him a chance to explain.

Each day, I send him away.

On the fifth day, I find myself exploding with frustration. "Don't you have a company to run? A life to lead? Something better to do than sit in my living room every morning?"

He looks up from the book he's been reading, his expression calm despite the dark circles under his eyes. "No."

The simple answer deflates my anger, leaving me uncertain how to respond. Each day, he looks more exhausted, as if he's not sleeping, not eating properly. Part of me—the vengeful part—is glad to see him suffer. But another part worries, despite everything.

"This is ridiculous," I mutter, turning away.

"Maybe," he agrees. "But I meant what I said. I'll be here every day, for as long as it takes."

"And if it takes forever?"

His eyes meet mine, steady and sure. "Then I'll be here forever."

The declaration should sound melodramatic. Absurd. Instead, it rings with a quiet certainty that makes my heart ache. This man, who manipulated and deceived me, who broke into my most private sanctuary, is also the man who stood beside me against my father, who showed me what freedom could feel like, who looked at me and saw something more than a pretty face on a billboard or a woman broken by tragedy and the sins of her father.

I turn away, unwilling to let him see the conflict in my eyes. "I'm going out with Ruby today."

"Tell her I said hello," he says simply, returning to his book.

The exchange leaves me unsettled for reasons I can't quite articulate. There's something about his patient persistence, his willingness to be humbled day after day, that feels more genuine than any flowery apology or dramatic gesture ever could.

Twenty minutes later I'm sitting at a café with Ruby nursing a cup of coffee. "Gotta give him points for persistence," I admit. "Most men would have given up by now."

She studies me over the rim of her coffee cup. "No way? Today, too?"

I nod.

"Why hasn't security been upgraded? Chains added to your door? I'd think that Archie would be all over that," she adds, referring to the head of security for all of Reed Tower.

I mumble a reply, then sip coffee.

"Sorry. I didn't quite get that."

I scowl, but answer. "I haven't told Archie."

"Uh-huh. Shall we discuss the works of Freud? I think someone's got some desires she doesn't want to acknowledge."

"Oh, please. It's infuriating. I just don't want to bother Archie. He's got more than enough on his plate."

She tilts her head, studying me. "I think you're impressed by his persistence."

I scowl at her, hating how well she knows me. "That's not the point."

She laughs. "Actually, I think you're a little turned on by it."

I ignore that part. It hits a little too close to home. "The point is—"

"The point is," she begins, talking right over me, "that he fucked up royally. He did something unforgivable by invading the one space that was truly yours." She leans forward, her expression earnest. "But Sasha, he also owned it. He didn't make excuses or try to justify it. He's just ... there. Showing up. Proving he means what he says."

"Since when are you on Team Liam?" I demand. "I thought you hated the Grimms."

"He's only half-Grimm. And he hates most of them, too. Besides," she continues before I can slide Leo into the conversation, "what matters is that Liam owned his fuck-up. Unlike certain other men we could name."

"He was Killiam."

"Oh, sweetie, I know it's hard." She reaches across the table for my hand.

"He was deliberately playing to my desires, knowing exactly what I wanted because he'd been watching me."

"Maybe. Or maybe it was the real him, connecting with the real you without the baggage of your families' feud. Without the walls both of you built in the real world."

The thought is simultaneously terrifying and compelling. But the truth is, I've seen the real Liam, at least I think I have. And maybe she's right. Because a lot of the things I love about him are the things that made Killiam so perfect.

Love.

Do I still.love him?

And even if I do, is that enough?

"I don't know what to do," I admit, the words barely audible.

Ruby squeezes my hand. "Yes, you do. You're just scared."

She's right, of course. Beneath the anger and hurt, there's a decision I've been circling since that first morning Liam showed up in my sitting room, his eyes haunted by exhaustion and remorse.

"What if I'm wrong?" I ask. "What if I forgive him and it happens again—different lie, same betrayal? Stealing my agency, my control, just like Father did?"

"That's the risk with anyone," Ruby points out. "But Sasha, think about what he did when he found out what your father was doing to you. He didn't just expose it—he stood beside you through all of it. When Desmond was a threat, he protected you. When the press was hounding you, he shielded you. When you needed to escape, he rescued you."

Put like that, the ledger seems more balanced than I've been willing to admit. Yes, Liam invaded my privacy and built a connection on deception. But he's also been there for me in a way no one else ever has, not even Ruby.

"I need to think."

Ruby nods. "For what it's worth, I've never seen you as happy as you were with him in Connecticut. Not ever."

The observation follows me back to Reed Tower, echoing in my mind as the elevator rises toward my suite. *Happy.* Was that what I felt in those peaceful days and passionate nights? The emotion seems too simple, too clean for the complex tangle of feelings Liam Grimm inspires in me. But beneath the complications, Ruby's right. I was happy with him. Hell, I was blissful.

Could I be again, knowing what I know now?

As I step into my suite, I find a note waiting on the coffee table, written in Liam's precise handwriting:

Can we talk over breakfast? - L

I stare at it, still trying to parse out my emotions, trying to truly weigh everything Ruby and I talked about. I'm still unsure. Am I ready to move beyond anger, to hear him out, to consider the possibility of forgiveness?

I pick up the note, running my fingers over the paper, imagining him writing it, hoping I'll respond. Imagining him returning to whatever sterile hotel room he's staying in, waiting for a sign that not everything is lost.

Making my decision, I reach for a pen.

FORTY-ONE
SURRENDER

The aroma of freshly brewed coffee and warm pastries surrounds me when I emerge from the bedroom the next morning. For a moment, I'm transported back to Connecticut—to lazy mornings on the terrace, watching mist rise from the valley below, Liam's presence a steady comfort beside me.

But this isn't Connecticut. This is Reed Tower, and the man arranging breakfast on my dining table carries the weight of betrayal on his shoulders, visible in the careful precision of his movements, in the tension that shows when he hears me enter.

He turns, and the hope in his eyes is so naked that I almost look away. I've never seen Liam Grimm like this—uncertain, exposed, stripped of the control he wears like armor.

"Good morning." His voice is carefully neutral despite the emotion evident in his expression.

"Morning," I reply, moving to the table where he's laid out a spread that reminds me painfully of our time together—croissants, fresh berries with cream, coffee in my favorite mug.

I take my seat, noticing that he's put my note at the center of the table. *Have breakfast waiting, and we'll talk - S*

I look at him—really look at him—for the first time since Maya dropped her bomb. He's lost weight, making the angles of his face sharper, more pronounced. I see shadows under his eyes, too, evidence of more than a few sleepless nights.

I want to pull him close and hold him tight, but I force myself to stay put. I'm still not sure if what I need can mesh with what he's capable of giving.

We eat in silence for a few moments, the tension between us so thick I almost feel I should add a third place-setting.

Finally, I'm unable to take the silence any longer. "Why Killiam?" I ask. "Of all the ways you could have interacted with me in Elysium, why choose to become the prince who Vale loved?"

He doesn't flinch from the question, though I see the effort it costs him to maintain his composure. "It wasn't planned," he says. "I'd been in there for months, watching you build this incredible world, seeing who you were when you thought no one was looking, and realizing I liked that woman." He draws a breath, lifts one shoulder in a tiny shrug. "I wanted to know you—not the woman your father let the world see. And in Elysium, you were real in a way you couldn't be anywhere else."

"So you manipulated me. You used Elysium to learn what I wanted, what I fantasized about, and you used what you learned to become closer and closer to me. To Vale."

"Yes. It was selfish and invasive and wrong. And that's exactly what I did."

The straightforward acknowledgment both surprises and disarms me.

"When did it change? When did it become more than surveillance?"

His brow furrows as he considers the question. "I'm not sure there was a single moment. It was gradual—seeing your creativity, your resilience, your determination to create something beautiful despite being trapped. I started looking forward to our meetings in Elysium more than I should have. And I started thinking about you even when I wasn't monitoring the system."

"Me? Or Vale?"

He meets my eyes. "I was learning that there isn't much difference."

I look away, because he's right.

"And after?" I say, once I've gathered myself. "When you took me from the gala and demanded *everything* as payment—was that just an extension of the game? Another way to possess me?"

"At first, maybe. I told myself it was about revenge, about using you against your father. But Sasha," he says as he leans forward, "from the moment you were actually in my life—the real you, not Vale—nothing went according to plan. You weren't what I expected. You were … more. Hell, Princess, you were everything to me. You *are* everything."

His words melt me a little, which is why I lash out, my voice sharpened by the pain in my heart. "You lied, dammit. Every day, every moment we were together, you knew this massive truth about us—about our connection—and you didn't say a thing."

"I was afraid," he admits, clutching his napkin like a life raft. "I've been through all kinds of hell in my life, and there's nothing I haven't faced down. But you fucking terrified me."

I shake my head, not understanding.

"Dammit, don't you get it? I was afraid that if you knew, you'd leave. That you'd never be able to look at me without seeing the violation. And since I couldn't bear the thought of losing you, what choice did I have but to stay silent?"

"Even if that meant our relationship was based on lies?"

"Yes." He doesn't attempt to soften or excuse it. "I did that. And I have to live with it, whether you forgive me or not."

We fall silent again, the weight of truth hanging heavy between us. I study him across the table, this man who has been both my jailer and my liberator, my deceiver and my protector. The contradictions seem impossible to reconcile.

"I don't know if I can trust you again," I say honestly, unable to look at him. "I want to," I say to the tabletop, "but I don't know if I can."

"I know." His voice is rough with emotion. "I won't blame you if you can't."

I lift my head, drawn to look at him by the intensity of his voice. "But if you give me the chance, I will spend every day proving that what we found in Tribeca and locked down in Connecticut was real. That what I feel for you is real, regardless of how it began."

There it is—the question that's been haunting me since Maya's revelation. *Was any of it real?* The connection, the understanding, the sense of finally being truly seen?

"I want to show you something," I say, making a decision. I stand, then lead him into my studio. I cross to an easel in the corner, removing the cloth that covers my most recent work. It's a painting of the Connecticut house, rendered in oils with painstaking detail—the glass and stone gleaming in morning light, the forest surrounding it in vibrant greens and golds.

"You painted this?" he asks, genuine surprise in his voice.

I nod. "I couldn't stop thinking about it. About the life we had there." I shrug. "I guess I was trying to hold on to a piece of it."

His eyes move from the painting to my face, and I see something like hope kindling in that vibrant blue. "It's beautiful," he says.

"It was," I agree quietly. "What we had there was beautiful, Liam. And I think … I think parts of it were real. The parts that matter."

"All of it was real for me," he says, his voice low and intense. "Every moment, every conversation, every touch. The deception was in how we got there, not what we found once we arrived."

I turn to face the window, the view of Manhattan spread out below, so different from the peaceful forest surrounding his Connecticut home. "There's something else I need to show you."

Moving to the window, I step onto the small fire escape outside.

"Sasha," he says, and there's so much joy in his voice that I know he understands.

"It's still there" I tell him. "The fear. But it doesn't control me anymore." I turn to face him, the wind tugging at my hair. "That's because of you. Because you showed me I was stronger than I thought. That I could face the things that frightened me."

Something shifts in his expression—hope warring with caution, as if he doesn't dare believe what he's hearing. When he extends a hand to help me back inside, I take it, and I don't let go once I'm safely back in the apartment.

"When I found out about Elysium, about Prince Killiam, I was shattered. I thought everything between us was just another manipulation, another cage built by someone who wanted to control me."

"It wasn't—"

"I was wrong," I say. "What happened in Connecticut was something new—something honest, despite how it began."

I see the hope on his face, and I take a deep breath. Then I say the words I've been pondering for days. "I think we're meant to be together," I tell him, looking down at our interlocked fingers. "All the twisted paths that brought us here … they led us to something real. Something worth fighting for."

The relief that crosses his face is almost painful to witness—a man who expected condemnation finding grace instead. "Sasha …"

I step closer, wanting to feel his warmth, to see the storm of emotions in his eyes. "We can't go back to how things were. But maybe we can build something new. Something based on truth this time."

He lifts his hand, then kisses the back of mine. Then he lets go and cups my cheek, his thumb brushing my lower lip in a way that's achingly familiar.

"I love you," he says, the words simple and devastating in their sincerity. "I have for longer than I've been willing to admit, even to myself."

"I love you, too," I whisper. "That's what scares me most."

When he kisses me, it's not the passionate claiming I've come to expect from Liam Grimm. It's gentle, almost reverent, as if he's afraid I might disappear if he asks for too much. I'm the one who deepens it, pressing closer, letting my body communicate what words can't fully express—that despite everything, despite the lies and betrayal, what exists between us is powerful enough to survive.

We stumble toward the bedroom, a tangle of hungry kisses and determined hands that can't get enough of each other. By the time we crash onto the bed, we're both half-undressed and fully desperate, tearing at our remaining clothes like they've personally offended us.

There's something frantic about the way we reach for each other now—like we need to erase the distance with our bodies that we've already bridged with words.

The rest of our clothes are ripped off, tossed aside, and then he's above me, looking down with an expression of such raw vulnerability that it takes my breath away. In this moment, stripped of all pretense and deception, Liam Grimm is more naked than I've ever seen him— not just physically, but emotionally. The man who always maintains control, who plans ten steps ahead, is utterly present in this moment, holding nothing back.

"I thought I'd lost you," he whispers, his voice rough with emotion.

"You almost did," I admit, reaching up to trace the line of his jaw. "I'm glad you didn't."

He lowers his head, pressing his forehead to mine, our breath mingling in the charged space between us. "I will never lie to you again," he promises. "Not about anything, no matter how difficult the truth might be."

"I'm holding you to that," I say, then pull him down for a kiss that closes the last of the distance between us.

What follows is unlike any of our previous encounters—more intense for the honesty that now exists between us, more passionate for having nearly been lost. He worships my body with hands and mouth, atoning for betrayal by bathing me in pleasure, and I respond in kind, claiming him as mine despite everything that should have torn us apart.

When he finally enters me, the sensation is both familiar and new. A fresh intensity. A deeper connection so that when that glorious release finally comes, it's shattering. A wave that crests and breaks, flinging us both into ecstasy. He collapses beside me, gathering me against him as if still afraid I'll disappear. I curl into his embrace, finding comfort in the steady rhythm of his heart beneath my ear.

"We should go back to Connecticut," he murmurs against my hair, his voice heavy with satisfied exhaustion.

"Yes," I agree, the thought of returning to the peaceful sanctuary of his home—our home—is deeply appealing. "But not yet. There are things I need to handle here first."

"Reed Cosmetics?"

I nod. "I can't keep avoiding my responsibilities. My mother's legacy deserves better than that."

His arms tighten around me. "Whatever you decide, I'll support you."

"I know," I say, snuggling close.

We lay in silence for a while, my finger tracing patterns on his chest as I let my mind wander. Minutes pass, maybe hours, and somewhere in there we begin to talk. The garden at the Connecticut house, plans to monetize Elysium, trips we want to take together, the future of Reed Cosmetics.

"I think I want to rebrand in a way that honors my mother."

"Lydia Cosmetics?" he suggests.

"Maybe. But maybe something even bigger than a name change. I don't know." I trace patterns on his chest, thinking. "And, of course, I still want to market Elysium."

"You'll be a busy woman." He nips my ear. "It's very sexy."

I laugh. "There's a way to motivate me to get busy. You'll help me?"

He strokes my hair, smiling in a way that tells me he likes it short just as much. "I will always help you."

I smile as we slide into an easy back and forth. There's still a wound from his betrayal, but it's overshadowed by the potential of what we might build together.

Eventually, conversation gives way to comfortable silence, and then to sleep, and for the first time since leaving Connecticut, I know I'll sleep soundly, his presence more powerful than the ghosts of the past that haunt Reed Tower.

FORTY-TWO
BROKEN

I wake to the sensation of fingers gently combing through my hair. Liam is propped on one elbow, watching me with an expression that makes my breath catch—tender, possessive, utterly unguarded.

"Creepy," I murmur, smiling to soften the word. "Watching me sleep."

A shadow crosses his face, and I remember how I'd gone off on him last night about watching me in Elysium.

I grimace. "Sorry. That's meant to be joke. Apparently, a bad one."

The tension eases from his expression. "We're going to need to work on your comedic timing," he says, pressing a kiss to my palm.

"Among other things," I agree. "Starting with breakfast. I'm starving."

He chuckles. "That, I can definitely help with."

As he rises from the bed, unabashedly naked and magnificent in the morning light, his phone chimes from the pocket of his discarded pants. He retrieves it, glances at the screen, and his entire demeanor changes in an instant—shoulders tensing, jaw tightening, the relaxed lover replaced by the strategic warrior.

"What is it?"

He frowns, and I'm certain he's debating whether to share whatever news he's received.

A chill cuts through me. "Dammit, Grimm. You promised. No more lies. No more secrets."

"I know." He sighs, then sits on the edge of the bed, the phone still in his hand. "Leo just texted. Your father is back in New York."

The words hit me like a physical blow, stealing the breath from my lungs. Victor. Back. After weeks of searching, of warrants and investigations, he's resurfaced—deliberately, no doubt. My father never does anything without calculation.

"How does Leo know?" I manage, my voice steadier than I expected.

"Sources in the NYPD."

I start to ask why Leo would have cop connections, but that's really not the point. "Does the NYPD have him in custody?"

"Not yet. But he's been seen in the financial district. And he's furious about the Reed Cosmetics situation."

Of course, he is. He never intended to let the company pass to me. And now I legally control my mother's legacy, the empire he's spent years claiming as his own.

"He'll come after me," I say, the certainty bone deep. "Try to force me to sign over control."

Liam's expression hardens, a glimpse of the danger that lives inside this man I've fallen for. "Let him try."

"Grimm—"

"He won't touch you," he says, voice low and fierce. "Not again. Not ever."

The vehemence in his tone should be frightening. Instead, I find it oddly comforting—this absolute certainty that he will stand between me and harm, whatever form it takes.

"We need a plan," I say, switching from fear to strategy. "There are arrest warrants out for him. If he's come back without his attorneys, then this isn't about trying to regain control of the company. It's about me."

Liam nods, and from his expression, I can see that he got to that conclusion before I did.

"I'm moving you to Grimm Tower. Ruby, too, if she wants. She can stay with you. I don't want you here. He knows his way around this tower too well, and a man like him would have escape routes. For all we know, he can get up to your suite from the sewer."

I look around the apartment, suddenly afraid my father might burst out from under the kitchen sink. But Liam's not wrong. "Okay," I say. In part because I'm scared, and in part because he's right.

Mostly because I know this is about my safety and he won't take no for an answer.

"What are you going to do?"

"Find him," he says. "Leo's already digging, trying to find out what Victor's planning."

I nod, strangely calm as a storm builds inside me—rage mingled with an odd anticipation. All my life, I've been at my father's mercy, subject to his control, his manipulation, his vision of who I should be.

Not anymore.

"I want to face him," I say, the words surprising even me. "Not hide. Not run. When the time comes, I want to look him in the eye and show him exactly who I've become. And I want the satisfaction of giving the evidence that puts that prick behind bars."

Liam studies me, something like pride flickering in his expression. "Are you sure?"

I nod, certainty growing with each passing moment. "More than sure. This ends when I say it ends. On my terms, not his."

"All right." He reaches for me, pulling me close, his lips pressing against my forehead in a gesture both tender and fierce. "I've got your back."

I sigh as I wrap my arms around him. Whatever my father is planning, I won't face it alone. I have Liam beside me, Ruby behind me, and most importantly, a newfound confidence in my own strength.

Let Victor Reed come. The princess is no longer locked in the tower—she's standing on the battlements, ready for war.

———

THE NEXT FEW days pass in a strange limbo as we wait for my father's inevitable move. Liam's suite at Grimm Tower has become command central, and he spends hours in his study with Leo as they organize the teams that are tracking my father. In my spare time, I work on Elysium, trying to build it out in a commercially viable way.

But most of my attention is on Reed Cosmetics, with Ruby and me working long hours to review operations, solidify my position with the board, and begin laying groundwork for the rebranding I envision.

"I've been going through the corporate archives," Ruby tells me one afternoon, spreading photographs across my desk. "Look at these —early campaigns from when Lydia was still alive."

The images show a strikingly different aesthetic than the princess-perfect strategy my father later developed. These are vibrant and empowering—women of all colors and ages, portrayed with strength and character rather than porcelain perfection.

"This was her vision," I say softly, touching one particularly powerful image. "Not the sugary, sanitized version my father created."

"I can't believe these were just shoved in a box in the basement archives."

I shoot her a sideways glance. "Clearly, you haven't met my father."

"Good point."

We share a grin. It's nice to have her at my side again. And now that she's officially the Vice-President in Charge of Marketing, she's no longer part of the Reed Tower staff.

"I talked to Vanessa Grady," I tell her, referring to a former board member who, I learned, was once my mother's best friend. "She told me all sorts of stories about me. Apparently, she was Lydia's best friend. She said I called her Auntie Van."

Ruby leans back in her chair. "Do you remember her?"

"I didn't before, but once she told me that, I started to. I thought maybe it was a fake memory—you know, wishful thinking. Me and my mom and Auntie Van at a park, the two of them taking turns pushing me on a swing, and a picnic with a watermelon. And the three of us having a contest to see who could spit the seeds the farthest."

"Who won?"

"Me," I say. "But I think they let me cheat." I smile, savoring the memory. "I called her when it came back—it was still fuzzy—and she said it was true. Every moment." I grin. "But she wouldn't confirm tossing the contest so I could win."

Ruby reaches for my hand and squeezes it. "The fucker tried to take that from you."

"And I'm going to make sure he rots in prison, spending every day left in his miserable life thinking about the harm he did to Lydia, to me, to god knows who else. Honestly, I don't think I've looked forward to anything more than testifying against him in court. Hopefully sooner rather than later. Seriously. Just thinking about it is better than ice cream."

"Liam and Leo will find him," she says. "And I'll be right there beside you when they lock the prison gate behind him."

I trace my fingertip over one of the pictures. "He took something important from the world when he killed her. Auntie Van said she was revolutionary for her time. She believed beauty products should enhance confidence, not prop up insecurity."

"I love that," Ruby says.

"Me, too."

It's a concept I'm determined to reclaim and get out into the market, and each day, Ruby and I work to tweak my mother's still-born campaign in a way that makes it both hers and mine. It's melancholy work, but I love every minute, because each new idea brings me closer to the mother I never had the chance to know.

Nights bring a different kind of intimacy—a new tenderness between me and Liam that wasn't possible when secrets still lingered between us.

"I never asked," he says one night as we lie tangled together in the darkness, "but what made you decide to forgive me? To give us another chance?"

The question catches me off guard, though I've asked myself the same thing many times. "Ruby, partly," I admit. "She reminded me that you owned your mistakes. That you didn't make excuses."

His arm tightens around me. "Remind me to thank her."

"Mostly, it was you. Showing up every day. Owning what you did and understanding that it wasn't just the deception of sliding into Killiam, but that you stole something vital from me." I smile at him. "But you get it now."

"I do," he says. He's silent for a long moment, his fingers tracing idle patterns on my skin. "I love you, Princess," he whispers.

"I love you, too, Grimm."

We're asleep when the call comes at 3:42 a.m.—Liam's phone

vibrating on the nightstand, casting eerie blue light across the ceiling. He answers immediately, fully alert despite the hour.

"When?" he asks after a moment of listening, his body going rigid beside me. "Are you sure? Keep monitoring. I'm on my way."

"What is it?" I ask, sitting up in bed as he pulls on clothes.

"We've got eyes on Victor." His voice is tight. Urgent. "And he's not alone. Bane's with him, along with what looks like a private security detail."

My heart pounds against my ribs. "Where are they going?"

"That's what I need to find out." He straps on a shoulder holster, checking a gun before sliding it into place—a stark reminder of the dangerous man beneath the lover I've come to know.

"I'm coming with you," I say, already reaching for clothes.

"No." His voice is firm, brooking no argument. "You stay here, where it's safe. Enhanced security is already on the way up. No one gets in or out without clearance."

"Liam—"

He crosses to the bed, cupping my face in his hands. "Please, Sasha. I need to know you're safe while I deal with this."

The intensity in his eyes stops my protest. This isn't about control —it's about protection. His desperate need to keep me from harm.

"Okay, but you stay in contact. I want to know exactly what's happening."

"I promise." He kisses me, brief but fierce. "Everything will be fine," he assures me, though the promise doesn't reach his eyes. "Stay here. Stay safe."

The next few hours are excruciating. Ruby joins me, but we don't talk. Instead, she sits on the sofa while I pace the suite, checking my phone obsessively for updates from Liam, which come in terse, infrequent texts:

Following Victor. In Tribeca.

Heading toward Brooklyn now. Bane separated, going elsewhere. Secondary team following.

He's stopped. Team's approaching with caution.

Then, nothing. An hour of silence that stretches my nerves to the breaking point. I call, but it goes straight to voicemail. I text, but there's no response.

Something is wrong. Terribly, catastrophically wrong.

"You don't know that," Ruby says. "Don't worry until you have to." Her expression, however, suggests that I should be worrying.

I'm about to ignore Liam's edict not to leave the suite when my phone finally rings—not Liam's number, but Leo's.

"What's happened?" I demand without preamble. "Where's Liam?"

"He's okay," Leo says, though something in his voice suggests otherwise. "But … There's been an incident."

I go cold. "What kind of incident?"

For a moment, he's silent. Then, "Victor Reed is dead."

The words hit me like a gut-punch, stealing my breath. "What?"

"Shot once, at close range. The shit had a weapon. He was threatening Liam. There were witnesses."

Dead. The monster of my childhood, the architect of my captivity, the man who poisoned and manipulated me—gone. Forever.

"So, it was self-defense?" My father tried to kill Liam?

A pause, then, "One-hundred percent."

It's the answer I want to hear, but I feel a chill up my spine nonetheless.

"I need to see Liam," I say, already moving toward the door. "Where is he?"

"Police station in Brooklyn. Giving his statement." Leo sounds tired, resigned. "I'll text you the address."

The ride to the station passes in a blur of conflicting emotions—shock, grief, relief, anger. The father I hate killed by the man I love. The finality of it is both liberating and terrifying. No more looking over my shoulder, no more fear of being recaptured and controlled.

But I heard the truth in Leo's lie, and now I can't help but fear that the cost of what Liam did is going to break both of us.

At the station, I'm directed to a small interview room where he's waiting alone, hands clasped between his knees, head bowed. He looks up when I enter, and the expression on his face cuts straight through me—part relief at seeing me, part dread at what he knows must follow.

"Sasha," he says, rising to his feet. "You shouldn't be here."

I glance around the room. "Can we talk in here?"

His brows rise, and I'm certain he knows what I'm going to ask. He nods.

"Was it really self-defense?" I hear the prayer in my voice. The hope that somehow, I've misinterpreted everything.

His gaze doesn't waver. "That's what the police report will say."

In other words, *no.*

No excuses. No justifications. Just the simple, devastating truth that makes my heart crack open.

"Why?" The word emerges as barely more than a whisper.

"He was planning to take you," Liam says, his voice flat, emotionless. "Tonight. He had Bane and a team of mercenaries ready. They were all set up to slide in with Grimm security. They anticipated we'd stay at my suite once this ball started rolling, and the plan was to snatch you there."

Snatch. I shiver. Both from what could have happened … and what did.

"How do you know all this?"

"Leo intercepted communications. He got one of the mercs to talk. By the time I had confirmation, Victor was already moving." His expression hardens. "I couldn't let him take you. Not again. Not ever."

"So you killed him." The words hang in the air between us, heavy with implication.

"I confronted him. He had a gun. It happened."

But we both know the truth behind the carefully constructed narrative. Liam tracked my father down and eliminated the threat permanently. Not in the heat of the moment, not in immediate self-defense, but as a calculated decision to protect me once and for all.

"You should have told me," I say, anger flaring suddenly. "You should have discussed it with me. My father, my life, my choice. Not yours."

"There wasn't time—"

"Bullshit," I cut him off, stepping closer as fury overtakes shock. "Dammit, Grimm, we talked about this, and then you just decided without me, anyway. Without even giving me the chance to weigh in. I told you I wanted him arrested. That I wanted to face the bastard in court, to have the world know exactly what he did to me."

"Sasha—"

"All your empty fucking promises, and still you took that from me. Decided for me, just like *he* always did. So you tell me, Liam, how the fuck are you better than my bastard of a father?"

He flinches as if struck, and I know my words have cut deep. "That's not—"

"You went out there planning to kill him. To eliminate the threat. To handle it."

He doesn't deny it, which somehow makes it worse. "I couldn't risk losing you," he says simply. "I couldn't take the chance that he might take you back into that nightmare."

The raw honesty in his voice defuses some of my anger, morphing it into something more complicated. Grief for a father I never really had. Confusion over moral lines that have been irreparably blurred.

"What happens now?" I finally ask.

"Legally? Nothing." He looks exhausted, the strain of the night evident in every line of his face. "The evidence supports self-defense. There were witnesses—including Victor's own people—who were more than happy to turn on him when the police arrived. I'll give my statement, and that will be that."

"I'm not talking about legally," I clarify. "I'm talking about us."

His eyes meet mine, vulnerable in a way I've rarely seen. "That depends on you," he says quietly. "On whether what I've done is … unforgivable."

The question hangs between us, demanding an answer I don't have. Do I walk away from the man who killed my father? The man who went to extremes to protect me? The man who, despite his methods, acted out of love?

But he's also a man who knew I wanted to confront my father—to see him ripped to shreds in a court of law—but killed him anyway, nullifying my decision and stealing my choice with one blast of a gun.

Is that a man I can forgive? And even if I can, is that a man with whom I want to move forward?

"I need time," I say finally. "To process all of this. To figure out how I feel. Because dammit, Grimm, this one cuts deep. We just fucking talked about this."

"I know," he says, accepting this with the same grace he showed during our earlier separation. And that's infuriating as hell, too.

There's a knock at the door, and an officer enters, telling Liam that they're ready for him. I leave the room with him, then turn the opposite direction and walk toward the exit without saying goodbye.

My father is dead. The man who imprisoned and medicated me, who stole my mother's legacy, then killed her. A man who treated me as property rather than a person.

That horrible man is gone forever.

The knowledge should bring relief, closure, perhaps even joy. Instead, it brings a complicated tangle of emotions I can't yet unravel.

Outside, the city is waking, the first hints of dawn painting the eastern sky.

My driver steps out, then opens the door for me. "Reed Tower," I tell him, then pull out my phone to call and update Ruby.

"There's going to be fallout from this," I say after I've run it all down for her. "We'll need to inform the board and get ready."

"I'll start working on your press statement." She pauses. "What are you going to do about Grimm? Can you forgive him?"

"I don't know," I say, because it's the only answer I have. "Right now, I don't have time to think about it." And that's a good thing. Because if I did, I think all I'd be able to do is cry.

FORTY-THREE

HARD RECKONING

By mid-morning, the news is everywhere: "COSMETICS MAGNATE VICTOR REED DEAD IN CONFRONTATION WITH GRIMM HEIR."

Similar headlines are plastered across every major outlet, each version more sensational than the last. Some paint my father as a tragic figure, others as the villain he truly was. Some portray Liam as a cold-blooded killer settling a family feud. Still others spin him as a hero who protected his former enemy—a woman with whom he'd fallen in love—from the father who'd abused her for most of her life.

The last reads like a romance novel and is the closest to the truth. I'm just not sure if it's a truth I can live with.

Reporters circle Reed Tower like vultures, their cameras and microphones ready to capture even the smallest tidbit to feed their ratings.

Inside, Ruby and I work with a crisis management team on the official statement that acknowledges my father's death, the past abuse that was revealed at the guardianship hearing, and the new revelation to the public that he killed my mother, his wife. Other than that, I've decided to say nothing. And I certainly won't say that I'm sorry he's dead, as that would be a lie.

But at the same time, I am sorry, because I'd wanted the chance to see justice served. To see him locked up and paying for what he'd done to me.

Liam took that possibility away, and while I don't know if I can forgive him for that, I do know it's not something I choose to talk about with the press. The world has had enough peeks into my life. It's time to draw the curtains and live outside the spotlight as much as I can.

"The board wants an emergency meeting," Ruby says, tablet in hand as she scrolls through the flood of emails and messages. "They're freaking out about stability, stock prices, public perception—you know, the usual corporate panic."

"Of course they are," I say with a tired sigh. "Schedule it for tomorrow. I need time to get my head straight."

"And this," Ruby continues, swiping to another screen, "is the official police report. They released it twenty minutes ago."

I scan the document, taking in the key points of the carefully worded narrative: Victor Reed, wanted for multiple charges. Confronted by Liam Grimm. An altercation ensued. Reed drew a weapon. Grimm fired once in self-defense. Multiple witnesses corroborated the sequence of events.

Clean. Simple. Believable.

And mostly bullshit.

I set the tablet aside, exhaustion hitting me in waves. "Any word on Desmond Bane?"

"Nothing solid. Leo's sources say he fled the scene before the shooting.

The thought of Desmond still out there sends an unpleasant chill through me. But I have bigger problems right now—the company, the press, the legal aftermath of my father's death.

And Liam. Always Liam.

As if summoned by my thoughts, he appears in the doorway, face carefully blank. "The press conference is set for four. Legal has prepared statements for both of us. They think we should appear together—show a united front."

The sound of his measured voice ignites something in me that I've been holding back since our return from the police station.

"Get out," I say quietly.

Ruby's head snaps up, eyes widening. Liam remains perfectly still, only the slight tightening of his jaw showing he's heard me at all.

"Sasha—"

"I said get out," I repeat, my voice steady despite the storm inside me. "Not just my suite. The tower. I don't want you here."

Ruby stands awkwardly. "I should probably—"

"No," I interrupt. "Liam is leaving. There's nothing to discuss."

Liam's eyes meet mine, searching for something—understanding, maybe, or forgiveness. When he doesn't find either, he nods once. "The statement—"

"Will be handled," I say, cutting him off. "I've managed press conferences without you before. I'll do it again."

Pain flashes across his face, quickly masked. Good. Let him hurt. Let him feel a fraction of the betrayal he tossed at me.

Without another word, he turns and leaves, his footsteps fading down the corridor. The moment the elevator doors close behind him, my composure cracks. I hug myself as I tremble, furious and scared and mourning the trust that has died between us.

"What the hell happened?" Ruby asks, urging me into a chair. "I mean, I know what happened with your father, but—"

"It wasn't self-defense," I say, forcing the words out past the knot of tears in my throat. "He went there planning to kill my father."

"Oh, Sasha."

"I wanted to see that bastard behind bars. Grimm stole that chance."

"What can I do?" Ruby asks, her hand warm on my shoulder.

I draw a deep breath, pulling myself together piece by piece. "Same as you've been doing. We focus on the company. Nothing else matters right now."

For a moment, I think she's going to argue, or at least ask about Liam. About what I'm going to do next. Thankfully, she doesn't. "Okay, then," she says. "One step at a time. Let's get through today."

I nod. "One step at a time."

The press conference passes in a blur of flashbulbs and shouted questions, and I deliver my statement with the composure expected of a Reed. If the reporters notice Liam's absence, they don't push it—not with the Reed legal team flanking me like guard dogs.

By evening, I'm emotionally and physically drained, and as the weight of the day presses down on me, I allow myself a moment of genuine grief—not for the father who had imprisoned and controlled me, but for the father I might have had in some other life, some other reality.

My phone rings, Liam's name lighting up the screen. I let it go to voicemail, unable to face his voice, his explanations, his justifications. Not tonight. Maybe not ever.

When sleep finally comes, it's broken and shallow, haunted by dreams of my father's face, of Liam's hands covered in blood, of towers with no exits and doors with no keys.

Morning brings little relief, but at least the immediate crisis is manageable. The board meeting goes as well as can be expected— questions answered with calm authority, a path forward outlined. I present my plans for rebranding as Lydia Cosmetics, honoring my mother's original vision while propelling the company into the future. If there are doubts, they're kept respectfully muted.

Days pass, then a week. Liam continues to call, to text, his messages increasingly desperate, increasingly raw. I read them all but respond to none. What is there to say? How do you begin to address such a fundamental breach of trust?

"He's a mess, Sasha," Ruby says one afternoon. "I've never seen him like this."

"Good," I reply, the word lacking the conviction I intend.

"Don't you think you should at least talk to him? Hear his side?"

I look up from the marketing reports spread across my desk, a flurry of thoughts and feelings kicking back up as they do whenever I think of him. Which is pretty much all the time.

The truth is, despite everything, I still love him. And I miss him with an intensity that frightens me. But at the same time, he stole something vital from me. Something he knew I wanted. And, yes, I know he feared that Victor would get to me before I could get him in a courtroom. But that doesn't change the truth. It doesn't give back what he stole.

"I can't," I say finally. "Not yet."

Ruby sighs. "Just think about it, okay? He loves you, Sash. He fucked up, but I truly believe he loves you."

"I know he does," I say. "I'm just not sure that's enough."

Even without him beside me, Liam Grimm stays in my mind, finding his way into my dreams, my thoughts. Funny things he'd whispered come back to me for no good reason. I shiver suddenly, certain I'd felt the brush of his fingers.

I try to ignore it, pouring all of my focus into reshaping Reed—no, Lydia—Cosmetics to reclaim my mother's vision while also working on expanding Elysium's reach. I sleep little and eat less, driven by a restless energy that's the only thing keeping me upright.

I'm tempted to lose myself in Elysium, but I don't. I'm too afraid that if Liam is there as Killiam, Vale won't have the fortitude to walk away. Especially since I'm feeling that fortitude fade in the real world.

It's nearly midnight on the twentieth day after my father's death when the elevator to my suite opens without warning. I look up from my laptop to find Liam standing in my living room, disheveled and haggard in a way I've never seen him before.

"You shouldn't be here," I say, my voice steadier than I expect.

"You need to start answering your phone," he counters, a flicker of his usual intensity briefly visible beneath the exhaustion.

I close my laptop and set it aside, but I stay seated on the couch. "Ruby let you up?"

He just tilts his head and cocks a brow, clearly insulted that I'd think he needed clearance.

Despite myself, I laugh.

"Just five minutes. That's all I'm asking for. Five minutes to explain, and then if you still want me gone, I'll go. For good this time."

The promise—or threat—of permanence makes me pause. Do I want him gone for good? The thought creates a hollow ache in my chest, an emptiness I can't ignore.

"Five minutes," I agree, gesturing to the chair across from me.

He remains standing, too agitated to sit. "I've been thinking about what to say, how to explain, for weeks now. And I realized there's no explanation that makes it right. No justification that erases what I did."

The admission catches me off guard. I'd expected defenses, rationalizations, clever arguments designed to minimize his guilt.

"So this is going to be a quiet five minutes?"

I see the hope bloom in his eyes, and wish I'd kept my snark to myself.

"I was wrong," he says simply. "Not just in what I did, but in how

I did it. I took a choice from you that wasn't mine to take, and the truth is I knew better, especially after our talk about Elysium."

He pauses, as if expecting me to say something. I just look at him, part of me still furious. And another part of me hoping that he knows what to say to get me through to the other side of that anger.

"He was going to take you," Liam says, his voice rough with emotion. "He had a plan, a team, a facility outside U.S. jurisdiction. He was going to drug you, imprison you, control you."

Bile rises in my throat, and my skin goes cold.

"I couldn't—" He breaks off, struggling for composure. "I couldn't stand the thought of you back in that nightmare. Not when I could stop it."

"So you appointed yourself judge, jury, and executioner," I say, though the words lack their earlier heat.

"Yes," he admits. "I did. I told myself it was protection, but it was also—oh, hell, it was like what your father did, I know that. I took a choice that should have been yours. Hell, I took it even though I knew you would have said no. You wanted him alive and tried and imprisoned. I just wanted him gone, because that was the only way I could be certain you could be safe. So, I did what I did. And the truth is, if I had to do it all over again, I don't know if I'd do it differently."

I gape at him. That really wasn't the speech I'd been expecting.

"But," he says, taking a step forward, "I do know that I'd tell you first. I'd let you try to talk me down, explain why I have to let the bastard live. Tell me all your worries about me being the one who ends up behind bars. And you'd be right. And I'd pull back, and we'd call in the authorities. He'd still be alive, but he'd be behind bars. I wouldn't have the satisfaction of killing him, but I'd have you. And that matters, Sasha. That matters so much. Because right now, not having you is killing me."

He's moved closer, and now he kneels in front of me, his hands on my thighs. He lifts one to my face, and I only realize I'm crying when he wipes away a tear. The brutal honesty of everything he's said has cut deep into my core, and I have to force myself not to pull him close.

"I'm not asking for forgiveness," he says. "I'm asking for a chance to earn your trust again. To prove that I can be the man you deserve."

I study him—the shadows under his eyes, the stubble darkening his jaw, the tension radiating from his shoulders. He looks as miserable as I feel, and I want to scream *yes*, but I have to be smart.

"I need time," I finally say. "Will you give me that?"

"It's not mine to give. Take the time you need. I'll be here when you're ready."

As he turns to leave, I find myself speaking before I've fully formed the thought. "Grimm."

He pauses, hope flickering briefly in his eyes.

"Thank you," I say. "For telling the truth. For not trying to justify what you did."

A ghost of a smile touches his lips. "I'm learning," he says. "Slowly, maybe. But learning."

FORTY-FOUR
SURRENDER

Liam watched her from across the café table, cataloging every micro-expression that crossed her face. The slight tension around her eyes had eased over the past weeks, the wariness in her gaze less pronounced each time they met. She was still guarded—he'd earned that—but the wall between them was crumbling, brick by painful brick.

The weeks following Victor's death had been the darkest of his life. Not from guilt—he'd never regret eliminating that bastard—but from the cold emptiness of her absence. He'd become accustomed to her presence, her warmth, her sharp intelligence cutting through his defenses.

Without her, the Connecticut house felt like a mausoleum, echoing with ghosts of what might have been.

"The rebranding is going well," she said, tucking a strand of hair behind her ear. A nervous gesture, one she wasn't aware of making. "The board has finally approved the name change to Lydia Cosmetics."

"Your mother would be proud." So was he. She was so much stronger than she knew. A woman who'd suffered no end of abuse and had essentially raised herself. A daughter determined to honor her mother's legacy, refusing to be defined by her father's shadow.

Her eyes lit briefly, and the flash of pleasure at his words was like a physical blow to his chest. He'd become addicted to her rare, genuine smiles, hoarding them like precious gems in the vault of his memory.

"There's still resistance to some of the changes I want to implement," she continued, then outlined her vision—diverse models, ethical sourcing, and technologies that would revolutionize the industry. Her hands animated her words, her passion evident in every syllable.

Liam absorbed every detail, not just her plans but the way her whole face brightened when she spoke of the future, the curve of her throat as she leaned forward, the pulse beating steadily at her temple. He'd always been observant, but with Sasha, the observation became reverence.

Their meetings grew more frequent as the weeks passed. Coffee evolved into lunch, lunch into dinner, and dinner into long walks through Central Park as twilight settled over the city. Never touching, always with that careful distance maintained between them, a boundary he wouldn't cross without explicit invitation. No matter how much he wanted to.

It was a strange purgatory for a man accustomed to taking what he wanted. Waiting. Hoping.

Liam Grimm, brought to his knees by the mere possibility of her forgiveness.

"I miss you," he admitted one evening as they stood watching the sunset paint the skyline in crimson and gold. Three simple words that cost him more than million-dollar deals or security empires ever had.

She turned to him, her face cast in light and shadow. "I miss you, too," she said, her voice barely above a whisper. "But I'm still ..."

"I know." He cut her off, sparing her the need to articulate what they both understood. "We have time."

Something softened in her expression, a surrender so subtle most would have missed it. But he'd made a study of her face, knew every micro-expression, every fleeting emotion. She was beginning to trust him again.

He hoped she'd decide that he'd earned it.

He knew he'd move heaven and earth to deserve it.

That night, he dreamed of her in the Connecticut house. She stood on the terrace, morning light turning her hair to molten gold. When she turned to him, her smile held no reservations, no shadows. Just Sasha, fully present, fully his.

He woke with her name on his lips and a decision crystallized in his mind. Before he could second-guess himself, he texted her. Simple. Direct. *Come back to Connecticut with me this weekend?*

Her response came faster than he'd dared hope: *Yes.*

As far as Liam was concerned, the weekend couldn't get there soon enough.

The next day, she asked him to meet her in her suite at Reed Tower. As the elevator ascended, he remembered the photo shoot on the roof of this building, a day that had set so many wheels in motion. Then, she'd been his bludgeon to use against Victor.

Now, she was his everything.

She was waiting when he arrived, composed but with tension evident in the set of her shoulders, the slight tremor in her hands as she motioned him to an overstuffed chair. He obeyed, though every instinct screamed to close the distance between them, to touch her, to claim her again.

"I've been thinking," she began, her voice steady despite the nervous rhythm of her fingers against her thigh. "About us. About where we go from here."

He remained silent, granting her the space to find her way through this conversation, even though he was terrified she'd shift in a direction he didn't want to go. Cancel the trip to the Connecticut house. Or worse, cut him loose altogether.

But he held his tongue, determined to let her get the first word in. And the last, if she wanted.

"What you did was wrong," she began, settling on the sofa, her hands twisting together in her lap. "Not just killing my father but making that decision without me. Taking away my choice in how to handle my own father, my own life."

"I know," he said, the inadequacy of the words bitter on his tongue. "It was unforgivable."

"No," she countered, and the word sent a jolt through him more powerful than any electric shock. "Not unforgivable. Just ... difficult to forgive. But I think ... I think I'm ready to try."

Hope crashed over him with such violence that for a moment he couldn't speak. "Sasha—"

She held up a hand to silence him "It's not because what you did was right. It wasn't. It was a hundred kinds of wrong. But these last few weeks, our coffees, our talks …" She trailed off with a shrug and a smile. "I see you, Liam. I see who you are, and who you want to be. I even see who we can be together, if we both keep trying." Her smile was quick and tentative. "I mean, if that's something you want."

"God, yes," the distance between them became unbearable, and he moved from his chair to kneel before her, taking her hands in his.

"I don't deserve you," he said, his voice rough with emotion.

"Probably not." A tiny smile danced over her lips. "But it looks like you're stuck with me."

The kiss started out soft and tentative, but that shattered in seconds, giving way to a wild intensity that surged between them like a living thing, as if every lost moment of their time apart was demanding its turn.

His hands moved over her with the ferocity of ownership—tangling in her hair, clutching her hips, teasing her ass. And her explorations were just as wild, ripping his jacket off his shoulder, yanking his shirt open so that buttons popped, sliding her hands along his rock-hard abs.

"Fuck the bedroom." She whispered against his mouth, then pulled him up onto the sofa with her. "Here. Now."

Liam groaned his approval, straddling her thighs as she lay back on the cushions. He hiked her skirt up around her waist, his fingers teasing along the edge of her panties. "I've been dreaming about being inside you again."

"Then it's time to make a dream come true."

The tease in her voice only made him harder, and he yanked her panties aside, too desperate for the feel of her to waste time on niceties. He thrust two fingers inside her, then groaned when he found her already slick and ready. "Christ, Princess," he growled, curling his fingers to hit that naughty little spot that made her cry out and buck against him. "Are you wet for me?"

"Only you." She wrapped her hand around his cock, stroking him with just the right pressure to make his hips buck. "Only ever for you."

He withdrew his fingers and positioned himself at her entrance, bracing his weight on one forearm while his other hand gripped her hip. They locked eyes, a moment of raw connection before he buried himself inside herin one powerful stroke.

The sensation was electric, even more so because of their time apart. Then Sasha rolled her hips, shattering his fragile restraint. He fucked her hard, each thrust driving deeper than the last, claiming her more thoroughly, his hold on her hip tight enough to bruise. To mark her as his. Because, dammit, he'd never let her go again.

She clawed at his back, her head thrown back to expose her throat to his hungry mouth.

"God, I missed this." He nipped at her skin, sucking and teasing, leaving a mark high on her neck where anyone could see it. "I missed the way you feel. The sounds you make when I'm deep inside you."

As if to prove his point, he shifted the angle, hitting her in a way that pulled a broken moan from her throat. "Oh, yes. Right there," she gasped, one hand fisting in his hair, pulling almost painfully. "Don't stop."

"Never," he promised, increasing his pace, driving into her with enough force to make the sofa frame creak beneath them. "Come for me, baby. I need to feel you come on my cock."

The crude words paired with the relentless rhythm of his thrusts pushed her over the edge. She shattered around him, her inner walls clamping down with enough force to draw a curse from his lips. He fucked her through it, prolonging her pleasure until she was trembling and incoherent beneath him.

Without warning, he wrapped his arms around her and rolled, reversing their positions so she was on top, straddling him, still joined. The change in position drove him impossibly deeper, pulling a gasp from both of them.

"I need to see you," he said as his hands clutched at her hips, guiding her movements. "I want to watch your sweet little cunt take all of me."

"Yes." She braced her hands on his chest, rising and falling on his length with increasing urgency. His hands slid under her half-unbuttoned blouse to cup her breasts, thumbs teasing her nipples through the lace of her bra.

"Take it off," he commanded, tugging at the fabric.

She complied, stripping off both blouse and bra, then tossing them aside. He leaned forward, his mouth immediately closing over one gorgeous peak as he sat up, then sucked hard enough to make her cry out and clench around him.

"That's it, Princess," he growled against her breast, one hand sliding between them to tease her clit. "Come for me again."

She drew in a ragged breath, then rode him harder, chasing the building pressure, her rhythm growing erratic as she approached the edge. "Liam," she gasped, nails digging into his shoulders. "I'm close. Don't stop. Please, please don't stop."

"Never," he promised, his eyes devouring her as she moved above him. "Look at you. Taking me so deep. Like you were made for me."

"I was." She ground down on him gasping. "We were made for each other."

Yes, he thought. *Oh, god, yes.*

The simple truth of it broke something open in him. His hands tightened on her hips as he took control of her movements, driving her down onto him with increasing urgency. "I love you," he said, the words more raw and honest than any he'd ever spoken. "Fuck, Sasha, I love you so damn much."

"I love you, too," she managed. "I need you, Liam. Wildly. Desperately."

Her words washed over him with the same force as his strongest orgasm. She was his. He was hers. And nothing would change that.

That realization, so powerful and true, drove him on. His fingers on her clit. His cock hitting that perfect spot inside her, all driving her rapidly toward another climax. "Grimm, I'm going to—"

"Yes," he urged, his voice strained with the effort of holding back his own release. "Give it to me. Let me feel you."

She came with his name on her lips, her body clenching around him in waves that seemed to go on forever. He followed a heartbeat later, his hips jerking upward as he emptied himself inside her with a hoarse moan.

For a long moment, they stayed locked together, both panting, sweat-slicked and trembling. Then Liam shifted, keeping her in his arms as he adjusted their position on the sofa, still joined, her body sprawled across his chest.

"That was …" he began, then laughed softly. "I don't even have words."

"Worth waiting for," she said, then pressed a kiss to the underside of his jaw. "Although I may have to reupholster the couch."

He chuckled. "Worth it."

"Oh, yeah."

He cupped her face, his expression shifting to something more serious, more vulnerable. "I meant it, you know. What I said."

"I know," she replied, no need to specify which words. "I meant it, too."

He finally withdrew, but only to gather her more comfortably against him. "Bed," he said firmly. "That was just the appetizer."

"Are you sure you're up for more?" she teased, though she could already feel him hardening against her again.

He flashed a predatory smile. "I've got to make up for lost time." He shifted their positions, then stood up with her in his arms. "Hope you didn't have plans for the rest of the night."

"Just a half-dozen really cute guys. But I'll cancel."

"Careful," he teased. "I'd hate to have to spank you."

She laughed. "No, you wouldn't."

"True," he said, then bent to kiss her. "And you'd like it, too."

Later—much later—they lay tangled in the sheets, her back to his front, his arm possessively draped over her waist. Their bodies were like a map of their reunion—bite marks on her neck and breasts, her ass still a bit red, and scratches on his back and shoulders. Both of them deliciously sore in the best possible way.

"What are you thinking?"

His fingers traced idle patterns on her hip, the earlier urgency replaced by something gentler but no less intimate. "That I've never felt this before," he admitted, the truth easier in post-coital darkness. "This … peace." He brushed a strand of hair from her face, cherishing her touch. Hell, cherishing *her*. "We walked through fire, Princess. And we came out stronger. Together."

She smiled, something bright and genuine that made his chest ache with feelings he was still learning to name. "Together," she echoed, settling back, her body fitting perfectly against his.

When morning came, he woke to find her watching him.

"Creepy," he murmured, smiling as he remembered their night—and morning—at the Celestial. "Watching me sleep."

"Just making sure this is real. That you're really here."

He reached out to touch her face, tracing the line of her jaw with gentle fingers. "I'm here," he assured her. "And I'm not going anywhere."

———

LIAM STARED AT HIS PHONE, the message from Leo sending ice through his veins. *Bane on the move. Sources confirm plan to abduct Sasha tonight. Team of six. Armed.*

He looked across the breakfast table at Sasha as she talked about her plans for Lydia Cosmetics, her face animated with passion for her mother's legacy. She was happy. Safe. At peace.

And Desmond Bane was about to fuck that all to hell.

He gripped his phone tighter. After everything he and Sasha had been through, they'd finally found their way back to each other. And, yes, he'd sworn to never make decisions for her again, never to steal her agency.

But this was different. This was her safety.

He stood abruptly, his chair screeching on the polished floor. "I need to head into the city."

"Everything okay?"

"Nothing I can't handle," he said, already calculating how quickly he could reach Bane and take the bastard out of the equation.

He kissed her forehead, lingering a moment longer than necessary. "I'll be back before dinner."

She nodded, then returned to her coffee, her expression worry-free. Why wouldn't it be? She trusted him.

Trust.

Still so fragile between them.

But this was different. More dire.

At least that's what he told himself as he walked to the door.

Except it was a goddamn lie.

He stopped, his hand on the knob. What the fuck was he doing? Repeating goddamn history, that's what.

This was exactly what he'd done before. Exactly how he'd justified killing Victor. Protecting her. Keeping her safe.

And keeping her in the dark through all of it.

"Fuck."

He turned around, then headed back to the dining area. She was still at the table, reviewing marketing materials for the rebranding.

"Forget something?" she asked, not looking up.

"Yes." He put his phone down in front of her with Leo's text visible. "The truth."

She read the message, her face paling. "Bane is coming here? Tonight?"

"Apparently." He took the seat across from her, forcing himself to stay calm. "My first instinct was to go after him myself. To handle it. To protect you without involving you."

She glanced toward the front door as understanding dawned in her eyes. "You were about to go after him. Like with my father."

He nodded. "I was halfway out the door when I realized what I was doing. Making the same damn mistake again."

She reached across the table, covering his hand with hers. "But you didn't."

"No." He turned his palm up, intertwining their fingers. "I didn't."

A smile flickered on her lips. "So, what should we do?"

The *we* sent a surge of something warm through his chest. Partnership. Trust. Something he'd nearly thrown away.

"We call the FBI," he said. "Anonymous tip. Leo's gathered enough evidence to convince them it's credible. They can intercept Bane before he gets anywhere near here."

"And if that doesn't work?"

"Then we have contingency plans. Together."

She studied him for a long moment, then smiled. "I'm proud of you."

Three simple words. Yet they hit him with more force than any praise he'd ever received.

"Don't get used to it," he said, the corner of his mouth quirking up. "I still have a reputation to maintain."

"Your secret's safe with me." She stood, tugging him to his feet. "Make the call. I'll pack a bag, just in case."

She paused on the way to the bedroom, looking back at him. "Thanks. For trusting me enough to tell me. For understanding that I need to know, too."

He nodded, something tight in his chest loosening. "Always. From now on. Count on it."

And as he dialed, Liam realized he'd finally, shaken off that damn need to control everything. The belief that he alone could protect what was his. The truth was, some threats couldn't be eliminated alone. Some battles were meant to be fought together.

FORTY-FIVE
HOME

The gavel comes down with a crack that rings through the courtroom, and I can't help smiling as Desmond Bane's face twists with rage. Twelve years, with the possibility of parole after eight. The judge's words still echo in my ears when Ruby squeezes my hand hard enough to hurt.

"Couldn't have happened to a nicer guy," she whispers, and I have to bite my lip to keep from laughing out loud.

Six months have passed since the FBI caught Bane and his goons before they could reach our house in Connecticut. Six months of actually living instead of just surviving. Six months of figuring out who the hell I am when I'm not being controlled by my father or drugged out of my mind.

I glance over at Liam, who hasn't moved a muscle since the verdict came down. His face is a mask, but I know that look by now—he's still running the numbers, still wondering if letting the legal system deal with Bane had really been the right call. Still thinking about how close he came to handling it his way.

When the courtroom starts to empty, he turns to me. "You okay?"

"Me? I'm better than okay. Are you?"

His response is a half-shrug.

I take his hand. "It's over, Liam. Really over."

"It is," he says, his voice firm, but I hear what's hidden underneath. The part of him that will never completely believe that Bane can't hurt me from behind bars. The part that will always be watching, calculating, ready to do whatever it takes to keep me safe.

I've learned to live with that part of him, just like he's learned to deal with my stubborn independence. It's our deal—he tries not to control everything, and I try to understand that his overprotectiveness comes from something real and raw and beyond his control.

"Let's get out of here," I say, grabbing my bag and standing up. The vultures are waiting outside—I can feel them already, cameras and microphones poised to tear us apart for a story that'll last less than five minutes on the evening news.

Liam's hand finds the small of my back, solid and warm. "Ready for the firing squad?"

I nod, squaring my shoulders and fixing my face in what my father always called my "public smile." I spent my whole life learning how to fake it for the cameras but, it's only been since he died that I've learned that a public smile doesn't always have to be fake.

The questions hit us like bullets the instant we push through the doors.

"Ms. Reed! How do you feel about the verdict?"

"Mr. Grimm! Any comment on Bane's threats during the trial?"

"Sasha! What's next for Lydia Cosmetics?"

I stop on the steps, letting them capture their moment as Liam stands like a sentinel beside me. His midnight blue suit was my pick this morning—it makes his eyes look like something that could drown you.

"Justice has been served," I say, keeping it simple. "Now we move forward. Together."

They eat it up, shouting more questions as security clears a path to the waiting car. Once the door slams behind us, I let out a breath that feels like I've been holding it for years.

"Nice," Liam says, and I can hear the pride under the word.

I smile at him. He knows I don't need coaching on how to handle reporters. It's one of the few useful skills my father accidentally taught me. How to lie with a smile. How to look confident even when my insides are liquid. How to keep your shit together when the world is watching.

The difference now is that I get to take the mask off when the cameras stop rolling. I get to be just Sasha—whoever the hell that is—with the people who matter.

As the car pulls away from the courthouse, I feel the adrenaline crash hitting me hard, leaving something else behind. Something hot and electric that makes my skin feel two sizes too small. I look over at Liam and find his eyes already on me, dark with something that makes my pulse skip.

"What?" I ask, though I know damn well what that look means by now.

"You were fucking incredible in there," he says, his voice dropping to that register that always makes me shiver. "So damn strong. So in control."

"I had good reason to be," I tell him, sliding closer, my eyes checking that the privacy screen is up out of habit.

His hand finds my thigh, fingers pressing just hard enough through my skirt to remind me of how strong this man is. "You drive me crazy when you're like that," he murmurs. "All powerful and untouchable."

I lean in closer, my lips almost brushing his ear. "Bet you'd like to touch me now though."

His grip tightens, and I can feel the restraint in him—the control that's always there, even when it looks like it's slipping. "Tell the driver to take us to the Celestial," he says, voice rough. "We need to properly celebrate before we head home."

The hotel's just a few blocks away—our own little hideout in the city where nobody gives a damn about the way his hand curls possessively around my elbow in the elevator, or how my body can't seem to keep a respectable distance from his.

The second our suite door closes, Liam's got me pinned against it, his mouth on mine with a hunger that leaves me dizzy. There's an edge to him today, something darker than usual that I know has everything to do with seeing Bane, with watching the man who tried to steal what's his.

"Do you know how fucking hard it was not to kill him when I had the chance?"

I tilt my head back, giving him better access for the kisses he's trailing down my neck. "You did the right thing."

His teeth scrape my collarbone, sending bolts of electricity straight to my core. "Did I?" His hands are already attacking my blouse buttons. "When that piece of shit looked at you in court, I wanted to tear his goddamn throat out."

It should scare me, this violence that lives under his skin. Instead, it lights me up like a match to gasoline. This dangerous, lethal man chose me. Chose to put my needs above his darkest instincts. It's heady and delicious and fucking sexy as hell.

"You're mine," he says, shoving my blouse off my shoulders. "And nobody's ever taking you from me."

"Never," I agree, my fingers fumbling with his belt. "I'm yours. Only yours."

We don't even make it to the bedroom. He lifts me onto the console table, knocking over some fancy vase that crashes to the floor. My skirt's up around my waist, and I hear the delicate rip of expensive silk as he tears my underwear away.

"I've been wanting to do that all day," he admits, dangling the ruined scrap from his fingers. "From the second you put on that prim little court outfit."

I laugh as his mouth crushes mine again. That's what I love about us—how we can switch from intensity to playfulness and back again in a heartbeat.

"Anything else you've been wanting to do?" I ask, my voice innocent as I, wrap my legs around his waist and pull him closer.

He reaches into his pocket and pulls out a length of silk I recognize as one of his ties. "Turn around."

The word sends heat flooding through me. I slide off the table and turn to face it as he pulls my wrists behind my back, binding them together with the tie. The position forces me to arch, pushing my chest forward.

"Christ, look at you," he mutters, his hands skimming down my sides to grip my hips. "So fucking perfect."

I hear his zipper, then feel the heat of him pressed against me from behind. One hand slides around to tease between my legs.

"Always so wet for me," he says, satisfaction dripping from every word. "Always so ready."

"Please," I whisper, already desperate for him.

He enters me in one hard thrust that knocks the breath out of me. The position—hands tied, bent over the table—leaves me completely at his mercy, and we both know it. There's trust in this, in the way I give up control to him. In the way he takes it.

"Look at you," he says, setting a rhythm that borders on punishing. "Like you were made for this. For me."

His words and the relentless pounding push me toward the edge fast. I'm almost there when suddenly he stops.

"Not yet," he says, voice strained with his own control. "Not until I say so."

He pulls out, and I whimper in protest. Then his hands are on me, turning me, lifting me. He carries me to the bedroom and lays me on the bed, my hands still tied behind my back.

"I want to see your face when you come. When you fall apart for me."

This time when he enters me, it's with maddening slowness—a deliberate tease that has me arching against the restraints, my eyes locked on his. "Liam, please ..."

"Please what, Princess?" His thumb finds my clit, circling with just enough pressure to make me crazy but not enough to push me over.

"Please let me come," I beg, beyond caring how desperate I sound.

He flashes a predatory smile. "Since you asked so nicely."

His rhythm picks up, his thumb matching his thrusts, and this time when I approach the edge, he doesn't stop me. The orgasm crashes through me like a tidal wave, tearing his name from my throat. He follows right after, his body tensing over mine, my name a rough prayer on his lips.

After, he carefully unties my wrists, pressing gentle kisses to the faint marks left by the tight knot of silk. It's this contrast that gets me every time—the fierce, possessive lover and the tender, careful man. The darkness and the light, perfectly balanced in one complicated package.

I curl into him as he wraps his arms around me, both of us sweaty and spent.

"I love you," he murmurs into my hair. "More than I ever thought possible."

"I love you too," I tell him, tracing patterns on his chest. "All of you."

We lie like that for a while, wrapped up in each other and the aftermath of something that felt too big for words. Eventually, we drag ourselves into the shower and get dressed for the drive back to Connecticut.

I curl against Liam as the car pulls away from the Celestial, heading north toward home. We spend most of our time there now, only coming into the city when we have to. I watch the Manhattan skyline shrinking behind us, remembering how I used to be terrified of open spaces. How just the thought of leaving the tower would send me into a spiral of panic.

Now I crave space—the woods surrounding our house, the lake we swim in on hot days, the endless sky at night so full of stars it makes my throat tight. It's taken a while, but time, the drugs finally out of my body, and my father's death took me most of the way. Liam took me the rest, literally opening the world for me.

"I've been thinking," I say as we cross the bridge, leaving the city behind. "About what's next."

Liam glances over, curious. "For the company?"

"For us."

His hand finds mine, our fingers twining together with the easy intimacy that still surprises me sometimes. "I'm listening."

"I want to sell the Reed Tower penthouse."

The words hang between us. I've been holding onto the place despite barely using it, unable to let go of that last connection to my childhood. Not to my mother—I have Lydia Cosmetics for that—but to the few happy memories that have come back to me. My mother singing me to sleep, teaching me to draw, chasing me around the tower in a silly game of tag. But those memories are of my mother, not the tower. And now that I have them back, I know she will always be with me.

"You sure?" he asks after I tell him all that. "You spent seven years there with her."

"I did. But even though I have so many good memories back, it's still the place where she died." I turn to face him. "The truth is, it's not home. It hasn't been for a long, long time. But you are, Liam. Wherever you are—that's home to me now."

Something raw flashes across his face, there and gone in a blink. "Princess ..."

"I'm thinking we keep Connecticut as our main place," I continue, letting him process. "Maybe get a small place in SoHo. Neutral territory. Not Reed, not Grimm. Just ours."

"Ours," he repeats, like he's testing how the word feels in his mouth. "I like that."

The countryside starts opening up around us, familiar and somehow still new. The last six months have changed everything. I still have nightmares sometimes—my father, the drugs, the years I lost to his control—but I never face them alone.

When they wake me up at night, Liam's there, his arms around me, his voice soothing me until the ghosts fade away.

He gets trauma in a way nobody else in my life ever has—the way it sticks to you, shapes you, blindsides you when you least expect it.

Now, he turns to smile at me. Have I told you how good Connecticut looks good on you?"

I laugh, delighted. "I'm glad. "It's the first place that's ever been mine," I tell him. "Well, ours."

He grins at the correction, and I marvel again at how this man— this complicated, dangerous, brilliant, fucked-up man—makes me feel safe. Seen. We've both lived in shadows our whole lives, and somehow, together, we've found our way into some kind of light.

The driver steers the car down the long drive to the house, trees arching overhead like a tunnel leading from the real world to our own magical realm. I roll down my window and breathe in the smell of pine and earth and flowers and greenery.

"We've come a long way," I say, watching the forest open to glimpses of the house ahead.

"That we have," he agrees, squeezing my hand.

When we reach the house, Liam insists on carrying me over the threshold like we're some newlywed couple instead of two people who've been living together for months. I laugh but let him do it, loving the easy strength in his arms as he lifts me into the foyer.

"What's gotten into you?" I ask when he sets me down.

"Just celebrating the victory," he says, but there's something else about him—a nervousness I've never seen from him.

He leads me into the living room, where a small wooden box sits on the coffee table. It's beautiful, made from dark polished wood with intricate carvings that catch the late afternoon light.

"What's this?"

"Something I've been meaning to give you," he says, guiding me to sit beside him on the couch. His face goes serious. "It belonged to my mother. One of the few things I have of hers."

My chest tightens at the vulnerability in his voice. Rebecca's death is a wound that never really healed.

"Elias gave it to me when I turned eighteen," he adds, running his finger over the carved surface. "It was one of the few nice things that man ever did for me. He told me it was her favorite thing, and she used it to hold other things that were precious to her."

"It's beautiful," I say, genuinely moved that he would share this with me.

From his pocket, he pulls out a tiny golden key. "I've only opened it twice. I've been saving what's inside for the right moment. For the right person.

The weight of what he's offering hits me like a punch to the chest. This man, who's spent his whole life protecting himself from vulnerability, is giving me something he's kept private all these years.

"You sure?" I ask.

He places the key in my palm, closing my fingers around it. "I'm sure. Because I trust you. Because I love you."

My throat goes tight as I carefully push the key into the lock. It turns with a soft click, and I gently lift the lid.

Inside, nestled on faded velvet, is a ring—a diamond on a delicate gold band that catches the light streaming through the windows.

"Liam …" I whisper, suddenly understanding. He takes my hand, his expression more open and vulnerable than I've ever seen it. "Sasha Reed, will you marry me?"

The question shouldn't surprise me—we've been heading here for months—but it does. Not the question itself, but the raw emotion behind it. The complete openness from a man who's spent his life hiding behind walls.

"Yes." I whisper, then louder, "oh, yes."

His smile is like sunrise—slow and beautiful and inevitable. He takes the ring from its velvet bed and slides it onto my finger. Perfect fit, because Liam Grimm would never leave something like that to chance.

"It's not an heirloom," he says. "Other than the box, I don't have any heirlooms. But I thought we could start our own traditions, collect our own heirlooms."

"I love that," I say as I gaze at the ring on my hand, feeling gooey and safe and loved.

The ring is a symbol that I belong to him. That we belong to each other. Not a cage, not a claim, but a promise. A partnership.

I glance at the box, then back to Liam. "She would have loved you," I say, the words coming from someplace deeper than thought. "She would have been proud of the man you are."

His arms go around me, pulling me close, and I feel the slight tremor in his body—this powerful man who's letting me see his heart.

"I love you," I say, the words still feeling new and precious on my tongue.

"I love you too, Princess," he replies. "Every difficult, extraordinary bit of you."

As he leads me toward our bedroom, I feel something settle inside me—a peace I never thought possible, a certainty about the road ahead. It won't be perfect. Liam will always struggle with his need to control everything, to protect what's his. I'll always push back, demand my space, insist on being an equal partner.

But we'll figure it out together.

And now, for the first time in my life, I'm not afraid of the future. I'm hungry for it.

EPILOGUE

The mountain air is crisp and clear as I stand on the terrace, sketching the sunrise over the valley. The Connecticut house— our house —glows in the early morning light, stone and glass and wood warmed by the promise of a new day.

Behind me, the door slides open, and Liam's warmth presses against my back as his arms encircle my waist. "You're up early," he murmurs against my hair.

"Just trying to capture the view," I say, leaning into him. "I still can't believe I can do this."

"Sketch or stand on balconies?" His words are a tease, but I hear the understanding, too.

"Be outside," I say. "Be anywhere I want to be." I turn in his arms to face him. "Be me."

His smile softens, and I see pride reflected in his eyes. "You've come a long way, Princess."

One year since Bane's conviction. Eighteen months since my father's death. And a lifetime since I was that frightened girl trapped in a penthouse, drugged and controlled by a man who saw me as property rather than a person.

Lydia Cosmetics continues to thrive, reclaiming my mother's vision with each new campaign. Ruby has proven herself an exceptional partner, her creativity perfectly complementing my strategic vision.

And Elysium ...

Elysium has exceeded all expectations. We launched the commercial version six months ago—a gaming platform that combines immersive experiences with the opportunity for users to build their own worlds, just as I once built mine. The therapeutic applications continue alongside it, drawing attention from mental health professionals worldwide.

My father would hate it all. The thought brings a smile to my face.

"What are you thinking about?" Liam asks, his hands warm on my waist.

"How different everything is. How much has changed."

"Regrets?" The question is casual, but I hear the undercurrent of vulnerability.

I shake my head firmly. "Not one."

He nods, seemingly satisfied, but I know him well enough to see the shadow that occasionally crosses his face—the memory of my father's death, of decisions that can't be unmade. Of the fine line between protection and control over which he still sometimes stumbles.

"We should get going," he says, glancing at his watch. "The board meeting—"

"You'll just have to drive fast," I interrupt, setting aside my sketch book and stepping closer to him. "There's something we need to take care of before we go."

"Oh, really?" he says, a familiar heat kindling in his gaze. "Is that so, Princess?"

I rise on tiptoes, then brush my lips over his. "That's so, Grimm."

His arms tighten around me, and I laugh he lifts me off my feet, then snuggle close as he carries me inside.

This is my life now. Not perfect, but real. Not a fairy tale, but a partnership built on truth and trust and love all tested and tempered by fire.

As Liam carries me to our bedroom, I catch a glimpse of the valley below, vast and open and brimming with possibility.

No more towers. No more cages. Just endless sky, and the promise of tomorrow.

Together.

UP NEXT: THE WOLF

Don't miss Ruby and Leo's story in THE WOLF, Book 2 of the Billionaire Brothers Grimm.

She spent her life running from monsters. But the most dangerous one was always behind her.

Leo Grimm has always lived for the chase—whether in the boardroom, the bedroom, or in the secrets buried beneath his family's name. Ruthless and relentless, he's never lost a hunt. Except once.

Ruby Ryder was the one obsession he couldn't shake, the one woman who slipped from his grasp. Now, she's back—terrified, desperate, and hunted by an enemy she can't outrun. And this time, Leo isn't letting her go.

He'll protect her … for a price. Her trust. Her surrender. Her heart.

But the closer Ruby gets to Leo, the more she realizes the real danger isn't the one chasing her—it's the man who almost caught her before. The man who left scars that never healed. The man whose family destroyed hers.

In the wolf's deadly embrace, Ruby discovers the ultimate seduction of surrender … as well as its all-consuming terror. Because once the wolf sinks his teeth in, he won't just own her body—he'll consume her soul.

SOME RAVE REVIEWS FOR J. KENNER'S SIZZLING ROMANCES...

I just get sucked into these books and can not get enough of this series. They are so well written and as satisfying as each book is they leave you greedy for more. — Goodreads reviewer on *Wicked Torture*

A sizzling, intoxicating, sexy read!!!! J. Kenner had me devouring Wicked Dirty, the second installment of *Stark World Series* in one sitting. I loved everything about this book from the opening pages to the raw and vulnerable characters. With her sophisticated prose, Kenner created a love story that had the perfect blend of lust, passion, sexual tension, raw emotions and love. — Michelle, Four Chicks Flipping Pages

Wicked Dirty CLAIMED and CONSUMED every ounce of me from the very first page. Mind racing. Pulse pounding. Breaths bated. Feels flowing. Eyes wide in anticipation. Heart beating out of my chest. I felt the current of *Wicked Dirty* flow through me. I was DRUNK on this book that was my fine whiskey, so smooth and spectacular, and could not get enough of this *Wicked Dirty* drink. — Karen Bookalicious Babes Blog

"Sinfully sexy and full of heart. Kenner shines in this second chance, slow burn of a romance. Wicked Grind is the perfect book to kick off your summer." — *K. Bromberg, New York Times bestselling author (on Wicked Grind)*

"J. Kenner never disappoints~her books just get better and better." — *Mom's Guilty Pleasure (on Wicked Grind)*

"I don't think J. Kenner could write a bad story if she tried. ... Wicked Grind is a great beginning to what I'm positive will be a very successful series. ... The line forms here." — *iScream Books (On Wicked Grind)*

"Scorching, sweet, and soul-searing, *Anchor Me* is the ultimate love story that stands the test of time and tribulation. THE TRUEST LOVE!" *Bookalicious Babes Blog (on Anchor Me)*

"J. Kenner has brought this couple to life and the character connection that I have to these two holds no bounds and that is testament to J. Kenner's writing ability." *The Romance Cover (on Anchor Me)*

"J. Kenner writes an emotional and personal story line. ... The premise will captivate your imagination; the characters will break your heart; the romance continues to push the envelope." — *The Reading Café (on Anchor Me)*

"Kenner may very well have cornered the market on sinfully attractive, dominant antiheroes and the women who swoon for them ..." — *Romantic Times*

"*Wanted* is another J. Kenner masterpiece ... This was an intriguing look at self-discovery and forbidden love all wrapped into a neat little action-suspense package. There was plenty of sexual tension and eventually action. Evan was hot, hot, hot! Together, they were combustible. But can we expect anything less from J. Kenner?" — *Reading Haven*

"*Wanted* by J. Kenner is the whole package! A toe-curling smokin' hot read, full of incredible characters and a brilliant storyline that you won't be able to get enough of. I can't wait for the next book in this series ... I'm hooked!" — *Flirty & Dirty Book Blog*

"J. Kenner's evocative writing thrillingly captures the power of physical attraction, the pull of longing, the universe-altering effect one person can have on another ... *Claim Me* has the emotional depth to back up the sex ... Every scene is infused with both erotic tension, and the tension of wondering what lies beneath Damien's veneer – and how and when it will be revealed." — *Heroes and Heartbreakers*

"*Claim Me* by J. Kenner is an erotic, sexy and exciting ride. The story between Damien and Nikki is amazing and written beautifully. The intimate and detailed sex scenes will leave you fanning yourself to cool down. With the writing style of Ms. Kenner you almost feel like you are there in the story riding along the emotional rollercoaster with Damien and Nikki." — *Fresh Fiction*

"PERFECT for fans of *Fifty Shades of Grey* and *Bared to You*. *Release Me* is a powerful and erotic romance novel that is sure to make adult romance readers sweat, sigh and swoon." — *Reading, Eating & Dreaming Blog*

"I will admit, I am in the 'I loved *Fifty Shades*' camp, but after reading *Release Me*, Mr. Grey only scratches the surface compared to Damien Stark." — *Cocktails and Books Blog*

"It is not often when a book is so amazingly well-written that I find it hard to even begin to accurately describe it … I recommend this book to everyone who is interested in a passionate love story." — *Romance-bookworm's Reviews*

"The story is one that will rank up with the *Fifty Shades* and Cross Fire trilogies." — *Incubus Publishing Blog*

"The plot is complex, the characters engaging, and J. Kenner's passionate writing brings it all perfectly together." —*Harlequin Junkie*

ALSO BY J. KENNER

For all of JK's Stark World and other titles,
please visit www.jkenner.com

Billionaire Brothers Grimm

The Tower

The Wolf

The Beast

The Stark Saga

He'd pay any price to have her…

release me

claim me

complete me

take me (novella)

have me (novella)

play my game (novella)

seduce me (novella)

unwrap me (novella)

deepest kiss (novella)

entice me (novella)

anchor me

hold me (novella)

please me (novella)

lost with me

damien

indulge me (novella)

delight me (novella & bonus content)

cherish me (novella)

embrace me (novella)

enchant me

interview with the billionaire

The Fallen Saint Series

His touch is her sin. Her love is his salvation

My Fallen Saint

My Beautiful Sin

My Cruel Salvation

Sinner's Game

Charismatic. Dangerous. Sexy as hell.

Meet the elite team of Stark Security.

Shattered With You

Shadows Of You

(free prequel to Broken With You)

Broken With You

Ruined With You

Wrecked With You

Destroyed With You

Memories of You

Ravaged With You

Hidden With You

Charmed By You

Tangled With You

Entwined With You

Craved By You

The Steele Books/Stark International:

He was the only man who made her feel alive.

Say My Name

On My Knees

Under My Skin

Take My Dare (includes short story Steal My Heart)

Stark International Novellas:

Meet Jamie & Ryan-so hot it sizzles.

Tame Me

Tempt Me

Tease Me

Touch Me

S.I.N. Trilogy:

It was wrong for them to be together…

…but harder to stay apart.

Dirtiest Secret

Hottest Mess

Sweetest Taboo

Most Wanted:

Three powerful, dangerous men.

Three sensual, seductive women.

Wanted

Heated

Ignited

Man of the Month

Who's your man of the month…?

Down On Me

Hold On Tight

Need You Now

Start Me Up

Get It On

In Your Eyes

Turn Me On

Shake It Up

All Night Long

In Too Deep

Light My Fire

Walk The Line

Royal Cocktail (bonus book)

**Bar Bites: A Man of the Month Cookbook(by J. Kenner & Suzanne M. Johnson)*

Blackwell-Lyon:

Heat, humor & a hint of danger

Lovely Little Liar

Pretty Little Player

Sexy Little Sinner

Tempting Little Tease

Rising Storm:

Writing as Julie Kenner

Small town drama

Rising Storm: Tempest Rising

Rising Storm: Quiet Storm

PARANORMAL

Demon Hunting Soccer Mom

Like Buffy… grown up!

Paranormal women's fiction

Carpe Demon

California Demon

Demons Are Forever

Deja Demon

The Demon You Know (short story)

Demon Ex Machina

Pax Demonica

Day of the Demon

How To Train Your Demon

ABOUT THE AUTHOR

J. Kenner (aka Julie Kenner) is the *New York Times, USA Today, Publishers Weekly, Wall Street Journal* and #1 International bestselling author of over one hundred novels, novellas and short stories in a variety of genres.

JK has been praised by *Publishers Weekly* as an author with a "flair for dialogue and eccentric characterizations" and by *RT Bookclub* for having "cornered the market on sinfully attractive, dominant anti-heroes and the women who swoon for them." A five-time finalist for Romance Writers of America's prestigious RITA award, JK took home the first RITA trophy awarded in the category of erotic romance in 2014 for her novel, *Claim Me* (book 2 of her Stark Trilogy) and the RITA trophy for *Wicked Dirty* in the same category in 2017.

In her previous career as an attorney, JK worked as a lawyer in Southern California and Texas. She currently lives in Central Texas, with her husband, two daughters, and two rather spastic cats.

Stay in touch! Text JKenner to 21000 to subscribe to JK's text alerts.

www.jkenner.com